THE PRINCE'S BLADE

Christopher Mitchell is the author of the epic fantasy series The Magelands. He studied in Edinburgh before living for several years in the Middle East and Greece, where he taught English. He returned to study classics and Greek tragedy and lives in Fife, Scotland with his wife and their four children.

BY CHRISTOPHER MITCHELL

THE MAGELANDS ORIGINS

Retreat of the Kell
The Trials of Daphne Holdfast
From the Ashes

THE MAGELANDS EPIC

The Queen's Executioner
The Severed City
Needs of the Empire
Sacrifice
Fragile Empire
Storm Mage
Soulwitch Rises
Renegade Gods

THE MAGELANDS ETERNAL SIEGE

The Mortal Blade
The Dragon's Blade
The Prince's Blade
Falls of Iron

Brigdomin Books Ltd
First Edition, November 2020
ISBN 978-1-912879-46-5

For the Scottish Health Service

ACKNOWLEDGEMENTS

I would like to thank the following for all their support during the writing of the Magelands Eternal Siege - my wife, Lisa Mitchell, who read every chapter as soon as it was drafted and kept me going in the right direction; my parents for their unstinting support; Vicky Williams for reading the books in their early stages; James Aitken for his encouragement; and Grant and Gordon of the Film Club for their support.

Thanks also to my Advance Reader team, for all your help during the last few weeks before publication.

DRAMATIS PERSONAE

The Royal Family – Gods and God-Children

God-Queen Amalia, Sovereign of the City; Ooste
Prince Montieth, Recluse; Dalrig

The Royal Family – Demigods

Aila, Bride
Naxor, Former Emissary of the Gods
Marcus, acclaimed Prince of Tara
Kano, Commander of the Bulwark
Yvona, Governor of Icehaven
Amber, Elder Daughter of Prince Montieth
Jade, Younger Daughter of Prince Montieth
Ikara, Former Governor of the Circuit
Lydia, Governor of Port Sanders
Doria, Courtier in the Royal Palace
Mona, Chancellor of Royal Academy, Ooste

The Mortals of the City

Rosers
Daniel Aurelian, Wolfpack
Lord Chamberlain, Advisor to the God-Queen

Dalrigians

Hellis, Grey Isle Captain

Icewarders

Yaizra, Convicted Thief
Hannia, Aide to Lady Yvona

Evaders

Emily Aurelian, Rat

Blades

Maddie Jackdaw, Young Sergeant
Rosie, Maddie's Younger Sister
Tom, Maddie's Older Brother
Hilde, Blade Captain
Quill, Wolfpack Sergeant

Hammers

Achan, Convicted Rebel
Torphin, Conscripted into the Rats

The Outsiders

Corthie Holdfast, Champion
Blackrose, Former Prisoner

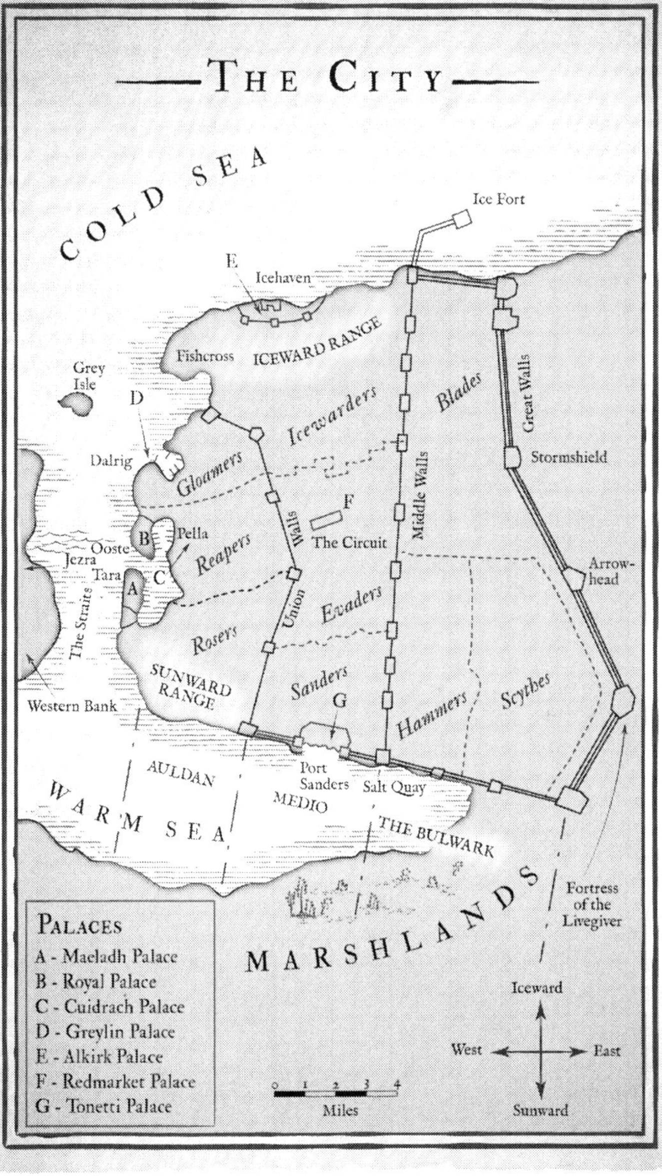
THE CITY
COLD SEA
Ice Fort
E
Icehaven
ICEWARD RANGE
Fishcross
Grey Isle
D
Dalrig
Icewarders
Blades
Great Walls
Stormshield
Gloamers
Middle Walls
F
Union Walls
The Circuit
B
Pella
Ooste
Jezra
Tara
C
A
Reapers
Arrow-head
Evaders
Rosers
The Straits
SUNWARD RANGE
Sanders
Scythes
Western Bank
G
Hammers
AULDAN
Port Sanders
Salt Quay
MEDIO
WARM SEA
THE BULWARK
MARSHLANDS
Fortress of the Livegiver
PALACES
A - Maeladh Palace
B - Royal Palace
C - Cuidrach Palace
D - Greylin Palace
E - Alkirk Palace
F - Redmarket Palace
G - Tonetti Palace
0 1 2 3 4
Miles
Iceward
West
East
Sunward

CHAPTER 1

NO RELIEF

Arrowhead Fort, The Bulwark, The City – 22nd Amalan 3420

Emily stood on the battlements of Arrowhead, the warm wind blowing her hair into wild tangles as the sun started to rise behind her. Her hands gripped the top of the wall, her knuckles white as she watched the growing light reveal the hordes of greenhides that had breached the Great Walls during the longest night of her life. They were swarming through every gate that had been left open or torn down, and a sea of them were marauding across the wide open spaces where the Blades lived. Smoke was rising from a few places, but the screams had faded away.

She turned her gaze to the empty skies, hoping to see a sign that the black dragon was returning. A few small specks were visible, but they were just the crows, come to see if they could share in the feast of human flesh that had been torn apart by the greenhides.

'Where are you?' she whispered, then turned for the stairs.

She hurried down the narrow spiral staircase that led from the battlements to Buckler's lair for what seemed like the hundredth time over the previous hours, her legs aching, and her head spinning from lack of sleep. She emerged into the depths of the lair, and noticed the glances of the exhausted Rats and soldiers that represented all that was left of the fortress garrison. Under ninety remained alive within the barricaded shelter. A few Hammers bowed to her as she approached Daniel.

He looked up from where he was sitting, his back leaning against a wall. 'Any sign of them?'

She shook her head.

Torphin glanced over. 'The dragon isn't returning. We should leave.'

'And go where?' said Sergeant Quill, her breastplate smeared with green blood.

'There's only one place we can go,' the Hammer leader said, 'into Scythe territory.' He looked at Emily. 'Is their wall still secure, my lady?'

'As far as I could see,' she said.

'That won't last long,' said Quill. 'The walls that surround the Scythes and Hammers weren't built to withstand greenhide attack.'

Torphin gave her a cold stare. 'Then why don't you tell us why they were built? What is their purpose?'

'You know the answer to that.'

'Yes, but maybe Lord and Lady Aurelian don't.' He turned to Emily and Daniel. 'The walls that go round the lands of the Scythes and the Hammers are there to make sure none of us can escape our bondage; to keep us all prisoners. We are slaves, nothing more, nothing less. Or should I say we *were* slaves, for the greenhide invasion, and your arrival, has changed everything.'

Daniel leaned forward, his elbows on his knees as Emily stood by his shoulder. 'I don't understand,' he said. 'That wall's there to keep the Scythes and Hammers in?'

Torphin nodded. 'Exactly.'

'I didn't know, either,' said Emily. 'We were only ever taught three things about the Bulwark: the Blades fight, the Scythes farm, and the Hammers build. No one ever mentioned that you were compelled, or that you were restrained from leaving.' She turned to Daniel. 'I think we should do as Torphin suggests, and enter the territory of the Scythes. There's a gate directly opposite the main entrance to Arrowhead fortress. If we can break through, and bar it behind us, then we can hurry towards the Middle Walls.'

'And what about the greenhides that are currently inside the fortress?' said Quill 'Have you forgotten about them?'

'No, but if we stay here, then they'll get in, eventually, and we'll all die. I'd rather take my chances running for it.'

Quill frowned. 'What about the dragon? I know Maddie, and there's no way she'd abandon the City.'

'But what if the dragon doesn't listen to her?' said Emily. 'Maddie can hardly make her do anything she doesn't want to do. The City walled her up and left her to starve to death; I'm not sure I'd want to help if I were her.' She glanced around at the gathered Rats and soldiers. 'The sun is rising, and more greenhides are entering the Bulwark with every minute that passes. If we leave, and try to break into Scythe territory, then many of us might die, but if we stay, we all die. Daniel?'

He nodded. 'I agree, but we need a different way out of the lair. We barricaded ourselves in too well, and there are hundreds of those things on the other side waiting for us.'

'We could try going along the battlements, my lord,' said Torphin.

Quill stood. 'Hold it everybody.' She sighed. 'I didn't want to have to do this, but I'm the only Blade here with any rank, and so that puts me in charge. We're staying here, and we'll hold out until we're relieved.'

Torphin stood to face her. 'The Blades don't rule me any more; you are no longer our jailors. Even if the Aurelians weren't here, I wouldn't do what you tell me.' He glanced at the other Hammers in the crowd and smiled. 'But they are here, aren't they? The Aurelians arrived, right at the moment the City needed them, when the walls have been breached. What more proof do you need? What other sign could you ask for? The wall that kept us imprisoned is now the only thing standing between the greenhides and all our trapped folk. All Hammers, raise your hands.' About forty lifted an arm into the air. Torphin nodded. 'And Scythes?' Another dozen raised their hands.

'More than half of us, eh?' He turned to Quill. 'We no longer accept your authority. The Aurelians will lead us now, not the Blades.'

Quill glared at him, then pointed at Daniel and Emily. 'You two are still under my command.'

'I'm a Rat,' said Emily, 'and I don't take orders from you. If the Hammers and Scythes trust me and Daniel to lead them to the Middle Walls, then I accept.'

Half of the crowd cheered, and raised their weapons into the air. Daniel got to his feet, his eyes unsure.

'I'm not a Rat,' he said, 'and Sergeant Quill is correct; I am under her authority, as are at least a dozen others from the Wolfpack that are here in Buckler's lair. Torphin is also right; the Blades have no moral authority to command the Scythes and the Hammers, not any more. We are not going to be relieved. There are no forces emerging from the gates of the Middle Walls to sweep the greenhides back out of the Bulwark, and the dragon has gone. I don't know anything about a legend of the Aurelians saving the Hammers, but that is where we should go. Sergeant Quill, you can stay here, or you can come with us, but we're leaving.'

The crowd roared again, and began to split. About sixty moved over to stand behind Emily and Daniel, leaving Quill with fewer than two dozen around her.

'It doesn't have to be this way,' said Emily to Quill; 'come with us. We should stick together, and then when we reach the Middle Walls, we can sort it all out. You're the best soldier here, Sergeant; please come.'

Quill stared at her, saying nothing for a long moment. 'Alright. We'll leave together, but that doesn't mean I'll forget what happened here.'

'Thank you,' said Emily. She turned to Torphin. 'The battlements?'

'No,' said Quill, 'the greenhides would see us right away, and they'd be waiting for us wherever we tried to come down. If we're going, you'll follow me; that's my condition.'

'There where do you suggest?'

Quill chewed her lip. 'Do we have rope?'

Thirty minutes later, the ninety survivors of the garrison were lowering themselves down the outside face of the fortress on a series of long ropes attached to the Dragon Port, the place from where Buckler had flown in and out of his lair. Below them was the channel that ran between the outer and inner walls of the defences, and it was crammed with greenhides, all staring upwards and baying, their claws snapping in the air. Halfway down the outside of the fortress was a long observation deck, cut back into the thick wall. Six ropes had been fixed, and Daniel descended in the first wave, while Emily and Quill waited until everyone else had lowered themselves to the deck before taking hold of the ropes.

Quill smirked as she began her descent. 'Don't look down, Lady Aurelian.'

Emily kicked out from the wall, the rope running through her gloves. She passed Quill, who glared at her, and reached the deck in a few seconds. Daniel was waiting, and he pulled her in as soon as her boots touched the solid stone.

He shook his head. 'Another thing you can do that I didn't know about.'

'I used to climb out of my bedroom window regularly,' she said. 'Once, it was so I could visit you.'

'I remember,' he said, taking her hand. 'It seems like a million years ago.'

She smiled. 'It's been an eventful marriage so far.'

'I'd kiss you, but all the Hammers are watching us.'

'I don't mind.' She put a hand up to his face and leaned in. Their lips touched and she felt his hand on her back pull her closer.

'Malik's ass,' muttered Quill as she landed on the deck beside them. 'Get your tongue out of his mouth, Rat.'

'Which way now?' said Emily.

'Follow me.' Quill set off, and the others followed her through a door. They went along deserted stone corridors, lit by small window slits that led to a view of the outer walls. Emily paused at one, her eyes lingering on where the body of Buckler lay. Greenhides were still swarming over it in their haste to get across the moat, while thousands were jostling and fighting each other to reach the front of the queue.

'The water level's starting to drop already,' said Quill, standing next to her. 'If Buckler's corpse slides into the moat or falls apart under the weight, it'll stop new greenhides getting in, but only for a few days.'

'Do the greenhides fear anything?'

'Not much, now that the red dragon's gone,' she said; 'fire and Corthie Holdfast, that's about it.'

They carried on, and descended a spiral staircase, their boots echoing against the walls. Quill raised a hand for silence when she reached the bottom and glanced to her left and right.

'We're safe for now,' she said. 'Through that door ahead of us is the back entrance of the Wolfpack Tower, but the entire yard will be crawling with greenhides, so we're going via the hospital to the left, and then out by the gatehouse. From now on, I want complete silence from everyone.'

Emily nodded, though her heart sank at the prospect of escaping through a hospital. Quill led the way, turning left at the bottom of the stairs and following a long passageway. It opened into a hall, and Emily saw the first bodies. Limbs were scattered as if thrown around, and blood streaked the walls and stone floor. Several torsos were lying hollowed-out, their heads missing. A shriek echoed off to the right, and Emily shivered. She felt for the grip of her sword, her fingers tracing the hilt as her eyes scanned every corner of the hall. Quill gestured and they moved off, padding slowly amid the sea of flesh. They passed a door to the right, which was lying open. Quill veered to the left around it, staying in the thick shadows by the far wall as they filed past. Outside, greenhides were running through the courtyard, though not as many as there had been before. Most were heading towards the main gates of the fortress, presumably, Emily thought, to chase down the prospect of fresh food.

Quill reached another door, and slid the bar to open it. She peered inside, then gestured to the others to follow.

Emily put a hand to her mouth as she entered the hospital ward and saw the devastation that lay before her. Beds were overturned, and blood covered the floor in a slick pool under their boots. Patients had been ripped to pieces, and were lying half-eaten from one end of the room to the other.

'No greenhides,' Daniel whispered to her. 'They move fast through places; maybe they'll have left Arrowhead by the time we reach the gates.'

Quill raised a finger to her lips. 'There's at least one open gate in the fort where more of them can get in.' She stopped, and tilted her head. 'I hear a voice.' She raised her hand for the column to stop, and they listened.

'I think it's coming from downstairs,' said Emily.

Quill marched them onwards until they came to a door and a stairwell.

'Everyone stay here,' she said, 'I'll take a squad down to check it out.'

She gestured to a few Blades, and they crept down the stairs while the others waited. Emily went to the other door and peered outside through the keyhole. A few greenhides were running across the yard, but their numbers had thinned out from before. One passed a few yards from the door, and she could see the red blood on its long claws. Its dark eyes swung towards the entrance, and Emily held her breath for a moment until it had passed by.

She felt a hand on her shoulder and jumped. Daniel nodded to the stairs. Quill and the Blades were leading a small group of patients up the steps. Most could walk unaided, but a few were on crutches, and needed help getting to the top.

'Found this lot downstairs,' said Quill. 'Every patient who could get out of the beds escaped when the greenhides swept through the hospital; they hid in the toilet until they had gone.'

Emily nodded.

'Can I speak to you alone?' said Quill.

'Yes.'

She walked across the landing to the corner, Daniel and Quill following her.

'I know what you're thinking,' said Quill, 'but I couldn't just leave them there. They'll slow us down, but their lives are worth as much as ours.'

'I agree,' said Emily; 'you did the right thing, Sergeant. Any survivors we find, we should try to bring into the group.'

'It'll make us a bigger, slower target,' said Daniel, 'but what else can we do?'

'Thank you,' said Quill. 'I was worried you'd object, and then the Hammers would mutiny again.'

Emily glanced up at the tall soldier. 'We're on the same side, Sergeant.'

They turned as one of the patients struggled, a Blade trying to restrain her.

'What's wrong?' said Emily.

The woman turned, her crutches squeaking on the floor. 'We have to go back. Tell these soldiers to unhand me at once; I'm a captain in the Blades. I order you all to go back.'

Quill saluted. 'Ma'am, go back where? The fortress has fallen.'

'You don't understand. There's someone here who needs our help.'

'Who?'

The woman glanced over the faces of the Rats and soldiers. 'Oh bugger, what's the point of keeping it a secret any more? There's another dragon under the fortress, in a hidden lair next to Buckler's. We can't leave her.'

Emily frowned. 'We know about Blackrose.'

'You do?'

'We freed her last night, then Sergeant Maddie climbed on her back and she flew away.'

'She flew away? But... the greenhides... She flew away?'

'She did,' said Daniel, 'and we waited hours for her to return, but she hasn't. So now we're leaving. We're going to break into Scythe territory and try to get to the Middle Walls.'

'And Maddie's gone too?'

'Yes,' said Emily.

'The yard's clear for now,' said Quill from the door. 'We should go.' She glanced at the Blade captain. 'Unless you have another plan, ma'am?'

'No,' she said. 'I'll follow your lead, Sergeant. You have a much better idea of what's going on.'

'Thank you ma'am. Captain...?'

'Hilde,' she said.

Quill eased the door open, as several Rats came forward to assist the less mobile hospital patients. The sergeant peered outside, then gestured for her squad of soldiers to follow her as she stepped out into the forecourt. The Wolves emerged from the hospital, followed by the Rats. To their left, the main gates of the fortress were twenty yards away.

'Go, go,' Quill said, ushering everybody and directing them to the gates. 'Hurry.'

Emily raced ahead, and entered the shadows of the entrance tunnel, five Hammers and Daniel close behind. She edged past an open door and glanced inside, where three bodies lay bloody and ripped on the floor, then she crept to the front of the tunnel. To her right, she could see greenhides roaming the open spaces of the Blade territory, the wide avenues and plazas teeming with the beasts. Directly ahead was the main road that connected the fortresses of the Great Walls, and beyond that was the concrete wall that marked the start of Scythe lands. The wall was tall but narrow, and had no battlements or towers anywhere along its length. She noticed a large closed gate a few yards from where she was standing, as Daniel, Quill and a few Hammers joined her by the corner of the gatehouse.

'The gate,' said Daniel; 'it's barred from this side.'

'Of course it is,' said Torphin, 'it's to keep the Scythes in.'

Quill turned, and signalled to the others to remain where they were, then the small group ran across to the barred gate.

'Quiet!' she hissed as the Hammers began to remove the crossbeams that barred the high doors. Emily stood by her, a hand on her sword hilt as she scanned up and down the road.

The first beam was lowered to the ground, and they began on the second, as others slid the iron bolts free. The second beam fell to the ground, and Quill pushed the gates open. She gestured back to the gatehouse of Arrowhead, beckoning for them to hurry. The Rats rushed over the road, bringing the patients from the hospital with them, as the crossbeams were dragged through the open gates.

'Greenhides!' called Daniel.

'Keep moving!' cried Quill. 'Everybody through the gates.'

Emily turned, her heart pounding as she saw a wave of greenhides running towards them from Blade territory. They were cramming onto the road that ran between the Great Walls and the Scythe wall.

'Wolfpack!' yelled Quill. 'Protect the others!'

The dozen or so remaining soldiers formed a thin cordon along the road as the others continued to cross and run through the open gates. Emily drew her sword to join them, but a small group of Hammers blocked her path, and started to push her and Daniel towards the gates. A few patients were struggling to cross the road, the Rats flanking them supporting their shoulders as the greenhides raced closer. Emily struggled to free herself from the Hammers, but they kept pushing her back.

The first greenhides reached the line of soldiers and swept through it, barely pausing to slash and rip their way past. One of the beasts leapt onto a small group of Rats carrying a patient across the road, its claws tearing through their flesh. Emily and Daniel were bundled through the gate, and the Rats began to push them closed. The last survivors out on the road were cut down in seconds as the gates edged shut. Every remaining Rat and soldier got behind the high doors, shoving and pushing them as the greenhides tried to get through. A claw flashed through the gap in the gates, ripping a Rat almost in half. Emily punched out with her sword, ramming it into the face of the greenhide, its tip entering the beast's left eye as it shrieked and fell back. The gates closed, but the pressure from the greenhides beyond was immense, and the Rats strained against it, each shoulder and arm against the doors to keep them from opening.

'Rats!' cried Quill. 'Get the beams back up!'

The crossbeams were lifted from where they had been dragged through, and were brought up to the gates. Rats with weighty tool bags over their shoulders rushed forward, and hammered long nails through the beams, fixing them to the inside of the gates. The pressure on the doors decreased as soon as the first beam was in position, and the rest of the survivors staggered back as the second beam was nailed in place. Emily pushed the hands of the Hammers from her arms and strode forwards to the gate, her fingers feeling the beams to make sure they were secure. Through a small crack she could see the hordes of greenhides on the road, feasting on the bodies of those they had slain.

She felt Quill's presence next to her. 'Five Wolves, six Rats and three patients; gone in under a minute. You were right; if we'd stayed they would have got us all. No one's coming to save us.'

'These gates won't hold forever,' Emily said, 'especially if the others are only barred from the outside. They're bound to work out how to get them open.'

Quill nodded. 'Yes. Once they've eaten their way through the rest of the Bulwark, then every one of them will be trying to get into Scythe and Hammer territory.'

They turned, and Emily glanced around for the first time since going through the gate. Ahead of them spread miles of fields, flat except for the small farmhouses and barns that littered the landscape. She walked forwards a few paces and crouched, feeling the freshly-tilled soil against her fingers.

She glanced at Torphin. 'How many Scythes live here?'

'About a hundred and fifty thousand, my lady,' he said. 'There used to be more, but the population of the Bulwark has dwindled over the last few centuries.'

'And the Hammers?'

'About a quarter of million of them live in a space half the size of Scythe territory, my lady.'

Daniel joined them. 'Presumably most of them will have made it through the Middle Walls by now?'

Torphin said nothing. 'We should be moving, my lord. It'll be slow-going accompanying the wounded from the hospital, but we need to make it to the Hammer wall before sunset, as the greenhides will most likely have broken through into Scythe land by then.'

The survivors got underway, with Quill leading them down a farm track that led to the nearest cluster of buildings. As they approached, four figures emerged from the farmhouse, all clutching weapons.

'Stay where you are,' and old man called to them, a long knife grasped in his hand.

Quill raised a hand for the column to halt.

'Don't they realise what's happening?' said Emily.

'Come with me,' said Quill, 'and Torphin, you too; bring a Scythe with you.'

The broad Hammer nodded, and gestured to one of the Rats.

'Stay here, Danny,' Emily said. 'If things get ugly, there should be one Aurelian left to keep going.'

'I saw you kill another greenhide,' he said. 'That's two now. If you can handle them, you'll be fine with a few Scythes.'

Quill, Emily, Torphin and the Scythe split from the group and began walking slowly towards the farmhouse, their hands empty and raised.

The farmer squinted at them as they approached. To his left were three others, all younger. One had a crossbow, while another was holding the leashes of three large dogs.

'You're in danger,' Quill called out to them.

'You have no right to be here, Blade,' the farmer shouted. 'We've done nothing wrong.'

'The greenhides have breached the Great Walls,' Quill went on; 'you have to leave, head for the Middle Walls.'

'The Middle Walls? It's sowing time, you fool; we can't leave.'

'They don't trust Blades,' muttered Torphin; 'with good reason.' He stepped forward a pace. 'I'm a Hammer, and this man to my left is a Scythe. The soldier speaks the truth; the Bulwark is breached. Greenhides have already penetrated the land of the Blades, and they'll be coming here next.'

'Nonsense, the greenhides will never get in here. You're just scaremongering. There ain't never been a single greenhide got in here, not in a thousand years. And if any does, we'll chase them away. My ancestors have farmed this land for generations, and it'll take more than a few greenhides to shift us.'

'Thousands have already been killed,' said Emily.

The farmer frowned. 'You might speak fancy, but that doesn't mean I have to listen to you.'

'But...'

'My lady,' said Torphin, 'some folk just can't be talked round.' He turned to the farmer. 'We want to cross these lands. We'll not disturb anything, or take anything, you have our word.'

'A cart would be useful,' said Emily, 'to transport the wounded.'

'Tough,' said the farmer. 'I ain't got no spare cart to sell you. You can cross my farm, but I'll be keeping a close eye on you.'

'Thank you,' said Quill.

She turned, and waved to the others, who began to walk up the track.

'This is crazy,' whispered Emily. 'They're going to get slaughtered.'

'I know,' muttered Torphin. 'Remember that things haven't changed here in a thousand years. We're lucky he's not setting his dogs on us.'

Daniel caught them up. 'Is there food or water? Can the farmer help us with...?'

'No,' said Quill. 'Tell the Rats to be respectful as we pass. Steal nothing.'

He glanced at Emily, who shrugged.

The survivors of Arrowhead trudged onwards, passing the first farm, then crossing a long stretch of open fields, lined with hedges and strips of tall trees. Far to their left they saw an enclosure with cattle grazing, and they could see armed Scythes eye them suspiciously as they followed the track towards Hammer territory. As the sun started its descent, the sound of screams echoed up far to their right.

'Hurry,' cried Quill. 'The greenhides have broken through the Scythe gates.'

Emily glanced around, but could see no movement anywhere. 'How far are we from Hammer lands?'

'Another mile,' said Torphin.

They carried on, and the last mile seemed to stretch on forever as the wounded stumbled down the track. The screams grew louder with every passing minute, and the Rats glanced over their shoulders with growing anxiety. A high wall appeared ahead of them, stretching from left to right at the far end of a line of fields.

'There are usually Blades here,' said Torphin, 'guarding the gates that connect Scythe to Hammer territory.'

Emily glanced around. 'It seems deserted.'

They reached one of the gates, and Quill thumped on it. 'Anyone there? We need through. Open up.'

The cries and screams were getting closer, and the Rats clustered by the gate, setting the wounded down.

'Open the gate!' cried Quill again, striking the wood with the hilt of her sword.

'We don't open to Blades,' called out a voice from beyond the gate.

Torphin strode forwards. 'Fellow Hammers,' he cried out; 'will you open for the Aurelians? We have them here with us, the heir and his wife, Lord and Lady Aurelian. Will you let the greenhides slaughter those sent to save us?'

The voice behind the gate fell silent, and Torphin gestured for Daniel and Emily to approach.

'Speak to them,' he said; 'quickly, before it's too late.'

'I am Emily Aurelian,' she called out. 'The greenhides are coming; please let us through.' She glanced at Daniel.

'And I'm... Lord Aurelian,' he said. 'Help us.'

They stood in silence for a moment, staring at the gates, then they began to swing open, slowly revealing a crowd of Hammers beyond. Most were armed with large tools rather than weapons, and they stared at Emily and Daniel.

'The Aurelians?' said one. 'Are we dreaming? Has the legend come to life?'

Quill pushed forwards, and the Rats squeezed through the entrance. A hundred yards down the track, the first greenhides came into view, racing toward them, a high shriek of blood lust echoing through the air.

The last of the survivors rushed through the gates, and the strong doors were pushed shut, and heavy beams placed on the metal supports to bar it closed. Emily glanced around. A huge crowd had gathered, filling the area between the wall and rows of narrow terraced streets. The Hammers stared at her, then slowly got down onto their knees, as a low chant of 'Aurelian' rose up. Daniel glanced at her.

Torphin stepped forward. 'We have brought the Aurelians to the land of the Hammers,' he said, getting down on his knees before them. 'They have come to save us.'

Emily took Daniel's hand, and swallowed.

CHAPTER 2

THE WALKING WOUNDED

The Cold Sea – 22nd Amalan 3420

Corthie watched the sunrise, his hands gripping the ship's rail, and the side of his shirt damp with blood. The pinks and reds of dawn were spreading out to cover the lower half of the sunward sky, while the thick dark line on the horizon grew almost imperceptibly larger with every passing moment. A warm wind was blowing into his face, and he savoured it after so many months of cold.

'A beautiful morning,' said the captain; 'the first of summer.'

Corthie turned. 'Aye. The first day without rain in two months. Is that Icehaven ahead of us?'

'Yes, but it's still a couple of hours away. Those are the hills of the Iceward Range that you can see on the horizon. The town sits at the bottom, next to the sea.' She glanced at him. 'I wasn't expecting to see you up on deck; I thought you'd received an injury getting out of the caverns.'

He smiled, suppressing the pain coming from his side. 'I'm fine.'

'Glad to hear it,' she said. 'Our little detour through the night seems to have worked. There hasn't been a single sighting of any Blade vessels, and we should have a clear run into town. Do you know what you're going to do when you land?'

'Not exactly,' he said. 'Yaizra and Achan were still sleeping when I woke up, and I left them in their bunks.'

'And the... other passenger?' She shook her head. 'I could hardly believe what Achan told me when I saw he was the only one waiting for the boat yesterday morning. What possessed you to rescue a prisoner from the castle?'

Corthie stared out to sea. 'We felt sorry for her, I guess.'

'Has she spoken?'

'No.'

'Have you any idea who she is?'

He shook his head.

The captain nodded. 'I don't want to seem harsh, but she's your responsibility. I agreed to take three fugitives off Grey Isle, not four. When we land, you'll be taking her with you.'

'Of course, aye. And thanks again, Captain; you saved our asses.'

She laughed. 'It'll be something to tell the grandchildren in years to come; that time I had a Champion of the Bulwark on my ship.'

'Former champion.'

'It'll be my story, and I'll tell it any way I like.'

He smiled.

'Hey!' cried a voice behind them.

They turned and watched as Yaizra approached from the top of the aft stairs.

'Morning,' said Corthie.

She stared at him. 'What in the blessed names of Amalia's ass are you doing out of bed, big lump?'

'I couldn't sleep,' he said. 'Between Achan snoring and the old lady mumbling all night, I was lying awake staring at the ceiling.'

She grabbed the edge of his cloak and pulled it wide, revealing the patch of blood soaking the side of his shirt.

The captain puffed out her cheeks. 'He told me he was fine.'

'Well, he's not fine; he's a damned idiot.'

'I'll let you two argue it out,' she said. 'We'll be docking in two hours; I'll speak to you before then.'

The captain turned and left them by the railings.

'Back to the cabin,' said Yaizra. 'Now.'

'What difference does it make?' he said. 'You heard her; we're nearly there.'

'But I'd managed to get the bleeding to stop, you oaf, and now look at it. We have two hours; you need to be resting.'

'I've done nothing but rest since I got onto this boat.'

'Corthie, you were stabbed yesterday. I know you want to be all big and manly, but I'd prefer you survived the next few days.' Her glare faded. 'There's breakfast.'

'Breakfast?'

'I thought that might grab your attention. Yes, a sailor brought food to the cabin, and right now, Achan is eating it all.'

'We can't allow that.'

'No, we can't. So, are you coming?'

Corthie sighed, and gestured towards the stairs. They walked along the deck, feeling the motion of the ship beneath them. He felt the pain in his side increase as he descended the narrow steps, and Yaizra shook her head as she watched him grimace. She led him to the small cabin and they went inside.

'He was up on deck,' Yaizra said as Achan looked up from a bowl of food. 'He blamed it on your snoring.'

Achan frowned. 'I don't snore.'

'Yes, you do,' she said.

Corthie staggered over to his bed and sat down, his hand clutching his side. He glanced at the old woman in the other bed. Her lips were still moving, but her voice had faded from a whisper into almost silence.

'She's not doing so well this morning,' said Achan, catching his glance. 'I managed to get her to take some water, but she's weakening.'

'I thought she would start to recover with that mask off her face,' said Yaizra.

'Maybe the pain was keeping her going.'

Corthie frowned. 'That doesn't make sense.'

'Yeah,' said Yaizra; 'I thought you told us she was a god?'

Achan shrugged as he filled two spare bowls with food. 'She is, well, she must be. No mortal could have survived that mask; it would have killed any of us sitting here, right? But say it is her, say it really is Princess Yendra, then what if she was tortured like that ever since the end of the Civil War? That's over three hundred years ago. Imagine what that's done to her self-healing powers.' He passed a bowl to each of them. 'Maybe her powers got swamped by the injuries caused by the mask, and that was all that was keeping her going? Now that the source of the injury has been removed, maybe she can finally give up the fight.'

Yaizra frowned as she picked up a spoon. 'You mean you think she's going to die?'

'I don't know, but she's definitely weaker than she was yesterday when we brought her on board.'

'It can't be her,' said Yaizra. 'Everyone knows she was executed for killing Prince Michael; it's in every school book in the City.'

'Everyone thought she was executed,' he said, 'but remember that it was supposed to have been carried out in secret, in the Royal Palace in Ooste. Thousands witnessed Michael die, but no one saw the execution of Yendra that supposedly followed. What if it was a trick, and they decided to punish her, but not kill her?'

'But the God-Queen hated her,' said Yaizra. 'Yendra killed her favourite child.'

'Yes, but the God-King and God-Queen separated right afterwards; what if they fell out over Yendra?'

She shook her head. 'We should have left her where she was.'

'But we didn't,' said Corthie as he ate.

Achan's eyes lit up. 'Can you imagine the reaction of the Evaders when they find out? That is, I mean, if it really is her, of course. They'll go crazy. She was loved by every one of them; her daughters too.'

'I thought they wanted rid of all of the gods and demigods,' said Yaizra.

'This will change everything. We should spread the word as soon as we land.'

Yaizra widened her eyes. 'Are you insane? It'll be hard enough trying to get off this ship without attracting attention, and you want to start a rumour that Princess Yendra has returned from the grave? We'd be arrested within minutes.'

'I'm with Yaizra on this,' said Corthie. 'Let's at least find somewhere to stay before we start with all that stuff.'

'Cheers, big lump.' She put down her bowl and stretched her arms. 'I'll be home soon; I can't believe it.'

Corthie glanced at her. 'Have you got relatives in Icehaven?'

'Oh yeah, tons. Sisters, cousins, uncles, but we won't be seeing any of them, not for a while, anyway. I want to keep away from the old gangs I used to be involved with.'

'Are your family all criminals?' said Achan.

She nodded. 'Mostly, though I wouldn't call them that to their faces.'

'They'd help us though, wouldn't they?' said Corthie.

'Yeah, but they'd suck me right back into the family business, which is what got me caught and locked up in the first place. They'll find out I'm back sooner or later, but I want to get settled before I have to face them.'

'Face them?' said Achan. 'Is there something you're not telling us?'

Yaizra stood. 'They're my family, and if I don't want to talk about it, then that's none of your business.'

She walked from the cabin and closed the door.

Achan looked over to Corthie. 'She killed someone, did you know that?'

'I thought she was a thief?'

'She is, or was, but you don't get sent to Tarstation for a bit of thievery. She's not a cold-blooded killer, I'm not saying that, but something went wrong on her last job when she was caught. And now I'm thinking that maybe her family might not be too happy to see her again.'

Corthie finished his breakfast and lay down on the bed, moving slowly to protect the injury in his side.

'I need to find Aila when we get to land,' he said.

Achan frowned.

'But I have no idea how to go about it,' he went on. 'She could be anywhere.'

'She's a demigod; she'll be living in luxury inside one of their palaces. You should forget about her, mate. Mortals have no business being with her kind.'

'Make your mind up,' Corthie said. 'A minute ago you were going on about Princess Yendra.'

'She's different; everyone knows that. Yendra and her daughters stood up for the mortals, fought for them, while the rest of the Royal Family did nothing.'

'That's not true. Aila told me that she helped Yendra in the war. She cares about the mortals.'

'I guess she'd be able to tell us if the old lady really is Yendra, I suppose.'

Corthie glanced over at the emaciated figure on the other bed. Her arms were lying across the covers, and her skin had a yellow tinge to it. A fresh bandage was over the top half of her face, and blood from her eye sockets had seeped into the material.

'If it is her,' he said, 'how would Marcus react?'

'She killed his father, and they were enemies before that, so I don't imagine he would be very happy. That's another reason we should get the news out quickly; it'll rattle him, and give him another problem to deal with.'

'Unless she dies.'

'Yeah.' He turned to the old woman. 'Come on, stay alive; the City needs you.'

His stomach full, Corthie managed to doze for a couple of hours, the motion of the ship soothing him to sleep. When he awoke the cabin lay in thick shadow, and he turned to see Achan and Yaizra packing up their things.

'What time is it?' he said.

'It's still early,' said Yaizra.

'Why's it so dark? I thought summer had begun.'

'The ship's gone under the shadow of the Iceward Range. Do you remember how I told you that Icehaven never sees the sun? The hills are too high.'

Corthie groaned. 'No sun?'

Yaizra shrugged. 'No greenhides.'

He swung his legs off the bed and winced in pain. He checked his side, and saw the fresh blood.

'Take your shirt off,' she said. 'We're going to have to put a new bandage on you.'

'Stop fussing; I'm fine. As long as you two carry Yendra, I can stumble along behind.'

'Remember, don't call her that once we're out of the cabin.'

'What should we call her, then?' said Achan.

'We'll say she's your grandmother,' she said. 'Granny Achan, that's what we'll call her.'

There was a light rap on their door, and it opened.

'We're approaching the harbour,' said the captain. 'The sailors have rigged together a stretcher for you to carry the old lady.'

'Achan's grandmother,' said Yaizra.

'Oh. Right. Achan's grandmother.'

Corthie pulled his boots on as the captain glanced around at them.

'We're going to berth somewhere nice and quiet, away from the main quaysides, so that you might, *might*, be able to get off the ship without too many folk seeing you. After that, then I guess you're on your own. If I had any money left I'd give you some, but this new ship took every coin I owned.'

'You've done enough, Captain,' said Corthie; 'thank you.'

He walked out into the corridor, where a sailor was holding up the new stretcher. Corthie nodded and took it, then passed it through to the cabin. Achan held it steady as Yaizra carefully moved the old woman onto the stretcher, then placed a blanket over her.

The captain gestured to the sailors in the corridor. 'Move her up onto deck, nice and slow.'

'Aye, Captain.'

The sailors took over, and carried the old woman on the stretcher up the steep and narrow steps as the others followed. Corthie went last, so no one would see him clutching his side and grimacing as he ascended the wooden stairs. He emerged onto the deck, and into the shadows of the Iceward Range. The hills towered high above a town that sat at their feet, and the harbour lay before them. The arm of a long breakwater swept towards them as they sailed.

'There it is,' said the captain; 'Icehaven. Think of it as a darker, rougher version of Dalrig.'

'Hey,' said Yaizra; 'I heard that. Take no notice of her, big lump; Icehaven's much nicer than scabby old Dalrig, and at least we haven't got a mad prince in charge.'

'Fair point,' said the captain, 'but I'd rather have a bit of sun, even if it meant keeping Montieth.'

'Is there a demigod that runs this place?' said Corthie.

'Lady Yvona,' said Yaizra, 'and I don't care what Achan says; she's always been good for the Icewarders.'

'Yvona?' said Corthie.

'The only surviving child of Princess Niomi,' said Achan, from where he was crouching by the old woman's stretcher.

'Let me guess; the rest were killed in the Civil War?'

'Yes, including Niomi herself. Lady Yvona withdrew from the conflict and made peace with Prince Michael after her mother's death.'

'Has she submitted to Marcus?'

'She will have done,' said the captain, her eyes on the approaching harbour, 'though it will have meant almost nothing. I doubt a single Blade has ever entered Icehaven.'

'We have our own town walls,' said Yaizra, 'and the hills shield us. We don't need the rest of the City, but they need us for coal, iron, silver and everything else that can be mined out of the ground. Lady Yvona has used that to leverage good deals for us, and no one goes hungry here, unlike in the Circuit.'

The captain frowned. 'It's just a shame that the locals hate outsiders so much. They don't even like their fellow Icewarders that live next to the Circuit on the other side of these hills.' She glanced at Achan. 'It might be better if you say nothing; your accent marks you out as being from the Bulwark, and they might report you to the militia. And Malik alone knows what they'll make of Corthie.'

They all watched as the ship sailed past the breakwater and entered the harbour. Along the busy waterfront stood a high row of grand, stone buildings, with a huge structure on the right side of the long quay. It rose above every other building in the town, and was fashioned from a granite so light in colour that it seemed almost silver.

'Alkirk Palace,' said Yaizra. 'Lady Yvona lives in a few rooms; the rest of it is taken up with the Icewarder government and a hospital.'

The ship banked left as sailors lowered the mainsail in the calm waters of the harbour basin. They passed a large fishing fleet, and piers lined with tall merchant ships.

'We're heading for the last wharf on the left,' the captain said. 'It's as far away as possible from the harbour master's office, where I'll have to report the boat's arrival. I want you to disembark the moment the gangway touches solid ground, and then I'll deny you were ever on board. Understood?'

'Aye,' said Corthie. He glanced at Yaizra. 'What's your plan?'

'Your part in it is simple; keep your mouth closed and follow where I lead.'

The vessel slowed to a crawl as the wharf approached. The far end of the docks were almost deserted, with just a few other boats tied up, several in a state of disrepair. A line of ramshackle warehouses backed onto the wharf, and then the streets and houses of the town spread back. Sailors jumped the gap when they were a yard away, and began to secure the ropes to the old cleats that studded the edge of the wharf. A wide, wooden gangway was placed into position, and the captain gestured to them.

'Farewell, and good luck.'

Yaizra and Achan picked up the stretcher, and Corthie followed them as they strode across the plank. Corthie turned and nodded to the captain, then stepped onto dry land. He was back in the City at last, six and a half months after he had been wrapped in chains and placed on a ship. Yaizra strode up the side of the empty wharf, then took a street leading to the left. High tenements of grey granite rose up on either side of the road.

'Everything here is grey,' said Achan; 'and it's cold.'

'This is as warm as it gets here,' Yaizra said; 'just be thankful we didn't arrive in winter.'

They reached a small square and Yaizra came to a halt. She and Achan lowered the stretcher onto a low bench, and Yaizra rubbed her wrists as Achan checked on the old woman.

'I think we got away unseen,' she said. 'The next step is getting to a house where we'll be able to stay for a couple of days.' She paused as the sound of footsteps approached. Voices drifted through the air towards them, and Corthie recognised the accent.

'Blades,' he muttered.

Yaizra raised an eyebrow. 'Get ready to run.'

Corthie felt the pain ripple from the injury in his side. 'Um... I'm not sure I can.'

A large group entered the square from the other direction, and Corthie relaxed as he saw they were civilians. Old men and women were walking with children, leading them by the hand, and carrying luggage. A cart was wheeled along with them, loaded with trunks and cases. The faces on each one of them were downcast and troubled.

Yaizra frowned. 'What in Malik's name are Blade civilians doing in Icehaven? Wait here.' She strode towards the group. 'Excuse me,' she said to them; 'what are you lot doing here?'

Most of the group ignored her, and some threw her glances of contempt.

'I'm getting a little tired of answering that question,' said an old man.

'We've lost everything, and the damn folk here are as unfriendly as any I've met.'

Yaizra glared at him. 'Go home if you don't like it.'

Cries of anger rose up from the group, and a few threatening gestures were aimed at her.

'Leave the girl alone,' said an old woman; 'she clearly hasn't heard.'

'Heard what?' Yaizra said. 'I just stepped off a boat.'

'The Bulwark's gone, love,' said the old woman.

'Eh?'

'The greenhides breached the Great Walls yesterday evening; and they overran it in hours. We were the lucky ones, we were close to the Middle Walls and could leave before those beasts could reach us.'

Corthie pressed his hand to his side and staggered over. 'The greenhides are in the Bulwark?'

'And what about the Hammers and the Scythes?' said Achan, his face as grey as the buildings.

'I don't know what happened down that end of the Bulwark, son,' the old woman said.

'What about the dragon?' said Corthie.

'Buckler fell, lad.'

Corthie felt winded, as if someone had struck him in the stomach. He stumbled back a step, his mind reeling.

The woman squinted up at him. 'Do I know you from somewhere, lad?'

'He's never been in the Bulwark in his life,' said Yaizra, 'so I doubt it. Are there more Blades like you here?'

She nodded. 'The road over the hills from the Middle Walls was full, love. There will be thousands of us here before nightfall, and thousands more in the Circuit and down in Port Sanders. Medio will be heaving with refugees this morning.'

'Thanks for letting us know,' she said, and the group carried on their way.

Corthie collapsed onto a bench. He felt numb, his mind unable to take in the enormity of what the woman had told them. He had grown to hate the Blades after being chased across the Western Bank and the Grey Isle, but had never imagined that the Great Walls could ever be breached. He pictured Blackrose in the lair at Arrowhead, and Maddie, and his old friends in the Wolfpack. If he had been there, he could have prevented it.

'I can't believe it,' said Achan, as the three of them sat staring into space. 'How could this happen?'

'It's happening right now, isn't it?' said Yaizra. 'As we sit here, thousands are being slaughtered.'

'How strong are the Middle Walls?' said Corthie.

'Not as strong as the Great Walls,' she said. 'Beyond that, I don't know.'

Achan started weeping, his head in his hands. 'Everyone I know will be dead.'

'Maybe not,' Yaizra said, putting a hand on his shoulder. 'The Hammers are closer to the Middle Walls than the Scythes. Many might have made it through the gates.'

'What gates?' said Achan. 'The gates that connect the Hammers to Medio have been walled up for centuries, to stop any of us escaping the Bulwark. Only Princess Yendra ever smashed one open, when she tried to free us in the Civil War, but they sealed it up again after she failed. Don't you understand? The Hammers and the Scythes are expendable! No one in the City cares what happens to us.'

Yaizra glanced away, then stood. 'Come on; we need to get moving.'

'Where is everybody?' said Corthie. 'With this news, I'd have thought that everyone would be out in the streets.'

'We'll find out soon,' she said. 'The house we're going to isn't far.'

Achan wiped his face and they lifted the stretcher. Corthie pushed himself up and staggered after them through the quiet streets. They turned away from the harbour, and went down a narrow alley bordered by rows of squat, granite houses. Yaizra checked no one was watching, then knocked on a door. The sound of a crying child filtered through, and Yaizra raised an eyebrow.

A young woman answered the door, a baby in her arms. 'What do you want? I…' Her mouth opened.

'Hi, Tami,' said Yaizra. 'Is that your baby?'

'What? No, no, it's my sister's. What are you doing here? I thought you… ah…'

'Can we come in?'

'Is that a stretcher? And who are these folk?'

'Friends,' said Yaizra. 'Can we stay over tonight? We're in a bit of a tricky spot.'

'Stay over? All of you? I don't know. I'm in here on my own just now.'

'Where's everyone else?'

'The whole town was mobilised before dawn, Yaizra. The militia went round door-to-door. I only got to stay because someone had to look after the baby.'

Achan coughed. 'My arms are getting sore.'

Yaizra glanced at the woman. 'Please? Can we come in at least?'

Tami frowned, then nodded. She opened the door wider and stood to the side as Yaizra and Achan carried the stretcher through. Corthie nodded to her as he grasped his side and squeezed past. They went into a room that held a fire and a small kitchen, and they rested the stretcher down on top of a table.

Tami stood by the door, the baby held close. 'You heard what happened?'

'Just ten minutes ago,' said Yaizra; 'I was on a boat last night.'

'Did you escape?'

'Yeah, and these two guys helped me do it. This is Achan, and this is, uh… big lump.'

Tami frowned. 'Is he injured?'

'He was stabbed yesterday.'

'What? You can't bring him here; what if he dies? And that old woman looks like she's already dead. You'll have to go before everyone gets back.'

'That could be ages, and we've nowhere else to go.'

'That's not true; you could go home.'

Yaizra lowered her eyes. 'I don't think I should.'

'Why?'

'Let's speak alone for a minute.'

The two woman left the room, and Tami closed the door behind them. Corthie took a seat and exhaled in pain.

Achan frowned. 'You need to lie down for, like, ten days.'

'Three would probably do it. In fact, I might have to close my eyes, just for a minute.

He leaned his head against the surface of the table, his head swimming with pain. He shut his eyes, and was unconscious within seconds.

When he awoke the room was in darkness. A noise came from his left and he opened his eyes to see Tami light a small oil lamp on the wall.

He groaned, and she turned, then started to back out of the room. 'Your friend, the uh, big lump, is awake.'

Yaizra walked through as he lifted his head from the table. She handed him a mug. 'Drink this.'

He sat up and raised the mug to his lips. Warmed brandy, mixed with something else.

'How you feeling?' she said.

'Terrible.'

'There's a bed waiting for you. We tried to move you from the table but, well, you were too heavy. Tami's letting us stay overnight.'

'Aye?'

'Yeah. Every able-bodied citizen is at the town walls, or helping the refugees find food and shelter. They've been streaming in all day through the gates, coming over the hill road from the Middle Walls.'

He noticed the table was empty.

'Don't worry,' she said, 'you-know-who's still alive. We put her in a bed, and that's where you're going.' She stuck out her hand. 'Come on, big lump.'

He put a hand on the table and pushed himself up, then took her arm and she helped him to the door.

'Say thanks to Tami for me,' he said, 'and where's Achan?'

Yaizra said nothing as she opened a door. Inside were four beds, and she led him to the closest one. The old woman was lying in the next bed along, with a fresh bandage on her face. The only indication that she was still alive was the soft movement of her lips as she voicelessly called for her daughter.

Corthie sat on the bed and let Yaizra change the dressing on his wound. The side of his shirt was dyed a deep red, and she peeled off the old bandage and wrapped a clean one round his abdomen.

'Why haven't you answered me?' he said.

She fastened a pin to the dressing and glanced up. 'Achan's gone. He disappeared while you were sleeping. I was speaking to Tami, then went back into the room and he'd gone. I think the loss of the Bulwark has hit him hard.'

Corthie nodded. 'He'll be back.'

'Maybe,' she said. 'And I have other news. It seems ridiculously insignificant compared to what's happening in the Bulwark right now, but I thought you might want to know.'

'Aye?'

'There was an announcement from the Royal Palace that arrived before the news from the Bulwark did. It concerns your Lady Aila.'

'Aila? Is she alright?'

'She's got herself a husband.'

Corthie blinked. 'What?'

'Sorry. She got married yesterday. I don't know how in Malik's name he persuaded her, but Duke Marcus has finally snared his bride.'

CHAPTER 3

THE TWO ROSES

The Cold Sea – 22nd Amalan 3420

Blackrose soared through the clear sky, the light from the two moons shining off the smooth surface of the Cold Sea. A red glow on the sunward horizon revealed the coming dawn, and Maddie gripped onto the harness as her eyes jerked open.

She had fallen asleep, and she blinked her eyes in the cold wind. In front of her, Rosie was huddled in, her head resting on the padded leather of the harness, and a strap round her waist to stop her from slipping off the dragon's back.

Land appeared ahead of them, the rocky cliffs of the Western Bank, and Blackrose glided towards it. She circled overhead a few times, then came down to land on a high outcrop of rock. She folded her wings in and turned her head.

'Good morning, my little Jackdaws,' she said; 'it's time to rest for a moment and collect ourselves.'

Maddie looked into the dragon's eyes. She wanted to ask her why she had abandoned the City and left the Bulwark when it was being overrun with greenhides, but she already knew the response she would get. 'How far did we fly?'

'About two hundred miles,' said Blackrose. 'I went iceward, then turned back when I realised it was getting too cold for you both.'

'I'm still freezing. We need blankets and warmer clothes if we're going to fly iceward at night.'

'We will fix this problem. First, wake your sister.'

'Why?'

'Because I wish to speak with her.'

Maddie put her hand on Rosie's shoulder and shook her gently. The girl's eyes opened and she woke with a start, jumping up and gazing around. Her eyes caught sight of the dragon and she let out a cry.

'Hush, smaller Jackdaw,' said Blackrose; 'I'm not going to eat you.'

Rosie glanced back and saw Maddie sitting behind her.

'It's alright,' Maddie said, 'we're safe.'

'Mum and dad...'

'I know.'

'Greenhides.'

Maddie felt her eyes start to well, and she glanced away. She couldn't break down; she needed to be strong for her sister.

'Where are we?'

Blackrose moved her head closer to Rosie. 'We are about one hundred miles from the City, little one. What is your name? In the hurry to gather you up, I neglected to ask.'

'Rosie Jackdaw.'

'Another rose? A little rose. How old are you, little Rose?'

'Fifteen.'

'Are you scared?'

'Of you? Yes, but I'm more scared of the greenhides. Are there any here?'

'No, I examined the nearby area before landing. There are no greenhides within fifty miles of this place. Are you happy to be alive?'

'Yes.'

'Good.'

Maddie frowned at the dragon, then turned to her sister. 'I think she's waiting for you to thank her for saving your life.'

'What?' said Rosie. 'Oh yes, sorry; thank you.'

'It was nothing, little Rose; you have your sister to thank. I intended to leave, and she insisted we try to rescue her family first. Now, please descend from my back, as my neck is straining turning to look at you.'

The dragon straightened her long neck and stretched it. Rosie and Maddie exchanged a glance, then unfastened their straps and started to climb down the series of knots and loops that ran across the dragon's flank.

'Thanks, Maddie,' Rosie said as they descended.

'Don't, Rosie. I mean, I'm glad you're alright, but I was too late to save mum and dad.'

'You still thought of us; in the midst of all that panic and terror, you remembered us.'

Maddie jumped the last yard, then helped Rosie down to the surface of the large, rocky outcrop. Ahead of them stretched the Cold Sea, its smooth waters starting to glow pink in the dawn light. To their right, the sun was rising, splitting the sky in reds and yellows.

Maddie stood next to her sister as they watched the dawn. 'Tell me what happened.'

'Mum woke me up,' Rosie said, 'and I could hear the bells coming from Stormshield. She told me to get dressed, and I did. As I was getting my boots on, the bells stopped, and I thought it was a false alarm. Then the screams started. I ran downstairs, and mum and dad were carrying swords and shouting about whether to run or fight, and then it was too late. I looked out of the window and saw them, hundreds of them, their claws shining in the light of the streetlamps.

'One of them burst through the front door and dad got dragged away, then another came in through the window. I ran back upstairs. Mum was right behind me, and then...' She put a hand to her eyes. 'Then they got her too. I went up onto the roof and barricaded the hatch by pushing the water tank over it. I'd moved my ballista up there because dad said it was too big for the garden, then I started shooting.'

She glanced at Maddie. 'It really happened, didn't it? The Bulwark has gone.'

'I was there when they breached the walls, and saw Buckler die.'

'How did you.. I mean, where did you find another dragon?'

'This is what I've been doing all this time, looking after Blackrose.'

The dragon turned to them. 'Maddie Jackdaw is my rider.'

Rosie looked from the dragon to her sister. 'The last time I saw you, you had a broken leg, and arm, and looked half dead. Was that the dragon?'

'Yes.'

'An accident,' said Blackrose. 'Had I intended to kill Maddie, she would be dead. I displayed my claws to Buckler, and she got in the way.' Blackrose raised her left forelimb and extended her claws. 'I managed to retract these just in time.'

Rosie stared at the thick, sharp claws. 'Can you breathe fire?'

'Of course. Do you not recall that I incinerated the greenhides surrounding your house to assist you to escape?'

Rosie's face darkened. 'Then why didn't you help the City? Why did you fly away?'

'Good question,' said Maddie. 'Why don't you answer her, Blackrose?'

'I will answer you, little Rose, despite the hostile tone you have adopted, because you are my rider's kin. My reason for refusing to help the City is simple; I despise it. The City held me in chains for more than ten years, and I was shackled when Buckler was slain, otherwise I would have done everything in my power to save him. Were it not for Maddie, I would have remained enchained within my lair, and the greenhides would have torn me to pieces, eventually. Would you help someone who had treated you so badly? Perhaps you would, but my heart is older than yours, and I have seen kingdoms come and go. I am sorry I couldn't save your parents, but I won't be sorry if the City is swept aside. Let the greenhides exult in the blood of my oppressors; may they feast upon the bones of Kano and Marcus; that's what I say. Does that answer your question, little Rose?'

Rosie stared at the dragon, saying nothing.

'What now?' said Maddie. 'Are you just going to fly about aimlessly?'

'I have brought us in this direction for a reason. Corthie Holdfast. Did you not tell me that he had been sent to a place along this coastline, called Tarstation?'

Maddie's eyes widened. 'I did. Are we close?'

'As I am uncertain as to its location, I cannot answer that. All I know is what you told me, that it was next to the Cold Sea, iceward of the City.'

'They burn oil there,' said Rosie. 'We'll be able to see the smoke from far away.'

Blackrose laughed. 'So that's where Maddie's common sense went; you got her share.'

Maddie glared at her. 'Hilarious.'

'And is Corthie Holdfast there?' said Rosie. 'The ex-champion? I thought he was dead.'

'We all did,' said Maddie, 'but we found out he was sent as a prisoner to this Tarstation place.' She frowned. 'What will we do when we get there?'

'If they have Corthie,' said Blackrose, 'then we rescue him. If they don't, then we shall look elsewhere. In either case, you are advised to stock up on everything you think you'll need – clothes, food, blankets, and secure it onto the harness.'

'How fast can you fly?' said Rosie.

'I'm a little slower than I was in my youth, but I can cover a mile every minute if I need to. My normal speed is a little lower than that, except when I am descending in a fast glide, or if the wind is assisting me.'

Rosie nodded, then peered up and down the length of the dragon. 'You're much bigger than Buckler was. Do you need a running start to take off?'

'I shall choose not to take offence at that question. The answer is no. Buckler was faster than I, this I admit, but that was on account of his youth, and my wings are more powerful than his were.' She stretched them out for Rosie to see, and the girl studied them, walking across the rocky outcrop to examine every inch.

Maddie watched as her sister asked the dragon questions about velocity and angles of ascent, and her mind drifted away. She sat down on the rock and gazed into the dawn, as images of the previous evening flashed through her mind. She saw Buckler being dragged down by the swarms of greenhides over and over, and then the image switched to the moment when the gate wouldn't close, and she had realised the outer wall had been breached. That part had been her fault. Their officer had been killed, and she had been in charge of the surviving Rats. If she had ordered the gate to be closed a few moments earlier, then the Bulwark might still be standing.

She started to rationalise it. There should have more Blades on the walls; there should have been a full company of them behind the outer wall to make sure the gates were closed irrespective of whether or not there were any Rats still out beyond the defences. That was what had happened countless times in the past, but Marcus had pulled every available Blade away from the Bulwark to carry out his petty power struggles. It wasn't her fault, she told herself, and yet the guilt remained, hanging over her like a weight.

Maddie heard Rosie sit down next to her. She passed her elder sister a hanky. Maddie stared at it for a moment, then realised that she had been crying, and tears were streaking her cheeks. She took it from her sister's hand and wiped her eyes.

'I wonder where Tom is,' said Rosie.

'Hopefully he's in the Circuit,' said Maddie, then she shook her head. 'There's a sentence I never thought I'd say. Imagine the Circuit being safer that the Bulwark.'

'Thousands of Blades will have escaped into Medio; Evader and Icewarder territory will be swamped with them.'

'And what about the Hammers and the Scythes?'

Rosie shook her head. 'They're all trapped. If they go outside their walls, the greenhides will get them, but if they stay, then the walls will be breached quickly, and... do I need to go on?'

Maddie nodded. 'Have you ever heard of a Hammer legend, about the Aurelians?'

'The last mortal prince of Tara?'

'I'm guessing that's a yes, then?'

'I know of it. It's a bit like the Redemptionist cult among the Blades; many Hammers believe that a mortal prince or princess will arise from the Aurelian line, who will unite all the mortals of the City and, well, I guess, save them or something. It's obviously a load of nonsense, I mean the Aurelian line was probably wiped out centuries ago.'

Maddie half-smiled. 'So you'd be surprised to learn that I met the heir to the Aurelians, and his wife? She was in my team in the Rats.'

'Wait, you were in the Rats? We'll come on to that in a minute. First, you met the Aurelian heir?'

'Yeah, and because of shortages, we had a lot of Hammers in the Rats, and they all went crazy when they realised the real life Lady Aurelian had been bundled off in a ship at night, and had ended up with us. Her husband turned up a few days later, looking for her; he'd given up all of his money and lands to become a Blade on the very day the Great Wall got breached. The Hammers went crazy about him, too. They didn't do anything I told them to, even though I was their sergeant.'

'You were a sergeant? You? How in Malik's name did *you* become a sergeant?'

'Through my skill and dedication,' she said. 'Nah, I was made a corporal because I was looking after a dragon, but when I got stuck in the Rats they promoted me to sergeant because they thought, "well, she's a corporal already, so she must be good". That's the kind of tortured logic that the Rats thrived on. I guess they're all dead now. The greenhides were storming Arrowhead when Blackrose took off and decided to fly away.'

'So the Aurelians are probably dead?'

'Yeah, though they could both fight, so maybe not.'

The dragon leaned her head down by them. 'Climb on, little Jackdaws, it's time to leave.'

Maddie and Rosie stood and walked round to the side of the harness. Rosie jumped and grabbed a handle, then pulled herself up with ease, while Maddie followed. Rosie sat, and placed her feet on the rests and Maddie got in behind her.

'I could adjust this,' Rosie said, gazing at the harness; 'make it more comfortable for two. I just need leather, some strong thread and a big needle. And some scissors, a knife and padding. And maybe some straps.'

'Make a list in your head,' said Maddie.

Rosie frowned. 'Are you telling me to shut up?'

'Is it working?'

Blackrose extended her wings, and took off, her height rising as Rosie stared in wonderment.

'The thrust ratio for Blackrose's weight is amazing,' she said. 'Her wing muscles must be like steel.'

Maddie rolled her eyes as the cold wind bit.

As Rosie had predicted, they saw the smoke rise from Tarstation long before the settlement came into view. The sunlight seemed duller that far iceward, and both Rosie and Maddie were shivering as the dragon soared along the ragged coastline. Sheets of ice stretched across to the horizon, but there was a great, dark stain by the edge of the sea, from where smoke belched upwards into the sky.

'What a mess,' said Maddie over the sound of the wind.

'Yes,' said Rosie, 'but without it, there would be no streetlamps or heating oil for winter, and the City would be cold and dark.'

'I knew all that.'

Blackrose descended closer, and circled high above the black stain marking the edge of the ice field. There was a large harbour, with several boats tied up, and a small settlement on a rocky promontory. Beyond that, stretched a camp with rows of huts enclosed by a fence, and a huge structure, with two tall chimneys. Tiny figures could be seen moving around the camp and the tar pits that spread out by the huge building.

'I shall give them a small demonstration,' said the dragon, 'and then drop you off by the harbour.'

Maddie nodded. 'Stay up on Blackrose when I get off,' she said to Rosie.

'Then how will I collect everything on the list you told me to make in my head? It runs to about four pages.'

'But it could be dangerous.'

'So? You mean more dangerous than the Bulwark?'

Maddie glared at her.

'You're only two-and-a-bit years older than me.'

'Rubbish; I'm nearly three years older than you, and you're going to have to do what I say.'

'Or what? You'll tell mum and dad?'

Maddie glanced away.

'Sorry,' said Rosie, 'that came out all wrong. I didn't mean it.'

'It's alright,' said Maddie; 'I forget too. Part of me thinks this is all a dream, and everything's fine back home.'

Blackrose plunged, and both sisters quietened as the wind rushed past them. The dragon swept its wings out and flew low over the settlement, and Maddie watched as dozens of faces stared up open-mouthed at them. The dragon banked left, then circled back round towards the harbour. She hovered a few feet over a long, empty pier, and Maddie jumped down to the wooden slats, followed a moment later by Rosie.

'Remember,' said Blackrose, 'Enquire about Corthie before anything else, then gather what you need. I will be keeping a close watch, and if you are threatened in any way, then I will bring down my wrath upon this miserable town, and render everyone and everything in it to ash.'

Maddie nodded, and watched as Blackrose ascended into the sky again. She glanced down and saw a sailor staring at them from the end of the pier.

'Hey,' said Maddie as she and her sister approached the man. 'Who's in charge around here?'

He didn't look at her, his wide eyes on Blackrose. 'Is that a dragon?'

'Yes, well done,' said Maddie. 'Now tell me who's in charge before the dragon decides to burn everything to the ground.'

'The governor,' he said, thumbing towards the small ramshackle collection of buildings on the promontory.

A small, wary crowd was gathering along the harbour front, staring upwards. A soldier spotted the Jackdaws walking towards them and pointed.

'You! Did you bring that beast here? What do you want?'

Rosie waved. 'We have a list.'

'We want to speak to the governor,' said Maddie. 'Could you escort us, please?'

'And why in Malik's name should I do that?'

'Because the dragon is watching, and if she sees you refusing to help, she might decide to eat you.'

'You're bluffing,' said another soldier, a crossbow in his hands.

'Nice bow,' said Rosie. 'Where did you get it? You're not a Blade, and that's Blade property. I'm a Blade; perhaps you should give it to me.'

She reached out for it, and the soldier slapped her hand away.

'Get back,' he shouted, 'or I'll shoot.'

'I wouldn't do that,' said Maddie. 'The dragon will definitely take offence if you shoot my sister.'

The crowd around them was growing, and she could see several angry glances directed at her and Rosie.

She raised her hand into the air. 'Don't make me do it. Take us to the governor, or something bad will happen.'

'Arrest them,' cried an officer barging his way to the front of the mob.

Maddie pointed towards a ship lying by a large pier to their right. Within seconds, the dragon was soaring down, and every pair of eyes on the harbour stared up. She swooped over the quayside, and opened her jaws. A great burst of orange and red flame rushed out through the air, and the ship that Maddie was pointing at erupted into flames, its sails and rigging consumed in moments, and the fires taking hold of the deck. Sailors leapt from its side, jumping into the freezing waters of the

Cold Sea amid screams of panic and terror. The crowd on the harbour broke, and many started running.

'I'll take that bow now, please,' said Rosie, plucking it from the staring soldier's hands.

Maddie glanced at the officer. 'Take us to the governor, unless you want everything else burned.'

The officer stared at the blazing ship as flames and smoke rose into the sky, then nodded.

'Clear a path!' he shouted, and the guards pushed the others out of the way. Maddie and Rosie followed the officer, the girl cradling the crossbow in her arms as they walked. More guards stood staring at them as they left the harbour. They reached a muddy track and walked towards a tall building, where guards and officials were gathering, all staring with horror at the burning ship in the harbour.

A man ran from the building, pulling on a long coat. 'Who is responsible for this?'

'We are,' said Maddie. 'Are you the governor?'

'I am,' he yelled. 'You'll hang for this; that ship was loaded with supplies.' He turned to the guards. 'Why are they not in chains?'

'See that dragon up there?' said Maddie. 'We're her friends, and she's pretty angry. She wants to turn the whole of Tarstation into a great big heap of nothing but ashes, and we're trying to restrain her. If you, or anyone else here, lays a finger on us, then every one of you will die. The ship was just a little demonstration of her power.'

The governor stared at her. 'Are you Blades?'

'Yes, we are. Now, if you help us, we'll be out of your way in under an hour, and no one here needs to die.'

He spat on the ground. 'What do you want?'

'Where is Corthie Holdfast?'

The governor laughed. 'Long gone. Is that why you're here? You're a little late; Blades arrived months ago to search for him, but he'd already escaped.'

'He escaped?'

'Yes. The last I heard he was on the Western Bank down by Jezra, or perhaps he had crossed to the Grey Isle.'

'So he hasn't been found?'

'Girl, we're the last to hear anything up here. Now, if you please, take your dragon and leave.'

'Not yet,' said Rosie. 'I have a list.'

'A list of what?'

'Of everything we need.'

'And do you have gold to pay for it?' cried the governor. 'And what about the ship? How are you going to pay for that?'

'We have no gold,' said Maddie, 'but you're going to give us what we need, if you want to live.'

'You're bluffing.'

'Eh, sir,' said the officer; 'that's what we told them down at the docks, and the dragon destroyed the ship to prove they weren't lying.'

'Time for a decision, Mister Governor,' said Maddie. 'What's a ship and a few supplies next to your life, and the lives of everyone in this dump?'

'I'll be reporting this to the authorities as soon as you're gone,' said the governor. 'This is extortion.'

'Go right ahead with that, but I'm not sure the "authorities" will care any more, not after the Great Walls were breached yesterday by the greenhides. The Bulwark has fallen.'

There was a gasp from the crowd surrounding them.

'See,' Maddie went on, 'all those Blades who were up here looking for Corthie should have been defending the City, only they weren't.' She shrugged. 'For once, you guys are getting the news early. When the next ship turns up here, you can tell them you already knew. That is, unless you try to stop us, or arrest us; then the ship that arrives will find nothing but a smouldering pile of ruins. I bet that big building thing would burn well.'

'It's called a refinery,' said Rosie.

'Yeah, the refinery, I knew that. It's full of oil, eh?'

'It would burn for days,' said Rosie.

'Ooh, that'd be nice to watch.'

'But the City would be cold next winter.'

'If any of it's left by then.'

'Good point, sister.'

Maddie turned back to the governor. 'Well?'

He glared at them. 'Let's see the list.'

'It's all in my head,' said Rosie. She pointed at a clear area of flat rock. 'First, I want a great sheet of tarpaulin over there, and then everything we need can be piled up on the middle. Right, I want water, clothes, food, oil, candles, kindling, canvas, blankets, tools, wood, leather…'

An hour later, the tarpaulin sheet had been filled with the contents of Rosie's list, and Blackrose circled overhead a few times, while the corners of the huge sheet were tied together with ropes. The governor had retired to his mansion, and was watching from behind the shutters of a window, as a collection of guards carried out Rosie's orders. Dozens of prisoners in the camp watched from the other side of a tall fence, their eyes wide at the sight of the great black dragon flying over the settlement.

When the tarpaulin was securely tied up, Blackrose lowered her body above it, and Rosie attached the ropes to each side of the harness, then clambered up to sit on her back.

Maddie glanced around at the guards who had helped. 'Thanks,' she said. 'Make sure you tell the governor who did this. It was the Jackdaw sisters, Maddie and Rosie; don't forget, alright?'

'Are you going to fight the greenhides?' said one.

She shrugged. 'I'm working on it.'

She reached up and grabbed a knot trailing from the harness and climbed up.

'I told her about Corthie,' said Rosie.

'Shall I burn it anyway?' said Blackrose as Maddie settled into the saddle next to her sister.

'Best not,' said Maddie, 'not after we told them we wouldn't.' She glanced over the side of the dragon, and saw the faces gaze up at them. 'Let's go.'

'That was good,' said Rosie as the dragon ascended, lifting the weight of the tarpaulin sack as she climbed into the air. 'Having a dragon with you makes all kinds of things possible.'

'Where are we going?' Maddie called out to Blackrose, as the settlement dwindled beneath them.

'Somewhere to rest,' the dragon said, 'and somewhere I can hunt. My hunger is growing, and my strength is still not what it should be. A mountain top, or a high cave beyond the reach of the greenhides, so I can sleep in peace without worrying if my two little Jackdaws will be safe.'

'As long as it's warm and dry, I don't care,' said Maddie, as the dragon stretched out her wings and soared through the sky.

CHAPTER 4
RECONCILED

Ooste, Auldan, The City – 22nd Amalan 3420

Aila opened the shutters covering the narrow window and let the summer sunshine enter the small room. Doria groaned from the bed as she shielded her eyes from the light.

'You're not dreaming,' Aila said; 'yesterday really happened.'

Doria pulled the blanket over her head.

'So this is what servants' quarters look like?' Aila went on. 'I was so tired when they brought us here last night that I didn't pay any attention.' Her eyes scanned the room. 'It's a bit basic, but it's better than the dungeons.'

She heard a noise coming from Doria. 'Are you crying?'

Doria whipped back the covers. 'Of course I'm crying. Our lives have been destroyed and we're prisoners here, trapped by the God-Queen. I've been living and working in this palace for nearly eight hundred years, and I've never been more scared than I am right now.'

Aila sat on the side of the bed, the red dress digging into her waist. 'If she was going to kill us, she would have done it last night.'

'No; she needed us last night, to move all of the sleeping mortals out of the salve mine. And you'll be fine, she won't kill the bride of Marcus.'

'I wondered when you'd bring that up.'

'How could you do it, Aila? He's our cousin. Do you love him?'

Aila hesitated. Could she trust Doria? She wasn't a bad person, but she was terrified and panicky, and might blurt out anything to the God-Queen if she thought it would save her.

Doria shook her head. 'The fact that you're not answering me means that you do love him, and you're ashamed, as you should be. You saw what he did to the God-King, and to my brother Naxor; he's a beast.'

'At least Naxor's alive.'

'For how long? Your new husband wanted to kill him there and then. You sicken me. When he returns to the palace, you'll be moved into his quarters, where you'll have to share his bed; how can you live with yourself?'

Aila said nothing, not wanting to admit the relief she felt that the Bulwark had been attacked, since it had meant that Marcus had departed the palace before they had gone anywhere near a bridal chamber.

Doria glared at her. 'Nothing to say?'

'Thank you for not telling them that I knew about the God-King.'

'Yes, well that was when I thought we were on the same side.'

'And which side is that?'

'I'm not telling you anything; not if you'll run off to your new husband and let him know what I've said. Princess Khora was wrong about you; so was Lady Mona.'

Aila lost her patience. 'For Malik's sake, Doria, you don't know what you're talking about. I've been fighting with the rebels for centuries while you've lived in a palace being pampered. Have you ever actually set foot in the Circuit? Have you any idea how most of the citizens of the City live? I was nearly executed alongside Yendra at the end of the war, but instead had to spend two hundred years as a prisoner, and you have the cheek to question my motives? I've risked my life countless times, while you fall to pieces the first time something goes wrong for you in eight centuries.'

Doria started to cry again, and hid her face in the blanket.

Aila sighed. 'I want to trust you, but I'm frightened. If I told you the real reason I married Marcus, then you might tell the God-Queen; not because you want to help her, but because you're scared too. Maybe there's a way we can help each other without giving away our secrets, like how Princess Khora allowed Naxor to keep secrets from her. She trusted him, but didn't want another god to be able to read his secrets from her mind.'

Doria lowered the blanket. 'Then you don't love Marcus?'

'I loathe him, Doria, with every fibre of my being. I think the God-Queen realises that, even without vision powers. She suspects me, I'm sure of it, and she's bound to ask you what I've said.'

'And what should I tell her if she does?'

'That I married him for peace, for the City. And it would have worked, if summer hadn't arrived early. If only I had waited one more day, then the Great Walls would have been breached, and I wouldn't have had to marry him.'

Doria frowned at her. 'You almost sound as if you wish the greenhides had attacked earlier.'

'I know; it's terrible. Thousands are being slaughtered right now, and I'm sitting here relieved that I didn't have to sleep with my husband. Malik's ass, I sound like a typical arrogant demigod, more concerned with my own problems than with the suffering of the mortals.'

'I'd rather the world ended in a fiery cataclysm than have to sleep with Prince Marcus, so I think I understand.'

They shared a wry smile with each other.

'What do they want with my brother?' said Doria.

'If I had to guess,' she said, 'then the God-Queen wants more than just information from him. I think she wants Naxor to do the same job for her that he did for your mother.'

'He would never work for her and Marcus.'

'No? Do you remember what my brother used to be like, before Marcus got hold of him?'

Doria glanced away, her eyes lowering. 'Yes.'

'Apparently it took Marcus a hundred years to break Kano. The man he is now is no longer my brother; he's unrecognisable. To me, my real brother died at the end of the war, and he's never coming back. I saw him kill your mother; he hacked her to pieces like an animal, and then he was going to willingly hand me over to Marcus. Naxor's strong, but so was Kano.'

'If the greenhides have broken through, then we might not have a hundred years.' She glanced at the door. 'I assume you've tried...?'

'Yes, it's locked, and I heard someone outside in the hallway.'

'Who? There were no guards or soldiers here last night, not after we'd dragged the last of them out of the salve mine.'

Aila shrugged. 'I don't know.'

Doria pulled the blanket from her and swung her legs over the side of the bed. 'I feel disgusting. I need to have a bath and change these clothes. And I need the toilet.'

'At least you're not wearing a fancy red dress.'

'Why didn't you take it off?'

'Because I'm wearing very little else, and I don't want to be caught running around the palace in my underwear.'

'If they let us go down to my quarters, I have plenty of clothes that will fit you; we're about the same size. And you can use my bathroom, after me, of course.'

Aila stood. 'Let's see if anyone's listening.'

She walked to the entrance and tried the handle. Locked. She began thumping on the door.

'Hey!' she cried. 'We need to get out. Is anyone there?'

Silence.

Doria got out of bed and wrapped her robes around herself. Like Aila, she was still wearing make up from the previous day, and it was smudged across her eyes from the tears. She walked to the only mirror in the small room and frowned.

Aila glanced at her. 'Do you reckon I could break this door down?'

'Probably not,' she said as she pulled her hair away from her face.

Aila hitched her skirt up and glanced at her bare feet. 'I should have worn boots under the dress.' She leaned back and kicked the door. 'Ow!'

She sat on the bed and rubbed her foot. 'I don't suppose you have a set of lock picks hidden about your person?'

Doria smiled.

'I thought not. Right, shouting will have to suffice.' She got back up and returned to the door.

'Let us out!' she yelled at the top of her voice. 'We need to pee!'

'Maybe they've gone,' said Doria, 'or maybe there's no one out there and you were hearing things.'

'I definitely heard the sound of boots earlier; I...' Her voice quietened as a key was placed into the door's lock. A moment later the door opened. Outside were two soldiers, armed and in Blade uniforms. Aila glanced at their faces, and took a step back. Their eyes were blank, and the skin on their features was greying and blotchy.

'What's wrong with them?' said Doria, staring.

Aila kept backing away from the door. 'They're dead.'

'What?'

'The God-Queen must have raised them,' said Aila. 'I've been inside Greylin Palace; Prince Montieth's guards were the same.'

The God-Queen appeared behind the soldiers. 'Well done, Lady Aila, you are correct. I find that mortals tend to ask fewer annoying questions if you kill them first. Now, come with me; we have a busy day.'

The soldiers stood aside, and Aila and Doria passed between them. The God-Queen began to stride away, and her two granddaughters followed.

'The soldiers are also here to prevent you from escaping the palace,' she said as they walked. 'I have imprinted your images into their minds and they will go to any lengths to keep you here. How I wish all mortals were so pliant.'

Aila eyed her. 'Where did you get them from?'

'I took advantage of the confusion that existed around here last night, and ordered a full company of Blades to enter the palace. They won't be missed. Absolutely no mortals are to be allowed within the royal quarters any more, lest any discover the truth about the fate of the God-King. You two have a role to play in this also, as you will soon see.'

She stopped at a door. 'Lady Doria, these are your new quarters. I've had your things brought up from your old rooms. Lady Aila, you will stay here also, at least until your husband returns. Go inside and get cleaned up. I want you in formal wear; gowns or long dresses, something suitable for a grand reception. You have one hour.'

Doria bit her lip. 'Are my old servants also here?'

The God-Queen gave her a look of withering contempt. 'Were you not listening? I said no mortals. I have dismissed your staff, so I'm afraid you'll have to do each other's hair from now on.'

She gestured to a soldier to open the door. 'Remember; one hour. If you are not ready when I call for you, you shall both be punished.'

Aila and Doria passed through the door, and it was closed and locked behind them. Aila glanced around the large room.

'Where are we?'

'A courtier's apartment,' said Doria.

Aila walked up to the windows and opened the shutters to let the sunlight spill in. The room was laid out around a large cold hearth, and there were two other doors. Aila opened one, and saw a bedroom. Lying on the floor were half a dozen large clothes trunks. She turned to see Doria disappear into the other room, then a moment later she heard the sound of water tumbling into a bath.

'Looks like we're sharing a bed again,' Aila called to her, 'though at least it's bigger than the last one.'

'You can take the couch,' Doria called back. 'The God-Queen did say these were my quarters.'

Aila frowned. 'Fine. Can I rake through your clothes?'

'No.'

Aila walked into the bathroom and went to the sink as Doria filled the bath. Steam was rising from the hot water, and Aila wiped the mirror clear.

'I've trying to have a bath,' Doria said.

'So? I need to wash my face.'

'I don't care,' said Doria, ushering Aila back out of the room; 'I want some peace for ten minutes.'

She closed and locked the door, leaving Aila standing in the sitting-room. She went over to a line of cupboards and started opening them. She smiled when she opened the third one along, and withdrew a half-full bottle of brandy. She took it to the long couch, sat down and uncorked the bottle.

An hour later, both demigods were almost ready. Aila had taken a quick bath after Doria, then her cousin had allowed her to choose one of her dresses to wear, after complaining about the smell of brandy on her breath. Doria unpacked an entire trunk that seemed dedicated to beauty, with brushes, make up, hair rollers, and a hundred other things that Aila couldn't even identify. They were just finishing their hair when a slow, dull thump came from the door.

Aila glanced at Doria, then got up to answer it. She opened the door to see the same two soldiers staring at her from their empty eyes. One gestured to his left.

'I think we're meant to follow them,' she said.

Doria got up and joined her, and the soldiers led them down a grand flight of stairs towards the open areas of the palace. They came to a door, and the soldiers opened it and motioned for them to enter.

The God-Queen turned to them as they walked in. She frowned.

'Well, you look marginally better than you did this morning, though wear something a little less dowdy next time. Right, smile.'

Aila narrowed her eyes.

'I said "smile". You are about to be confronted with a large, and rather agitated crowd of mortals that have come to beg me to save the City. I need you to radiate a calm confidence. You will say nothing, I repeat: nothing, when we go next door into the hall. You will listen to what I say, and remember it, and you will smile. No, not like that, Doria; you look like a grinning child. Remember, the inhabitants of the Bulwark are being slaughtered, and the mortals tend to get upset about these things. A serene smile is what's required. Hmm, that's a little better. Aila, you will stand on my right, Doria on my left. Do not scratch your nose, fidget, glance around, or make any noise at all. Right, follow me.'

They approached a large set of double doors and one of the soldiers opened them, letting in a hubbub of noise from the two hundred or so mortals standing in the large hall beyond. The God-Queen strode through the doors, and every mortal fell to their knees at once. She walked up onto a dais and sat in the large, gilt throne in the centre as Aila and Doria took their positions, standing slightly behind the throne to each side.

A courtier that Aila recognised from the salve mine stood, his head bowed. 'Your divine Majesty, the august and almighty ruler of the City, your government begs you to speak in our hour of need.'

The God-Queen raised a hand to quieten him. 'Thank you, Lord Chamberlain. We have come from the presence of the blessed God-King, and the words we speak shall be his Majesty's words also, for we are in complete concord and agreement about what is to be done. The people of the City require a sign from their leaders, and it is this: the God-Queen and God-King are successfully reconciled.'

Aila watched the crowd as the God-Queen spoke. Some looked confused, others elated at the idea that their monarchs had got back together. A few aimed glances at her or Doria, but almost all attention was on Queen Amalia.

'Together,' the God-Queen went on, 'we shall unite this City again, and we shall prevail over the challenges that afflict us. The marriage of Lady Aila and Prince Marcus serves to reinforce this message; that the ruling family is once again ready to lead. From them will spring a new dynasty of gods and demigods to serve the City and secure our future. As for the present, Prince Marcus is already commanding our armed forces from his base on the Union Walls, and we have issued a joint order to mobilise the entire City. Every citizen is expected to work to repel the invaders, and martial law is hereby declared, with Prince Marcus as Commander-in-Chief. Under the last government, infrastructure and maintenance were sadly neglected, so therefore labourers shall commence the full renovation of the Union and Middle Walls with all haste. Unfortunately, necessity dictates that we must temporarily abandon the Bulwark, but remember that your God-King and God-Queen were here before even the Union Walls were built. We have seen the greenhides at the very walls of Tara and Ooste; we defeated them then, and we shall defeat them now. Cowardice and defeatism will not be tolerated, and your message to the people will be one of unity and fortitude.

'Until further notice, the Royal Chambers of this palace are completely out of bound for all mortals, excepting a single company of soldiers that we have already selected. The God-King requires privacy, and we shall respect that. The burdens of leadership weigh heavily upon us all, and the God-King's shoulders have borne more than any mortal could comprehend. Anyone found to be in breach of this rule shall be dealt with accordingly. Lady Doria and Lady Aila shall remain here as our courtiers, and shall see to our needs.

'Lord Chamberlain, you shall return to Maeladh Palace immediately, and take up the reins of the Taran government, as we shall remain here with the God-King. Our reconciliation is rooted in mutual trust, love and respect, for we are the City, and when we flourish, the City flourishes. That is all.'

The hundreds of mortals in the hall glanced at each other, and many looked as if they wanted to speak.

'Your divine Majesty,' said Lord Chamberlain, still kneeling. 'we thank you for your words, and bow before your limitless wisdom. May I please ask about Lord Naxor, and the events of last night?'

The God-Queen nodded. 'Very well. Lord Naxor, hurt and angry about the death of his mother, entered the Royal Palace last night to speak with us. However, he first used his powers to send you all to sleep, for which I have admonished him. We have spoken to our grandson, and calmed him. He wishes to apologise to you all for the discomfort you suffered, and is once again a full member of the Royal Family, ready to do his part to protect the City.'

'My thanks, your Majesty.'

'We shall now retire to our chambers. If you have any questions, please direct them to Prince Marcus. As Commander-in-Chief during this crisis, he has full authority over all areas of policy.'

She stood, and the assembled crowd all lowered their heads.

Lord Chamberlain raised a hand. 'A cheer for our blessed monarchs!'

The crowd let out a half-hearted cheer amid a smattering of applause. The God-Queen glanced at Aila and Doria, then they descended the dais and processed back into the smaller side room.

'Is that true about my brother?' said Doria once the door was closed.

The God-Queen frowned at her. 'You're as gullible as those mortals. Of course it wasn't true. Your foolish brother tried to kill me, and I'll not be forgetting that soon. And besides, I haven't yet had a chance to properly interrogate him.'

'Then where is he, your Majesty?'

'Locked in a cell, chained, and with a restraining mask on his face. Do you remember those?'

Doria's face fell.

'A what mask?' said Aila.

'A god-restrainer,' said Queen Amalia. 'A delightful invention that keeps those with vision powers under control. If you were to wander down by the cells, you'll no doubt hear him screaming. I recall Michael having to put Khora in one when she was causing trouble at the start of the Civil War; she never crossed us again after that. Doria watched as it was fitted to her mother; you can ask her about it later.'

Aila glanced at her cousin, but her eyes were directed at the marble floor.

The God-Queen smiled at them. 'The soldiers will now escort you to the kitchens. You two will be responsible for preparing your own food until we work out the new arrangements. Doria, you are now my personal body servant; you had plenty of practice with the God-King, report to me once you have eaten; and Aila, I need you to get your husband's rooms ready. His clothes and possessions should be arriving by ship from Tara today, and I want him to feel at home whenever he returns. Off you go, then.'

Aila and Doria bowed, then left the chamber, escorted by four soldiers.

'What does "body servant" mean?' asked Aila as they walked along the marble corridor.

Doria shook her head. 'I'll have to wash her, dress her, feed her; be her slave, basically. Whatever she wants, whenever she wants it. From brushing her hair to opening doors for her; everything.'

Aila puffed out her cheeks. 'What a nightmare.'

Doria glared at her. 'I'd rather do that, than do what you'll have to do for Marcus.'

'Damn, you're right. Fancy a swap?'

Doria said nothing.

'And what's a god-restrainer?'

'A mask.'

'Yeah, I know that, but what's so special about it?'

'Can we talk about this another time?'

'What's wrong with now?'

Doria halted in the corridor. 'Fine. It's a horrible metal mask that covers the top half of your face, only there are nails on the inside.'

'Nails?'

'Yes, and they hammer it into your head, one nail for each eye, then strap the mask on. I was forced to watch as Prince Michael put one on my mother.' She shook her head, her eyes distraught. 'She was in that thing for a month; it nearly destroyed her. She looked old and haggard when they took it off again, and she screamed for days as her eyes slowly healed.' She lifted her head, staring into Aila's face. 'And that's why my mother didn't join the rebels in the Civil War. That's why she followed Prince Michael, even though she hated him; she couldn't face going into the mask again.'

Aila stared at Doria, her mouth open. 'I'm sorry. I had no idea.'

'And now my brother's wearing one, because he tried to rescue you, cousin.'

The soldiers gestured to them to move, and they trudged on towards the kitchens.

Aila was summoned by a dead soldier after they had eaten, and led to the front of the palace, where huge crates were piled up in a large chamber. An officer from the Taran militia was there, waiting for her.

'These are the prince's possessions, ma'am,' he bowed, keeping half an eye on the undead Blades towering over them.

'Thank you,' said Aila. 'How are things in the City?'

The man immediately backed away. 'They're fine, ma'am; everything's fine.'

Aila frowned. 'Dismissed.'

'Thank you, ma'am,' he said, and hurried from the room.

Aila glanced at the huge soldiers. 'I can see why Montieth made your kind wear masks; your flesh is starting to turn a funny colour.'

The soldiers said nothing, their eyes expressionless.

'Right then,' she said. 'I want all of these crates carried up to the quarters I share with the prince. Please.'

The soldiers began work, lifting the crates and moving them away. Aila skipped by them and ascended the stairs to her new apartment. She had been given a set of keys, and she unlocked the main doors and went inside. She opened up all of the shutters and went into every high-ceilinged room except for one. There were two receptions rooms, a study, an enormous bathroom, a dining room and the bedroom, which she kept closed, unable to bring herself to look at the bed. Each room was well-apportioned, with wood panelling painted in white, and everything looked clean and fresh.

'This is way more than Marcus deserves,' she said to the first soldiers to enter; 'put that crate down over there, please.'

They dropped the crate onto the floor, then turned for the door.

Can you speak?

She blinked. *Mona?*

Yes. How are you, dear?

Alive. The God-Queen's keeping me here. She doesn't trust me, but she hasn't killed me. She's just waiting for Marcus to break me in, I suppose.

At least you're alive. I can't locate Naxor. I've searched everywhere. Does he live?'

They put something called a god-restrainer on him.

There was silence for a while, and Aila walked to the window and gazed out at the view of the bay.

I told him not to go, Mona's voice said, *but he wouldn't listen to me. I saw what one of those things did to Khora; is there any way you can help him?*

I don't know. I'm being shadowed by soldiers wherever I go; soldiers that the God-Queen killed then raised from the dead. She told the government that she and the God-King have reconciled.

She did? And what was their reaction?

Many looked as though they didn't believe it, but what could they say in front of her? And it doesn't matter; once the news gets to the people, they'll believe it. What should I do?

Escape, if you can. Rescue Naxor, if you can. If both are impossible, then wait for Marcus to return and we will finish what we planned.

Even now, when the City is under threat?

Especially now, Aila. Marcus doesn't care about the people of the City; he would sit and watch them be ripped to shreds by greenhides if it meant he could cling onto power. He must die.

I'll try. It's nice to hear a friendly voice.

I'm proud of you, cousin. Stay strong.

The voice disappeared from her head and she sighed as she sat on the arm of a chair. She glanced at the growing pile of crates, and got to work.

CHAPTER 5

THE AXE OF RAND

Icehaven, Medio, The City – 23rd Amalan 3420

Corthie opened his eyes and glanced around, unsure where he was. He felt the pain in his side, but it had lessened a little, and he was able to sit up in bed. He saw the old woman in the next bed along, and remembered. He was in Icehaven. He swung his legs off the mattress and placed his feet onto the cold, stone floor.

He gazed at the old woman as the fog of sleep lifted from his mind. He could see the thin cover slowly rise and fall, but her mouth had stopped moving, and she was no longer mumbling the name of her daughter Kahlia. He reached out and took her hand, but it felt cold, as if the life in her was receding. She was slipping away, and seemed even frailer and more emaciated than she had been in the prison cell on Grey Isle.

With one hand on the bed post, he pushed himself to his feet and staggered to the door. He opened it, and saw Yaizra and Tami standing in the kitchen to his right.

'Hey,' said Yaizra. 'You should be staying in bed.'

'Are you making breakfast?' he said. 'And where's the toilet?'

Yaizra raised an eyebrow. 'See? He doesn't listen to a word I say.' She pointed. 'That way, big lump.'

He went to a small, dark toilet and relieved himself, then washed his hands in the freezing water that sputtered from the old tap. He splashed some onto his face to wake himself, then walked through to the kitchen.

'Thanks for letting us stay, Tami.'

'You're certainly looking a lot better this morning,' she said, her eyes glancing at the bandage wrapped round his abdomen.

'Aye, I am. Last night was a bit rough with all that walking. I think I might have been a bit delirious with the pain.'

Yaizra nodded. 'Do you remember what I said about your little demigod?'

Corthie squinted for a moment, then groaned. 'I do now. Aila married Marcus? But she hated him.'

'Who know what goes on in that family?' said Tami. 'And they're cousins. I mean, that's just wrong.'

'The God-King and God-Queen are back together too,' said Yaizra. 'The news was in the morning paper. An urgent bulletin for the citizens of the City, that was how they put it, as if knowing that our rulers have a happy marriage will help beat the greenhides. Ridiculous.'

'At least our Lady Yvona's normal,' said Tami.

'Is she?' said Corthie. 'I hadn't heard of her before coming here.'

'Exactly,' she said. 'She just gets on with running Icehaven, and stays away from the affairs of the rest of the City.'

Corthie nodded. 'Any sign of Achan?'

'No,' said Yaizra. 'I don't think he'll be back, to be honest. He's probably at the Middle Walls by now, searching for any surviving Hammers.'

Corthie shook his head. 'I still can't believe she married Marcus. I thought it might be difficult getting back with her, that she might have moved on, but I wasn't expecting this. Did he capture her?'

Tami leaned over to the paper recycling bin and removed a scrunched up newspaper. She flattened it out and looked at the small print.

'It says here,' she said, 'that Lady Aila travelled to Ooste of her own accord, and asked Lady Mona to contact her brother Prince Marcus on her behalf. The prince set off immediately, and they were married the same evening.' She glanced up. 'Sounds a bit rushed, but it looks like she gave herself up.'

'That's if you can believe it,' said Yaizra. 'They print whatever the palace tells them to.'

'The God-Queen married them in person,' Tami went on, her eyes back on the newspaper, 'and then she visited the God-King, and that was when they reconciled.'

Yaizra laughed. 'The palace would have seen a lot of action last night, eh?'

Corthie frowned.

'Sorry, big lump. Look, you're miles better off without her. Find yourself a nice mortal girl. What about Tami? She was only saying this morning that she quite fancied you.'

'Hey!' Tami yelled, her face turning red.

'You know,' said Corthie; 'I think I might go and lie down again.'

'Come on,' said Yaizra. 'Tami's not that bad.'

'You cow,' said Tami. 'I should kick you back out onto the street.'

'I'm only winding you up.'

'See what I've had to put up with for the last few months, Tami?' said Corthie. 'I should have left her in Tarstation.' He half-smiled. 'The news about Aila has knocked me sideways, I'll admit. I really thought that she liked me, and now I feel stupid and a bit broken, to be honest. You got any brandy?'

'Somewhere,' said Tami.

Yaizra lifted her hand. 'No way. You're not using booze at this time of the morning because you're feeling down; it'll only make it worse, and you need to be resting your side. In fact, you shouldn't even be walking.'

Corthie laughed. 'You sound like my sister when my mother got stabbed. She couldn't walk, but she wanted to go to this ale festival, so she got two men to carry her all they way there so she could get drunk.'

Yaizra frowned. 'Your mother did that?'

'Aye, and that was the night she let me drink ale for the first time.' He sat on a chair by the kitchen door. 'Fine, no booze. You're right, it'll only make me maudlin.'

'Do you miss your family?' said Tami.

'Aye. They will come for me, I know it. I hope it's soon.'

'Where are they?'

'He's a former champion,' said Yaizra; 'where do any of them come from?'

Tami shrugged. 'The stars?'

There was a crashing sound of wood being ripped as the front door to the house was smashed in. Tami's eyes widened as she stared down the hallway. Corthie jumped to his feet, ignoring the flash of pain in his side as he reached Yaizra. He turned, and saw a mass of militia guards advancing, their crossbows pointed towards the kitchen.

Corthie glanced at her. 'Should we fight?'

'Are you crazy?' said Yaizra, raising her arms high as Tami did the same.

'Get down on your knees!' cried one of the soldiers. 'Hands clasped behind your head.'

Corthie watched as the two women did as the soldier said, then followed them, his knees hitting the cold floor of the kitchen as he placed his hands behind his neck.

Soldiers streamed into the house, several going into the side rooms, while others filled the kitchen.

'Corthie Holdfast?' said one of the soldiers, pointing a crossbow into his face.

'Aye.'

'You're under arrest.'

A sound came from the bedroom. 'She's in here, Captain.'

'Be gentle,' said Corthie, 'she's very frail.'

'We have our orders,' said the officer. 'Bind his hands.'

Two soldiers moved round to either side of Corthie, and looped cords around his wrists.

'What about us?' said Yaizra.

'What about you?' said the officer. 'The orders said to arrest the champion and the old woman. Are you also wanted by the militia?'

'No.'

'Then shut up.'

'Where are you taking them?'

The officer glared at her. 'Alkirk.'

'Can we come?'

'It's a free town,' he said. 'No one will care if you follow us. You won't get past the guards at the palace, though.' He gestured to Corthie. 'On your feet.'

Corthie stood, his wrists tied behind his back. He pulled on a slim thread of battle-vision. There were at least twenty soldiers in the house, and with the injury in his side he reckoned he only had an even chance of escaping. Maybe if he was sent to Marcus, he could ask Aila why she had married him.

'This way,' said the officer. 'There's a wagon waiting outside.'

Corthie took a few steps forward, then paused as soldiers came out of the bedroom, carrying the old woman on a stretcher. They strode towards the front door, then Corthie felt the end of a crossbow nudge him in the back and he started walking.

Behind the soldiers, he heard Tami and Yaizra follow. A small crowd had assembled on the street to watch, and another dozen or so soldiers had formed a cordon around a large wagon. The old woman was slowly lifted up and placed into the back, and Corthie was marched out of the house. Several in the crowd stared at him, and he glanced back to see Yaizra at the door of the house, a pained expression on her face.

'I'll come to the palace,' she said. 'If this was Achan, I'll kill the little runt.'

Corthie was pushed up into the back of the wagon, and six soldiers got in next to him, each with their crossbows trained on his body. The officer was the last to climb up, and he raised his hand to the driver, who cracked the whip. The wagon started to move off, pulled by a team of six ponies, as the rest of the soldiers flanked it on either side.

Corthie glanced at the soldiers. 'How did the Middle Walls hold up last night?'

'Keep quiet, prisoner,' the officer muttered.

'I've killed more greenhides than anyone in this City,' he said, 'so why am I under arrest?'

'Maybe if you'd done your job instead of skulking in the back streets of Icehaven, the City wouldn't be in this position.'

'I was stabbed, you cheeky little asshole. I don't skulk. I was imprisoned miles from anywhere in the ice fields, then I escaped and made it all the way back to the City, and you call it "skulking"?' He smiled. 'I forgive you. No apology necessary.'

He glanced down at the old woman on the stretcher, and for a split second thought she was dead. He leaned a little closer, then saw the rise and fall of her chest, and he let out a breath. Why had they arrested her also? He could understand why he was being picked up by the militia, but why would they take the old woman and ignore Yaizra, who was genuinely wanted by the authorities? Yaizra had blamed it on Achan, and he hoped it wasn't true.

The wagon took a right at a large crossroads, then headed along a wide avenue parallel to the harbour front, which Corthie could see every time they passed a side street. Gulls flocked over the masts of the ships, screeching and wheeling through the air. Ahead, he saw the large palace of Alkirk rise above the rooftops of Icehaven, its silver-grey stone almost gleaming in the shadows that bathed the town. The streets were almost empty of traffic, and the wagon made good progress. It went round to the rear of the palace, and pulled up within a large walled yard.

The captain jumped to the ground, and ordered the soldiers to form up as Corthie stood. With his hands bound, he had to step forward, then leap from the back of the wagon, and he landed next to the captain, who eyed him with a wary expression.

'If I was going to resist arrest, Captain,' he said, 'I would have done so by now.'

Soldiers carried the stretcher down and they marched towards the palace, Corthie walking in their midst as other members of the militia and palace officials stared from a distance. They walked in through a narrow entrance, and ascended a set of stairs. At the top, the officer led them into a large, stone chamber, where more soldiers awaited them.

'Major,' he said, saluting another officer, 'here are the prisoners as requested.'

The major stepped forward, her eyes tightening as she glanced at Corthie. 'Has he shown any signs of aggression?'

'No, ma'am; he cooperated fully.'

She nodded, then turned her attention to the old woman on the stretcher, a frown forming on her lips. 'Clear the room, please. Leave two guards only by the door.'

The captain saluted. 'Yes, ma'am.'

The stretcher was placed across the backs of two chairs, and the majority of the soldiers present filed from the chamber, with a pair remaining by the entrance, their crossbows ready. The last soldier out closed the door and the major turned back to Corthie.

'You certainly fit the description of the former champion. Why are you in Icehaven?'

'I arrived yesterday, but I had no opinion about where in the City the ship was going to dock; I just wanted to get back.'

'I assume you sailed from the Grey Isle?'

'Aye.'

She nodded. 'Why did you allow yourself to be arrested?'

'I was stabbed two days ago, by a Blade when I was escaping the island; if you lift my shirt you'll see the bandage. But I also wanted to see what you would do with me. I've heard about the Bulwark, and I'm wondering if I'd be of more use to the City fighting the greenhides rather than getting executed. Are you going to hand me over to Marcus?'

'That remains to be seen. Do you know how our militia found you?'

'I guessing you got visited by a guy I know, who told you a crazy story about me, and about who the old woman might be.'

She frowned. 'He pestered me for hours. I didn't listen to him at first, but now I'm glad I did. Even if the old woman is not who he claimed her to be, we still have you.' She took a breath. 'I need you to swear an oath before we move on.'

'What kind of oath?'

'You must swear not to harm anyone within this palace; if you do, then the sentence of death that hangs over you shall be carried out.'

'Alright, I swear.'

She nodded, then turned and walked to the far wall, and opened a door that lay flush and hidden into the panelling.

'My lady,' she bowed, as a tall woman in flowing yellow robes entered.

'My name is Yvona,' she said, as she approached Corthie and the stretcher; 'the Governor of Icehaven.'

He nodded. 'I'm Corthie Holdfast.'

She stared at him. 'I know you didn't kill Princess Khora. I know you were set up, and who was responsible, though I will not utter their name. I imagine you have returned for revenge?'

'Not really,' he said. 'I'm angry about what happened to me, but I don't want to get involved in the politics of the City.'

'Then why did you come back?'

'Don't laugh,' he said, 'but mostly because I'm in love with Lady Aila.'

She raised an eyebrow, but her expression remained serene. 'She was there with you when Princess Khora died, wasn't she?'

'Aye, she was.'

'Did she love you too?'

'She never told me, but I believe so.'

'Did you hear about her marriage?'

'Aye, and to be honest, that was another reason why I didn't resist arrest.'

'I wouldn't put any store by it, if I were you.'

'What do you mean?'

'I know Aila. We haven't spoken or been close in a while, but one thing I can say with certainty is that she would never marry Marcus out of love. No, I suspect she was either coerced into it, or she has an ulterior motive. I know which of those two options I prefer.'

Corthie said nothing, wondering why the demigod was flirting so close to denouncing Marcus in front of him. Her words had made him feel a little better, though he felt worry for Aila replace the disappointment.

'Let me ask you,' she went on; 'how would you feel about fighting the greenhides again?'

'Sure,' he said, 'once my injury has healed in a few days.'

She frowned. 'I sense no injury on you.'

'Are you using powers?'

'I am a healer. If you had a wound, I'd sense it. I sense nothing from you...' She narrowed her eyes. 'Absolutely nothing, as if you weren't here.'

'I block all powers, well, those sent through the air. Put a finger on my arm.'

The demigod reached out with her hand and touched Corthie.

'Oh,' she said. 'I sense you now, and I can feel the wound in your side, as well as several other smaller injuries, and some mild toothache that's been bothering you for a while. There, that should do it.'

Corthie felt a surge of power ripple through him, removing every ache and pain he felt in his body. The wound on his side closed up, and he felt better than he had done in months. He powered up his battle-vision, and felt his senses explode.

'So, it's true,' she said, her hand still on his arm; 'battle-vision, and an extremely virulent strain. I can also feel the shield that protects you from airborne powers, though I can scarcely believe such a thing is possible. My, you are an interesting mortal.' She turned to the officer. 'Remove the cords that bind his hands.'

'Yes, ma'am.' She walked round behind Corthie and cut the bonds from his wrists.

'Why do you trust me?' he said to the demigod.

'If Aila loved you, then she must have deemed you trustworthy.'

'But I could be lying.'

She peered at him, then shook her head. 'I get the feeling you're a terrible liar. Your eyes give you away.'

'I'm not sure if that's a good thing or not, but thanks for healing my wound.'

'Prince Marcus will discover that you have returned; there's little I can do to control the tongues of all that live and work in Icehaven, but I shall protect you as far as I am able, if you are prepared to fight the greenhides. No Blade forces have ever entered this town, and Marcus might rage, but I do not believe he would send soldiers to apprehend you while the current crisis exists. This is what I offer you – fight against the eternal enemy, and I shall stand between you and Marcus.'

'Alright. One thing, though, what about Aila? If she's in danger I should help her.'

'Another thing I know about my cousin is that she's more than capable of looking after herself, and with Marcus basing himself on the Union Walls, she is in no immediate danger from him.'

Corthie nodded. 'How do I know that you're not lying to me?'

'You don't. Hopefully I have shown that by trusting you, you can trust me. If you don't then you are free to depart Icehaven, but I would no longer be able to offer you protection.'

'I want to agree, Yvona, but can I first see what you make of the old woman we rescued from the Grey Isle?'

She smiled. 'I've been concentrating on you, because I can hardly bring myself to even look at the woman you have brought. The story your colleague told me was too incredible to believe, and I have refused to nurture any hope that it might be true.'

They both turned to glance at the stretcher. 'She's fading,' he said. 'She seemed more alive when she still had that nail-mask strapped to her face.'

Yvona closed her eyes for a moment, and took a long, slow breath. She and Corthie walked over to the stretcher where it lay placed across the backs of two chairs. The old woman was still, her mouth open a little.

'I fear to do this,' Yvona said as she raised a hand; 'I fear what it might mean.'

She reached out and placed a hand onto the old woman's shoulder, then her face crumpled into tears. She slipped down to the floor, on her knees by the stretcher, her hand still in contact with the old woman's skin. Yvona's chest heaved as she wept, the tears spilling down her face.

'My lady,' said the Major, approaching.

'Don't touch me,' Yvona cried. 'Stay back.'

'Who is she, my lady? Is it really her?'

Yvona removed her hand from the old woman, and lowered her face. Corthie reached out a hand and she took it, pulling herself to her feet. She wiped her face.

'Bring her to my personal quarters,' she said, 'and you too, Corthie, come with me.'

The two guards by the door were called over and they lifted the stretcher. The major led the way, and they walked in silence through the hidden doorway, and into Yvona's private rooms. She gestured to a door, and the major opened it. Inside was a small bedroom, with a tall, narrow window letting in the light from outside.

'Set her down here, gently, and remove the stretcher,' she said.

The soldiers did as she asked, and the old woman was placed onto the bed. Yvona gestured for the two soldiers to leave, then turned to Corthie.

'This is Major Hannia,' she said, 'my closest advisor. When you fight the greenhides, she will be your commanding officer.'

Corthie nodded.

'Take a seat, both of you.'

Corthie and the major sat by the bed, and Yvona did the same. She leaned over and took hold of one of the old woman's hands.

'It's true,' she said; 'this is Princess Yendra. I felt the three hundred years of torture that she has suffered, and the grief she feels for her three daughters. Her life force is that of a god, though it has been damaged, perhaps irredeemably so. I think I have enough power to stop her dying, but possibly no more than that, and it may take several healing sessions to even get that far.'

The major's eyes widened. 'Princess Yendra? Achan was telling the truth.'

'Yes, and I'm very grateful that you listened to him.'

'Should I have him released from custody, my lady?'

'Yes. Then find him and Corthie suitable rooms where they can stay while they remain under my protection.'

'There's one other friend,' said Corthie; 'a woman, an Icewarder who helped free Yendra from the Grey Isle.'

The major frowned. 'Achan didn't mention her.'

'He probably didn't want her to get into trouble. She was sent to Tarstation as a criminal, and we escaped together. She's wanted by your militia.'

'What's her name?' said the major.

'If I tell you, will you arrest her and throw her back into prison?'

'Do you vouch for her?' said Yvona.

'Aye.'

'Then she will not be re-arrested if she stays with you and Achan in the palace. If, however, I discover that her crimes were of an extremely serious nature, then I must retain the right to have her punished. What did she do?'

'She was a thief. I think her family are all thieves. But I also think she might have killed someone, I'm not sure.'

The major frowned. 'Is her name Yaizra, by any chance?'

Corthie said nothing.

'Not many Icewarder thieves are sent to Tarstation,' the officer said. She glanced at Lady Yvona. 'She did murder someone, my lady, but it was one of her own kin, during a robbery. She was sent to Tarstation for her own protection, to ensure her family didn't seek revenge upon her within the prison here in Icehaven.'

'I didn't know that,' said Corthie.

'Is she one of the Tornwings?'

'She is, my lady,' said the major.

'Then find her, but keep it quiet if possible. My protection now also extends to her.'

'The Tornwings?' said Corthie.

'They are the most powerful criminal family in Icehaven,' said the major.

'Leave me,' said Yvona. 'I shall start the first healing session with the princess.'

Corthie and the major stood. The demigod glanced at Corthie. 'Thank you for bringing my aunt back from the dead, champion.'

'You are a complete asshole!' Yaizra yelled at Achan. 'My life is ruined because of you. Why couldn't you keep your mouth shut?'

'But I didn't mention your name to anyone,' he said; 'I kept you completely out of it.'

Corthie leaned on the rooftop railings and glanced at them. Yaizra had been found by the militia outside the gates of the palace and brought up to the top floor, where rooms had been set aside for her, Corthie and Achan.

'It was me who told them,' said Corthie. 'The major mentioned that the Tornwings would be after you, so I figured you'd be safer here.'

Yaizra's eyes widened. 'Don't say their name.'

'We're on a roof, Yaizra, there's no one else around. Anyway, why didn't you tell us your family wanted to kill you?'

'Cause it's none of your business.' She peered at him. 'You're moving differently.'

He lifted the side of his shirt and showed them the smooth skin where the injury had been.

His two friends gasped.

'Lady Yvona healed me, just like she's trying to heal Princess Yendra just now.'

'So it really is her,' said Achan. 'Look, I'm sorry for sneaking off like that, but I was trying to do the right thing. Yendra might have died if we hadn't brought her here.'

'Well, that's great for Yendra,' said Yaizra, 'but what about us?'

'I made a deal with Yvona,' Corthie said. 'She'll protect me from Marcus if I fight the greenhides, and she'll protect you two as well.'

There was a cough behind them and they turned. Major Hannia was standing on the wide, flat roof, with a few soldiers next to her.

'Major,' Corthie nodded.

'I heard you mention fighting the greenhides,' she said, 'and I have brought something upstairs for you to see. It's been displayed on the wall of the palace's feasting hall for hundreds of years, only being taken down to have its wooden handle repaired or replaced.' She beckoned to the soldiers and they approached. Two of them were carrying something long, which was covered in a sheet. The major removed the covering to reveal a heavy war axe.

'This is the Axe of Rand,' she said. 'It belonged to Lady Yvona's eldest brother, after whom it is named. He was the only warrior in Icehaven strong enough to wield it. The metal used in its construction is exceedingly rare, and the only other weapon I know of that uses the same material is the Just; the blade that Prince Michael once owned, which is now in the hands of his son Marcus.'

Corthie stepped forwards. The axe had a long, darkwood handle wrapped with leather strips. The head was double-sided, with a large axe blade opposite a thick spike. He picked it up, and hefted it in his right hand.

The major smiled. 'How does it feel?'

'Good,' Corthie said. 'I've trained with axes this size; I like it.' He glanced at her. 'When do I start?'

'As soon as possible,' she said. 'I've ordered the weapon smiths to prepare a new set of armour for you, and it should be ready by tomorrow morning. Rest for the remainder of today, for Lady Yvona expects you to fight at dawn, Champion of Icehaven.'

Yaizra raised an eyebrow. 'Champion of Icehaven? Malik's ass, we'll never hear the end of this.'

CHAPTER 6

INTO THE FURNACE

Hammer Territory, The Bulwark, The City – 23rd Amalan 3420

Emily lay awake in bed, her elbow propped up under her left side. The small, attic room was bathed in the reds and purples of the night sky coming through an open window, which was also letting in the distant sounds of screaming and greenhide shrieks from over the wall in Scythe territory. It had been a long, warm night, and she had hardly slept, though that was partly due to sharing a bed with Daniel again. Despite the fear and exhaustion, or maybe because of it, they had fallen into each other's arms as soon as they had been left alone in the room.

The window had been closed then, and she wondered if she should shut it again to block out the sounds that were drifting over the wall. It had been uncomfortably warm with it closed, and she reckoned the cooling breeze was worth the sounds that came with it.

Outside their door were dozens of Hammers; the survivors from Arrowhead, and many more who had gathered once they had heard the Aurelians were there. Many had bowed before her and Daniel, and some had even wept tears of joy as if their prayers had been answered. It had made Daniel uncomfortable, but Emily had run with it, smiling and waving at the wide-eyed crowds. Beyond that though, she didn't know what else she was supposed to do. She could fight, but she had no battle-vision; she was just a mortal like the rest of them. Arriving on a dragon would have been impressive, but Buckler was dead and Black-rose had gone. What could she and Daniel offer the Hammers except a vain hope? They could try their best to lead them to the Middle Walls, but if the greenhides broke through the Hammer wall, it would be carnage.

She glanced down at the sleeping form of Daniel. He had seemed almost overwhelmed at first by the events that had overtaken them, but she could sense he was almost ready to lead. He had led soldiers before and had been trained how to do it. With her it was different; she had accepted the role of Lady Aurelian without any difficulty, and leading seemed natural to her. It was her upbringing, she supposed. She might be an Evader, but she had been raised as a Roser, and taught to view herself as superior to the folk of the lesser tribes, and even though she knew the truth about her origins, it was hard to shake off.

She noticed the horizon grow pinker and she got out of bed, pulling on the clothes that were hanging off the back of a chair. Some of the Hammers had suggested that, as Lady Aurelian, she should wear a dress, but she had ignored them, preferring the Rats uniform. It was designed for movement and agility, and had a dozen pockets to store things in. How was she supposed to fight in a long, flowing dress?

'Is it morning?' said Daniel, rolling onto his back.

'Nearly. We should get moving. We're only three miles from the Middle Walls.'

'As a raven flies, maybe, but it's like a maze out there. Row after row of narrow, identical streets, with every brick house looking the same as the others. And all those chimneys belching out smoke, and covering everything in soot. I hadn't imagined anywhere like this could exist.'

'The sooner we're out of here, the better.'

'And then what? Will the Hammers still expect us to lead them once we've made it into Medio?'

She stood and pulled her hair back, tying a piece of ribbon round it to keep it in place. 'Let's worry about that at the time.' She glanced at him. 'Do you think Torphin was being a little evasive about the Middle Walls last night?'

'What do you mean?'

'Do you remember I suggested that we carry on to the gates? After all, we were tired, but we could have walked another three miles.'

'I got the feeling he was hoping that word of us would spread, and that he wanted time for all the Hammers to hear that we'd arrived.'

'But why are so many of them still here? Why aren't they all fleeing towards Medio?'

'I don't know. Maybe they've been slaves for so long, they've forgotten how to think for themselves.'

'I doubt that. I think many of them hate the Blades, and have been looking for an opportunity to do something about their conditions.' She frowned. 'It's going to be hard to live up to their expectations.'

'I don't know if we can, or should. Already we're claiming to be something we're not, and my parents would no doubt be furious to discover we're being referred to as Lord and Lady Aurelian. Not that I give a rat's ass about what they think, but are we doing the right thing? Maybe we should quietly explain to the Hammers that this legend of theirs is, well... bollocks, frankly.'

'I don't think that's a good idea.'

'But we're not here to save them, Emily.'

She shrugged. 'Maybe we are. Maybe there's a higher power at work. Fate, or a plan of some god or other.'

He climbed out of bed and started to dress in his Wolfpack uniform. 'I didn't think you were superstitious.'

She gave him a glance. 'I think you're confusing superstition with religion.'

'They're the same thing as far as I'm concerned.'

'Did you never pray to the gods; not even as a child?'

'No.'

'Alright, then how do you explain the two of us being a legend in a place we knew nothing about? And you arrive, on the day the walls are breached, and lead the survivors here?'

He shrugged. 'The names of hardly any mortals are known from the ancient days of the City. We remember Maeladh and Cuidrach because palaces were named after them, but we know nothing about their lives. The only person from more than two thousand years ago that anyone learns about is Aurelian, because they were that last mortal rulers to stand up to the gods.'

Emily raised an eyebrow. 'Historically accurate, but I choose to interpret it differently. For today, at least, I'm fully prepared to be Lady Aurelian if it helps the Hammers escape the greenhides. After that? We can worry about tomorrow when it comes, Danny; let's just survive today.'

He walked round the bed towards her and took her hands. 'You got one detail wrong,' he said. 'I didn't lead the survivors here. If anyone did, it was you and Sergeant Quill. I think I was in shock for half the time.'

'You did fine.'

He put his arms round her waist and she kissed him, her hands on his chest as she forgot about everything else for a moment.

The sound of raised voices echoed up from the floors below, and they turned.

Emily frowned. 'That sounds like Captain Hilde. We should probably go downstairs.'

She picked up her sword and buckled it to her belt, and they opened the door. Four Hammers were waiting outside their room, each armed with a variety of homemade weapons. They bowed their heads as Emily and Daniel squeezed past on the narrow landing. The stairs were also busy with more people, who stared at the Aurelians as they descended, their eyes wide.

The sound of arguing voices rose as they entered a large room, which was packed with people. The dozen or so Blades stood separate from the majority of Hammers, but everyone quietened as Emily and Daniel entered.

'Good morning, my lord, my lady,' said Torphin. 'Please sit.' He gestured for a couple of civilians to get up from their seats.

'No need,' Emily said to them. 'We can stand.'

Hilde glared at them from where she sat, her crutches leaning against the wall behind her. 'So you two are the ones who have tried to usurp the legitimate authority of the City? What gives you the right to give orders?'

'The people,' said Emily, 'from whom all authority ultimately derives.'

Torphin chuckled as the Blade officer scowled.

'We all want the same thing,' Emily went on; 'to deliver the civilians trapped in the Bulwark to safety.'

'That's not all these... people want,' said Hilde. 'They are trying to overthrow the last thousand years of stability; they want anarchy.'

Emily smiled. 'They want to be free.'

Hilde shook her head. 'They're rebels. They're almost as bad as those treacherous Evaders.'

'I am an Evader,' said Emily. 'I might not speak like one, but it's the truth. Now, what is the disagreement over? It is merely about who is in charge, or are there differences over what we should do next?'

'The Blades want us to travel down to the harbour at Salt Quay,' said Torphin.

'Why?' said Emily. 'Even if the port is still held by City forces, there wouldn't be enough ships to carry everyone away.'

'But it's the only route out,' said Hilde.

Emily frowned. 'But what about the gates through the Middle Walls?'

The room fell into an uncomfortable silence.

'What are we not being told?' Emily said.

Torphin frowned. 'There are no gates that lead from Hammer territory into Medio, my lady.'

Emily felt a ripple of anger and despair flow through her. 'That can't be true, surely? There have been gates on every map of the City I've ever laid eyes on.'

'It's another dirty little secret of the City, my lady,' said Torphin. 'The gates were walled up centuries ago, to make sure none of us lesser folk could taint the rest of the City.'

She glared at Quill. 'Did you know this?'

The sergeant nodded. 'Everyone in the Bulwark knows it. The only gate that's ever been opened between Hammer lands and Medio was when Princess Yendra tried to drag the Bulwark into the Civil War three hundred years ago. She smashed down the wall that blocked the gatehouse and sent her soldiers through, in order to foment rebellion. That's when Marcus was appointed Commander of the Bulwark; he sent the Blades down and resealed the gate.'

'Typical Blade,' said Torphin; 'she suffers from a selective memory. She omitted to mention that the Blades massacred thousands of Hammers, then crossed into Medio and did the same to twenty thousand Evaders. *Then* they resealed the gate.'

'Salt Quay is wholly inadequate for our needs,' said Daniel. 'If Princess Yendra could smash down a gate in the Middle Walls, then we can too.'

'You fool!' cried Hilde. 'If we smash down a gate, what do you think will happen next? The greenhides would pour into Medio, and the City would be lost forever.'

'The soldiers on the Middle Walls will open the gates for the Aurelians,' said Torphin. 'The City cannot ignore destiny. And,' he went on, glancing at Captain Hilde, 'if you call Lord Aurelian a fool again, there will be consequences.'

'Let's not fight each other,' said Emily. 'We should be moving. We'll make our way to the Middle Walls as planned, and see what transpires.'

The Hammers in the room began to move as if an order had been given.

'Remember,' said Torphin, 'each Hammer should take nothing with them except a weapon and small bag of possessions. Send out word, have the people start to make their way to the walls. The Eighth Gate is the closest to our current position.'

There was a flurry of activity as the Hammers started to gather things and leave the room.

'May I have a word, my lady?' Torphin said.

'Of course,' said Emily.

'I see that you have chosen to wear your Rat uniform this morning,' he said.

'Yes?'

'Many of us feel that Lady Aurelian should not be dressed as such a lowly warrior, my lady. If you were to wear something more formal, such as I suggested last night, then the people would see you more easily. Otherwise, they might assume that you're just another Rat.'

'How am I supposed to fight in a dress?'

Torphin frowned. 'You shouldn't be fighting, my lady; the risk is too high. We cannot afford to lose you.'

'If I'm going to lead, it'll be from the front, Torphin,' she said. 'I'll not hide behind the people I'm supposed to be saving.'

Torphin frowned again, but said nothing.

They walked to the front of the small house and Emily gasped as she saw the hundreds of people out on the street. She glanced at Daniel standing next to her and smiled.

'Are they here for us?' he said.

'They are,' said Torphin. 'Raise your hands, let them see you.'

Emily and Daniel clasped each other's hand and raised them high, and the crowd erupted with cheers and cries. Parents held children up so that they could see, and people were climbing up onto the roofs of the terraced brick houses to get a better view.

'There are thousands more,' Torphin said. 'Word has spread to every Hammer for miles around.'

'Is the wall around Hammer territory still holding?' said Daniel.

'Yes, my lord, but I estimate that at least one of the entrances will be breached by nightfall.'

'Let's go, then. The Eighth Gate.'

A large group of armed Hammers cleared a path down the street, and the Aurelians began walking. The few remaining Blades kept close behind, their expression anxious as they glanced at the masses of Hammers everywhere.

'Sergeant Quill,' said Emily, 'please walk with us.'

The soldier frowned, but moved up to flank Emily's right side.

'How are you this morning, Sergeant?'

'How do you think? You're leading an armed rebellion against the rest of the City.'

'So we should remain here and die?'

'I don't know any more, to be honest. I know the Hammers hate us, but this is the first time I've ever been inside their land. I'd like to say that I had no idea what was going on here, but it wouldn't be true. We all knew that the Scythes and Hammers were little more than slaves, but we ignored it. It seemed to us Blades that it had always been this way. I know that's no excuse.'

The crowds flowed through the streets like a tide, as thousands of Hammers began to abandon their homes to join the march. The narrow alleys that linked the rows of housing were filthy, piled up with refuse, with raw sewage running down the open gutters. The houses themselves were coated in a layer of black soot and pollution from the numerous chimneys that were still belching out smoke into the sky. They passed lumber yards and coal yards, and dozens of small charcoal stacks. A huge tannery appeared to their right, and the stench coming from it made Emily's eyes water. They crossed a bridge over a water channel that stank from the refuse streaming from the tannery, and Emily almost threw up. Torphin raised his hand and they halted on the other side, the flanking group of Hammers clustering around Emily and Daniel as the main crowds carried on.

'What is it?' Emily said.

Torphin pointed sunward. Approaching down a narrow street was a group of soldiers, running.

'Blades?'

'Yes.'

The soldiers got closer, and one of them noticed Hilde's officer insignia.

'Ma'am,' he cried; 'the greenhides are coming this way.'

'Have they broken through the wall?' said Emily.

The soldier gave her a glance, then turned back to Captain Hilde. 'We tried to get into Salt Quay, ma'am,' he said, 'but the garrison inside wouldn't let us enter. The greenhides have surrounded the port, but Lord Kano managed to escape on a boat. We broke into Hammer land, but the greenhides followed us through.'

Torphin glared at them. 'You mean you fools let them in?'

The soldier spat on the ground. 'Since when did Hammers think they could talk like that to Blades?'

'The Hammers have mutinied,' said Captain Hilde, leaning on her crutches. 'They are no longer recognising our authority.'

'You can join with us, or leave,' said Emily. 'It's your choice.'

The soldier scowled at her uniform. 'Shut your face, Rat.'

Emily could sense the Hammers' anger grow, so she stepped forward and punched the soldier in the face before anyone else could react. Blood gushed from his nose. He reached for the hilt of his sword, then glanced at the large number of Hammers closing in.

Sergeant Quill pushed the soldier back. 'You'd do well not to insult Lady Aurelian again. She's right, come with us or get lost.'

A high shriek rose from the streets sunward of their position, and everyone turned.

'Here they come,' said Daniel.

'Get the civilians away,' cried Emily. 'All Blades and armed Hammers should remain between them and the greenhides. We'll cover the retreat to the Middle Walls.' She glanced around, and saw an enormous building towering up a hundred yards from the bridge they had just crossed. 'What's that?'

'The ironworks,' said Torphin.

'It looks like a fortress. Is it defensible?'

'Yes, ma'am.'

'Then we lead the greenhides in that direction. If we can hold them there for a while, the civilians should be able to reach the Middle Walls.'

'Let's go!' Quill yelled, and they began to pull back.

Some of the Blades split off, and fled back across the bridge, scattering into the nearby streets.

'Cowards,' Torphin cried at them.

'Leave them,' said Emily. 'The greenhides will rip them to shreds.'

They hurried along the road, seeing the crowds ahead of them continue their march. The high façade of the ironworks grew closer, and Emily could see smoke belching from its four tall chimneys. Carts filled with coal and wood lay by one of the entrances, and they raced towards it.

'Use the carts to block the street,' Emily called out; 'force the greenhides into the ironworks. Sergeant Quill, can you work out a plan?'

She nodded, and gestured to the soldiers to follow her. Daniel appeared by Emily's side.

'You should retreat with the others, Danny,' she said.

'No chance. If you're fighting, then I am too.'

'But if one of us gets killed, at least the other will survive,' she said. 'If we both die, then the Hammers might lose hope. It has to be you, Danny; you're the heir. Torphin, please make sure Lord Aurelian is escorted to safety.'

'Yes, my lady.'

'But...' Daniel said. 'I can't lose you again.'

'You won't,' she said. 'I'll meet you at the Eighth Gate.'

He took her hand as Torphin ushered two burly Hammers to Daniel's side.

'This is wrong,' he said. 'You shouldn't be facing the greenhides in order to keep me safe.'

'Would you do the same for me if it were the other way around?'

'Of course I would.'

'Then go, Danny. Get to the Middle Walls.'

'My lord?' said Torphin.

Daniel frowned, but allowed the two Hammers to escort him away.

'A brave decision, my lady,' said Torphin as they watched Daniel pass through the barricade that was being constructed across the road. 'You are everything the legend foretold you would be.'

Emily turned away, and saw Quill organising the Blades by the entrance to the ironworks.

'Sergeant,' she said, 'will this work?'

'You mean, will it slow them down? Probably. Will it get us all killed? Also probably.'

'Here they come!' cried a Hammer.

Emily glanced down the street. On the far side of the bridge the greenhides were coming into view. Some kept running by the side of the stream, while others shrieked and turned when they saw the Hammers by the barricade.

'Everyone inside the ironworks!' yelled Quill. She eyed Emily. 'You too, Aurelian.'

'You usually call me "Rat".'

Quill pushed her towards the entrance. 'Whatever you are, you're not just a Rat any more.'

They rushed into the dark, vast hall of the ironworks. To their right were heaps of coal and charcoal, piled up along the high wall, while rows of forges ran down the centre of the hall. Two enormous furnaces sat at the far end, their openings glowing red hot.

'We lure them in,' cried Quill to the other fighters, a group of both Blades and armed Hammers, 'and then we run.' She pointed at two soldiers. 'Secure the entrance by the ore bins. Everyone else, scatter, and stay low.'

Emily followed Quill as she ran down by the sides of the forges. Racks of half-finished armour and weapons were stacked by the wall, and the sergeant picked up a steel breastplate from a heap.

'Here,' she said to Emily, 'put this on.'

Emily stood with her arms out as the sergeant strapped the armour over her chest, buckling it at her shoulders and back.

'It might impede your movement a little,' said Quill with a smile, 'but it's better than trying to fight in a dress.'

'Thanks. Why are you helping me? I thought I was leading a rebellion?'

'I saw you send your husband away; that took guts. I'm not saying I believe in any of that legend crap, but you've already killed two greenhides, which is only one fewer than I've managed in six years of service.'

She put a finger to her lips as the noise from outside increased. Quill had posted two soldiers by the main entrance as bait to draw the enemy in, and Emily watched them sprint away as the first greenhide appeared, silhouetted in the doorway. Quill and Emily crouched behind the forge as the greenhide shrieked and bounded in, its large legs powering its heavy body. A hail of crossbow bolts whistled through the air, striking the beast on its left side. Three embedded themselves in its thick, green armour, but one struck its neck, and the creature fell, its momentum carrying it into a forge. It cried out, then stilled.

'One down,' muttered Emily.

'Only five hundred million to go,' said Quill.

The entrance to the ironworks became crowded with more greenhides, each jostling and pushing to get through into the building.

'It's working,' Quill said. 'They're coming.'

The sliding door at the entrance was ripped from its rollers and a surge of greenhides poured into the hall, fanning out as they searched for humans. 'This way!' cried a soldier by the furnaces, waving his arms in the air to get their attention. Emily's eyes widened at the speed with which the greenhides began to move through the ironworks.

'Pull back!' cried Quill, getting to her feet, her sword drawn.

The soldiers and Hammers began running towards a small door at the far end of the hall, next to large bins where the raw iron ore was stored. Greenhides overtook a group of Hammers as they ran, their claws ripping down their backs. A soldier raised his shield and lunged at one, but a beast's forelimb swung, and took his head off in a single sweep.

Quill raised her sword. 'Furnaces, now!'

A small team by the main furnace began swinging sledge hammers at the base of the chimney, the noise ringing through the hall. The greenhides swerved in that direction, racing toward the huge furnace. The Hammers stood their ground, each one swinging until, with a deafening roar, the furnace buckled and its iron seam split. A torrent of red hot coals burst from the side of the furnace, showering the approaching greenhides. They screamed as the coals rained down on them, the flames lighting up the interior of the hall.

Emily raced after Quill as the fighters withdrew. More greenhides were still entering the ironworks, but the flames were forcing them away from the centre of the hall. The stench of burning greenhide flesh filled the air as the bodies piled up.

The Hammers and soldiers began racing through the narrow gate and back out into the street as the greenhides swarmed closer. Emily drew her sword, and stood by Quill.

'You should get out now,' the sergeant said.

'If you're standing here, then I will too.'

'You're an idiot.'

'Then so are you.'

The last Blades formed a thin cordon between two large forges as the others continued to escape the building. The flames in the centre of the hall were growing, and sparks had ignited the heaps of coal that sat by the other entrance, adding to the smoke and heat. The soldiers joined their shields together; without one, Emily positioned herself to the left of the line, where Quill's shield offered her some protection. The greenhides slammed into them, their claws and teeth flashing, and the line of soldiers was pushed back. Two went down, their shields slashed to ribbons. Emily lunged out with her sword, the blade stabbing deep into a greenhide's abdomen. It barely reacted, and swung its claws, raking them across Emily's breastplate and sending her flying backwards. She hit the side of a forge, winded, her armour scored. The greenhide leapt at her, but fell onto her sword as she held it up, the blade passing through its chest as it collapsed onto her.

Emily was pushed to the ground, the weight of the greenhide pressing against her. Its face was only inches from hers, and she realised it was still alive, its long teeth bared as it tried to bite her. She felt its breath on her cheek and she leaned her face away, the teeth reaching for her. It shrieked out in agony as another sword struck its neck, and Emily was sprayed in thick, green blood. She felt hands grab her shoulders, and looked up to see Torphin and another Hammer drag her out from under the body. They pulled her through the narrow entrance, and the door was slammed closed and barred. A second later the door bulged outwards as greenhides collided with it.

'Can you walk?' cried Quill.

Emily pushed the hands from her shoulders and scrambled to her feet. 'I can run if that's any help.'

Quill laughed, a manic gleam in her eye. She had green blood all across the front of her armour, and her sword had several notches down its edge.

'Run!' she cried, and the survivors raced down the narrow street, passing the soot-stained brick houses on either side. Emily glanced back as she ran. Smoke was pouring out of every window of the iron-works, and she hoped that the greenhides inside were roasting.

Quill raised her hand as they reached an open square, with tall brick buildings on all four sides. She walked along the line of panting Hammers and Blades.

'How many did we lose?' said Emily.

'A dozen,' said the sergeant.

'What now? The Middle Walls?'

'Yes, though be prepared. I heard what Torphin said, but I wouldn't count on the gates being opened.'

'We have to try.'

Quill nodded. 'Let's go.'

They hurried through the deserted streets, and Emily saw the high line of the Middle Walls loom in the distance. They were as high as the inner walls of the Bulwark's defences, but lacked an outer wall and a moat. Figures were moving on top of the battlements, and there were catapults and ballistae sitting on platforms next to the regular towers that punctuated the length of the wall. Quill veered to the right, towards a tall gatehouse, and they emerged onto a wide road packed with Hammer civilians, all tightly pressed. Thousands were crammed into the streets leading to the gatehouse, all trying to push forwards.

'Clear a path for Lady Aurelian!' yelled Torphin, and the crowds turned. Emily could see the terror in the faces as they made their way through the crowd. A few eyes lit up with hope when they saw her, but most were glancing over their shoulders as the sound of the approaching greenhides increased.

'If the greenhides get here before the gate is opened, the Hammers will be slaughtered.'

'Then we'd better get it open,' cried Quill.

Torphin and the others shoved their way through the tight crowd, until they reached a wide, open area in front of the gatehouse. The crowd was packed in, but were leaving a clear space in front of the old gate, where several bodies lay, all riddled with crossbow bolts.

Daniel was standing at the front of the crowd, just out of crossbow range. He was calling out to the soldiers on the battlements above the gate, pleading with them. Emily reached his side, and stared. The gate was, in reality, a stone wall, the arched opening completely blocked up.

'Stay back!' yelled a voice from the battlements. 'If you approach, we will shoot.'

'There are thousands of Hammers here,' Emily shouted back.

Daniel turned, and puffed his cheeks when he saw her. She took his hand.

'You're covered in blood,' he said, his eyes widening.

'None of it's mine.'

'Where are the greenhides?'

'We managed to slow them, but they'll be coming soon.' She glanced at the gatehouse, her eyes catching on the sprawling corpses.

'What do we do?' he said.

Emily frowned. 'We have no choice,' she said; 'we'll have to attack.'

CHAPTER 7

OASIS

The Warm Sea – 23rd Amalan 3420

'Look,' cried Rosie, the wind blowing through her hair; 'the City.'

Maddie gazed down. In the distance she could see the Straits that separated the Western Bank from the City. They were flying high above it, but she could make out the fog and mist of the Clashing Seas as a grey patch, and beyond that, the bay where Ooste, Pella and Tara sat. The enormous statue of Prince Michael was visible on the headland next to the cliffs that shielded Tara from the sea.

'Wow,' said Rosie; 'Auldan looks beautiful from up here. I can't spot any greenhides, so the Middle Walls must be holding. Do you think anyone can see us?'

'If they can,' said Maddie, 'we'll be a little dark speck in the sky. Folk'll think we're just a seagull.'

'They're called gulls; there's no such thing as a "seagull".'

'I knew that.'

'No, you didn't.'

'Why do you always have to correct me?'

'Because you're always wrong.'

'I'm not wrong about you being a pain in the ass.'

The dragon banked a little to the right, and headed in the direction of the sun. The Warm Sea flashed beneath them, and the coastlines of the City and the Western Bank began to fade into the distance.

'I thought we were supposed to be looking for Corthie?' said Maddie. 'He won't be sunward of the City.'

'Who cares?' said Rosie. 'It's bright and warm this way; I'm sick of ice and cold.'

'We were only there for one day.'

'And one night, and I froze the whole time, even with the blankets we got from Tarstation. An icy cave is not my idea of comfort.'

'But we left all our stuff there,' Maddie said. 'We'll have to go back.'

Below them, the wide Warm Sea seemed to merge seamlessly into the edge of the vast marshlands that spread for hundreds of miles. Dozens of ships were sailing through the area where the sea mixed with the marshes, harvesting reeds and seaweed for the City, while hundreds of birds circled above the wetlands.

'The sea's so small compared to the marshlands,' Rosie said, leaning over the dragon's flank to look downwards, thick straps keeping her secured to the harness. There were no hills visible for miles in either direction, just the endless sweep of flat, featureless marshes. It was getting warmer the further the dragon flew, and Maddie could feel the heat from the sun's rays on her face. She pulled off the heavy winter's coat that she had worn since they had taken off from the snow-capped mountain, and stuffed it into a bag that was buckled by her side. Rosie had already made several adjustments to the harness, adding in more straps, and places to store things. She had kept busy with it for the entire evening, while Maddie had shivered by the small fire by the cave's entrance.

'That's better,' she said, feeling the warm air on her arms. 'I was getting as sweaty as Malik's crotch after a night with the God-Queen.'

'I thought I could smell something. When did you last have a bath?'

'Um... three or four days ago? It might be longer; I can't remember.'

'That's something else we need to think about.'

'You're going to think about me not having a bath?'

Rosie squinted at her. 'No, we need to think about how we're going to clean ourselves, you know, wherever we end up. If we're not returning to the City, and assuming that Blackrose can't just fly forever, then we're going to need somewhere to stay; somewhere better than the ice cave.'

Maddie frowned, then gazed down at the vast marshes. Aside from her annoyance that her sister was right, she felt almost dizzy at the thought that they might never return to the City. The Bulwark had been lost, and there was nothing they could do about that, but if the Middle Walls were holding, then the City might survive, even if Blackrose continued to refuse to help. She settled into the saddle, the warm breeze lulling her to sleep.

She awoke when Rosie nudged her with an elbow.

'Look,' she said; 'the marshlands are finally ending.'

Maddie blinked. 'And what's past them?'

'Desert.'

Maddie glanced ahead. The last few miles of marshlands petered out into a thin strip of scrubby wasteland and then, beyond that, a golden, sandy desert stretched out to the horizon.

Rosie pointed upward. 'And see how high in the sky the sun is?'

Maddie lifted a hand to shade her eyes. 'That's weird.'

'It's only weird if you don't understand the reason behind it. If you'd paid attention at school you would know all about it. If you go sunward far enough, the sun never sets, and if you go iceward far enough, it never rises.'

A few green areas were dotted around close to the border with the marshlands, and Blackrose started to descend in wide, lazy circles. The temperature rose the lower they went, until Maddie was sweating again as the dragon landed on the golden sand.

Blackrose swung her head round to face them. 'I shall drink at this oasis and rest for a moment, and you two can wash in the cool water under the trees.'

Maddie frowned. 'Can you hear everything we say when we're flying?'

'Yes. My hearing is far superior to yours, as is my eyesight and, unfortunately, my sense of smell. Off you get.'

Rosie and Maddie unbuckled their straps and climbed down. They jumped onto the sand and ran for the shade of the small group of trees by the oasis. Maddie sat in the shade and started unlacing her boots. Rosie had brought the water bottles, and she filled them in the pool as the dragon sniffed the water.

'It's clean,' she said. 'From what I know of this world, there will probably be no more sources of water sunward of this point. Would you agree, Little Rose?'

'Why are you asking her?' said Maddie as she lowered her bare feet into the water. 'Ooh, that's nice.'

'Apparently there are more sources of water,' said Rosie, 'but they run deeper under the surface, and are hard to get to. The City has sent out several expeditions, but none have made it beyond two hundred miles or so before having to turn back. It's the same iceward. Well, I mean, it's the opposite, but with the same results. Beyond a few hundred miles, it's impossible to live.'

'Impossible for humans to live,' said Blackrose. 'I could happily stay on the ice mountain where you slept last night. I don't mind the cold, and I prefer flying in the dark. The sunlight here is harsh on my eyes.'

'The greenhides love it down here,' Maddie said. The dragon and Rosie turned to look at her. 'That's right, isn't it?'

'Yes,' said Rosie; 'the eternal enemy love the sun, but they also need fresh water. I read that they burrow under the hot sand for water, and lie out in the sun all day. They worship the sun, I think.'

Blackrose emitted a low laugh.

Rosie frowned. 'Did I get something wrong?'

'For a city of humans who have faced the greenhides for thousands of years, you appear to have learned little about them.'

'What is there to learn?' said Maddie. 'They're vicious beasts who want to eat us, and they number in the gabrillions.'

'Are you not curious about where they came from?'

'Who cares? The other side of the world apparently. The world is round.' She glanced at her sister. 'I remember that from school.'

'All worlds are round,' said Blackrose, 'or round-ish. If, however, they were native to this world, then humans would not have had a chance to evolve, as the greenhides would have wiped them out long ago. I have seen greenhide worlds, and continents on worlds where no animals live but them. I also remember when the gods unleashed them upon my world. Their plan didn't succeed, as my world consists of dozens of archipelagos, and the greenhides cannot swim. The islands that they did reach were devastated utterly.'

Maddie noticed that Rosie was staring wide-eyed at the dragon, her mouth open.

'This is the first time my sister's heard any of this,' she said. 'She doesn't know anything about the war you fought against the gods, or that you're a queen.' She smiled. 'It feels nice actually knowing something that she doesn't.'

Blackrose tilted her head. 'We will explain it all to you in time, Little Rose. Maddie has had the advantage of listening to my words for a lot longer than you have.'

'A queen?'

'Yes, Little Rose, I was a queen on my world, and one day, I shall reclaim my throne.'

'Yeah?' said Maddie. 'That's the first time I've heard you say that.'

'I confess that back in the fortress, I had all but given up hope of ever tasting freedom again. Now that I have, my spirits are returning.'

'Blackrose,' said Rosie, her voice quieter than usual, 'can I ask you something?'

'Yes?'

'Do the champions come from the stars?'

'In a way, I suppose, but not any star that you can see at night from here. And the stars are only other suns, of course.' She leaned over and drank from the pool, then lifted her head again. 'I thought I told you girls to get clean?' She lifted a forelimb and nudged them both, sending them flying into the pool.

Rosie's shriek was drowned out by the splash they made, and Maddie plunged through the cool waters. She swam for a moment then surfaced.

'This is bliss,' she said, floating on her back in the pool. She gazed up and saw the long leaves of the thin trees above her head. Beyond, the sky was the bluest she had ever seen, and the sun was beating down with an intensity she had never felt before.

They washed, then laid their clothes out on the sand, where they dried in minutes.

'We should have put a hairbrush on the list in Tarstation,' said Maddie as she gazed at her reflection in the water. 'I look like a scarecrow.'

'Are we still going to search for Corthie?' said Rosie, as she leaned against a tree in the shade.

Blackrose edged her way into the pool, easing her bulk down into the waters. 'Yes, but I admit I am a little confounded as to how we go about such a thing. I can hardly land on the roof of one of the City's famed palaces and demand to know where he is. I would need someone to spy for me, to determine his location, and to possibly make contact with him.'

'If he's in the City,' said Maddie, 'he'll be fighting the greenhides. You know what he's like; he has a sense of duty.'

'Meaning I don't?'

'Basically.'

'That sits well with me. I feel no sense of duty towards the City. My only hope for it is that Corthie survives, along with the Quadrant.'

'The what?' said Rosie.

Maddie waved her away. 'Later.' She turned back to the dragon in the pool. 'What about Lady Aila? Do you not care what happens to her?'

'She was supposed to find Lord Naxor and the Quadrant. She did neither.'

'Lady Aila?' said Rosie.

'She's a demigod,' said Maddie.

Rosie rolled her eyes. 'I know who she is; I just wondered what in Malik's name she has to do with Blackrose.'

'She and Corthie were… you know.'

'No, what?'

'Use your imagination, because I'm not going to spell it out for you.'

'Eww.'

'I hadn't realised you were such a prude.'

'I'm not, it's just, well, she's eight hundred years old, and he's what? Eighteen or nineteen? It's a bit yuck.'

Maddie frowned. 'I hadn't thought of it like that.'

'Like what?' said Blackrose.

'The age difference,' said Rosie.

'Corthie's a mortal,' said the dragon. 'It wouldn't matter if he was eighteen or eighty; as far as Aila is concerned, he will wither and die before her in the blink of an eye. If you are going to feel sorry for one of them, then it should be for her.'

'Their love is doomed,' said Rosie. 'Whatever happens, it won't end well.'

'But look at all the other demigods,' said Maddie. 'Each one of them had a mortal as one of their parents, right? Prince Isra had an enormous harem, and Lady Aila's mother would have been in there. The thing is, no one remembers the names of any of the mortal parents of the demigods, so I reckon they just don't care.'

'What about Princess Yendra?' said Rosie. 'She married a mortal man called Laven, and they had three daughters together. After he died, she never went with another mortal again. She must have loved him.'

'Maybe, but that was the exception. Yendra was weird in lots of ways. She actually cared about mortals, for one thing. That's what got her killed in the end.'

'No, it wasn't,' said Rosie. 'It was that fact that she stomped on Prince Michael's head that got her executed.'

'The gods of the City are all worthless,' said Blackrose. 'Except perhaps Amalia. Her powers are extensive.'

'How do you know about her?' said Maddie.

'I'd heard her name mentioned as one of the rebel gods. Theoretically, that would put her on the same side as me in the Great War. She was part of a group that included Nathaniel, one of the legendary world builders. I think this world may well have been created by him. One of his earlier works, judging by the numerous flaws in its construction.'

'I think I need to lie down,' said Rosie. 'There's too much going on in my head. Is any of this true, or am I dreaming?'

'I am a dragon,' said Blackrose, 'and I do not lie. I prevaricate on occasion, if I wish to conceal something, but I never knowingly state a falsehood. What about you, Little Rose? Do you always tell the truth?'

Rosie glanced away. 'I don't think I'll answer that.'

'You are wise not to, for you would have to either lie or shame yourself.'

'Malik's ass,' said Maddie, 'I'm starting to feel how Hilde must have felt when I arrived. Should we think about where we're going to be sleeping tonight? I vote not the ice cave.'

'I agree,' said Rosie. 'It was too cold to sleep.'

'Then we shall search for a suitable place,' said Blackrose. 'Somewhere along the narrow strip between the ice and the desert; somewhere the greenhides cannot reach.'

'And then we need to fly back and get all our stuff,' said Maddie.

'Indeed. It is good that I love to fly.' She pulled herself from the pool, and spread her wings out in the bright sunshine to dry. 'Climb up; I kept the harness out of the water.'

'Maddie,' said her sister as they walked towards the dragon, 'while we fly, could you start telling me everything about the gods and the other worlds? The Quadrant too.'

'I guess so,' she said as she grabbed the ropes and climbed up to the saddle.

Rosie scrambled up after her, and got into position in front of her elder sister. They buckled the straps, and Maddie felt the intense heat of the sun drum down on her as the dragon beat its wings and took off. They soared upwards into a cooler breeze and Maddie smiled again, feeling the rush of the wind on her face. She glanced at her sister.

'Right,' she said. 'There was a war, eh... some gods invaded the dragon place where Blackrose was queen, and there's another, totally different place, where Corthie lived with his sister, who has the powers of a god, and she's looking for him, right?'

Rosie squinted at her. 'Something tells me that Blackrose is going to have to correct most of this when we land.'

The dragon flew over the desert, keeping the marshlands close to their left. After a while, she veered slightly iceward, and the monotonous marshes passed under them for hours as Maddie talked about what she remembered. The sun had lowered in the sky when Rosie nudged her and pointed. Ahead of them, the marshlands had narrowed to a small strip, and the land rose. The Warm Sea came into view, and then the walls of the City. The long breakwaters of Port Sanders poked out into the sea like pincers, and along from them, the much smaller harbour of Salt Quay marked the position of the Bulwark. At that distance, no movement was visible, but where the walls ended, the land was covered in a thick layer of what appeared to Maddie to look like ants, swarming over the plains in front of the Great Walls.

Maddie's mouth opened as they flew closer. The sea of greenhides spread for mile after mile, an unbroken carpet of life, all moving in the same direction, towards the City. She heard Rosie break down and sob at the sight, but Maddie felt empty. Her home, her life, it had all ended; no, not ended; changed. She thought of all the people who had died, and who were still dying, for pockets of the Bulwark would still be holding out. All those poor Scythes and Hammers, trapped between walls built by the Blades to control them. Thousands of Blades would have been torn to pieces, but at least many of them could run for the gates in the Middle Walls. The bulk of the Blades of fighting age would also still be alive, she realised, as they would have been serving in Auldan or Medio at the time of the breach. She hoped their brother Tom and the gatehouse sergeant from Arrowhead were among them.

They flew on, shifting their course to head along a line halfway between the ice and the desert, but there seemed to be no end in sight to the greenhides, and Maddie felt a raw despair take hold of her. Would the City ever be safe? How could it hold out against such numbers, such overwhelming odds? Surely it would fall one day, and she had been cursed with a life that had coincided with that inevitable fact. If she had been born at any time in the previous thousand years, she would have known nothing but peace.

'Mountains,' said Rosie, pointing ahead. 'At last, something that's not just greenhides.'

'Thank Malik,' Maddie muttered.

The jagged edge on the horizon grew larger as they approached, and soon the vast expense of the mountain range loomed into sight. The land rippled and rose up in a ragged line, cutting across the middle of the plain for a hundred miles.

'This is as far as the Children of the Gods got a thousand years ago,' said Rosie. 'They cleared the greenhides as far as these mountains, and none returned for a few hundred years.'

'I wish I'd lived then,' said Maddie. 'Imagine never having to see those green monsters.'

As they got closer, Maddie made out several valleys that snaked through the mountains, along which the greenhides were reaching the plain. To their left, some of the mountains were capped in snow, and had bands of dark forest clinging to their flanks, while to the right, towards sunward, the slopes were brown and barren. Blackrose continued on in a straight line, and they began to fly between the high peaks, as forests and grasslands sped by beneath them.

Blackrose began to circle over the peaks and ravines, her gaze directed downwards. Several mountains were so high that their summits were lost in a thick bank of cloud, and the dragon flew through it, and Maddie shivered in the cold, wet air. Blackrose dived again, out of the clouds, and soared down, the ground rushing towards them. She headed for a small, green valley enclosed on all sides by high ridges and peaks, circled over it a few times, and then went in to land. A waterfall tumbled down the face of a sheer cliff at one end of the little valley, and Blackrose landed by the large pool at its base, where a stream set off down the hillside.

Maddie and Rosie climbed down, and jumped onto the thick grass that covered much of the valley. Maddie gazed around. Clusters of trees heavy with the blossom of early summer sat by the banks of the small stream, and the entire valley was bathed in the reds and pinks of the lowering sun.

'What do you think?' said Blackrose. 'This valley is far from any of the paths the greenhides take through the mountains, and it has fresh water, and shelter in the caves by the pool.'

Maddie knelt by the waters. She could see to the bottom, where small, silver fish darted though the weeds and rocks. She put her hand in, and felt the chill from the mountain water.

'This is perfect,' said Rosie. 'It has everything we need, except for food.'

'I shall hunt, Little Rose, and bring back meat for us to share.'

Maddie frowned. 'I hope you're not talking about greenhide meat.'

'Of course not, I would never eat one of them. I will hunt in the valleys iceward of here, where it is too cold and dark for them, and find the other creatures that live there. But first, I must return to the cave we departed from this morning, to fetch your supplies. Remove what you need for tonight from the harness, for I shall be gone until at least dawn tomorrow.'

'Are you going to leave us here?' said Rosie, her voice high.

'You'll be safe, Little Rose, and I can fly faster without worrying about you two on my back.'

The Jackdaw sisters unfastened the bags from the dragon's harness, and dropped them onto the grass, then Blackrose extended her wings.

'Explore our new home,' she said, 'and I shall return.'

'Don't be long,' said Rosie.

They watched as Blackrose ascended back into the sky, circled, then flew away.

'She will come back, won't she?' said Rosie.

'I certainly hope so.'

'What do we do now?'

'You're the smart one,' Maddie said; 'why are you asking me?'

'Because you're my big sister, and I'm a bit scared.'

Maddie glanced at her, an eyebrow raised. She felt a few sarcastic responses on the tip of her tongue, but she suppressed them. Apart from Blackrose, her sister was all she had left. 'We'll be fine. Why don't we get all of our bags into a cave, and then we can explore together?'

Rosie nodded.

They picked up the bags and carried them by the left side of the pool, where several dark openings led away into the side of the cliff. None were large enough to accommodate a dragon of Blackrose's size, but they were dry and airy. They picked a shallow cave with a large opening, from where the whole stretch of the small valley could be seen, and unpacked their blankets, and the food they had brought. Once settled, they left the cave, and walked down by the tree-lined banks of the stream, passing under branches heavy with blossom. Tiny flowers carpeted the grass, and birds were calling to each other from the tops of the trees. The light was starting to fade, and the sun dipped below the edge of the ridge, casting the valley into shadows. They picked up armfuls of dry wood from the ground, and followed the stream to where it disappeared, plunging down into an underground channel.

They walked back to the cave, carrying their bundles of wood with them. They built a small fire on the barren rocks next to the cave's entrance, and lit it with the matches Rosie had stowed away in one of their packs. The temperature was dropping, so they gathered their blankets and sat by the fire, watching the flames as night fell.

A noise came from one of the trees, and Rosie jumped.

'It's fine,' said Maddie. 'It'll be a bird or something. We're safe here; the valley is enclosed on all sides.'

'But greenhides can climb mountains.'

'Why would they, though? They're all rushing headlong towards the plains so they can queue up to get into the City. They're not going to come up here.'

'But what if they do?'

'They won't. Blackrose wouldn't have left us somewhere that was vulnerable.'

'She deserted the City; what's to stop her doing the same to us?'

Maddie smiled. 'I'm her rider, and Buckler once told me that dragons never desert their riders. It's an honour thing for them.'

Rosie nodded, but her eyes remained tight and troubled. 'I miss mum and dad. It's like, it's only just dawning on me what happened. We've lost everything.'

Maddie took her hand. 'Not everything. We've got each other.'

Rosie moved next to her, and Maddie put an arm over her shoulder and pulled her close.

'Everything's going to be alright,' Maddie said. 'You'll see.'

CHAPTER 8
BEGUILED

Ooste, Auldan, The City – 23rd Amalan 3420

'Good morning, granddaughter,' said the God-Queen as Aila entered the throne room. 'Have you finished preparing your husband's quarters?'

'Not yet,' said Aila. 'Marcus has a lot of things.'

'You know, if you prove to be a good wife, then in a century or so I might elevate you to the level of Princess of Pella. I understand your brother Kano has been petitioning for this honour to come to himself, but after his mistakes with the former champion I doubt he would be worthy of the title of prince. I hardly think you're suitable either, to be honest, but Marcus has chosen you, so he must see something that has so far eluded me.'

Aila said nothing. She glanced around the large, empty chamber, wondering why she had been summoned. She had been told which dress to wear, and her feet kept getting caught in the long robes that flowed to the marble floor.

A tall door opened and Doria entered. Aila hadn't seen her since they had eaten together in the kitchens the previous evening, and her cousin looked worn out.

She approached the throne, her eyes acknowledging Aila, then she bowed before the God-Queen.

'The delegation from Dalrig has arrived, your Majesty.'

'Yes? And who has my son sent in his stead?'

'Prince Montieth has commissioned Lady Amber to attend the palace, your Majesty.'

'Amber? I've not laid eyes on her in five hundred years.' She turned to Aila. 'You were in Greylin Palace recently, were you not? You must be familiar with Lady Amber.'

'I met her there, yes.'

The God-Queen waited, as if expecting Aila to say more, then frowned. 'How helpful, thank you.' She turned back to Doria. 'Let her approach the throne.'

'Yes, your Majesty.' Doria bowed again, and returned to the door.

The God-Queen eyed Aila. 'You need to be of more use, dear.'

'I thought I was supposed to say nothing when I was summoned to the throne room?'

'Don't try to be clever with me. If I ask you a direct question, I expect a proper answer.'

Doria reappeared at the entrance, with Lady Amber by her side. They walked in, and approached the dais where the God-Queen sat.

Doria bowed low. 'Lady Amber of Dalrig, your Majesty.'

'I can see who it is, girl,' the God-Queen said.

Amber stood motionless, not lowering her head in a bow, or even averting her eyes as she stared at the God-Queen.

'Well, Lady Amber,' the God-Queen went on, 'does the government of Dalrig have anything to say?'

Amber frowned. 'My father wishes for peace.'

'Ahh, so Montieth has opened his eyes at last, has he? It's a pity that it took the fall of the Bulwark for him to come to his senses.'

'The fall of the Bulwark is the only reason I am here, grandmother. Were it not for that, Dalrig would remain unpolluted by the inept rule of Duke Marcus.'

The God-Queen's face tightened, and her eyes narrowed at Amber.

'We propose a truce between our forces,' Amber went on, 'to ensure that the defence of the City from the greenhides is not compromised by any more silly little invasions by the idiot duke. Trade must resume immediately, otherwise we shall not assist you in any way. Understand also, that our armed forces will never serve under the command of the duke, as he has proved incompetent to lead...'

'Enough!' cried the God-Queen, her temper flaring. 'How dare you come here and try to dictate terms to me, your sovereign and monarch. I should flay your skin from your body for the disrespect you are showing me.'

Amber stood firm, her lips forming into a smile. 'You forfeited all authority when you appointed your most stupid grandchild as a pretend prince. These are Dalrig's terms. Accept them, and the Gloamers will fully cooperate in the defence of the City; reject them, and Dalrig will stand alone.' Her eyes flickered over to Aila. 'I'm surprised to find you here, cousin. Lady Doria has always had a servile nature, but I thought you disliked being confined? At least that was the impression you gave me, when you were a guest in my father's palace. I remember you telling me how much you loathed Duke Marcus, yet here you are, married to him.' She shook her head. 'I'm a little disappointed.'

Aila cringed.

'I see now that you are trying to provoke us,' said the God-Queen. 'You remind me of Montieth, when he was younger; a most contrary child. You think that because you possess the same powers as me I would be unable to destroy you? Would you like to put that theory to the test?'

'Do as you please, grandmother; I am not afraid to die. Unlike you, I do not cling onto life, nor do I overindulge in salve. Judging by your youthful appearance, my queen, I doubt the same could be said about you. Now, where is grandfather? I would like to speak with him, to learn if you have truly reconciled.'

'The God-King and I have never been happier,' she said. 'That is all you need to know. Before casting aspersions at another's home life, you should examine your own. Tell me, where is your sister?'

'Jade is currently residing at the sunward end of the Circuit, as I'm sure you already know, grandmother.'

'And what are you and your father doing to rein her in?'

'Nothing. She deserted us, fooled by Lady Aila's words into thinking she was a friend. If she returns of her own free will, then we will forgive her, but until then she'll have to look after herself. What she happens to do in the Circuit is of no concern to me or my father. Some days, I think he may have already forgotten about her. But this is an irrelevance; do you accept our terms or not?'

The God-Queen raised her hand, and Amber's face greyed. She cried out in agony and slipped down to her knees, her hands reaching for her throat.

'Do you feel that?' said the God-Queen. 'Of course you do; the decay, the rot, the death. I know you're strong, Amber, but my power is magnitudes greater. I can reverse your self-healing powers, so that they turn on you. Your extremities would be the first to go, then your hair and teeth, as the rot spreads to every part of your body.'

Amber cried out again, as the skin started to peel and fall from her face. Blood came from her eyes, trickling down her green-tinged cheeks.

'That's better,' said the God-Queen; 'that seems to have stopped your impertinence. Now, where were we? Oh, yes; the terms. Tell your father that we accept your offer of a truce, and expect your borders to open immediately. The Gloamer armed forces shall remain on the Union Walls, to assist in the garrisoning and repair work, and Dalrig shall cede Fishcross to the Blades as a permanent Cold Sea port. That is all; you may leave.'

The God-Queen lowered her hand and Amber collapsed onto the floor, panting as blood seeped through her clothes onto the cold marble.

'Lady Doria,' said the God-Queen; 'please escort our honoured guest out of the palace.'

Doria ran over to where Amber was lying on the floor as the God-

Queen got to her feet and strode from the chamber. Aila stepped down off the dais and walked over to Doria and Amber.

'You've got a lot of guts,' she said, kneeling by her cousin.

'More than you,' said Amber as she struggled up. Her skin was starting to heal itself, but the sores across her face were oozing and angry-looking. They stood. 'Tell me, cousin,' she went on; 'why did you leave Greylin, only to marry Marcus? We would have protected you from that outcome.'

'You were holding me as a hostage, Amber. I might have stayed if I'd been free to leave.'

'My father remains very angry with you.'

Aila's thoughts went to the stolen vial of salve. 'Why?'

'Why do you think? You lured Jade from the palace, then abandoned her in the middle of the Circuit.'

'I saw things in that palace,' Aila said, 'things your father was doing. It's not right, Amber, you must know that.'

Her cousin shrugged. 'What my father does to a few mortals is of no concern to me.'

'What does he do to them?' said Doria.

Amber glanced at her. 'He experiments on them. He's always looking for ways to allow dead mortals to be of more use to us. If he succeeds, then maybe we wouldn't need any living mortals in the City, and the undead could serve us. He's a visionary.'

Doria's face fell. Oh.'

Amber took a breath, her skin restored.

'Are you alright now?' said Aila.

She shrugged. 'My father has done much worse to me over the years. Goodbye.'

Amber turned and strode from the throne room.

'She scares me a little bit,' said Doria. 'Does she not have any fear in her at all?'

'I guess a thousand years with Prince Montieth has made her that way. Jade's even worse; at least Amber's intelligent. Jade is... well... not exactly... Damn it, I should have bought her that cat.'

'I'd better go, the God-Queen will be wanting me.'

Aila nodded. 'And I have to carry on unpacking Marcus's stuff.'

They left by separate doors, and Aila passed the cordon of undead soldiers who guarded the private chambers of the palace. She was ascending the stairs to Marcus's rooms when she heard a loud clatter from the hallway below her. She went to the side of the stairs and gazed down. A woman was striding along the marble corridor, wearing leather armour, with a sword strapped to her back. Aila frowned. Her clothes seemed foreign, and she was walking with a confident air, her expression guarded. The woman glanced up as if sensing someone was watching her and their eyes locked.

'Who are you?' Aila called down to her. 'How did you get past the guards?'

The woman gazed at her for a second as she walked to the base of the stairs.

'Did you hear me?' said Aila. 'Who are you?'

'Are you the queen?'

Aila frowned at the strange accent. 'No.'

'Do you know where Corthie Holdfast is?'

'What? Corthie?'

'Are you deaf?' the woman said as she bounded up the stairs towards her. 'Yes, Corthie Holdfast. Is that name familiar to you?'

Aila's mouth fell open. 'Are you... are you his sister?'

The woman frowned. 'No, of course not. His sister sent me. Do you know where he is?'

'He was last seen on the Grey Isle, but I doubt he's there any more,' Aila said. 'The City tried to execute him, but he escaped.'

'I know all that. Karalyn Holdfast read the mind of someone called Vana.'

'She's my sister.'

The woman eyed her with suspicion. 'If you don't know where he is, then you are no use to me. Where is the queen?'

'I'm a prisoner here,' Aila blurted out before she could stop herself. 'I can help you find Corthie. He trusts me. We were... close. I love him.'

The suspicion in the woman's eyes turned to disgust. 'Are you saying you were involved romantically with him? How old are you?'

'Nearly eight hundred.'

'You're a god?'

'A demigod, like Vana.'

'Is it normal here for demigods to get involved with children?'

'Corthie's not a child. He's young, but he's a man.'

The woman took a step back, and she eyed Aila up and down. 'Tell me something about him so I know you're not lying.'

'He has green eyes, and he said his sister and mother have the same. He said his sister is the most powerful mortal ever. And he has a brother that he doesn't like. He kept telling me that his family would come for him.'

'I'm not his family,' said the woman. 'I... owe a lot to Karalyn Holdfast. I promised to help her find her lost brother.' She nodded. 'Alright. What's your name?'

'Aila.'

'My name is Belinda. If you're a prisoner, then why don't you try to escape? I don't see any chains on you.'

'The soldiers,' she said; 'they won't allow me to leave.' She leaned in to whisper. 'They've been raised from the dead.'

'By a soulwitch?'

Aila frowned. 'A what?'

'A mage who can do that.'

'Corthie talked about mages with me. He said that mortals on your world have powers, but it's not like that here. Only gods and demigods have powers. It was the God-Queen herself that raised the soldiers.'

'What else can she do?'

'She has the full range of life and death powers,' Aila said, 'she's the most powerful god in the City.'

Belinda snorted. 'Let's go.'

She turned and started back down the stairs.

'Wait,' said Aila. 'Where are we going? Can I get changed first? If I have to run, I don't want to do it in this.'

Belinda frowned. 'Can you fight?'

'Yes.'

'Very well.'

Aila rushed off towards Marcus's quarters, with Belinda striding alongside. The woman's eyes seemed oddly cold, as if she had no particular attachment to what she was doing. They entered the rooms of the prince, and Aila slipped her dress off and started to get dressed in her older clothes, the ones she had worn when pretending to be Stormfire. A thought occurred to her as she fastened on her belt.

You see me as Corthie.

Belinda's expression didn't change in any way. Aila smothered a gasp and dropped her disguise. Like Corthie, Belinda must be shielded from the powers of others.

'Are you a mage?' she said.

'No.'

'So you don't have any powers?'

'I'm a god.'

'The Holdfasts have got gods on their side?'

'Just me. They killed all the other gods on their world.'

'*Their* world; not yours?'

'As I said, I'm a god. Do you have a map?'

'A what? Eh, yes. I think Marcus has a few somewhere.'

She finished dressing and rushed over to a large trunk, filled with scrolls, books and maps. She pulled out one of the City and passed it to Belinda.

The woman gazed at it. 'Where are we?'

'Here,' Aila said, pointing, 'Ooste.'

'And if Corthie was on Grey Isle, where would he go next? Dalrig seems the closest.'

'Maybe. Listen, I have another two cousins trapped here in the palace. We need to rescue them too.'

'Only if they can help find Corthie, or a Quadrant.'

Aila blinked. 'Don't you have one? How did you get here?'

'Karalyn Holdfast doesn't need a Quadrant to travel between worlds.'

'Then why isn't she here?'

'She doesn't need a Quadrant, but she does need a lot of power. She drained the two demigods we found on Lostwell, but it was only enough to send one person. I volunteered.'

'Go back a bit. She drained two demigods? You mean Irno and Vana, my brother and sister?'

'Yes.'

'Are they alive?'

Belinda frowned. 'Yes. Karalyn doesn't like to kill people; it's her major flaw. She could rule all the worlds if she wished, but she just wants to get her brother and go home. She should have killed me, twice, but each time showed me mercy.'

Aila puffed out her cheeks and fell into a chair. 'Well, I'm grateful that Vana and Irno aren't dead, but how are you planning to travel back?'

'There are two Quadrants in this world, and I intend to take one.'

'And when you find Corthie?'

'I shall return with him to Lostwell, and my debt to Karalyn will be paid.'

Aila leaned over to lace up her boots, but also so she could avoid Belinda's piercing gaze. Her thoughts raced as she tried to look ahead. If she could get out of the palace, then they could start looking for Corthie, but she realised that she wasn't sure if she wanted Belinda to find him, not if she was only interested in rescuing him, and would happily let the City fall to the greenhides.

'You tell me something about Corthie,' she said, 'so I know you're not lying.'

Belinda looked impatient. 'I love him too, but not in the same way that you do. He used to read me stories every night, when I lived in the Holdfast townhouse, and he was kind to me, like a sweet little brother.'

'Did he tell you that he killed a god?'

Belinda nodded. 'I was in the townhouse when it happened. Corthie smashed his head in.'

Aila rubbed her face.

'Alright,' she said, standing; 'I'm ready. After we leave the palace, we should go via the Royal Academy. I have some things hidden there that I need to collect. Before that, we need to rescue Naxor and Doria.'

'No. Your cousins are superfluous. I'll take you, and only you. Do you have any powers?'

Aila bit her tongue. 'No.'

Belinda shook her head. 'I thought you said you could fight?'

'I can, but I don't have battle-vision.'

Belinda walked to the door of the room and opened it, and Aila followed. They retraced their steps and descended the grand stairs to the ground level, where a group of soldiers were standing on duty by the doors to the main areas of the palace. They had been supplied with masks to hide their decaying features, and their lifeless eyes shone through.

'Stay behind me,' Belinda said as they approached the guards.

Aila nodded and took a step back as Belinda drew her sword. The four soldiers turned to her, and raised their maces. One also lifted a gauntlet-clad hand to bar their way. Belinda swung her blade and sliced the hand off at the wrist, then rolled under a wild mace blow. She sprang up, cleaving the head from one of the soldiers, its helmet bouncing off the marble floor as the corpse toppled over. Belinda moved like lightning, her battle-vision faster that Aila's eyes could follow. She slashed out, and another soldier fell, then swung low, hacking through the legs of another. The last soldier lunged at her, and his head went flying a moment later. Belinda glanced at the four bodies, then sheathed her sword.

'The undead do not bleed the same,' she said, peering downwards at a decapitated body.

'We should probably go.'

'How long were they dead for,' Belinda said, 'before they were raised?'

'I've no idea; does it matter? Listen, I'm not sure I can leave without Naxor. Doria will be fine, but Naxor is being tortured right now, and we need to help him.'

Belinda shook her head and placed her hand on the door.

'Belinda!' cried a loud voice.

Aila frowned, and turned. The God-Queen was running down the hallway towards them, the look on her face one of joy and surprise.

She approached, then halted a few yards away. 'Is it really you? Am I dreaming?'

'My name is Belinda,' she said, 'but I've no idea who you are.'

'What? But... You're joking? It's me. Amalia.'

Aila edged backwards from the two gods, a sour feeling developing in her stomach. The God-Queen knew her?

'I don't know any Amalia,' said Belinda. 'Do you know where Corthie Holdfast is?'

'This is the God-Queen,' said Aila.

Amalia turned to her. 'And how do you know Belinda? What's going on?'

Belinda sighed. 'I may have known you in my old life, but all of my memories were destroyed a few years ago. I'm here to collect Corthie Holdfast, and I warn you; do not hinder me.'

'You lost your memories?' the God-Queen said. 'I didn't know that was possible for a god. Is Nathaniel here too; did he come with you?'

'Nathanial is dead.'

The God-Queen lifted her hands to her face and broke down in tears. Aila stared, unable to believe the change that had come over her. Doria emerged from a door and hurried over.

'Your Majesty, what's wrong? Who is this woman?'

'Please,' said the God-Queen as tears streamed down her face; 'Belinda, please, you must tell me what happened. Come and sit down, just for a moment. You were my best friend for centuries, you owe me that much.'

Belinda scowled. 'I'm not your friend now.'

'I beg you, please.'

Doria and Aila share a glance, their mouths open.

Belinda turned to Aila. 'I will tell Amalia what I know; she even might be of assistance to us.'

The God-Queen glanced at Aila in confusion, then seemed to remember herself. She wiped her eyes and straightened. 'Doria, fetch some wine. I shall talk with Belinda in the day room.'

Doria bowed. 'Yes, your Majesty.'

Aila followed as Amalia led Belinda to a small reception room, with white-painted walls and a tall window facing sunward. She showed Belinda to a seat, and then sat down opposite her. Aila edged onto a couch, watching them both.

'You really don't remember me?' said the God-Queen.

'I have no memories of my old life.'

'What happened? The last time I saw you and Nathaniel, you were with Agatha and her friends, talking about your plans for Nathaniel's new world. You were waiting for it to be finished when Malik and I came here and founded the City.'

'Do you know who Corthie Holdfast is?'

'Yes, but why are you looking for him?'

'His sister wiped my mind completely clean; memories, language, everything. I was trying to kill her at the time, so I don't particularly blame her for what she did. Everyone else thought she should have killed me. She and Corthie belong to a family called the Holdfasts, and I'm helping to find her brother. Once I've done that, we shall leave this world. Can you help me?'

'What happened to Nathaniel?'

'He got trapped inside the world he had made, and the Holdfasts killed him. Apparently that's why I went there, to seek revenge. I took Agatha and five others. The Holdfasts killed all of them too.'

Amalia stared at her. 'And you serve these creatures? The Holdfasts? Are they gods?'

'No, they're mortal. Nathaniel made a mistake. He wanted to create a world filled with mortal mages, and he succeeded, but one strain was too powerful for him or for any other god to resist. The dream mages. Karalyn is the mightiest of them.'

'I ask you again, Belinda; do you serve them?'

'I do.'

Amalia's eyes hardened. 'How far back do your memories go?'

'A few years.'

'Do you know that you have been alive for over thirty millennia? You and Nathaniel were two of the oldest gods in existence. Malik and I were children in comparison, and even though Malik and Nathaniel were brothers, the age difference was immense. I looked up to you; you were powerful, beautiful; everything a true god should be. And now, you're telling me that you serve a family of mortal god-killers?'

Belinda smiled. 'You're not going to persuade me to change my mind. I'm not the same person you once knew.'

Doria walked in with a tray and set in down onto the low table between Amalia and Belinda.

'Thanks,' said Aila.

The God-Queen glanced at her. 'Why are you still here? Be gone, now.'

Aila chewed her lip for a moment. 'No, I think I'll stay. I'm going to help Belinda find Corthie.'

'You wretch,' cried Amalia. 'I should strike you down.'

'If you do, I will kill you,' said Belinda. 'I need Aila for now. Let her stay. Tell me more about who I was. Tell me more about Nathaniel. Were we together long?'

The God-Queen slowly turned away from Aila and smiled. 'Long? You were devoted to each other for ten thousand years. I don't think there has ever been a bond between gods that has lasted as long as you did with him. Malik and I were together for almost five thousand years, but I hated him for long periods of that. With you and Nathaniel it was true love.'

'Why should I believe you?'

Amalia laughed. 'Read my mind if you don't.'

'I can't.'

Amalia's laughter stopped. 'What? What do you mean?'

'When Karalyn wiped my mind, she blocked every one of my powers, including my ability to self-heal, so that I wouldn't try to kill anyone when I woke up.'

'You have no powers?'

'I have battle, line and range-vision, and I have self-healing. I can heal others, also.'

'Is that it? Belinda, you used to have the full range of god powers. How can you serve someone who did this to you?'

'Because she's the only one who can restore my powers.'

Amalia nodded. 'Ah, now I think I begin to understand.'

'Tell me more.'

'Of course, yes,' said the God-Queen; 'however, I have two conditions. Firstly, I ask that you stay here, tonight, as a guest in the palace. I will talk to you, and tell you everything about your old life that you want to know. One night. Also, I ask that we talk alone, without my grandchildren prying.'

'And tomorrow?' said Belinda.

'Tomorrow you can leave and begin your search for Corthie.'

'I'm taking Aila too.'

'If you must, though I wouldn't bother if I were you; she's utterly useless.'

Belinda glanced over at where Aila was sitting. 'Out.'

'Screw you, Belinda,' Aila cried. 'You came here to do something, and the God-Queen's beguiled you with her sobs and stories about how you were friends. She's trying to play with you; don't you get it?'

The god's eyes narrowed. 'Leave. We shall speak in the morning.'

Aila stood. The God-Queen glanced up at her, a tiny smirk on her lips. 'I think we'll be having words in the morning too, Lady Aila.'

Doria got up and bowed, then the two demigods walked to the door. They went into the hallway, and Doria closed the door behind them. Aila smothered a scream of frustration, and clasped her face. She pushed Doria out of the way and ran across the hallway, towards the tall doors where Belinda had slaughtered the guards. Maybe, she thought, the way would still be clear and she could flee, anywhere, just as long as she could get out of the palace.

She turned the corner, and saw four fresh soldiers standing by the doors, the bodies gone. She skidded to a halt, then stumbled to her knees.

She was a prisoner again, of the palace, the City, and the world. She lowered her face; wondering if she would ever be free.

CHAPTER 9

THE CHAMPION OF ICEHAVEN

Icehaven, Medio, The City – 24th Amalan 3420

'It's quite a sight,' said Major Hannia, 'one I hoped I'd never live to see.'

Corthie nodded as they stood on the high walkway of the Middle Walls, gazing down at the mass of greenhides occupying the Bulwark. The last three-mile stretch of the Middle Walls ran across a ridge of the Iceward Range, and sheer cliffs dropped to the Bulwark. In the distance, the line of the Great Walls was visible, and between it and the base of the cliff the ground was swarming with the eternal enemy.

'This is the safest part of the Middle Walls,' the major went on. 'If you look directly below us, you'll see the stairs that were cut into the side of the cliff hundreds of years ago; once the Blades in this area had used them to escape, we tore down several sections. The greenhides are good climbers, but they'll never scale these cliffs in numbers, and the First and Second Gates are secure.'

'Then what does Lady Yvona need me to do? Would I be better put to use down in the Circuit?'

'Lord Kano is based there, with most of the surviving Blades. It's probably best that you stay clear of him, and there is still much you can do for the Icewarders. As you know, every citizen in Medio and Auldan has been mobilised, and thousands are working on repairs to the walls; in some places they are constructing a new wall directly behind the old where it is weak. If you look to the left, you'll see where we have a problem.'

She pointed along the ridge towards iceward. Corthie could see the First Gate, and then the land dropped at a steep angle down to the shores of the Cold Sea, where a fortress lay. Beyond the fortress, a long wall projected out into the waves like the breakwater of a harbour. At its far end rose a tower, just visible in the dawn light.

'There was a weakness in the Middle Walls when they were first built,' the major said, 'which meant that, in winter when the seas froze, the greenhides could simply walk across the ice and bypass the defences altogether. Our solution was to construct the long sea wall, to block them, but it's been crumbling for generations, and there's a potential breach where the wall joins the fortress.'

She started walking down the slope towards the sea, and Corthie followed.

'What we need you to do,' she said, 'is clear the area in front of the weak point, so that we can repair it properly without the workers being slaughtered. The materials are prepared and the labourers are waiting, all they need is time to work.'

'Alright,' he said; 'I can do that. Is my armour ready?'

'Yes; it should be waiting for us at the bottom of the hill.'

'When I fought before, in front of the Great Walls, I had a team to support me; the Wolfpack. We would screen the Rats who did the repairs to the moat.'

'Yes, I've been briefed on that. Unfortunately, you will have to fight alone, as we cannot risk opening one of the postern gates in case the greenhides break through.'

'Then how will I get into the Bulwark?'

She glanced at him. 'You'll see.'

They climbed down a set of steps from the walkway, and joined the road that ran behind the wall. It was busy with wagons and workers, and repairs were happening to almost every section of the defences.

Heaps of cut timber and shaped blocks of stone lay piled every twenty yards, much of it coming from the forests and quarries that covered the Iceward Range of hills.

'Normally every tree in the City is counted,' said the major, catching his glance, 'and the quarries only used for prestigious building projects, but all those rules and regulations have been suspended in the crisis. The forests will take years to recover, but we must do whatever it takes to survive.'

'There are lots of trees on the Western Bank.'

'Yes, and ships are heading out there every day, but the shores on the other side of the Straits are dangerous in summer, with greenhides attacks common. Many ships do not return.'

'And where is Marcus? If Kano is leading the Blades in the Circuit, what's the new prince doing?'

The major frowned. 'He's based himself at the largest fort on the Union Walls, in Reaper territory, ostensibly so he can coordinate the overall defences, but I don't know what he's doing there. Thousands of Reapers are repairing the Union Walls, just as everyone in Medio is fixing the Middle Walls. It might be a sensible approach, but it doesn't look good to the Icewarders or anyone else in Medio.'

The road started to zigzag down the steep slope, but there were stairs cut into the rock that followed the direct route down, and the major and Corthie took them to avoid the queues of wagons on the road. The area at the bottom of the slope was packed with people and supplies, gathered behind the high walls of the fort that sat at the end of the Middle Walls. Corthie and the major entered the fort through a side door and came into a triangular forecourt, filled with soldiers wearing the uniforms of the Icewarder militia. They cleared a path for Corthie, many staring at him.

'Word will reach Kano and Marcus that you are here,' the major said; 'there's little we can do about that. Lady Yvona is anticipating a summons from the new prince, or a demand that you be arrested, but she will ignore it.' She halted by a door. 'Lady Yvona is placing a great deal of trust in you, champion; she is risking a serious rupture with the God-Queen by protecting you. Do you understand?'

'Aye. I'll try not to get killed.'

'It's not just about the way you fight,' she said, 'it's about what you say, and how you act when you're on this side of the walls. I beg you; don't let her down.'

They entered a tower through the door, and the major showed Corthie to a chamber where a set of armour had been laid out on a table.

'The armourers worked through the night to fashion this for you,' the major said. 'Put it on.'

Corthie took his coat off and stood with his arms stretched out, and soldiers began strapping padded linen to his body, before attaching the plates of armour.

The major gestured to another table where the Axe of Rand lay. 'And please, try not to lose this. It'll cut through the thick skin of any greenhide, better than any other blade in the City, but it's irreplaceable. The ore it was forged from has long been exhausted, but its symbolism to the Icewarders is even more important.'

Corthie smiled. 'I'll try not to break it.'

The major nodded. 'Do you need anything else before you go out?'

'I don't think so. I've eaten tons, but I'll need food and drink when I get back; some brandy would be nice.'

The soldiers stepped back, and Corthie moved around in his new armour, feeling the weight press against him. It didn't fit as well as the armour the Blades had made for him in Arrowhead, but they had been given much more time than the Icewarder armourers. He picked up the helmet and slid it on over the padded hood, then grasped the Axe of Rand with both hands. He rolled his shoulders, and drew on some battle-vision to clear his mind, feeling his energy increase.

He nodded. 'I'm ready.'

The major led him to a door, and they ascended a flight of steps, emerging out onto the battlements of the small fort. The din from the greenhides roared in his ears. They were massed around the base of the fortress wall where it met the long breakwater. Several seemed to be trying to burrow under the junction of the two walls, where the stonework had partly collapsed.

'Do you see what they're doing?' the major said. 'If that section of the wall is undermined much more, they could bring it down, and the road to Icehaven and the rest of Medio would be open to them. We have hundreds of workers ready to fix it, but they can only do so if the area is cleared of greenhides first.'

'How long will they need?'

'A few hours.'

Corthie scanned the terrain. The ground was barren and rocky, with high points and slopes of rough shingle that stretched to an abandoned old wall by the shore. The area between the walls formed a rough triangle that he would have to clear and dominate.

The major pointed to a crane sitting on the battlements. 'This is how we intend to lower you down, and retrieve you, once the work is complete. It can handle huge blocks of stone, so it'll bear your weight with no difficulty.'

Corthie walked over to the crane, and it was then that he noticed the thousands of faces watching him. Every soldier standing on the walls, and every worker and member of the militia that were waiting to fix the wall junction was staring at him.

'You don't mind an audience, do you?' said the major.

'Not at all. If I can hear them shouting and cheering it'll help.'

She took a breath and stuck out her hand. He took it. 'Good luck,' she said.

A small cluster of soldiers were operating the crane, and Corthie strode forwards and grasped the large iron hook that dangled at the end. He nodded to the soldiers, and they began to turn the winch, lifting Corthie off the battlements as he held on with his left arm, his right clutching the long axe. They swung him out over the wall, his feet hanging free, and he looked down at the mass of greenhides. They had seen him, and were snapping their claws upwards, and swarming across to his location.

'Don't worry,' he cried to them, 'there's plenty of time for you all to meet me.'

He felt his excitement build, and wondered if he was supposed to be scared. He knew others would think him insane for not being frightened, but in truth he was looking forward to dropping into the greenhides, so he could give himself over to what he had been born to do. Kill.

He lifted his axe in a gesture to the crane crew, and they stopped lowering him. He glanced down to time his jump, then let go of the hook. Claws reached out for him as he fell. He swung the axe, and felt it slice clean through the forelimbs of a greenhide, and he grinned. He landed onto the back of another beast, and rammed the axe-spike down into its brain, then got to work as the howls and shrieks closed in.

Three hours seemed to pass in the blink of an eye as Corthie fought alone at the place where the two walls met. The pressure from the greenhides waxed and waned. He would slaughter all those around him until they retreated, then a fresh batch would arrive, and the pattern would be repeated, until the mounds of slain grew around him, and the ground was slick with greenhide blood. He climbed the highest heap of dead during a short lull, vaguely aware that someone was shouting his name, but his battle-vision was so occupied with every movement of the greenhides that he suppressed it.

'Come on, ya cowards!' he yelled at the greenhides as they kept their distance from him, swirling by the base of the mound of corpses. His eyes scanned them, taking in every detail in his battle-vision haze. He was about to leap down to chase them when the voice shouted again.

'Corthie!'

He glanced back, and blinked. The battlements were crammed with cheering soldiers, and he smiled and waved, then noticed the major by the crane, gesturing urgently for him to return. He almost frowned in disappointment, and glanced back at the masses of greenhides swarming around the mound. He jumped down and bounded towards where the hook was dangling. He sprang onto the back of a greenhide and launched himself upwards, gripping the hook's chain in his left gauntlet, and the crew winched him up. The soldiers on the wall let out a deafening cheer, and he held up the axe, its edge glistening with green blood. The crane swung round, and Corthie dropped onto the battlements, where a crowd of soldiers pressed round him, hugging him, or just trying to touch him. Some were in tears, while others were laughing, and he smiled.

The major barged her way through. 'Give him room!'

Corthie nodded to her. 'Did I do alright? Did you get the wall repaired?'

'It was repaired almost an hour ago, Corthie,' she said, 'and I've been shouting on you ever since. It was like you were lost in your own world out there.'

He nodded, then turned to gaze down from the walls. His eyes widened at the sight of the heaps of slain. 'I did kill quite a lot of them, didn't I?' He powered down his battle-vision, and began to feel a dozen places where he hurt. A wave of exhaustion swept over him, and he staggered as the soldiers reached out to steady him.

He laughed. 'I might need that brandy now.' He staggered again, then toppled over.

Corthie awoke, and the first thing he saw were the dozens of faces in the dark chamber, all staring at him.

'Hello,' he said.

'He's awake!' cried one, and more folk crammed into the room. All were wearing the uniforms of the Icewarder militia, and they crowded round the bed, touching him as he lay there.

'Everybody out!' yelled the major. 'The champion needs to rest.' She and a few other guards began shoving the militia soldiers from the room. Some grabbed onto Corthie's arm, trying to stay, but they were pulled off him as he laughed. When the last had been evicted from the room, the major closed the door. She picked up a chair and brought it over to the bed.

'How long was I unconscious for?'

'About four hours,' she said. 'How do you feel?'

'In pain. I must have picked up quite a few knocks and cuts without realising it.'

'A carriage is ready for you, to take you back to Icehaven, Lady Yvona is expecting you in Alkirk Palace. She will be able to heal you there.'

'How's the wall looking?'

'It's repaired. Listen, word has already spread about what you did. Folk in the Circuit will have heard about it by now; in fact the entire City has probably heard about it. I imagine Lord Kano will be furious at the news.'

Corthie laughed. 'What a shame.'

'Please take this seriously, champion. If you return to Alkirk Palace, then Lady Yvona intends to announce her protection of you publically, and she will warn Marcus not to intervene.'

'*If* I return?'

'Yes, if. Lady Yvona wants to make sure you understand the consequences before this is taken any further. If she provides protection, then you will be expected to swear allegiance to her, in public, making sure everyone knows that you see Lady Yvona as your sovereign. You would be Champion of Icehaven.'

'For how long?'

The major blinked. 'An oath is not measured in time, champion. If you swear, then you will be bound to her and to Icehaven forever. You will live in the palace, with every luxury and comfort you desire, and you will be treated as if you were Lady Yvona's brother.'

'She wants me to replace Rand?'

'In a way, though I beg you not to put it to her like that.'

Corthie moved up on the bed, grimacing from the aches and pains covering his body. 'I have two problems.'

The major frowned. 'Yes?'

'Aye. First, I don't know how long I'll be in the City for. It might be years, but I can't say. My family will come for me at some point, and when they do, they will take me home.'

'Your friend Achan said something to me along those lines. It's been five years since you were taken from your home, yes?'

'Aye, about that.'

'And your second problem?'

'Aila. I need to know about her marriage to Marcus. If she tells me that there's no hope for me and her, then I'll accept it, but I need to know.'

'How does that square with your desire to go home? If you love Lady Aila, would you stay in the City for her?'

'If she loved me in return.'

The major pursed her lips and nodded.

'I'm happy to work for Lady Yvona,' he said, 'and I'll do what I did today as often as she wants; she seems like one of the more decent demigods running the City, but I can't promise I'll remain here for the rest of my life.'

'I shall travel ahead of you,' she said, 'so that I can discuss this before your arrival.'

'Will she be angry with me?'

'She is risking her position, her status, and perhaps even her life to shield you from Marcus and the God-Queen. She might find it hard to understand why you do not feel like reciprocating.' She stood. 'I will leave now. There is an escort of elite guards outside this chamber who will escort you back to Icehaven.'

Corthie nodded, and watched as the major walked from the room. He wondered what he would do if his sister turned up at that moment. If she insisted that they leave immediately, then he didn't know what he would say to her. He loved having battle-vision, but knew it was also the source of his troubles. Without it, none of the gods or demigods would care about him and he would never have been abducted from his home in the first place.

He got out of bed, and pulled on the fresh set of clothes that had been laid out for him, noticing the bruises and bandages that covered much of his body. Once he had dressed, he opened the door and saw a squad of armoured soldiers waiting. They bowed before him.

'This way, sir,' said one.

They flanked Corthie as he walked through the hallway, then they emerged into the triangular forecourt of the fortress. Standing in the open air were hundreds of the Icewarder militia, with many more up on the battlements, or leaning out of the windows that ran up the sides of the tall towers. A deafening roar rose up from them as Corthie appeared, and he raised his arms, and turned slowly, smiling at them. A carriage was waiting by the gates, and two soldiers were sitting on its roof, holding up the Axe of Rand for all to see. The din rang in his ears as the guards pushed through the thick crowd, while hands reached through to touch him as he passed.

He climbed up into the carriage, and it moved off, driving through the crowd and out onto the main road beyond the gates. Corthie glanced out of the window as hundreds of labourers mobbed the carriage, banging on the windows and cheering.

Four miles separated the iceward end of the Middle Walls from the gates of Icehaven, and it seemed as though every yard of it was busy with traffic, and with people out to get a glimpse of the champion. The soldiers on the roof held up the axe for the entire journey, and onlookers cheered as they passed. The streets of the town were quiet, with few people about, and Corthie wondered if they were all working on the walls.

He climbed down from the carriage to another ovation, as the palace staff and guards cheered his arrival, and he was escorted up the stairs of the palace to the rooms that had been set aside for him and his two friends. The major was there, waiting for him.

'Lady Yvona would like to see you in private, champion,' she said.

'Sure.'

She gestured to a door, and Corthie went through and entered Yvona's private study, which had a tall window overlooking the harbour and the Cold Sea. He limped over to a chair and sat, as the demigod looked up from the documents on her desk.

'Champion,' she said.

'Call me Corthie.'

She nodded. 'I understand that you are refusing to swear allegiance to me?'

'Did the major explain why? This is not my world, and though I have grown to love... aspects of it, it will never be my real home.'

'Do you care if it falls?'

'Of course, aye. I don't want to see the greenhides get into Medio or Auldan; I didn't want to see them in the Bulwark, but I can't commit the rest of my life to you. I will pledge, however, to stay until the threat diminishes.'

She gave him a wry look. 'That could be interpreted in a multitude of ways, for as long as the greenhides remain on this world, then we are threatened.'

'I guess I meant I'll stay until the Bulwark is retaken, and the Great Walls are secure again.'

'That might be never, Corthie.'

'I know.'

'And what about Lady Aila? I personally feel that this is the easier of the two problems to solve. Either she loves you or she doesn't. If she loves you, and wants to be with you, then we shall have to work out how to make it so. I care nothing for what Marcus thinks, and would happily steal his bride if it will make you stay. We need to send her a message, somehow. Anyway, apologies, I am forgetting myself.' She stood, and leaned over to place a finger on his hand.

He felt her healing powers surge through him, repairing every cut and bruise on his body.

'That feels amazing,' he said.

'It's the least I can do, Corthie, after what you did for me today.' She sat again, and smiled at him. 'I still intend to announce you to the public, but we shall shelf the full oath for now, if you are willing to promise to stay here while the current emergency endures.'

'I can agree to that.'

She took his hand again, clasping it in hers. 'What do you want, Corthie? Name it. If I can give you anything you need, or desire, then tell me.'

'All I really want is a chance to see if I can make it work with Aila. My expectations are low, and I'm prepared for her rejection; well, as prepared as I can be. What's killing me is not knowing.'

She smiled. 'What is it about my cousin? First Marcus, and now you? She has bewitched you both.'

'I have an idea about who to send with a message, but can I ask you how Yendra is today?'

'Of course. Do you want to see her?'

They stood, and Yvona unlocked a side door. The old woman was lying on a bed in the small room. She still looked frail and weak, but her breathing had improved, and some colour had returned to her skin.

'She's seems a bit better,' he said.

'Yes, she is no longer dying. I've managed to stabilise her, but it'll take many more sessions before we can expect much else. Her eyes might never grow back, and I don't know if she'll ever speak again.'

'Achan will be disappointed; he has a thousand questions for her.'

'If she doesn't recover, it won't just be your friend who will be disappointed. Some, however, might well feel relief. She had enemies who would not be pleased to learn she is alive, and her enemies roughly align with yours. Marcus, the God-Queen, Kano, all would pause if they knew Yendra had returned.' She glanced at him. 'Rest now for a while, then come here again before sunset, for that is when I intend to speak publicly to the people of Icehaven, with you at my side.'

He nodded. 'I'll be there.'

He went to his rooms and found them empty, so he climbed the steps up onto the roof. Yaizra and Achan were sitting there, looking out over the town, and he walked up to them.

'Look who it is,' said Yaizra; 'the big lump's a champion again. How many did you kill, because the stories I'm hearing are too ludicrous to be true.'

He sat. 'I didn't count.'

'Liar.'

He laughed. 'When I'm out there, I'm only thinking of one thing, and it's not keeping count.'

'Hundreds, they're saying,' said Achan; 'heaps of greenhides, piled up.'

'I may have made a heap or two.'

'I wish I could have seen it,' said Achan.

Yaizra shuddered. 'I'd be too nervous to watch. One little mistake, and Corthie's head goes flying through the air? No thanks.'

Corthie glanced at her. 'You were a good thief, aye? You were good at sneaking about and getting into places where you're not supposed to go?'

She returned his glance. 'Why?'

'Just answer the question.'

'I was excellent, yes.'

'Good. Now, how do you fancy a little trip to Ooste?'

'Ooste? Why in Malik's name would I go there?'

'I need you to go to the Royal Palace, and pass on a message from me to Lady Aila.'

'You could get a courier to do that.'

'Aye,' he said, 'but I need you to do it without Marcus or the God-King or Queen finding out.'

She raised an eyebrow. 'You're asking me to break into the Royal Palace to find out if a demigod fancies you? Yeah, I could be up for that.'

CHAPTER 10

THE EIGHTH GATE

Hammer Territory, The Bulwark, The City – 24th Amalan 3420

Flames lit up the night sky, sending pillars of smoke rising in a rough arc spreading out from the vicinity of the Eighth Gate. On one side of the flames huddled the tens of thousands of fleeing Hammers, while on the other, the hordes of greenhides bayed and shrieked as they tried to find a way through the inferno. As well as the fires, the Hammers had destroyed every bridge, and barricaded every street that led to the gate, but still, the Blades had refused to open the way into Medio.

Emily lay curled up on a chair, in a house close to the gates, trying to catch a hour's sleep before the assault was due to begin. She had been up all night, organising the fires, and sitting at the meetings where the Hammer leadership had planned their next move. Shields had been fashioned from doors and nailed-together planks, and the squads of workers had been drilled on what to do. A thousand things could go wrong, and each one was trying to force its way into Emily's mind.

She felt a hand nudge her and she opened her eyes.

'Hi, Danny,' she said.

'You look exhausted.'

She sat up, her eyes heavy.

He smiled. 'You were never good in the mornings.'

She glanced at the window, and saw traces of pink smear the horizon. 'Damn, is it dawn already?'

'Drink this,' he said, passing her a warm mug.

She sniffed. 'The horrible tea. Where did you find it?'

'They drink it here too, apparently. Helps with getting ready for a long shift in a factory.'

She sipped it. 'Yuck.'

'I can't believe how far we've come in two days,' he said. 'Last night, every Hammer listened to our words as if we were only capable of speaking wisdom.' He shook his head. 'A Rat and a private, and they're listening to us?'

'You might not realise it, Danny, but you've been training for this all your life. You have more military experience than anyone else here.'

'Quill knows more than me.'

'Alright, apart from her. What I meant was, you're the only trained officer. Hilde might be a captain, but I think that was only because she looked after a dragon. They listened to you because you spoke sense.'

'Don't underplay your own part. You've taken to this as if you were born for it.'

Emily stretched as she felt the tea wake her a little. 'Maybe I was.'

They stood, and walked passed several sleeping forms on the way to the front door of the house. They stepped outside, and strode towards the cordon of armed Hammers that stood in a semi-circle around the walled-up gate in the Middle Walls. The Blades had allowed them to retrieve those who had fallen under a flag of truce, but since then had called out that they would shoot anyone who approached. Emily could see them up on the battlements of the gatehouse, and along the walls to either side, looking down on them. She wondered if any felt guilty about what they were doing; if they were gazing down on the Hammers with any pity in their hearts.

'Good morning, my lord, lady,' said Torphin, bowing as the approached. 'Are you ready?'

'We are,' said Emily. 'Should we try one last time to reason with the Blades?'

'No,' said Daniel. 'We've already tried a dozen times, and it might alert them.'

Emily nodded. 'Alright. Torphin, please fetch Sergeant Quill.'

The Hammer frowned slightly at the mention of the Blade's name, but bowed and walked away.

'He doesn't like her,' Daniel said.

'Mistrust runs deep here, just as it does in Auldan. If the City survives, it will need to somehow heal itself of these divisions.'

'And how would it do that?'

'I don't know; a charter maybe, that proclaims all tribes as equal, and every citizen has to follow the same rules and laws. At the moment the rich get away with murder, and the poor are murdered for nothing.'

'My dear Emily,' he said, 'I do believe you have become a radical.'

'I wish my father could see me now. Lord Omertia, I mean; I don't think I'll ever discover who my birth father was. Some drunken, thieving Evader no doubt.'

He raised an eyebrow at her.

'I'm allowed to say it,' she smiled; 'I'm one of them.'

Sergeant Quill appeared beside them. She glanced up at the battlements in silence.

'Good morning, Sergeant,' said Emily. 'We are ready to commence the operation. Is everyone ready and in position?'

'They are.' She lowered her eyes. 'Is there no other way?'

'If you can think of one, then I'd gladly hear it.'

'So, I'm about become a traitor; a Blade fighting other Blades?'

'Their commanders have lost their moral authority, Sergeant. Most Blades, if they search their hearts, will realise that the orders they have been given are wrong.'

'Maybe, but it won't stop them from carrying those orders out. Many will die.'

'So that many more can be saved.'

Quill nodded. 'It that weren't the case, then I wouldn't be doing this.'

She took a whistle from a pocket and clasped it in her hand. 'Everyone in the first few companies are volunteers; they understand the risks. When I blow this, it will begin, and there will be no way to undo it. History might never forgive us.'

Emily glanced up at the tall Blade. 'We're not part of history; we're making it. Blow the whistle.'

'Yes, ma'am.' Quill lifted the whistle to her lips and gave two short blasts.

At once, two groups of Hammers began emerging from the side streets, carrying large shields over their heads. Others also held wooden beams, and together, they sprinted for the gates. The Blades took a few moments to respond, and by the time the crossbow bolts started to fly down, the groups were in position, holding up two lines of shields that stretched back out of bow range.

Emily nodded to Quill, and she blew on the whistle again. Dozens of Hammers rushed forward with slings, and began peppering the battlements of the gatehouse with stones. As the Blades crowded the walls to shoot back, another group of Hammers appeared, each carrying mallets, pickaxes and sledgehammers. They ran under the protective lines of shields towards the walled-up gate.

Emily kissed Daniel. 'This is where I leave you. First one through.'

Daniel nodded. 'Last one through. Good luck, my queen.'

She smiled, then ran along the line that marked the range of the Blades' crossbows, and ducked under one of the raised shields. Bodies were starting to fall as the bolts rained down on them, but as soon as a Hammer was struck, another would run to take their place. Emily moved under the line of shields, hearing the thuds above her head as bolts struck the wood, then she reached the gate. The walled-up section was located two feet within the arched tunnel marking the entrance, and anyone who could squeeze in there was safe from the missiles falling from above.

The workers had already started on the wall when she reached them, swinging their pickaxes and hammers. Some were kneeling, and driving chisels into the ancient mortar, which was falling away in large chunks by their feet. A man a yard to Emily's right fell, a bolt striking him in the eye, and she picked up his shield and held it aloft, covering the head of a worker as he swung his pickaxe into the wall.

She gazed at the Hammers dismantling the wall as she held up the shield. She thought about saying some words to encourage them, but each was absorbed in their job, and she didn't want to be a distraction. Her arms started to ache under the weight of the shield, and her heels sunk into the soft ground as more bolts thudded above her head.

'Look out!' cried one of the workers as a section of the wall collapsed, sending stone blocks tumbling down.

Emily glanced back at Quill. The sergeant gestured to show that she had seen what had happened, then blew on her whistle.

'Take this,' Emily said to the man next to her. 'I'm going through.'

She passed the shield to the Hammer and raced forward, taking a moment to breathe under the protection of the arched tunnel, then she scrambled up the heap of stones to the gap that had been created. It was dark beyond, but she didn't know if Blades would be posted there. She drew her sword as she crouched against the stones, then turned to the workers.

'As soon as I'm through, get back to dismantling the rest of the wall.'

'Yes, ma'am,' one cried.

Emily peered up into the gap, her eyes seeing nothing but gloom. An old, stale odour was coming from the arched tunnel, but there was no sound, so she pulled herself up and through the gap. She dropped down to the ground inside the tunnel, her eyes adjusting.

The tunnel was about six or seven yards long, and was sealed at the other end with a wall similar to the one she had just scrambled through. She heard a voice behind her, turned and saw a face silhouetted against the gap in the wall.

'Ma'am?'

'It's safe,' she called back. 'There's another wall. Bring torches and soldiers.'

'Yes, ma'am.'

The light in the tunnel got a little brighter as more blocks were removed from the first wall behind her, and she noticed a side door to her left. She sheathed her sword and walked up to it. The wood crumbled in her hand as she touched it, and she felt the rotten fibres fall to the ground. She turned back to the wall at the far end of the tunnel, and put her ear to it, wondering if a hundred Blades with crossbows were waiting on the other side.

'Ma'am?' she heard behind her.

She turned, and saw the tunnel fill up with armed Hammers. The first wall was halfway down, and through it, Emily could see the hail of missiles continue to fall. The ground outside was carpeted with the bodies of fallen Hammers, all riddled with bolts. Sergeant Quill hurried into the tunnel, bringing more soldiers with her.

Emily approached her. 'Give me five minutes before you order the workers to start dismantling the other wall.'

'Five minutes? Dozens will die in that time; they're taking a pounding out there, and the greenhides have breached the line of fires.'

'But it could be a trap; there could be a thousand Blades with ballistae and crossbows lined up on the other side of the wall. I'm taking a squad, Sergeant; give me five minutes.'

Quill frowned. 'Alright. What are you doing to do?'

Emily pointed at the side door. 'If we can get into the gatehouse from there, we can throw the Blades out, and the Hammers will be able to get through without being cut down.' She gestured to a squad. 'Follow me.'

She raced to the door, then directed one of the soldiers to break it down. He kicked it square in the middle with a heavy boot, and the door cracked and splintered.

'Torch,' said Emily as she drew her sword.

She clambered through the shattered doorframe, and entered a dark hallway, filled with the same stale odour as the arched tunnel. She strode along it, the soldier behind carrying a lit torch in her hand. Damp was rising up the walls, and the hallway seemed abandoned. They came to a set of stairs at the end, and ascended, Emily creeping up as quietly as she could. The stairs ended with a door at the top, which opened with a push and a creak, and she stepped into a chamber, lit by a series of openings in the walls to the left and right. Directly ahead of her stood a great portcullis, its chains rusted and lying broken on the stone floor. She ignored it, and raced to the windows to her left. She gazed out into the morning light of Medio, the sun starting to rise to her left. Below lay the old road that led away from the gatehouse, beyond which the fields and orchards of Sander territory spread into the horizon. She gazed at the trees and fields for a moment, then glanced down, and saw the lines of Blades that she had feared. They had built a high barricade in a loop around the blocked-up entrance, and had crossbows and bolt-throwers standing ready.

She turned to one of the soldiers. 'Go down and tell Sergeant Quill to delay the destruction of the second wall. Tell her to give me fifty soldiers, and we'll clear the gatehouse.'

'Yes, ma'am,' she cried, and ran for the stairs.

She walked back to the ancient portcullis. Although old, it seemed robust and heavy. The slot that it was designed to go down stood a few inches from where it sat, propped up by metal beams.

'If we could move this,' she said, 'we could reseal the gate once the Hammers are through.'

She was still walking around it when Quill appeared, with soldiers at her back. The sergeant glanced at the portcullis, then gazed out of the narrow windows at the ranks of Blades.

'Damn it,' she muttered.

Emily glanced at her. 'We need a team working on the portcullis while we clear the gatehouse of Blades.'

The sergeant nodded at a soldier. 'See to it; bring up a squad of workers with their tools.' She turned to Emily. 'Where next?'

'Upstairs. That's where the Blades are, shooting down from the battlements.'

'Yes, but how do we get there?'

Emily pointed at the doors leading from the room. 'Through one of those, I imagine.'

Quill sighed. 'What are we doing?'

'We're thinking on our feet, Sergeant.'

'Right.' She gestured to the soldiers. 'One squad, remain here to protect the workers, the rest, line up behind those doors. When I blow the whistle, break down all three at once and get your asses through. Remember, the doors are old, and might have been bricked up on the other side. If that happens to your line, get into one of the others. Make for the stairs, and head up.' She paused. 'Kill anyone who tries to stop you.'

Quill led the way to the central door, and Emily took her place behind her as the soldiers formed up into columns. The sergeant blew her whistle and a great noise broke out as the lead soldier in each line smashed into the door, using hammers and axes. The left hand door fell away to reveal a wall, but the other two opened out into hallways, and the soldiers rushed through. Emily drew her sword again and followed Quill as she ran through the broken entrance. The hallway was lit by oil lamps burning on the walls, and the smell was different from the other rooms of the gatehouse, it felt lived-in. The passed an open doorway and saw a room inside, piled with storage jugs and crates, then came to a spiral staircase.

'Go up first, Sergeant,' Emily said. 'Your Blade uniform will give us a few extra seconds.'

Quill frowned, but nodded. She gripped the hilt of her sword, and charged upstairs, Emily a step behind her. The sergeant burst out onto the battlements, and into a crowd of Blades on the rooftop of the gatehouse, a square of battlements surrounding them. The first Blade turned, and saw Quill race towards her. She hesitated for a moment, and the sergeant struck her down. Emily dashed to Quill's side and parried a blow aimed at the sergeant as the rest of the Hammers flooded the rooftop. A Blade lunged at Emily from her left, but a Hammer laid him low with a swing of his pickaxe. Emily pushed forward, and confronted a Blade who was trying to reload his crossbow. Without hesitating, she plunged her sword through his throat, feeling her training take over, her mind almost separate from her actions. Heavily outnumbered, the Blades were pushed back against the battlements, and the last dozen threw down their weapons and raised their hands in the air.

'Get more reinforcements up here,' said Emily as Quill glanced at her. 'We need to be able to repel any counter attack. Take the prisoners downstairs.' She walked to the edge of the battlements as Quill listened. To either side of the gatehouse, Blades were staring up from the walkway at the top of the Middle Walls. 'There will be old gates that open onto the walls; we need to find them and block them.' She turned to the side facing Medio. 'Move the ballistae over here and get them ready to loose on the Blades below, and instruct the workers in the tunnel to commence the destruction of the last wall.'

She walked over to the side that faced the Bulwark as Quill translated her orders into practical steps. She leaned against the battlements and gazed at the enormous mass of Hammers crammed into the area in front of the gate. The barrage from the battlements was still continuing from the walls to either side of the gatehouse, but the rate had decreased. Some along the walls had stopped loosing, and were looking down at the Hammers, but doing nothing.

Beyond the huddled crowds of Hammers, the arc of fire was still burning, but she could hear the screams coming from the outer reaches of where the masses had gathered. At each location, the greenhides would be tearing their way through the crowds, and dozens were being slain with every minute that passed. Emily felt sick as she watched, then she turned away, her glance falling down toward the entrance that had already been dismantled. Daniel was standing directly before the gate, ushering in the columns of reinforcements that she had asked for, and hundreds of Hammers were entering the tunnel. She smiled at the sight of him, then heard Quill cough behind her.

'We're ready to start loosing onto the Blades,' she said, 'and teams are working on the wall.'

Emily nodded and they walked over to the battery of powerful ballistae that had been dragged over to face Medio.

'Loose one,' said Emily, 'but aim it a few yards in front of them. Let's give them a warning first.'

Quill nodded, then gestured to one of the crews. They adjusted the angle of the ballista, and shot a yard-long bolt down at the Blades by the gate entrance. It exploded into the road a few paces from the barricade they had constructed, sending dust and sparks flying. The Blades on the road glanced around, their eyes wide, then someone pointed upwards.

Emily raised her arm. 'The Hammers will be coming through that gate in a few minutes,' she shouted down, her hands cupping her mouth. 'If you attempt to hinder them, we will destroy you from up here.'

An officer stepped forward, his hands raised. 'Who are you?'

'I am Emily Aurelian, and the Hammers have taken control of this gatehouse. If the Blades attack us, we shall defend it to the death.'

'I have orders from Commander Kano to ensure the Middle Walls are not breached, by anyone.'

'The greenhides are approaching, but there's still time to get most of the Hammers through, and we will take responsibility for resealing the gate. All I ask is that you do not attack your own people, the folk of the Bulwark. We have a dozen Blades as prisoners. We shall send them through the wall first, as a sign we don't want to kill anyone.'

The officer stood for a moment, then walked back to the barricade without another word.

Quill glanced at Emily. 'I'll get the prisoners down into the tunnel.'

'And make sure they're let go,' said Emily. 'We're not going to use them as shields.'

The sergeant nodded. 'Understood.'

'Oh,' said Emily, 'can you make sure work is being done on the portcullis; we're going to need it.'

'Yes, ma'am.'

Quill hurried towards the stairs and disappeared as more Hammers arrived. One of them approached Emily.

'There are over three hundred Hammers inside the gatehouse now, ma'am,' she said. 'and Lord Aurelian sends you his greetings.'

'Thank you.'

'Lord Aurelian estimates that it will take two hours to get everyone through the gates before the greenhides arrive, my lady.'

Emily nodded. 'Please let him know that I understand. We will hold the gates open until the last possible moment.'

A crash distracted her and she looked down over the battlements to see blocks of stone tumbling onto the road in front of the gate. More blocks followed a moment later, and then a dozen Blades emerged from the tunnel, their hands raised in the air.

'Prepare the ballistae,' Emily said to the crews, 'but do not loose unless I expressly order it. If the Blades pull back, we will not attack them.'

Her heart pounded as she watched the freed prisoners run across the road. The soldiers at the barricade let them pass, and she could see the officer question them. She watched as more Blades got involved in the discussion, and she almost felt that time had stopped at that moment, as the future of so many lives hung in the balance.

The first Hammers appeared in the new breach, their arms raised, and in the front row Emily saw Quill among them. The Blade officer stood frozen for a moment, then he gestured to his soldiers, and they began hauling the barricade away, clearing the road for the Hammers. Emily gasped in relief, and felt a tear slide down her cheek. The slow surge of Hammers began to quicken as they emerged into the fields of Medio, and within minutes hundreds were pouring through the gatehouse, flooding the area behind the Middle Walls. The Hammers on the rooftop cheered.

Emily wiped her cheek. 'Get these ballistae moved to the other side. It's time to fight the real enemy.'

'Yes, ma'am,' cried one, and the crews got to work.

Emily turned away, unable to keep the smile from her face as she watched the current of Hammers flow through the tunnel. The greenhides were coming, but she knew it was a moment she would treasure forever.

For the next two hours, the flood of Hammers continued through the gatehouse unabated. The Blades on the Medio side remained by the road, but did nothing to intervene. Dozens of local militia arrived from the direction of Port Sanders, but there were too many Hammers for them to control, and the refugees were allowed to spread outwards, moving through the fields and outer suburbs of the sunward end of the Circuit.

On the side facing the Bulwark, things were grimmer. The crowds became more exhausted, and fear rippled over them as the greenhides slashed and cut their way through the mass of flesh towards the gatehouse. Emily could see them approach from all three directions, pushing inexorably closer to the Eighth Gate. The Blades and Hammers on the battlements kept up a steady stream of bolts as the greenhides came into view, but it made almost no difference to their numbers.

'Ma'am,' said a guard as Emily gazed down at where Daniel remained by the entrance to the gate.

'Yes?'

'A Blade officer is asking permission to enter the gatehouse to speak with you.'

Emily nodded. 'My permission is granted.'

The guard bowed and ran for the stairs. Emily turned back to look at Daniel. He was still ushering the Hammers through the gates, but the greenhides were less than a hundred yards away, hacking the rear lines of the tightly-packed refugees to shreds. The screams rose to a constant pitch and Emily grimaced at the sound.

She heard a cough and turned.

'Lady Aurelian, I believe?'

'Yes?'

'I am Captain Ganning of the Blades.'

She nodded, waiting for him to continue.

'Commander Kano has sent me here to place you under arrest, ma'am.'

She smiled. 'And do you intend to try?

He glanced round at the fifty armed Hammers on the roof of the gatehouse. 'I think that would be unwise, both for me personally, and for the future of the City. I estimate close to a hundred thousand Hammers have travelled through this gate in the last two hours, and each one is mentioning the name of you and your husband. It seems that you are the leader of these people and as such, I would rather be negotiating with you instead of trying to arrest you.'

'So you are prepared to disregard the orders of the Commander of the Bulwark?'

'I will assume that the commander did not fully understand the situation here when he issued the orders. My primary concern is how you will reseal this gate once the last of the Hammers are through.'

'Understandable,' she said. 'You can observe and report back to the commander.' She glanced at the shrinking crowd of refugees still crammed by the gate. 'It won't be long now.'

A pack of greenhides was ripping though the Hammers to the left of the clearing by the Eighth Gate, and Emily saw Daniel glance up towards the battlements, his sword raised.

She turned for the stairs. 'Follow me, Captain.'

She went down to the middle level of the gatehouse and squeezed past the Hammers guarding the doors that led to the walls. She entered the room directly over the entrance tunnel, where a team had been working on the portcullis since their arrival. The enormous iron gate had been shifted a few inches, and was being propped up by a dozen beams. New chains were attached to the top, and a pulley with weights had been rigged up.

'Is it ready?' she said to the supervisor.

'Yes, ma'am,' the Hammer said, bowing to her as the Blade officer watched. 'Just say the word, and we'll drop it.'

Emily felt her heart pound, but she kept her features steady, not wanting to show her fear and anxiety in front of the officer. She gestured to him, then crouched down by an opening in the floor that gave a view of the inside of the tunnel. Below, the heads of dozens of Hammers could be seen fleeing towards Medio. The screams were getting closer, and the Hammers kept glancing back as a near panic swept through them.

The officer knelt by her side. 'I would recommend dropping it now, ma'am.'

'No,' she said. 'My husband will the last one through.'

'Lord Aurelian? Is he still down there?'

'He is.'

The screams rose again, much closer, and the numbers of Hammers fleeing lessened. Emily raised her hand to the team by the portcullis. 'Any moment... wait.'

She saw Daniel at last, running down the tunnel, leading the last band of refugees as the greenhides closed in behind them, He pushed them ahead of him, his sword drawn, and bundled them over the midway point.

'Now!' Emily cried.

The workers pulled away the beams supporting the portcullis, and the great mass of iron fell, its weight driving it down through the wide slot in the floor. Chains strained and creaked, and the floor vibrated as it smashed downward. The first greenhides were charging through the tunnel as the portcullis rammed home, filling the width of the gate, its spikes impaling two greenhides as it crushed them. The entire gatehouse reverberated with the clang as it settled into place, and dust floated down onto the heads of everyone in the chamber.

One of the workers stared. 'Did it work?'

Emily gazed down, unable to tear her eyes away. On one side of the portcullis, the greenhides were pressing up against it, their momentum crushing those in front as thousands tried to get through the tunnel. She leapt up and raced for the stairs. The officer followed her as she ran down to the side door where they had entered the gatehouse, and she burst out into the tunnel, the portcullis two yards to her right. Greenhides were crammed against it, their claws reaching through gaps in the iron latticework. Many were already dead in the crush, and she stared, her ears filled with their shrieks.

Emily started to cry in relief, as if the weight of a hundred thousand lives had been lifted from her shoulders. The guards, refugees and workers stood around her in silence as she wept, then she felt a hand on her shoulder and she turned.

Daniel.

'We did it,' he said, putting a hand against her cheek.

Emily tried to speak, but pulled him close instead, sobbing into his chest. They embraced, hugging each other a few yards from the portcullis, amid the howling screams and shrieks, and the stares from the others gathered there.

Sergeant Quill approached. She pulled a hanky from a pocket and passed it to Emily.

'Thank you,' she said, wiping her eyes.

'We have a team ready to block up the side door and to rebuild the wall on this side of the tunnel,' Quill said. 'Also, there are one or two people outside who want to see you.'

Daniel nodded, and they walked out from the tunnel, into the sunshine of a summer's afternoon. A cart was parked by the entrance, and a pile of stone blocks was sitting next to it. Torphin was there, and he gestured for Daniel and Emily to climb up onto the cart. Daniel jumped up, and reached down with a hand. Emily took it and he pulled her up. The noise hit her as soon as she stood, and her mouth opened. Arrayed in front of them was the largest crowd she had ever seen, stretching for a mile in every direction. Every face in the crowd was turned to them, and the noise fell away to an utter silence as Torphin raised his hand.

'You were here,' he cried, 'the day the legend became real. It was foretold the Aurelians would save the Hammers, and today they have. The first one through, and the last one through.' He lowered his arm, and knelt on the ground before the cart where Daniel and Emily were standing, and the rest of the crowd did the same, every one of them falling to their knees in silence, and bowing their heads.

Emily gazed out at them, seeing the clusters of children and old folk, each carrying the one bag they had been allowed to bring, each one alive because of what they had done.

'Behold,' Torphin cried into the silence, 'Lord and Lady Aurelian, the rightful rulers of the City. To them, and to them alone, do we pledge our lives, our love, and our allegiance.'

Emily and Daniel raised their hands, and the crowd erupted as the voices of a hundred thousand Hammers split the air.

CHAPTER 11

HAPPY RETURNS

The Eastern Mountains – 24th Amalan 3420

'Wakey, wakey,' said Rosie, nudging her sister's shoulder, 'and happy birthday.'

Maddie groaned and opened her eyes. Daylight was coming into the cave from the entrance a few yards away, and she shivered in the cold air.

'It's beautiful and warm outside,' Rosie said, 'and I've made you breakfast.'

Maddie sat up. She frowned at Rosie. 'You're in a cheery mood this morning.'

'Things always seem better in the sunshine; come and look.'

She pulled her blanket off and they went to the entrance of the cave. Maddie gazed out at the little valley. Her sister was right; it was beautiful. Birds were singing from the branches of the trees as blossom floated down onto the grassy banks of the small stream, while the waterfall to their left was glistening in the rays of the sun. The sky was a deep pink, and the bare mountain peaks were reflecting its warm glow.

Rosie scampered down the slope to where a small fire was burning by the side of the pool. It was in the same place as the fire they had sat round the previous evening, and the stones surrounding it were blackened with soot. Next to it, Rosie had laid out a blanket on the grass, and on it were a few bowls and mugs.

Maddie smiled. 'A birthday breakfast? It's been a while.'

'How does it feel being so ancient?'

'I'm nineteen; I've not even peaked yet, though eighteen was pretty eventful.'

She walked down and joined Rosie by the pool. She sat, then yawned and stretched her arms, feeling the sun on her skin. Her sister passed her a bowl with the leftovers from their evening meal, and Maddie started to eat.

Rosie glanced at her. 'I'm going to ask Blackrose to take me back to the City.'

'What? Why?'

'To look for Tom, and to fight the greenhides.'

'But it's too dangerous.'

'What's the alternative, that we stay here in this little valley, hiding for the rest of our lives?'

'But we've only been here one day.'

'And Blackrose said she wanted a spy to find Corthie for her. I could do that, as soon as I've found Tom.'

Maddie frowned. She still harboured hopes that the dragon could be persuaded to fight for the City, but also knew that finding Corthie could help with that.

She shook her head. 'You're too young to go on your own.'

'But you can't come with me; you're bonded to Blackrose, and I understand that. Where she goes, you go. And let's face it, I probably know how to look after myself better than you. I can find Tom, and let Corthie know where Blackrose is.'

'And how in Malik's name would you find Tom?'

'He'll be on the Middle Walls, probably. He'll think we're all dead, and I can't bear to imagine what he's going through. Let me do this, Maddie.'

'Mum and dad would say no if they were here.'

'Would they? They let me build a ballista on the roof of our house; they knew I could handle myself.'

'Alright, say you go back and find Tom, and then you find Corthie? What good will it do if Corthie can't reach this little valley? We're two hundred miles from the Great Walls, and about a trillion greenhides stand between us. Not even Corthie could kill that many.'

Her sister frowned. 'Easy. I arrange for Blackrose to return at a later date, and I'll have Corthie with me by that point.'

Maddie narrowed her eyes. 'Smart ass.'

'Where would be the best place for Blackrose to drop me off? It needs to be safe, but not too close to the City, as I don't think Blackrose wants to be seen. How about the Grey Isle? I could get a boat to Dalrig from there. Or maybe the hills of the Iceward Range at night?'

Maddie put her bowl down, her appetite gone. 'Why are you doing this on my birthday?'

'What's wrong?'

'How can you ask me that? You're saying you'd rather go back to the nightmare in the City than stay with me. What am I supposed to do? I'll be alone.'

'Hardly, you'll have a massive dragon for company.'

'Blackrose won't take you back; she knows you're too young.'

Rosie raised an eyebrow, but said nothing.

'I'm right.'

Rosie shook her head. 'Blackrose tolerates me, but she loves you. I'll ask her when she gets back; I think you might be surprised.' She stood. 'I'm going for a walk.'

Maddie frowned as her sister strode away down by the bank of the stream, then she turned back to her breakfast.

Maddie was lying on the blanket in the sunshine when she felt a shadow pass over her. She opened her eyes, and saw Blackrose hovering over the valley, her enormous wings beating. The dragon lowered the tied tarpaulin to the ground, and Rosie unbuckled the straps, then Blackrose circled and landed next to the pool. She had the body of an animal clutched in her front claws, and she placed it onto the grass next to Maddie.

Maddie grimaced at it, and got to her feet.

'Good morning, my rider,' the dragon said. 'Did the night pass peacefully?'

'Yeah, it's nice up here.'

'I'm glad you like it. I have brought food.'

'Thanks for bringing our stuff,' said Rosie. 'How was all the flying?'

'Wonderful. I soared far iceward, into temperatures that would have frozen you solid to my back, then returned via the desert, with the stars to guide my way.'

'It's Maddie's birthday today,' said Rosie.

'The dragon swung her head round to face Maddie. 'Is it?'

'Yeah.'

'Nineteen?'

'That's right.'

'In commemoration of this day, you can select the first portion of the meat I have brought. I made the kill, but you should have the honour.'

'Eh, thanks,' Maddie said, trying not to sound ungrateful as she eyed the ripped corpse of the large goat that Blackrose had dumped onto the grass beside her.

'I can start cooking it,' said Rosie.

'If you must,' said the dragon. 'Leave my share raw, if you please, Little Rose.'

Maddie watched as Rosie built up the fire, and then used a knife to gut the goat, scraping the skin from the meat and bones.

'Stop looking at me like that,' she said as she noticed Maddie's glance. 'I skinned the New Year goat at home.'

'I thought I'd put a stop to that horrible tradition.'

'Well, you weren't at home last New Year, so mum and dad bought one for the family, and let me prepare it.' She grinned. 'It was delicious.' Her smile fell. 'That was only two months ago; it seems like a lifetime.'

She turned to the dragon. 'Blackrose, I have a plan; do you want to hear it?'

'Of course, Little Rose.'

'Alright. First, you fly me to the Iceward Range in the City, and drop me off there. I'll find Corthie, and then you come back after a few days... maybe ten, I'm not sure? Whenever we agree, I'll have Corthie with me. How does that sound?'

'It sounds like an excellent plan.'

Rosie gave Maddie a glance. 'Thank you. We should probably do it soon.'

'I need to rest after my flight,' said Blackrose, 'but I could take you there tonight. Shall we say ten days? That should be enough time for you to find Corthie.'

Maddie glared at them.

'Is something troubling you, rider?' said the dragon.

'Rosie's too young to go wandering around the war-torn City on her own.'

The dragon tilted her head. 'She seems perfectly capable to me. And didn't you say that your older brother is there? He can look after her, surely? Is he a good brother?'

'He is,' said Rosie, 'and I'll find him before I search for Corthie.'

'See?' said Blackrose. 'Nothing to worry about.'

Maddie jumped to her feet and stormed away, her frustration boiling over. She hurried up the slope and strode into the caves, feeling the air cool around her. She glanced back, and saw the dragon and Rosie deep in discussion. Her sister had been right; Blackrose didn't really care about Rosie, just as she didn't care what happened to the inhabitants of the City.

She turned, and cracked her right knee off the side of a jagged rock. She suppressed a cry, and clutched her leg as blood poured down her shin. Tears came to her eyes, of pain and anger, and she limped deeper into the caves, so that the others wouldn't be able to see her cry.

The caverns were lit by a series of shafts in the porous rock. Some shafts went directly upwards, and let in the sunlight, while others channelled down from the waterfall, and she was soaked with spray as she passed one. An eerie light permeated the caves, and she paused as she noticed markings on a wall. She peered at them, and made out some shapes. It was a drawing, or painting, and showed small stick-like figures chasing a large beast with horns. Next to it was another picture, of what looked like slain people, lying on their sides in rows, and in the third picture a stick-figure was holding aloft a jewel or a stone that seemed to be glowing. Maddie squinted at the pictures. Rosie would be interested in seeing them, she knew, but she wasn't yet ready to speak to her sister.

She limped onwards as the cave wound into the side of the mountain. She noticed scrape-marks on the walls on either side, as if the cave have been extended, or tunnelled through, and it felt strange to imagine that other folk had lived there long before. The beast in the picture had not been a greenhide, and she wondered if the people had been there before the eternal enemy had first appeared. She walked on, her curiosity overcoming the pain from her bleeding knee. She turned a corner and sensed a dim glow, but it wasn't coming from any shaft that she could see. She narrowed her eyes. It as was if streaks in the rock itself were glowing. A light grey, almost silver rock seemed embedded within the walls of the cave, and there was evidence that some had been gouged out. She placed her fingers on the edge of the grey rock; it was soft and yielding, and then she pulled her hand away, feeling a tingle spread up from her fingertips. She gasped. It was almost the same feeling as when Lady Jade had healed her on the road to Pella.

She frowned, and took a knife from her belt. She raised it to the grey stone and cut out a tiny piece, then examined it closely. It seemed to glisten and sparkle with its own light. Without really knowing what she was doing, she lowered the knife and smeared the crumbly rock over the cut on her knee.

A cry of pain left her lips and she slid to the ground, clutching her leg. She felt the tingle too, but the agony outweighed it.

The pain ceased as abruptly as it had started and she panted for a moment, then gazed at her knee. The wound had gone, and the skin on her leg had healed. She wiped her hand over it, brushing away the last of the crumbly rock, then stood and flexed her knee. It felt fine. She picked up the knife and went back to the wall. She had a pouch on her belt, and she gouged out a large chunk of the grey rock and dropped it in, being careful not to let it touch her skin.

When the pouch was full, she turned, and hurried back to the cave entrance, almost forgetting all about her sister's plan. The dragon was basking in the sunlight when she reached the little valley, her wings extended on the grass.

Her sister glanced up from the fire, where she was arranging cuts of meat onto skewers. 'Are you alright?'

'Yeah,' said Maddie. She walked over to the blanket and sat down. 'I found something in the cave.'

'A mountain bear?' said Blackrose.

Maddie frowned. 'No. Is that likely? Anyway, have you heard the rumours about this almost mystical substance that keeps the gods and demigods looking young?'

'Salve?' said Rosie. 'I've heard about it.'

Maddie placed the pouch onto the blanket and removed the cord that was tying it. 'Do you reckon this is it?'

Rosie reached out with her hand.

'Wait,' said Maddie, 'don't touch it.'

Blackrose extended her neck so that she could take a look. 'It doesn't look like the salve I've seen,' she said, 'but that might be because it hasn't been refined. On my world, the gods would drink a silvery liquid from a little vial or bathe in its vapours. It does glisten in the same way, however. Have you tested it?'

'I cut my knee, and then a smeared some on, and, by Malik's ass it hurt, but only for a minute, and then my leg was healed. Look.' She showed them her knee. The blood was still streaked down her shin, but there was no wound.

'My rear limb still aches from the chains that bound me in Arrowhead,' said Blackrose. 'Perhaps I should apply some. Was there much of it in the cave?'

'Tons. I think a lot might have already been taken, but there's loads more.'

'If it is salve,' said the dragon, 'then we must keep this location a secret. Wars are fought over this substance. This world, as far as I know, is the only source of it. I was paid for in salve, when the demigod from the City bought me on Lostwell, and so too was Corthie, I would imagine. It is worth more than any other substance in the known worlds.'

Maddie grinned. 'So we're rich?'

Rosie picked up the pouch. 'How do you refine it? It looks like there a lot of contamination, with grit and stones; that's maybe why it hurt. There must be some process for purifying it.'

'If the gods fight over it,' said Maddie, 'then why don't they just come here and take it for themselves?'

Blackrose glanced at her. 'The location of this world is kept secret. If the gods knew how to find it, then rest assured they would come, and this world would be dragged into the great wars. When Lord Naxor purchased me, he used intermediaries, trusted friends that he knows on Lostwell, but he takes a risk every time he travels there. If one of the ruling gods were to capture him, they might discover how to get here.' She turned to Rosie. 'You are correct, Little Rose, but I do not know the process for refining salve. I imagine that only a certain few gods or demigods in the City are aware of it.'

'There's something I don't understand,' said Rosie. 'If it makes the gods look younger, then why doesn't Maddie look any different?'

'Let's see if it is salve first,' the dragon said. 'If either of you girls would do me the favour of putting some onto my leg, I'd be grateful.'

Maddie and Rosie stood, and walked alongside the flank of the dragon until they came to her right rear limb. Rosie picked up a broad leaf from the grass, and Maddie smeared some of the crumbly rock onto it from the pouch.

'It stung my knee,' Maddie said, 'so maybe we should stand back once it's on.'

Rosie nodded and they both peered at the red weal across Blackrose's limb, left by the shackles that had once imprisoned her. Maddie took the leaf, and rubbed it against the wound, then both of them hurried back a few steps. Blackrose swung her head round to watch.

'Isn't it sore?' said Maddie.

'A little, but I have a very high tolerance for pain.'

'Malik's ass, look at that!' cried Rosie, pointing.

Maddie glanced at the dragon's limb; it had healed, the black scales smooth and lustrous where the weal had been. Blackrose stretched her leg out.

'Much better,' she said. 'It's definitely salve; I remember the feeling from long ago.'

Rosie and Maddie returned to the fire and sat.

'I could use this,' the dragon said. 'If I were to return to Lostwell with a large batch of salve, it would open every door I need, and I could buy whatever I desired. Even in an unrefined state, it would still be worth more than a mountain of diamonds.'

'How does it work?' said Rosie.

'I have no knowledge of that,' said Blackrose, 'and, as you mentioned, it has different effects on mortals and gods. To mortals, even those as strong as I am, it acts as a healing balm, as you have seen, but for gods and demigods it must work on their immortal self-healing powers somehow, and it not only heals them, but it rejuvenates them as well. Without it, gods do age, though very slowly. I was very young, but I remember when it first appeared, nearly three hundred years ago. No one knew where it came from, and the gods went quite mad with their desire for it. They still don't know where it comes from, only that it can be bought on Lostwell, thanks to Lord Naxor.'

'The mortals of the City are never allowed to have any,' said Maddie; 'it's for gods and demigods only.'

'There are seams of it in the hills behind Tara and Ooste,' said Rosie, 'accessible from the palaces there, but I've never seen any until now. Maybe I should take some to the City, and distribute it to the wounded.'

Maddie frowned, the memory of her sister's plan coming back to her. 'Are you still serious about that?'

'Yes. Blackrose and I discussed it further when you went off to the caves. We're leaving tonight. I don't know whether you want to come or not.'

'Why does it have to be tonight, on my birthday?'

'The sooner it is done,' said Blackrose, 'the sooner we shall find Corthie. I have also talked with Little Rose about the importance of locating the Quadrant. Corthie may already have it in his possession, of course.'

Maddie shook her head. 'She's too young for this.'

'I disagree; she is mature for a mortal of her age. She is not offering to kill anyone, or do anything dangerous. All she needs to do is find her brother and Corthie Holdfast. Have a little faith in your sister; she has the same Jackdaw courage as you, my rider.' Blackrose turned away, and leaned over the carcass of the goat. 'I shall eat now, and then sleep, so that I am ready for tonight's flight.'

Maddie showed Rosie round the salve cave once Blackrose had fallen asleep in the sunshine, and they hacked off a few more pieces and dropped them into a bag. As Maddie had expected, Rosie was enthused by the cave paintings, spending ages examining each one in detail. Neither of them brought up her impending departure, and they went back outside and sat by the dwindling fire to eat.

The goat had been slowly roasted over the fire, and Maddie ate until she was full, then lay down on the blanket to let her dinner settle. Rosie collected a jug from the tarpaulin and opened it, then filled two mugs.

'What's that?' said Maddie as Rosie handed her a mug.

'Ale.'

'You took ale from Tarstation?'

'Yes. I thought we might need some.'

'You're too young to be drinking. Wait; what am I saying? We're about to send you into a war zone where you might get killed. Drink up.'

'I'm not going to get killed, and you're not sending me anywhere. This was my idea. By this time tomorrow, I'll be in the Circuit, and I will have already spoken to a few Blades. I know which battalion Tom was serving with, and I have gold if I need to pay for anything.'

'Gold?'

'Yes, it was on my Tarstation list. I asked for a hundred sovereigns. I'll also take a crossbow, so I can defend myself, and if any officers ask who I am, I'll just tell them the truth, that I lost my parents in the Bulwark and I'm searching for my brother.'

'You make it all sound so simple, but these things are never simple. What if the Iceward Range has already fallen to the greenhides?'

'Then Blackrose will bring me back.'

Maddie sipped the bitter ale. 'I was hoping we'd have more time together. Three days, and you're already sick of me.'

'Oh Maddie, don't be silly. My opinion of you has gone up a lot over the last three days. I loved you before, but I also thought that you were... eh, how do I say this, a bit useless? I couldn't have been more wrong. You're a dragon-rider, and I'm proud that you're my sister.'

Maddie lowered her eyes. The sun was setting below the rim of the mountains towards sunward, and the valley was falling into shadow.

'Do you want me to pass on a message to Tom?'

'Yes,' said Maddie, 'tell him he was right in the end about me getting sent to the Rats; he always said I would. And tell Corthie that I hope everything works out between him and Lady Aila.'

'Why did you get sent to the Rats?'

Maddie glanced at the sleeping dragon. 'Take a guess. Kano was annoyed at her, and I was there. I was only in the Rats for twenty days. The craziest thing about it was that I was responsible for a whole team, and I had to give orders to folk who were lot older than me. I had no clue what I was doing; Buckler once rescued me when I was dangling from a moat bridge.' She sighed. 'Poor Buckler, that was a nasty way to go. I'd never tell Blackrose, but he was showing off at the time. That's all it took; one little mistake.' She glanced at Rosie. 'Promise me you won't show off; you have to be careful.'

'I promise. Don't worry.'

Maddie snorted. 'Easy to say.'

'And what will you do while I'm gone?'

'I don't know, I guess it depends on what Blackrose wants. I'm going to try to persuade her to help the City, but you've seen how that's gone so far. Maybe once she's seen it tonight, she might change her mind.'

'Are you going to come along?'

Maddie shook her head. 'I can't stand the thought of the journey back without you. Listen, if something's happened to Tom... I mean, if he's... you know what I'm trying to say, then you'll come back here in ten days, yeah?'

Rosie glanced down. 'Yes.'

'Good. Do you need a hand to pack?'

The two sisters gathered up some things, and dragged the contents of the tarpaulin into the cave. The supplies they had taken from Tarstation filled an entire wall of the cave, and Maddie was impressed with how thorough Rosie had been with her list, though she decided not to mention that fact to her sister. They lit a lamp as the sky darkened, and Rosie packed a small bag, stowing the salve and the gold near the bottom. She selected one of the two crossbows they had taken, and fitted the strap so it sat over her shoulder.

The dragon was awakening when they were finishing the preparations, and she stretched her wings in the cold night air. Maddie and Rosie walked to the cave entrance.

'I'm going to stay here,' said Maddie.

'Very well, rider,' said Blackrose. 'Come, Little Rose; climb up and I shall take you to the City.'

They walked down the small slope to the side of the pool, and Rosie strapped her pack and the crossbow to the side of the dragon's harness. She turned.

'We'll see each other soon, sister.'

Maddie nodded, though she couldn't suppress the knot forming in her stomach. She stepped forward and embraced Rosie, squeezing her tight.

'Take care, little Rosie.'

Her sister turned to the dragon and scrambled up the ropes to the saddle. Maddie took a few steps back so that she could see her, and smiled at how small she looked on the dragon's back.

Blackrose swung her head round to face Maddie. 'I'll be back before dawn, and then it shall be you and I again, my rider.'

She beat her great wings and rose into the air, and Maddie watched until the tiny speck in the night sky was swallowed up by the darkness.

CHAPTER 12

DELIVERANCE

Ooste, Auldan, The City – 24th Amalan 3420

Aila sat in a deep armchair, her legs drawn up as she stared at the door. Another night in the palace had passed, and she had spent it alone, locked inside Marcus's quarters after soldiers had escorted her there the previous day. She had slept fitfully on the chair, the side door to the bedroom remaining unopened and ignored, and her clothes felt grimy in the warm air.

She threw the thin blanket to the floor and stood, rubbing her face, her eyes on the door. All around her were half-empty crates and trunks, and Marcus's things were scattered across the floorboards. She had looked through his possessions, searching for a weapon or something else she could use, but had found nothing. Marcus loved clothes, but not much else, it seemed. Aila pulled her eyes from the door, and walked over to open the tall shutters, letting the dawn light flood the room, turning the white-painted walls into shades of vibrant pink. The glare made her scrunch her eyes up for a moment. She slid a bolt free and pushed one of the windows open a few inches to let in some air. She could smash the glass, she thought, but it was a long way down to the ground outside. Jumping out of a four-storey high window was something to consider if Marcus himself entered the apartment, but not before.

She walked back to the front door of the rooms and tried the handle again, checking it was still locked for the hundredth time. She had kicked and punched the door many times throughout the night, but no one had responded. She could see the shadows of at least two soldiers under the bottom edge of the door, so she knew they were out there.

Belinda had said that she would come for her in the morning. Aila didn't trust the strange god who had appeared in the palace, but she needed to be ready. She rummaged in her own bags for some clean underclothes and hurried into the bathroom, where she washed in the warm water that flowed from the golden taps, before redressing quickly, her ears listening for any sounds from the hallway.

She emerged from the bathroom freshened up, her nerves ragged. She paced up and down across the polished floorboards, turning to check that the sun had risen, then collapsed back into the armchair, suppressing a scream of frustration.

Why had Karalyn Holdfast sent a god in her stead? They couldn't have known that Queen Amalia would recognise her, but sending Belinda, who seemed to have had a fractious relationship with the Holdfasts, had clearly been a gamble. If the God-Queen had truly turned her, then the gamble had failed.

She stared at the door, but nothing changed. She leaped up in a rage, and began breaking some of Marcus's things. She picked up a ceramic statuette of his father Prince Michael and hurled it against the wall, where it shattered into a cloud of dust and a thousand fragments. She pictured the God-Queen hammering a restraining mask onto her face, and picked up a painted, wooden box. She threw it against the marble fireplace, and it splintered, the contents spilling out. She frowned, and crouched down by the mess she had made.

Letters, tied in a bundle.

She picked the entire bundle up and sat back onto the armchair. She flipped through the many envelopes; all were addressed to 'My Son, Marcus'. She frowned and pulled one from the bundle at random. She opened the envelope and took out the letter from within. The paper was old and yellowed, and the inked script had faded in places. She skipped past the cold and formal greetings from Prince Michael to his son, and started reading.

Taken individually, each mortal life is worthless; their existence is justified solely by their duty to serve us, and to glorify our name. The only danger that could arise from them is if they were to unify against us, but that outcome has been rendered impossible by the careful division of the mortals into nine separate, competing tribes. Foster the divisions, and the mortals will remain malleable and pliant.

Aila frowned. None of the content surprised her; she remembered Prince Michael's attitude towards mortals, and Princess Yendra's response. She slipped the letter back into the envelope and pulled out another.

The morning slipped by as she worked her way through the bundle of letters. She hadn't realised that she had been looking for a mention of her own name until she discovered it, halfway down a page.

I have decided that your desire for your cousin is no longer to be suppressed. So many demigods have been slain in my sister's foolish uprising that I fear for the future of our rule over the mortals of the City. Without fresh blood, the Royal Family is doomed to wither away over time, therefore I shall remove the ban on cousins intermarrying. Take Lady Aila into your possession, and from her womb a new line of demigods shall arise, and the City shall have heirs.

She raised an eyebrow at the last line, and was about to select another letter when something else caught her eye.

In your new role as Commander of the Bulwark, one of your first tasks will be to utterly stamp out the ridiculous fantasies among the Hammers that a mortal shall arise to redeem them. That hope was destroyed centuries ago, when the last mortal prince was deposed. Since that day, the vision of mortal unity and rule has been wiped from the histories of Auldan and Medio, to the degree that no one now remembers how close the Aurelians came to overthrowing our rule; and it irks me that this vain belief has lingered among the Hammers. As far as the mortals of the City are concerned, I am the eternal

Prince of Tara; the crown once borne by the Aurelians has passed to me, and the great sword of state, which they once wielded, is in my hands. The Crown and the Just must remain in our grasp forever, for there is no going back.

Aila remembered meeting the young Aurelian officer in Pella after he had carried out an atrocity in the Circuit. Michael's lessons had been well learned, it seemed. A family that had once stood up for the mortals had been turned into an instrument to oppress them instead. She had been born a thousand years after the Aurelian's failed uprising against the gods, and knew about it only as a ridiculous footnote to the history of the City; the futile attempt of a vain prince to resist the inevitable, and an expression of the ingratitude shown by some mortals towards the benevolent rule of the gods.

She considered ripping the letters to pieces once she had worked her way through them, her mind spinning with the relentless hatred and arrogance evident on every page, but instead she tied them back into a bundle. Burning them in front of Marcus would cause him more pain, she thought, and she slid them into her bag.

The day passed. No one appeared with food or drink for her, so she drank the water from the bathroom taps, and paced the floor as her stomach rumbled. Her mood soured with every hour that went by. The God-Queen would be coming for her, whenever she recalled her grand-daughter's disobedience from the previous day, and jumping from the window began to look more appealing.

The sun was setting, and Aila had returned to the armchair, when a noise outside the room disturbed her from her frustrated lethargy. She bolted upright on the chair, her hands trembling a little as the footsteps outside the door grew louder. She eyed the window. If it was Marcus or the God-Queen, she would jump. If she was lucky, she might only break one leg, and would be able to limp or crawl away before the soldiers got her.

The noise outside the door rose, as if a struggle was taking place, then the door was kicked in. It swung on its hinges, battering off the inside wall of the room. In the doorway stood Belinda, a sword in her hand. Next to her lay two soldiers on the floor of the hallway, both decapitated.

Aila stared as the god approached.

'Are you ready to leave?

'What?'

Belinda frowned at her. 'I told you I was coming for you; are you ready to leave?'

'Now?'

'Yes, now. Hurry, otherwise I will leave you here.'

Aila stood and swung her bag over her shoulder. 'What about the God-Queen?'

'I have subdued her; she will not notice us going.'

'But, I thought...'

Belinda glanced at her, a small smile on the edge of her lips. 'You thought Amalia was going to change my mind? Why does everyone doubt me? If I say I'm going to do something, then I do it. Amalia seemed to think that if she told me everything about my history, then I would help her, but I was already aware of the kind of person I used to be.'

Aila joined her by the door, and glanced down at the bodies of the two undead soldiers. She stepped over them, and Belinda led her to the stairs. The corridors and hallways of the private quarters were deserted, and lay in silence.

'We have to rescue Naxor.'

Belinda glanced at her. 'Why? And it had better be a good reason. Feeling sorry for him isn't enough.'

'He has vision powers; he'll be able to help.'

Belinda smiled. 'Alright, let's get him.'

'Do you know where he's being held?'

'Yes, Amalia told me,' she said as they changed direction and took another passageway; 'once she started talking, she poured everything out to me, and it look longer for the opium to take effect than I'd anticipated. That's why I wasn't here for you at dawn.'

'You were up all night with her?'

'And all of today.'

'Smoking opium?'

'She was melancholy, and wanted to talk about her recollections of when I used to be her best friend.'

'And you betrayed her anyway?'

'Don't be stupid. How could I betray someone I have no memory of? And you should cease complaining. If Amalia had got her way, right now you would be in a restraining mask awaiting the return of your husband. She loathes you, and would have killed you were it not for the fact that this Marcus person is in love with you.'

They came to a spiral staircase, and ascended a tower that stood on the sunward side of the palace. At the top of the steps was a door, and Belinda lifted a boot and kicked it down with one blow, the lock splintering and falling to the ground. Aila rushed into the small, dark chamber. Naxor was lying on the floor, writhing in agony, with chains attached to his ankles and wrists. The top half of his face was covered in a thick, iron mask, from which blood was trickling. She knelt beside him as Belinda examined the chains.

'It's alright,' Aila said, 'we're here to help you.'

'Don't waste your breath,' said Belinda, 'he's in so much pain that he probably can't hear you.' She withdrew a leather purse from her belt and unrolled it onto the stone floor, revealing a set of lock picks and tools. 'I'll deal with the shackles if you take the mask off.'

Aila grimaced as she reached out with her hands for Naxor's face. Her fingers went through his blood and sweat-soaked hair, searching for the buckle at the back of his head. He cried out, and Aila checked that the spiral stairs were still deserted.

'It's fine,' said Belinda; 'Amalia put him up here so she wouldn't have to listen to his screams.'

Aila pushed Naxor's head to the side and grasped the buckle with her right hand. She pulled it, and the clasp came free. Naxor let out another cry as Aila ripped the mask from his face. She shuddered at the sight. His eyes were dark pits of blood.

'Out of the way,' said Belinda. She shoved Aila to the side and placed a hand onto Naxor's chest. His body spasmed, but Belinda held him down. The blood in his eye sockets stopped pouring out, and then his eyes began to regenerate in front of them. Aila gasped as she watched. The process took a few moments, then Belinda lifted her hand as Naxor lay still.

Aila turned to her. 'You're healing powers are beyond anything I've ever seen.'

'Yes. Imagine if I had all of my powers. Amalia said I used to rule entire worlds before I switched sides in the War of the Gods.'

Naxor groaned and opened his eyes. 'Aila? Where am I?'

'We're in the Royal Palace; we're escaping. This is Belinda.'

His eyes widened as he gazed at the woman. 'You?' He tried to scramble away, then realised the shackles were still attached to his wrists and ankles.

'Stop moving,' said Belinda; 'I'm trying to free you.'

Naxor stared at her. 'I saw you on Lostwell.'

'I know.'

He glanced at Aila, his eyes wild. 'She's with the Holdfasts!'

'Yes,' said Aila, 'she's here to find Corthie. Now, shut up for a minute so she can remove the chains.'

Belinda picked up her tools and picked the locks on his ankles first, and the chains fell free.

'Why is she rescuing us?' Naxor whispered.

'Because we're going to help her find Corthie.'

'We are?'

Aila nodded. 'Yes.'

'But where's the God-Queen?'

'Sleeping, I think.'

'Then who healed me?'

Belinda glanced up from where she was working on his wrist shackles. 'I did. We can put the mask back on if you're unhappy in any way.'

Naxor shook his head. 'That was the worst nightmare I've ever lived through. Where is it?'

Aila passed him the bloody mask.

'Malik's ass. Just looking at it makes me feel sick. What happened?'

'Don't you remember? You tried to send the God-Queen and Marcus to sleep, but they were wearing these things in their eyes that protected them.'

Belinda removed the shackles from his right wrist. 'They have those here? The eye-shields?'

'Yes,' said Aila. 'Little transparent disks.'

Belinda moved to the last shackle.

'And what happened then?' said Naxor. 'I remembered Marcus coming at me with the Just.'

Aila nodded. 'Yes. After that, the soldiers brought the God-King out of the caverns, and Marcus executed him.'

Naxor stared at her. 'Malik's dead?'

'Yeah. The God-Queen couldn't stand the sight of him so salve-addled.'

'And she's just going to let us walk out of the palace?'

Aila shrugged. 'That's what Belinda says.'

The final shackle fell loose, and they got to their feet as Belinda packed her tools back into her belt. Naxor cast a suspicious eye towards the god.

'Can we trust her?' he said.

Belinda frowned at him. 'I just unshackled you. Are you trying to read my mind? You won't be able to.'

Aila shook her head. 'That was a bit rude, cousin.'

'I had to try,' he said. 'She has the same kind of protective shield around her as Corthie does.'

'Listen, both of you,' Belinda said, as they stood at the top of the stairs. 'I'm taking you with me, but I'll be honest; I'm perfectly capable of finding Corthie without your help, and if you betray me, or hinder me in any way, then I'll abandon you. Your fate is of no interest to me; however, if you help me, I will protect you. Naxor, I want you scanning the area wherever we go; tell me if anyone is approaching. Aila... just don't get killed.'

She turned, and hurried down the spiral staircase, and the two cousins followed. Naxor raised an eyebrow at Aila as they descended, but said nothing. They emerged from the old tower into the brightly-lit hallways of the palace.

'What about Doria?' whispered Naxor. 'Is she in the palace?'

'I guess so,' said Aila.

'Are we going to get her too?'

Belinda turned. 'What powers does she have?'

Naxor frowned. 'None.'

'Then no. Two demigods are enough for me to look after.'

They strode along the passageways towards the front of the palace, then Belinda slowed as they reached the top of the grand staircase that led out of the private quarters.

'Hello,' said the God-Queen, standing at the bottom of the steps. 'Going somewhere?'

'Yes,' said Belinda. She started to descend the stairs. 'I advise you not to try to stop me, Amalia.'

The God-Queen laughed. 'To think I stayed up with you all night talking, telling you the innermost thoughts of my heart, and you do this as soon as I fall asleep? Do you take me for a fool?'

'You're a fool if you think you can change my mind.'

Aila and Naxor followed Belinda down the stairs, keeping close to her.

'So it comes to this?' said the God-Queen. 'My best friend stabs me in the back. Aila, Naxor, remain where you are. I'm going to have to kill an old friend, and I don't wish for you to die. Not yet, at any rate.'

Belinda drew her sword, halfway down the stairs. 'Get out of my way, Amalia.'

'You don't scare me,' said the God-Queen; 'you've already told me about the loss of your powers. That was a mistake.' She raised her hand. 'It's not too late, even now. If you kneel before me, and beg forgiveness, I will stay my hand. You would be a useful ally, Belinda, even in your diminished state.'

Belinda carried on down the stairs.

The God-Queen shook her head. 'You leave me no choice. I will rot the flesh from your body, and you will feel pain like you have never known.'

'Then try.'

The God-Queen glared at her, then staggered back a step, gasping. She stared at her hand, then at Belinda, her eyes wide. 'No.'

Belinda reached the bottom of the stairs and plunged her sword into the God-Queen's stomach, driving the blade clean through. 'Not quite as diminished as you thought,' she said, as blood stained the front of the God-Queen's dress. She pushed her off the blade, and the God-Queen fell to the floor. Belinda stood over her, the tip of her sword against Amalia's throat.

Aila and Naxor raced down the stairs, and stood watching as Belinda placed a boot onto the God-Queen's torso.

'This is the last warning you'll get from me, Amalia,' Belinda said. 'I don't want to kill the ruler of the City, not because I care about you, but because every soldier here would be hunting me, and that's an inconvenience I could do without. You will send no one to pursue me, understand? If you do, or if you do anything to obstruct or even annoy me, then I'll back here for your head.'

Before the God-Queen could respond, Belinda rammed the blade into her chest, and ripped it down her abdomen, all the way to her stomach.

Aila cried out, her hand to her mouth, as the God-Queen screamed, blood spilling from her as she writhed on the marble.

Belinda turned to them. 'Let's move.'

She headed for the main entrance of the palace, with Aila and Naxor running after her.

'You just sliced open the God-Queen,' Naxor said, his eyes wide and staring.

'She'll live,' muttered Belinda.

'Will she?' said Aila. 'I'm not sure I could recover from that.'

'You wouldn't,' said Belinda, 'but Amalia is a full god. It might take a while, but she'll get over it.'

They reached the edge of the private quarters, where four undead soldiers stood by the doors.

Belinda drew her sword again. Naxor opened his mouth to speak, but Aila raised a hand to quieten him.

'Let her do her thing.'

Naxor stared as Belinda tore through the soldiers, slicing through arms and necks until the four guards were reduced to a heap of bodies on the floor. She stepped over them and pushed open the doors. They strode through into a large hall, and Naxor hurried out in front.

'Let me lead,' he said; 'I know every inch of this palace. We can leave from a quiet side door rather than risk meeting too many people by the front.'

They followed him through an arched opening, and down a narrow service corridor to a row of storerooms. He paused for a moment, his eyes hazy.

'Belinda,' said Aila; 'I have a confession.'

Belinda frowned.

'I do actually have a power.'

'Oh, that's better than I was expecting. What kind of power?'

'It doesn't work on you, which is why I didn't say, but I think I'm going to have to use it in a minute. I can change my appearance, so that people looking at me think I'm someone else.'

Belinda nodded. 'Like a kind of vision power?'

'Yes. People see me differently, but I don't physically change.'

'Can you make yourself invisible too?'

'No, and I can't change into inanimate objects or anything like that.'

'Alright, that's good to know. I guess I'd only just met you when you lied to me, so I can see why you might not have trusted me at the time. I hope you trust me now.'

'Yes. I'm a little scared of you, but I trust you.'

Belinda smiled. 'Thank you.'

Naxor came out of his trance. 'The route is clear if we hurry now. Come on.'

They raced down the passageway, then through a door and down some more stairs. To the left the sounds of a busy kitchen echoed out, but they ran on, and Naxor opened a tall door. He peered outside, then beckoned the others. They walked out into the dark evening, a few lamps illuminating the palace courtyard.

Aila concentrated. *You see me as a palace guard.*

Naxor blinked when he saw her. 'Hey, tell me when you're going to do that, I nearly panicked.'

Belinda turned.

'I'm looking like a palace guard,' Aila said. 'It should help us walk out of here.'

They strode across the courtyard. A few workers glanced over as they unloaded a wagon piled high with supplies, but no one challenged them. They exited the palace grounds via a gate, and walked through the deserted streets of Ooste.

'The Royal Academy first,' said Aila, 'and then we can plot our next move.'

'Someone's following us,' said Belinda.

'I know,' said Naxor. 'I'll deal with it. Keep going, and I'll meet you at the academy.'

He darted off to the side, and disappeared into the shadows.

Mona gasped as she opened the door.

'Don't worry,' said Aila; 'we're not staying.'

'Come in; quickly,' she said, standing to the side as Aila and Belinda entered the academy keep. 'What's happened? Who is this?'

'This is Belinda,' said Aila; 'she helped me and Naxor escape. Belinda, this is my cousin, Mona. She's on our side.'

Mona glanced at the woman in strange armour. 'Naxor has escaped too?'

'He's on his way here,' said Aila, as Mona continued to stare at the god.

'Would you stop doing that?' said Belinda. 'Why is everyone trying to read my mind?'

Mona took a step back. 'My apologies. It was very impolite of me; I'm afraid I'm a little suspicious of everyone these days. Your protection though, how is it done? It is very impressive.'

'She has the same shielding as Corthie,' said Aila, 'and that's who we're looking for.'

'Ah, I see,' said Mona. 'Come and sit; we can talk. I have news of Corthie Holdfast for you.'

They went into a small reception room close by and Mona directed them to a couch while she poured some wine into three glasses.

'Am I to assume,' she said, 'that Belinda is one of the people that Naxor mentioned was looking for Corthie? A Holdfast?'

'She works with the Holdfasts,' said Aila.

Mona brought over a silver tray and placed it onto the low table in front of them.

Belinda took a glass. 'You said you had news about Corthie?'

'Yes; he is in Icehaven.'

Belinda took the map out of a pocket and unfolded it. 'Icehaven? Yes, I see it. Maybe fifteen miles by road?'

'About that,' said Mona, 'although travelling there at the moment might be difficult.'

'Why?'

'Because of Corthie's presence. Lady Yvona, the governor there, has claimed him as her champion, and he has been fighting the greenhides on the stretch of the Middle Walls controlled by the Icewarder tribe. Very successfully too, I might add. The news reached us this evening that he was acclaimed by the crowds outside Alkirk Palace, and Lady Yvona announced that all roads between Icehaven and the rest of the City will be closed, to prevent Prince Marcus or Commander Kano from attempted to seize her new champion.'

'There are too many names for me to follow,' said Belinda, 'but can you clarify something for me – they're making Corthie fight?'

'I doubt anyone's making him do it,' said Aila. 'I think he enjoys it.'

'From all reports,' said Mona, 'he's the best fighter the City has seen since the days of Michael and Yendra.'

'We shall go to Icehaven,' said Belinda. 'Did you have a bag to collect here, Aila?'

'Yes, that's right.' She turned to Mona. 'Do you remember that bag I left here? I'll need it, please. Oh, and there's a lot still to tell you.'

'I'll retrieve your bag, and you can tell me everything when I return.'

Mona rose from her seat. The door burst open as Mona was walking towards it, and Naxor entered. He saw Mona and embraced her, laughing.

'Glad to see you well, cousin,' she said. 'Who's that with you?'

Aila squinted past the figure of Naxor by the door. A woman was standing a few paces away.

'This is Yaizra,' he said. 'She was following us because she was looking for Aila. I brought her in through the back door, Mona, to avoid anyone seeing us. I've read her mind; she's safe.'

The young woman walked into the room, and her glance settled on Aila.

'You were looking for us?' said the demigod.

'Yeah. Are you Lady Aila?'

'I am.'

'I was outside the palace gates when I recognised Lord Naxor leaving. I was sent here by Corthie; he has a message for you, well, more of a question, I guess.'

'You know Corthie?' said Belinda, leaning forward on the couch.

Yaizra's eyes flicked over the god. 'I was in Tarstation with him, and we escaped together and made it to Icehaven.'

Naxor strolled over, sat, and poured himself a wine. He smiled. 'I already know what she's going to say.'

'Shut up,' said Aila, her nerves jangling. She faced Yaizra. 'What did he want to ask?'

'Well,' she said, 'he's a bit upset about you getting married to Marcus.'

Aila cringed. 'He knows about that?'

'The whole City knows,' she said. 'Where have you been; locked in a palace?'

'Yes, as a matter of fact.'

'Oh. Well, yeah. Everyone knows, and you broke Corthie's heart. He's my friend, and well, you'd better have a good reason.'

Aila glanced at Mona, then back at Yaizra. 'The truth is I had a plan to kill Marcus on our wedding night, but the Bulwark was over-run, and he left for the Union Walls.'

Yaizra nodded. 'Fair enough. Corthie's question is this – do you want to go to Icehaven to be with him? He loves you.'

Aila's face broke into a smile. 'Yes. I mean yes, I'll come to Icehaven.'

Naxor laughed. 'Your face! Actually,' he said, peering at her; 'your face looks a lot younger than when Corthie last saw you. He might be in for a shock.'

'I know,' she muttered.

'Thank you for bringing us this news, Miss Yaizra,' said Mona; 'please sit and have a drink with us. And tell me, please, how do you intend to get through the roadblocks that Lady Yvona has set up?'

Yaizra grinned. 'Easy.' She pulled a folded paper from a pocket on her coat. 'This is signed by Lady Yvona herself. It'll get me and whoever's with me through any roadblock. Her ladyship knew that Corthie was sending me here, and approved.'

Aila glanced at her cousin. 'You should come with us, Mona. Ooste isn't going to be safe for you if the God-Queen discovers you've helped us.'

'Thank you, but no,' she said. 'Someone needs to remain here, and I can keep you up to date via my vision powers, and let you know what's happening.'

'That would be useful,' said Belinda. 'Thanks.'

Aila turned to Naxor. 'What about you?'

He took a sip of wine. 'I think I'll come along with you to Icehaven for now.'

She smiled. 'Good. So, when do the four of us leave? Considering what Belinda did to the God-Queen in the palace, it should probably be soon.'

Mona frowned. 'What do you mean?'

'She got in my way,' said Belinda. She glanced at the others in the room. 'I let her live.'

'There's one thing I don't understand,' said Aila. 'If you were going to do that to the God-Queen anyway, why did you stay over last night? Did you want to find out more about your past?'

'In a way, but that wasn't the reason.'

'Then why?'

Belinda smiled, and unclasped a side buckle of her chest armour. Hidden inside was a copper-coloured sheet of metal, shaped into a quarter circle.

Aila squinted. 'What's that?'

'It's a Quadrant,' said Naxor. He shook his head. 'Belinda's stolen the God-Queen's Quadrant.'

CHAPTER 13

OPPOSING FORCES

Icehaven, Medio, The City – 25th Amalan 3420

The carriage moved through the teeming crowds of Icewarders that lined the streets of the town.

'It appears,' said Major Hannia, 'that news of your trip beyond the Middle Walls this morning has already reached Icehaven.'

Corthie smiled as the crowds tried to push through the line of soldiers to reach the carriage. His body was aching, and he was looking forward to another healing from Lady Yvona. He noticed Major Hannia was writing in a journal.

'I'm logging your times,' she said, catching his glance. 'You were out fighting for four and a half hours today, then needed to rest for three.' She nodded. 'Quite similar times to yesterday. Do you always require the same rest period after using battle-vision?'

'It depends,' he said. 'Back at the Bulwark, some nights wouldn't be as intense as others, and I wouldn't need to rest at all, but I'm on my own here, so I need to use a lot more of my powers. I could last a lot longer out there, but then I would need to sleep for an entire day. That would be fine too; I'll do whatever Yvona asks.'

Hannia raised an eyebrow.

Corthie laughed. 'Alright, everything except swear undying loyalty. Did you hear the pledge I read out last night in front of the palace?'

'Yes. It was cleverly worded, and should satisfy most people, but I could read between the lines.'

Corthie glanced out of the window at the cheering crowds. 'They don't seem to mind.'

'You rescued an entire garrison who had been stranded on the Sea Wall for four days. Three hundred soldiers; men and women whose families had almost given them up for dead. That's all anyone will be thinking about today, champion. And tomorrow, and the next day. But what about a year from now? I worry that Marcus will harbour this grudge for a long time, and eventually, he will seek revenge upon Lady Yvona.'

Corthie shrugged. 'Then maybe I should kill him.'

'What? And the God-Queen and Commander Kano too?'

'The City would be better without them.'

Hannia stared at him and shook her head. 'You're talking about the three most powerful beings in the City; and if the God-Queen and God-King have truly reconciled, there would be four to contend with. Mortals can't just go around killing gods like that.'

'Why not?'

'You can't... they're gods.'

'Aye, bad gods. They might have once been good for the City, but now? Why isn't the God-Queen on the Middle Walls, using her death powers to destroy the greenhides? She could kill hundreds a day, and relieve the pressure all down the line of defences. Marcus and Kano could flank her and use their battle-vision to keep her safe; so why are all three of them hiding behind the mortals they're supposed to be protecting?

The major said nothing.

'You know the reason, don't you?' Corthie went on. 'They don't care. We mortals mean nothing to them; we're just expendable slaves.'

'But Lady Yvona isn't like that.'

'I know. I didn't say that all of the Royal Family were bad. Naxor was alright, and I like Yvona. And Aila, of course.' He lowered his voice. 'And you-know-who, if she ever recovers from her injuries. I've heard a lot of good things about her. My mother was the ruler of a realm in my world, but there the people selected her by voting, and if they don't like her, they can vote her out again. Maybe they should try that here.'

'Icehaven has the most advanced voting system of anywhere in the City,' Hannia said. 'All property owners have a say in the government, though Lady Yvona holds a veto over some areas. Remember that Icehaven was on the side of the rebels in the Civil War, at least until Princess Niomi was murdered.'

She glanced out of the window as the carriage reached the gates of Alkirk Palace. 'I know you're tired, but there's something I would like to ask of you.'

'Aye?'

'When you were resting in the fort on the walls, I received a message stating that a hundred or so of the town's dignitaries were gathering at the palace today to welcome your return. I would be obliged if you could spend an hour with them, talking and shaking hands and so on.'

Corthie groaned.

'Sorry.'

'I'll do it,' he said; 'for you and Yvona. If you could get me a bath and a hot meal ready for afterwards, I'd be grateful.'

'Of course,' she said. 'Thank you.'

'Has there been any word from Yaizra?'

'Not that I know of. The ship she boarded yesterday would have got into Dalrig around sunset, so I would hope she has delivered your message by now. You aren't worried, are you?'

'Worried? I'm terrified.'

'Surely it can't be as nerve-wracking as facing all those greenhides on your own?'

He shook his head. 'I'm not scared of the greenhides, but the prospect of Yaizra returning alone, with a message that Aila's not interested, or that she's in love with Marcus?'

'You must be prepared for the worst, I suppose. What will you do if she rejects you?'

'I don't know. The first thing will be to ask if I can do a twelve hour shift beyond the walls tomorrow to take my mind off it, and then I'll probably drink myself into oblivion. Don't worry, I'm not like Marcus; I can take no for an answer. It doesn't mean it won't hurt, though.'

'Lady Yvona is considering offering you a private harem within the palace, if it doesn't work out with you and Aila.'

Corthie frowned at her. 'Marcus offered me the same once. Tell her thanks, but no. I don't want a harem.'

'She'll be glad to hear that. She wasn't keen on the idea, but she... very much wants you to stay.'

The carriage ground to a halt in the large courtyard at the rear of the palace. Outside, dozens of well-dressed men and women were lining up in the sunshine.

'There they are,' said Hannia. 'A few words to each should suffice. Thanks again.'

'It's fine. I had to do a lot of stuff like this when I was younger, especially after my mother was elected leader. I'll be on my best behaviour.'

The carriage doors opened to a loud cheer and applause. Corthie went to the steps of the carriage, suppressed the aches and pains that rippled through his body, then smiled and waved.

Two hours later, Corthie emerged from his grand bathroom with a towel wrapped round his waist, his skin pink from the hot water, and his wet hair dripping onto the carpeted floor.

'Afternoon,' said Achan, glancing up from the table where he was reading. 'I heard you outdid yesterday's efforts. They're saying you killed five hundred greenhides.'

'They're exaggerating,' Corthie said. 'I wasn't keeping a strict count, but it was more like two hundred.'

Achan stared at him. 'Two hundred? How is that even possible?'

Corthie shrugged as he walked over. 'I just keep swinging the axe. I never thought I'd find a weapon as good as my old Clawhammer, but the Axe of Rand might be it; its blade is stronger than anything I've ever used before, and stays sharp no matter how many greenhides it hacks through.'

He sat at the table. Plates and bowls over-flowing with food were sitting waiting for him, and his stomach rumbled from the smell of roasted meat.

'The palace staff brought that here for you,' Achan said; 'they 're getting more used to your appetite.'

Corthie smiled, and picked up a fork. 'What you reading?'

'A history of the City.'

'Why? I thought you already knew all about that.'

'Did you hear what happened yesterday, down by Sander territory?'

Corthie shook his head as he ate.

He grinned. 'A hundred thousand Hammers made it through the Eighth Gate, despite Kano trying to stop them.'

'Why would he try to stop them?'

'Well, they're saying it was because they didn't want to risk a breach in the Middle Walls, but we all know the real reason – they don't value the lives of the Hammers. I mean, a hundred thousand is amazing; a miracle, but that's still less than half of the entire population. More than that are dead, ripped to shreds by the greenhides. But, I thought they were all going to die. The Hammers pushed the Blades out of the gatehouse, and then resealed the entrance once the refugees were through. And that's not even the strangest part; they were lead by two Aurelians.'

Corthie paused between mouthfuls. 'Who?'

'Do you remember when we were on the Grey Isle, and I told you who that prison was originally built for? Almost two thousand years ago, Prince Aurelian was sent there in chains, where he died. For some reason that I've never understood, the Hammers have a legend about how the Aurelians would return, and unite the mortals of the City.' He shook his head. 'And it seems to have happened. Two Aurelians turn up out of nowhere, and lead the Hammers to safety.'

'It could be a hoax.'

'I know; half of me thinks it must be. The only way to be sure is to go down there myself. The Hammer refugees are clustering round the Eighth Gate, keeping the Blades away, but I should be able to get through. I need to go, just to witness it, and to find out if any of my family or friends made it out.'

Corthie nodded. 'Of course. You should go.'

'Kano must be soiling himself with fear; he has you up here, iceward of his position, and a hundred thousand Hammers sitting sunward of him. On top of all that he has to somehow control the Evaders in the Circuit.'

'Poor guy,' Corthie said. 'My heart bleeds for him.'

'I'll wait until Yaizra returns, then I'll go. You need at least one friend here.'

'Thanks.'

There was a knock at the door and Major Hannia entered. Her eyes wandered over Corthie's bare chest for a moment, then her eyes met his.

'Sorry for interrupting,' she said, 'but Lady Yvona is hoping you will speak to her.'

'Aye, sure,' he said. 'I'll get dressed and find her. Is she in her study?'

'Yes.'

He nodded and stood as the major left their quarters.

Achan glanced at him. 'You could be a king here if you wanted it.'

'I can't imagine anything duller,' he said as he strode to his room. He dried his hair, then pulled on a fresh set of clothes. His wardrobes had been sparse when he had moved into the palace, but Lady Yvona had commissioned garments for him in his size, and more had been arriving each day, the fingers of the town's seamstresses and tailors working through the night to create outfits for the champion.

He walked out into the hallway beside their rooms and went to Lady Yvona's study. He knocked on the door, and opened it when he heard the governor's voice.

'Champion,' she said, smiling from behind her desk as he walked in.

'First of all, my thanks for what you did today. Three hundred Icewarder families will never forget it, and neither will I. Sit, please.'

'It's no problem,' he said as he took a seat; 'I'm glad I can help.'

'Major Hannia has been working hard to make sure everything here is to your liking; food, clothes and your quarters and so on, so I've decided to make it her full time job. I've reallocated her other duties so that she devote all of her energies to see to your needs. She'll be your chief-of-staff, as it were.'

'Thanks. Can she still come to the wall with me every day? I like her being there.'

'Of course; wherever you go, she will remain close by if you need her. I need to prepare a reception for the families of the soldiers you saved today; many will be attending the palace later this evening. I was hoping you might be able to spare five minutes?'

'To speak to them? Sure.'

She smiled. 'Thank you.'

'It's part of the job, and you're the boss.'

They stood.

'Can I see Yendra?' he said.

'Of course. Just please remember to lock the door on your way out. It remains the case that only you, Major Hannia, your two friends and I are aware of her identity, and it needs to be kept that way for now.'

He nodded.

'I shall see you later, champion.'

She glided from the office, her pale yellow robes trailing behind her. Corthie turned, and went to the side door that led to the small bed chamber. He unlocked the door, and entered. The shutters were half-open, and a grey light was hanging in the air. He sat by the bed and gazed at the old woman. The blanket covering her was rising and falling, and she looked a little better than she had the previous day.

'Yvona's healing must be working,' he said aloud. 'You seem healthier than ever. I like Yvona, your niece, but she's trying so hard to please me that I feel a little suffocated. I wish I could swear allegiance to her, but how could I tell my sister that I was never coming home?' He smiled. 'You're a good listener, Yendra; I might start coming here to tell you all of my problems. My biggest one is Aila. No, that's not right; she's not the problem, it's my feelings for her that are confusing everything. In some ways it would be easier if she rejected me, then I would be able to turn my back on the City when the time came, and walk away without any regrets. You knew her well, didn't you? I remember she said that you mentored her, and she was with you at the end, when the war finished. I'd love to hear some stories about her wild youth. She really admired you, I hope you know that.'

Yendra's hand moved an inch across the covers, and Corthie stopped talking. He took her hand and squeezed it gently, then nearly jumped in surprise when she squeezed it back.

'Yendra,' he said; 'can you hear me?'

The old woman squeezed his hand again.

'You're safe, in Icehaven. Lady Yvona is caring for you.'

She moved her lips. 'Aila?' she gasped.

Corthie laughed. 'You spoke. Aila's not here, but hopefully she'll be coming.'

'What... what year?'

'Em, it's thirty-four, twenty, and it's the month of Amalan.'

'Khora?'

'I'm sorry, she's dead. Marcus did it; he's taken over the City, and the greenhides are occupying the Bulwark. Wait, sorry, I shouldn't be telling you things that'll worry you. Everything's going to be fine.'

'Your voice... you saved me from the prison... from the mask.'

'Aye, me and a couple of friends. We didn't know who you were, but we couldn't leave you like that.'

'Who are you?'

'I'm Corthie Holdfast; I fight greenhides.'

'Thank you, Corthie.'

'Who did it to you? Who put the mask on?'

'My father.'

'The God-King? Asshole.'

'My mother wanted to... kill me. They fought; that's the last thing I remember. After that, it was just... the mask.'

'It's off now; you're going to get better.'

The old woman didn't respond.

'Are you alright?'

'I'm so... tired...'

He felt her grasp loosen against his hand, and the sound of her breathing slowed as the old woman drifted back to sleep.

He smiled. 'Sweet dreams, Yendra.'

He let go of her hand and went back through into Yvona's study, locking the door behind him. He needed to tell the demigod about what had happened. He went out into the hallway, and saw Major Hannia leave his quarters.

'Ah, there you are, Champion,' she said.

Corthie hurried over to her. 'Yendra just spoke to me.'

Hannia's eyes widened.

'She asked what year it was, and who I was, and we had a proper chat for a few minutes; she was lucid.'

'We must inform Lady Yvona immediately.'

'Aye, that's just what I was about to do. You do know where she is?'

'Downstairs in the reception hall, I think.'

They turned for the stairs.

Corthie glanced at her. 'What were you wanting me for?'

'I was just going to go over my new job with you.'

'Aye, that's right; you're my chief-of-staff.'

'Yes. I'll be moving into quarters directly opposite yours, so that I'll always be available if you need me; and we need to start talking about your staffing requirements.'

'My what?'

'Your servants. You'll need cleaners, cooks, a housekeeper. I could get you a tailor, and someone to look after your hair.'

He frowned. 'A cook, fine; but I can look after my own hair.'

She glanced up at him. 'Hmmm.'

'I've had servants before, and not one of them has ever touched my hair.'

'It might benefit from a little trim.'

'No chance; I like it long. I've been growing it since Tarstation.'

'Very well; you're the champion.'

They came to the bottom of the stairs and went through a set of tall doors into a large hall. Lady Yvona was standing talking to a small group of officials in the centre of the chamber, and Corthie and the major walked over to her. They waited until Yvona turned to them.

'Ma'am,' said Hannia, 'could we speak to you alone for a moment?'

'Certainly,' she said. She raised a hand to the officials and walked a few paces away with Corthie and Hannia.

Corthie leaned in. 'Yendra spoke to me; she was lucid for a few minutes.'

Yvona gasped. 'What did she say?'

'She asked some questions, and I told her that you were looking after her. She said that it was the God-King who put the restrainer mask on her.'

'Is she still awake?'

'No. She fell asleep again. She was weak, but she wasn't rambling, and she could hear what I was saying.'

Yvona smiled, her eyes alight. 'This is excellent news. I felt her get a little bit stronger during this morning's healing session; I just need to keep it up.' She took a slow breath. 'This is exciting. If ever I needed guidance from someone like her, it's now.'

A courtier approached, and curtsied. 'My lady, guests have arrived in the palace, and they are asking for you.'

Lady Yvona raised an eyebrow. 'The reception isn't due for another few hours.'

'They're not from the soldiers' families, my lady. One of them is the champion's friend, who has been staying in the palace, a Miss Yaizra.'

Corthie's heart jumped. 'Yaizra's back?'

'Yes, sir,' she said. 'Two of the others are your noble cousins, my lady; Aila and Naxor.'

'Send them up,' said Yvona.

'Yes, ma'am.'

Corthie watched as the courtier hurried away, then glanced at Yvona. 'I'm going down with her.'

Yvona smiled. 'Go, and good luck, champion.'

He raced after the courtier, and caught up with her on a flight of stairs heading towards the ground floor of the palace.

The courtier glanced at him.

'I thought I'd tag along,' he said, trying to hide his nerves.

They reached the bottom of the stairs, and the courtier led him into a small room, where three women and a man were sitting.

Corthie glanced round the room. His eyes flitted over Yaizra, then he saw Aila. She caught his glance and stood. They gazed at each other, and for a moment neither moved, the world stilling around them. She smiled, and they rushed forward and fell into a tight embrace. Corthie reached round her back with his arms and pulled her close, his face in her hair. She touched his cheek, and he moved his face. Their lips touched and Corthie felt his mind spin.

'Hi, Corthie,' she said, draping her arms around his neck.

'Hi.' He laughed. 'How have you managed to get younger? You're just as beautiful, but you look like you've lost a few years.'

'Eh, yeah. I had a bit of an accident with some salve. And what about you? Your hair's looking... long.'

'Aye, do you like it?'

She shook her head and laughed. 'Malik's ass, I missed you.'

'Me too; every day.'

'I was worried that you'd forgotten about me.'

'And I was a little concerned when I heard you got married.'

'I married Marcus so I could get close enough to kill him, that was the only reason.'

Corthie felt a tap on his shoulder. 'Remember me?'

He turned, and his mouth fell open. 'Belinda?'

She grinned at him. He disentangled from Aila and gave Belinda a hug.

'I can't believe it,' he said; 'is my sister here?'

'No, it's just me.' She shook her head and frowned at him. 'You don't look the same. I mean I know it's you, but you've aged.'

'Of course I've aged; it's been five years.'

Belinda's frown deepened.

The courtier coughed. 'Excuse me, but Lady Yvona has asked for everyone to please follow me upstairs to the reception hall.'

'Excellent,' said Lord Naxor, who Corthie noticed sitting by the wall. 'Anything to move on from having to watch my cousin kissing the champion.' They followed the courtier out of the chamber, and Corthie looked for Yaizra.

'Hey, thanks,' he said.

'No problem, big lump. I had a fun time; looking forward to my own bed though.'

'Are you seeing this palace as your home now?'

'Yeah, well it is, I guess, for as long as you're here.'

He nodded, then glanced at Belinda as they began to ascend the stairs. She looked exactly the same as when he had known her before.

'It's good to see you, Corthie,' she said. 'Your family miss you. I missed you too.'

'How are they all?'

'Karalyn had twins. Your mother's... the same as always. Kelsey's fine, and Keir got married to a soulwitch.'

'Who, Thorn?'

Belinda frowned. 'Yes.'

Corthie nodded, wondering if she had a plan to take him home. He assumed she did, but something within him didn't want to hear about it. His eyes flickered over to Aila, who was walking with her cousin Naxor. He might have been prepared for either her or Belinda's arrival, but both at the same time? One was a reason to stay, the other the instrument of his departure. Aila caught his glance and smiled, and he moved to her side.

'It must be nice to see Belinda again,' she said.

'I think I'm still in shock, to be honest. Last time I saw her, she was still very shy and quiet after my sister wiped her mind, and now she's being sent on missions to other worlds. Wait, has she told you what my sister did to her?'

'Yes, she mentioned it. She was trying to kill her at the time?'

'That's right, she used to work for these gods who were hunting my family. Anyway, how have you been?'

'Not great, Corthie, if I'm honest. Terrified mostly. Of Prince Monti-eth, then Marcus and the God-Queen.' She lowered her voice. 'And now Belinda a little bit.'

He raised an eyebrow and kept his voice low. 'Why would you be scared of Belinda?'

'Have you ever seen her fight?'

'No. Well, I watched her practise, but then she went away with my elder sister, and my father was murdered. My mother took me back home, and I never saw Belinda again.'

'Your father was murdered? You never told me that.'

He nodded. 'A god killed him. He saved the lives of my brother and younger sister, but he couldn't save himself.'

She took his hand. 'I'm sorry.'

They walked into the large reception hall, where lady Yvona and Major Hannia were waiting, along with a small crowd of servants and guards.

'Greetings, cousins,' Yvona said, rising from her chair, a smile on her lips. 'I was hoping Aila would come, but Naxor too? This is a surprise.'

'It's been a while,' said Naxor.

'It has. I understand that both of you have had some difficulties with the present regime ruling our beloved City?'

Naxor laughed. 'That's one way to put it. The God-Queen had me in an old-fashioned restrainer mask, and they made Aila marry Marcus. It's been a fun time.'

'Thanks for letting us shelter here,' said Aila.

'You're very welcome,' said Yvona. 'Sit, please, and take some refreshments. Miss Yaizra, my thanks to you for delivering my cousins safely here. And may I ask about the fourth member of your party?'

Corthie sat next to Aila round the table as servants offered wine and a selection of drinks and food. He reached out and took her hand under the table, and she smiled at him.

'This is Lady Belinda,' said Naxor.

'I'm not a lady,' she said. 'I'm here to take Corthie home.'

Yvona's smile dropped for a second, then resumed. 'And do you have a timescale for that, Miss Belinda?'

The god glanced round the table. Her gaze fell on Corthie and Aila. 'Soon. We can discuss it again in a few days.'

'Very well,' said Yvona. 'You are all welcome to stay. The God-Queen and Prince Marcus will no doubt be displeased by what is occurring in Icehaven, and my actions in bringing you here will have cast me into the role of a rebel.'

'We understand the risks you are taking,' said Naxor, 'and thank you for it. Could we dismiss the guards and servants for a moment?'

Major Hannia got to her feet, and ushered the soldiers and serving staff from the room.

'You stay, Major,' Yvona said. 'It will save me having to repeat it all to you later.'

Hannia bowed and retook her seat.

Naxor kept his gaze on Yvona. 'The God-King is dead.'

Yvona stared at him, her eyes narrow.

'And the God-Queen...' Naxor went on, 'well, it's safe to say that Aila and I aren't too popular with her, especially after Belinda almost killed her.'

'What?'

'She's immune to god powers,' said Aila; 'just like Corthie.'

'She knows I could beat her any time I wish,' Belinda said. 'She won't want to face me again.'

'And once you have gone?' said Yvona, her voice rising. 'If you take Corthie with you, you shall be leaving us a little exposed.'

'The internal affairs of the City are of no concern to me. Corthie was abducted from his home and family, and my job is to put that right, not to get involved with who rules.'

'Let's concentrate on one day at a time,' said Yvona. 'The greenhides are at the gates of the Middle Walls and, frankly, we depend upon Corthie's strength to keep us safe. He has killed more greenhides in the last two days than the rest of the mortals of this City put together. This morning he saved three hundred soldiers who had been stranded in a small fort on the Sea Walls. Can we rely on him tomorrow?'

'Aye,' he said. 'I'm going out tomorrow, and the next day.'

Belinda glanced at him, her expression unreadable. 'To fight?'

He nodded.

'I don't approve,' she said. 'Your sister, aunt and I have been searching worlds for you, and Karalyn would never forgive me if I allowed you to get killed. Are you going beyond these Middle Walls?'

'Aye.'

'Then I shall go with you to watch your back.'

'Alright,' he said. 'How's your battle-vision?'

She smiled. 'Adequate.'

Naxor snorted. 'She's a killing machine. I'd take her up on that offer, Yvona, before she changes her mind.'

'I rarely change my mind,' said Belinda, 'and I'm not doing it for the City.'

Corthie laughed. 'This will be fun.'

Aila gave him a glance as the room quietened. His smile fell away as he noticed the serious faces around him.

'I have no objection to Miss Belinda fighting alongside Corthie,' Yvona said, 'as long as it doesn't interfere with his task.' She glanced at the major. 'Please make preparations for Miss Belinda to join our champion tomorrow morning. Allow her full access to the town's arsenal; she may select any weapons and armour that suit her.'

'Thank you,' said Belinda.

Yvona smiled, but her eyes remained troubled. 'I am having fresh quarters prepared, and the kitchens will have a welcoming meal ready for you in an hour or so. I'm sure we all have much to discuss, but I do not think we are yet ready for any major decisions to be taken.'

'Cousin,' said Naxor, a slight smile on his lips; 'may we talk alone?'

Yvona frowned. She glanced from Yaizra to Naxor, and he nodded. 'Very well. Major, please show the others to their rooms while I speak to Lord Naxor.'

Hannia stood, and the rest of them got to their feet, leaving Yvona and Naxor alone.

'This way, please,' the major said, leading them from the hall.

They went upstairs, and the major halted outside the door to their quarters. 'Corthie lives here with Yaizra and another friend, Achan; and on this side of the hall, I have rooms prepared for Lady Aila, Lord Naxor and Miss Belinda.'

Belinda shook her head. 'I'll be staying in the same rooms as Corthie.'

The major glanced at him. Corthie shrugged.

'Is there a problem?' said Belinda.

'No, I can make the arrangements,' said the major. 'Lady Aila, will I show you your rooms?'

'Eh, alright,' she said.

'I'd like to see them too,' said Corthie.

'Of course,' said the major. She unlocked a door opposite the one leading to his quarters, and gestured. 'Here we are.'

Yaizra smirked at Corthie. 'See you later, big lump.'

He went through the door with Aila, then turned.

'Thanks, Hannia,' he said, his hand on the door, 'but I think I'll show Aila round. Bye.' He swung the door shut and turned to her. 'I thought we were never going to be left alone. It was painful sitting there, listening to everyone talk, when all I wanted was to be with you.'

She gazed up at him. 'Who is Belinda to you?'

'A friend. I was thirteen years old when I last saw her; she was like a lost sheep back then. She's a little more assertive now.'

'Assertive? Corthie, she's a maniac.'

'She's not; you just have to know how to take her. Let's not argue over Belinda.'

Aila walked into the apartment and put her bag down onto a chair.

'What's wrong?' he said.

She turned to him. 'She wants to take you home. Why are we bothering?'

'I thought you wanted to be with me?'

'I do, Corthie, but I can't bear the thought of you leaving, and the closer we get, the harder it will be.'

'Let me deal with that,' he said, unable to take his eyes off her.

He walked over to where she was standing.

'I've dreamed of this moment,' he said, his hand touching her face; 'through months of running and hiding, and being chased by Blades and greenhides. Sometimes I almost gave up hope, but it was the thought of being with you that kept me going. I love you so much it hurts, and I never want to be parted from you again. Do you feel the same, Aila?'

Her eyes pierced him. 'Yes.'

'Then nothing else matters.'

She closed her eyes and they kissed, then he picked her up and carried her to the bedroom.

CHAPTER 14

ALL IN

Tara, Auldan, The City – 25th Amalan 3420

Emily smiled at Quill from under her hood. 'Welcome to Tara.'

The sergeant glanced round at the busy streets in the light of the summer sun. Rosers were out shopping, or sitting at tables outside cafes and taverns, while birds were singing from the branches of the blossoming trees that were lining the avenues. The water was sparkling by the harbour, where lobster boats were unloading their catches as gulls screeched overhead.

'It's exactly how I pictured it,' said Quill. 'It's beautiful, but it makes me angry at the same time.'

Emily pointed at a row of grand houses. 'I used to live a few streets beyond there.'

'Have you always been rich?'

'My adopted family was well off, but they had nothing compared to the wealth of the Aurelians.'

'Are you going to visit them too while we're here?'

'Who, my adoptive parents? No. I have nothing to say to them.'

They fell silent as a group of well-dressed Rosers passed them on the pavement.

Quill glanced at them, then turned back to Emily. 'Are you not worried you'll be recognised?'

'Not while we're wearing these clothes,' she said. 'People look at that first here, and they'll assume we're Reaper peasants. Our accents will give us away; you sound very much like a Blade.'

They took a side road away from the harbour and entered Prince's Square. Elegant couples and families were out strolling, and small groups were chatting on the flagstones, while their Reaper servants hung back a few paces.

Emily glanced away. 'I'm so embarrassed at how I used to think. I really did believe that Reapers were only good at being servants, and that Evaders were all filthy criminals. I was just like the others in the Taran aristocracy; I thought I was better than everyone else.'

Quill eyed her. 'A hundred thousand Hammers would agree with that last statement. Malik knows what they'll do if they discover you've slipped out for the day with a Blade.'

'I'm sure Daniel can handle things.'

'That's not what I meant. If something bad were to happen to you here, then the Hammers would march on Tara and burn the place to the ground. You have a responsibility towards them now, and you shouldn't be doing anything this reckless.'

She frowned. 'Is this reckless? We'll be back at the Eighth Gate by nightfall. I don't see the problem; it needs to be done.'

'Your husband didn't seem to agree.'

'No, Daniel thought it was a stupid idea, but he still supported me when I told him I was going.' She smiled. 'And I brought you along as back-up. Do you regret coming with me?'

Quill shrugged. 'I've always wanted to see Tara.'

They went down another street and came to the cliff face, where a set of steps ascended the slope.

'This leads to Princeps Row, where all of the huge mansions are,' Emily said as they started to climb, 'along with Maeladh Palace, of course, which is now empty, I guess, if the God-Queen and Prince Marcus have moved out. Daniel and I were with the crowds in the harbour when Marcus arrived, and we watched the God-Queen anoint him as the new prince.'

Quill smirked. 'Taking your rightful throne?'

'I wasn't married to Daniel then, but that's pretty much what I said to him at the time. I think Daniel spent a lot of his youth wishing he wasn't an Aurelian; the burden of expectation on his shoulders overwhelmed him, and that was before he knew anything about the beliefs of the Hammers.'

'But I'm guessing it didn't overwhelm you?'

Emily smiled. 'Not particularly.'

They reached the top of the steps and turned to gaze down at the view. The town of Tara spread out before them, the red tiled roofs and tall trees shimmering in the bright noon light. Beyond, the blue waters of Warm Bay glistened, and dozens of tiny sails were visible all the way to Pella on the opposite coast. To the left, the white façade of the Royal Palace could be seen, almost buried into the flank of the hillside across the bay.

'This is the image most Rosers see when they picture the City,' Emily said. 'Not the Circuit, and certainly not the Bulwark.' She stretched her arms out. 'This is what they imagine.'

Quill said nothing as she stood next to Emily at the top of the cliff. Emily took a deep breath, savouring the scents of home.

'Right,' she said, 'let's go and visit the mother-in-law.'

They turned away from the cliff's edge and took a tree-lined path leading towards a road that ran along the hillside. The great mansions of the richest families in the City stood hidden among the trees and thick hedges, and Emily glanced up and down the street to make sure there was no traffic. They stepped out onto Princeps Row, and walked towards the Aurelian mansion.

Emily's heart started to race as they approached the huge house. Maybe Daniel and Quill were right, and she was making a mistake, but she couldn't remain on the Middle Walls without at least trying. They turned up the driveway, their boots crunching on the gravel, and Emily led Quill to the side door of the mansion. One of the Reaper servants noticed them approaching and hurried over.

'This is private property; you can't come in here.'

Emily smiled at the man, and his eyes widened.

'Miss,' he said, 'you're back.'

'I am,' Emily said. 'Did you miss me?'

The servant continued to stare, but said nothing.

The side door opened and the housekeeper came outside. 'Who's this? What's going on?'

'I have come home,' Emily said. 'Is Lady Aurelian in?'

The housekeeper joined the servant in staring at her.

'Oh dear,' said Emily, 'I appear to have taken you by surprise. Don't worry about showing me in; I know my way around.'

She strode towards the door, with Quill a step to her left. The housekeeper rushed to block her, his hands raised.

'What are you doing?' said Emily. 'Are you trying to stop me from getting into my own home? I am an Aurelian, and I don't require an appointment.'

He looked uncertain for a moment, then turned and ran into the house.

'He'll be off to tell Daniel's mother we're here,' she said. 'A pity, I would have liked to have surprised her.'

Quill chuckled as they entered through the side door into a small hallway. 'Maybe you should have gone with your original plan and broken in.'

'I know,' she said, 'but that would have made it look as though I didn't belong here, when I do.'

They strode through the hallway, passing the kitchens on the right. To their left, raised voices emerged from an open door, and Emily smiled.

'Ah, there she is,' she said; 'this way.'

They went into a large, brightly lit chamber, where the huge bay windows were letting in the daylight. Lady Aurelian was standing by a table, talking to the housekeeper, her eyes narrow.

'Good afternoon,' said Emily from the doorway. 'What a lovely day; the waters of the bay are crystal clear, just like my conscience. How's yours, Lady Aurelian?'

Daniel's mother stared at her for a long moment as several expressions crossed her features. For a while, Emily thought that she was going to erupt, but slowly her composure reasserted itself.

'My conscience is quite untroubled, thank you. Did you have a pleasant trip?'

'Which one? The journey here today, or the one where I was kidnapped and bundled into the back of a wagon at midnight?'

Lady Aurelian glanced at the housekeeper. 'Some refreshments for our guests.'

'Yes, my lady,' he bowed, then hurried from the room.

'This is Sergeant Quill,' Emily said, gesturing to the tall woman. 'After what happened the last time I was here, I felt it wise and proper to bring a professional soldier with me in case you tried to have me abducted again. Are you in the mood for a civilised chat?'

Lady Aurelian smiled. 'Take a seat.'

Emily and Quill walked into the room and sat on a long, low couch, while Daniel's mother went to her chair by the window.

'I don't need to have you abducted,' she said to Emily as she sat; 'you're wanted by the City authorities for a multitude of crimes, including treason. If I wished to have you removed from the house, I could simply call upon the Taran militia.'

Emily smiled. 'So you've heard about what Daniel and I did? Good, that saves me having to explain it all.'

'Your... followers are illegally occupying a fort on the Middle Walls, and hindering all attempts by the Blades to have you arrested. I must say, you are either very foolish or very brave to expose yourself by coming here.'

'Where else would I go? Daniel and I have done much to glorify the Aurelian name in the last few days; so much so that Lord Chamberlain must be beside himself with rage. Come on, it must make you a little proud.'

Lady Aurelian's features remained stern for a moment, then they softened into a broad smile. 'Yes, I am a little proud. I could scarcely believe what I was hearing last night when the news arrived. My son and his wife, leading a hundred thousand Hammers through the Middle Walls; having to fight both Blades and greenhides at the same time. The name of Aurelian is now known throughout the City. Before we go any further, I must ask; how is Daniel? I miss him very much.'

'He's well. Healthy and strong, and growing into the leader he was born to become.'

'And what about you? The stories I heard involved you leading the assault on the gatehouse, and it was you the Blade officers were negotiating with. It sounds like you aren't doing too badly either.'

'Daniel and I are a partnership.'

'He hates me for what I did to you, doesn't he? I misjudged him, and I underestimated you.'

'He loves you, but he's angry. He thought me coming here today was a foolish idea, and tried to talk me out of it, but I felt you deserved to hear the truth from one of us, rather than from the news sheets. I forgive you for what you did to me, I want you to know that. As far as I'm concerned, it's in the past; over. The only thing that matters is the future.'

'So you didn't come here to mock, or to rub my face in your triumph?'

'I'm an Aurelian and you are Lady Aurelian. I want a reconciliation. We can help each other.'

'Even after I tried to have your marriage annulled?'

'I don't take it personally. You did it because I'm an Evader, not because of anything I'd done. You liked me before you discovered that.'

'I did, yes, but the fact remains that you *are* an Evader. You will never be a Princess of Tara if you are an Evader, and neither will your children. The bloodline would be broken.'

Emily leaned forward on the couch. 'And what if my ambitions stretched beyond Tara?'

Lady Aurelian said nothing for a moment, then the silence was broken by the arrival of the housekeeper wheeling a trolley into the room.

'I have brought the refreshments you requested, my lady.'

Lady Aurelian nodded. 'That other thing we were discussing; do *not* proceed with that.'

The housekeeper bowed as he unloaded a tray onto the table. 'Very good, my lady.'

He opened a bottle of wine, and unwrapped a plate of small cakes, then bowed and left the chamber.

'Thank you,' said Emily. 'I trust we will not now be interrupted by the arrival of the militia?'

'Indeed,' said Lady Aurelian. 'I had to consider contingencies.'

'Perfectly understandable.'

'Beyond Tara? My dear Emily, I knew you were ambitious, but what exactly are you saying?'

'Who better to unite the mortals of the City than a Roser and an Evader? A member from each of the two tribes most opposed to each other? Who else could do it? I'm not saying it's likely at this stage, but it's not impossible. Are you aware of the legend the Hammers have concerning the Aurelians?'

'I thought the news sheet had made that part up.'

Emily smiled. 'Sergeant Quill, you know a lot more about the legend than I do; could you please tell Lady Aurelian about it?'

The sergeant put down her glass. 'Alright, I'll give it a go.'

Lady Aurelian raised an eyebrow. 'A Blade?'

'Yes, ma'am, that I am. This is my first time in Auldan; I was posted on the Great Walls until the greenhides broke through. The Bulwark's always had legends and myths among the three tribes that lived there, and many of them revolve around a figure who will arrive and liberate or... save the people. The Blades have a cult called the Redemptionists, who went crazy about Corthie Holdfast when he was fighting on the walls, but before that it was a dragon; what I mean is that it changes from year to year who they perceive as their saviour. It's not the same for the Hammers. They've been devoted to the Aurelian family for centuries, maybe longer. They have very few books, and many can't read or write, but they've passed on legends about your family, about a Prince Aurelian who once ruled the mortals and fought against the gods, but lost.'

'That part's true,' said Lady Aurelian.

Quill nodded. 'I know; Emily's told me all about it. Well, I saw the way the Hammers reacted when they heard that she'd joined the Rats.'

'Sorry, the Rats?'

'A company of misfits and criminals who got sent out beyond the lines to do all of the dirty work. That's where Emily ended up.'

'Oh.'

'There were so many Blades serving in Medio and Auldan, that the Rats had to get a batch of Hammers in, to fill up the spaces. The Rats have a high casualty rate, you see. Within a few days Emily had a following, and then when her husband arrived and the greenhides broke through, the Hammers revolted. Emily and Daniel led them all the way to the walls and into Medio.' She smiled. 'You can see why the Hammers now believe the legend is true. To boil it down for you, ma'am, Emily and Daniel now have one hundred thousand Hammers behind them, and those Hammers are spreading the word to the Evaders in the Circuit, and soon? Who knows? The crowds acclaimed them as the true rulers of the City and, after what they did, who's to say they don't deserve it?'

Lady Aurelian raised an eyebrow. 'I can think of a few who might object. The God-Queen for one, and Prince Marcus. Without a god or demigod on your side, any revolt would be doomed from the start.' She glanced at Emily. 'I admire what you're trying to achieve, I admit it. I would apologise for what I did, but in some ways it seems to have been the making of you. And Daniel too, tell him I'm very proud.' She sighed. 'However, my earlier point stands. Any war between mortals and gods would only end the same way as the last failed revolt led by the Aurelians two thousand years ago.'

Emily frowned. 'There must be a way we can win.'

'Have you considered contacting Icehaven?'

'No, why would I?'

Daniel's mother took a sip from her wine glass. 'Lady Yvona has declared that she no longer recognises the authority of Prince Marcus, and has enticed an old Champion of the Bulwark to her side.'

'A champion?' said Quill. 'Who?'

'The Holdfast boy. Apparently he's rather good at killing greenhides. So good in fact, that Lady Yvona has given him her full protection, and has let him use the Axe of Rand.'

Quill shook his head. 'Corthie's there? Malik's ass. Oh sorry, ma'am, it's just that Corthie was my friend. I was one of his two sergeants in the Wolfpack.' She glanced at Emily. 'This could help us. If we can get word to Corthie, then Commander Kano would have to guard both his sunward and iceward flanks.'

Emily nodded. 'And he has the Axe of Rand? That weapon was last wielded in the Civil War. Lady Yvona must trust Corthie if she's given him her brother's axe.' She smiled at Lady Aurelian. 'Thank you.'

'There's more,' she said, 'only this time not so promising. You are aware that Prince Marcus has based himself on the Union Walls?'

'Yes,' said Emily.

'Well, he might be there, but the government is still shuttling between the Royal Palace in Ooste and the palace here in Tara. Lord Chamberlain is now in charge of the administration, here at Maeladh.'

'Lord Chamberlain's in Maeladh Palace?' said Emily, her eyes narrowing. 'Perhaps I should pay him a visit.'

Lady Aurelian blinked and shook her head. 'Are you mad? You'd throw away your position by putting yourself in his hands? No, my girl, not while we have some momentum. The time for silly risks is over if we are considering revolt.'

'But I took a risk to come here.'

'Yes, and you were foolish for doing so. I am a little upset with Daniel that he allowed you to come with only one sergeant to protect you; I betrayed you both, and sent you off to the Rats to die.' She gave Emily a wry smile. 'You have much to learn; you shouldn't have trusted me. The fact that I'm receptive to your words should not let you forget that.'

Emily smiled. 'I'll try to remember.'

'Good. Now, Lord Chamberlain has been summoning various nobles to his staff since he assumed virtual control. Naturally, the Aurelians have not been invited, but I have many paid agents among the Reapers that work in the palace, and word has reached me of the plans the government is considering.' She paused, and glanced out of the window. 'It seems that some in the Taran aristocracy are viewing the greenhide invasion as an opportunity.'

Emily shared a glance with Quill.

'Yes,' said Lady Aurelian, turning back to them. 'An opportunity to rid themselves of the Evaders, the troublesome Icewarders, and now the mutinying Hammers; all in one fell swoop.'

'But,' said Emily, 'how would they... oh. The Middle Walls.'

'Did you know that thousands of Reapers are busily repairing the Union Walls? The government is spending what it has on sealing Auldan up tight. You might call it prudence, a precaution, but I know that certain shipments of building stone have been diverted from the Middle Walls to the Union Walls. Once the repairs have finished, were the greenhides somehow to breach the Middle Walls, then who would die?'

Emily's throat contracted, and she thought she was going to be sick. She put a hand to her face.

'But what about all the Blades in Medio?' said Quill.

'That will be the sign,' said Lady Aurelian. 'If they start to withdraw to Auldan, then you will know that this rumour has substance to it; for that's all it is at present, a rumour, pieced together by a dozen different reports from my spies. The evidence is circumstantial at best but, Emily, my dear, does this plan not sound like something that could have come out of Lord Omertia's mouth? Lord Chamberlain thinks in a similar way to your adoptive father; is this not something they would do if they had the chance?'

Emily lowered her head. 'They'd be rid of the Evaders at last.'

'And the rebel Hammers, and the rebel Icewarders. Not even Corthie would be able to kill all of the greenhides if the Middle Walls were breached. If such a plan exists, it would have to be approved by the God-King, the God-Queen, and Prince Marcus, and therein lies our hope, for surely the God-King wouldn't stand by and watch as his people are abandoned to be slaughtered like animals.'

'Are you saying the God-Queen would?' said Emily.

'Yes. I don't think she cares about the mortals of the City, except for maybe a few of her pets like Chamberlain. And as for Marcus, well... spoilt, arrogant, incompetent; need I say more?'

'Thank you for the warning,' said Emily, the nerves coiling in the pit of her stomach. 'I believe them capable of this; it fits with all of the Roser rhetoric that I've heard for years. It would take the City back to the old days, when there were only three tribes, and the rich Rosers and Gloamers will rule, with the Reapers as their slaves.'

'You forgot about the Blades,' said Quill; 'they'd end up as Marcus's personal army, to garrison the Union Walls.'

Emily nodded 'Yes.' She raised her eyes. 'There is much to be done.'

'And how can I help?' said Lady Aurelian.

'You would help us?'

'Have I not already provided you with useful information? Of course I will help you; frankly, I have no choice. You and Daniel have started an uprising against the rule of the gods of the City, and have done so in the name of the Aurelians. If I were to denounce you, then the family would irrevocably split, and die. I'm afraid it's all or nothing, my girl. So, how can I help?'

'Food and gold,' said Emily.

Lady Aurelian nodded. 'I thought as much. Feeding one hundred thousand Hammers will not be an easy enterprise, nor will it be cheap. Do you need administrators? If you're the new rulers of the City, you'll need staff, and if the Hammers are illiterate, then I can provide a large team of Reaper clerks to assist you in the mundane day-to-day affairs. How are you for weapons?'

'We're a little short of crossbows.'

'I'll see to that as well. Be aware that I will delay any public pronouncement in your favour, as my usefulness would decrease if I were arrested or forced into hiding. It might take some time to win over my husband, as he is rather risk averse. However, he loathes Marcus, and dearly loves both you and Daniel. I broke his heart when I had you sent away, and this, I hope, will prove to him that I deeply regret my actions.' She smiled at Emily. 'That's as close to an apology as you'll get from me.'

'No apology is necessary,' said Emily, 'as I've already forgiven you. Everything that you've said makes sense. There is one thing however, that I feel I should apologise for.'

'Yes?'

'Many of the Hammers refer to me as "Lady Aurelian". I corrected them for a while, but lately I've found it easier to let them say it. The legend stated that it would be a Lord and a Lady who would save them and I don't want to, well, disappoint them, I suppose.'

'That's easy to resolve,' she said. 'Let them call you that, because my words are your words. When you speak, you speak for me also. You, after all, will be in the heart of the maelstrom, and from your record so far I trust that you would never abuse the name of Aurelian.' She smiled. 'Is Daniel called Lord?'

Emily laughed. 'Yes. You should see him; on his first day beyond the walls he saw a million greenhides storm the Bulwark; and now thousands of Hammers kneel before him and call him "Lord".'

'I imagine he hates that.'

'He does, but it's growing on him.'

'You know, Emily,' she said, 'I'm glad Daniel married you. Whatever happens to the Aurelians, whether we rise or are destroyed, we shall do so together. Now, I don't mean to be rude, but you should leave. I'm sure you were careful, but if someone saw you on your way here, then you should be gone before anyone from the militia turns up at the door. I have a spare carriage; take it, and travel to our villa in the Sunward Range. I shall send one of my personal agents along with you, so that no one questions your authority on the estate. There are plentiful food reserves stored there, and gold, which I'm sure you already knew, having read every page of the family's accounts. Take what you need.'

'Thank you,' said Emily trying to control the smile on her lips. She felt her eyes well for a second, and she took a breath, bringing her emotions under control. 'This means more than I can say.'

'The Aurelians have been waiting for nearly two thousand years for this opportunity,' she said, taking Emily's hand as she looked into her eyes. 'Together, we shall win, or die.'

CHAPTER 15

THE NEST

The Eastern Mountains – 25th Amalan 3420

Maddie peered through the undergrowth clinging to the edge of the cliff. Far below her was a long, narrow ravine that twisted through the mountains. A stream cascaded down the steep slope, spraying water through the air that glistened in the sunlight. At the base of the valley, the flow of greenhides was unceasing. They entered the ravine from the left, filling the floor of the narrow defile, and surging like a tide. Far to the right, the valley turned, and the greenhides disappeared, charging and jostling their way down towards the plains that led to the City.

Despite their relative proximity, Maddie felt safe. The sides of the cliff were sheer, and impossible for any creature without wings to scale. Instead of being afraid, she felt a profound sense of sadness. The City was doomed, one way or another. She and the other Blades had always joked about there being uncounted numbers of greenhides, but seeing the unceasing flow surge down the ravine, and knowing that there were many other paths through the mountains that were being similarly used, she could see the truth in the joke.

She considered starting a rockslide. There were a few large boulders sitting near the top of the cliff that she might be able to shift, and she imagined the carnage at the bottom of the valley that would result, picturing the giant rocks crushing the greenhides. It would give her two minutes of satisfaction, but would make no difference to their numbers, and would only alert them to her presence. She was fairly sure her little green valley was secure on all sides, but if enough of the greenhides swarmed around it, they might find a way in.

She crept backwards through the undergrowth, keeping quiet as the ravine pulled out of sight. She turned onto her back, and slid down a short bank at the top of the cliff, then got to her feet. The path back down was difficult, and she took her time, scrambling over the rocks and through thick thorn bushes. She found the stream that led to her waterfall where it danced down from the huge ridge that dominated the iceward flank of the valley, and caught a glimpse of the trees and pool at the bottom. Lying stretched out on the grass was the dragon, sleeping in the warm rays of the sun, her black scales shimmering.

Blackrose had returned in the hours before dawn, alone. She had been tired and, after briefly muttering that Rosie was fine, had gone to sleep, leaving Maddie's thoughts racing. Her sister was in the City again, which at least meant that the City was still standing, but beyond that she knew nothing about what was going on. She followed the stream to the top of the waterfall, then climbed down the rough slope to the grass at the bottom. Blackrose had brought back another dead goat, and its carcass sat staining the ground by the side of the pool as flies buzzed around. Maddie grimaced. Unlike Rosie, she had no idea how to prepare an animal for cooking, and even less desire to touch it.

She glanced at the dragon. Her eyes were closed, and the breath from her nostrils was blowing the tall grass back and forward like a breeze. Maddie wandered to the cave and picked up an apple from a crate. She glanced at the tools and equipment that Rosie had ordered at Tarstation, lying stacked against the side of the cave. Without her sister there, all of it just looked like firewood to Maddie; she didn't know how to build a ballista, or whatever it was that Rosie had been planning.

Impatience weighed her down, and she lay on the pile of blankets, staring at the cave wall as she listened to the sounds of the waterfall a few yards away. The little valley was beautiful, but without Rosie to keep her company, it felt like a prison. She got back up and strode towards the dragon.

'Hey, Blackrose.'

Nothing.

'Blackrose!' she cried. 'Wake up.'

One of the dragon's eyes cracked open. 'This had better be an emergency.'

'It is. I'm fed up.'

The dragon's eye remained on Maddie for a moment, then she raised a forelimb and pushed her into the pool.

Maddie shrieked as she tumbled headfirst into the water. She flailed around, then got her head above the surface, spluttering.

'That's what you get,' said Blackrose, 'if you wake a sleeping dragon. You're lucky you're my rider.' She lifted her head and yawned as Maddie glared at her.

'Well?' said Blackrose. 'What's bothering you?'

Maddie paddled to the edge of the pool and pulled herself out into the sunshine, dripping water onto the grass.

'I don't know,' she said. 'I was alone for all of last night, worried about Rosie, and then you came back and fell asleep. I'll go crazy if I have to wait another ten days before you go back to see her; I need to do something.' She sat on the warm ground. 'I actually hoped that you'd bring her back last night, but then I felt guilty, because that would mean that the City had fallen.'

'The Bulwark was quiet when I flew over it,' the dragon said, 'but I could see the thousands of greenhides gathered there, sleeping in the light of the moons. The humans on the other side of the wall weren't sleeping; hundreds were busy, repairing battlements and building throwing machines.'

'Did you take her to the Iceward Range?'

'Yes, it's the quietest place inside the walls of the City. I landed by an old quarry, in the middle of a forest, unseen by any eye, then I watched her climb down and hurry away through the trees. She's a brave girl; she wasn't in the least bit frightened. You, on the other hand? I can smell your anxiety from here.'

'She's a child; we shouldn't have let her go.'

'But if she finds Corthie, then I shall be one step closer to being able to leave this world at last.'

'Is that all you care about? Yourself? You'd happily put Rosie into danger if it gets you what you want?'

'Is this what you woke me for? I don't have time to indulge you in your silly arguments.'

'That doesn't make sense; you have nothing but time, because you'd rather lie about here sunbathing than doing anything useful.'

Blackrose stretched out on the grass. 'I cannot deny that.'

'I need to do something, Blackrose.'

'Skin the goat.'

'No, thanks; I won't be touching that thing.'

The dragon lowered her head onto the grass next to her. 'Then tell me, what do you want to do?'

'Go flying.'

'Should I take you over the City so you can check that it's still there?'

'No, I want to go the other way.'

Blackrose tilted her head a little. 'The other way?'

'Yes, east. I was watching the greenhides from the top of the cliff while you were sleeping. They all enter the mountains from the east before crossing to the plain in front of the City.'

'Of course they do, Maddie; there is no other direction they could come from.'

'But there must be a source; a place where they originate. There were never any child-greenhides at the walls, but they must exist. I think we should fly out, and follow them back to... wherever that happens to be.'

'And if we did this, then will you cease harassing me?'

Maddie pursed her lips. 'Deep down, you probably realise that the answer to that is "no".'

'One needn't delve too deeply to realise that. Will you at least promise to desist from harassing me for the rest of today?'

'Alright. I promise to try.'

'Fine. I will devour the goat, and then we shall be on our way. Shall I leave you any?'

'No thanks; I've gone off meat.'

'Then what are you going to eat; weeds?'

'There's still food left from Tarstation; I'll eat that until it runs out, and then I'll think of something.'

The dragon gave her a look, then turned to the goat. Maddie got up, and walked into the cave. She went to the pile of her things, and pulled an extra tunic over her clothes so that she wouldn't shiver when Blackrose soared high into the sky. The sound of the dragon's teeth crunching the bones of the goat came through from outside, and Maddie decided to wait until Blackrose had finished. The sight of the dead goat had made her want to throw up, and reminded her of the blood and guts she had seen when the greenhides had breached the moat.

The noise died away, and she peered outside, where nothing remained of the goat apart from a dark stain on the grass. Blackrose had her nose lowered into the pool and was drinking, and Maddie admired her for a moment. The black scales were sleek and gave off a dull sheen in the sunlight, and the muscles in her wings and limbs were as hard as granite. A ridge of hardened scales ran down her spine, ending in a long tail that curled through the grass like a snake.

She raised her head from the water and sniffed the air, then turned to Maddie. 'Climb up, rider.'

Maddie walked down the little slope and went to the flank of the dragon. She grabbed hold of a knot in the harness ropes and pulled herself up onto the saddle at the centre of the dragon's shoulders. Slipping the belt round her waist, she buckled the straps and pushed her feet into the holds.

'I'm ready,' she said.

The dragon tilted her head to show that she had heard Maddie, then beat her wings and rose from the ground.

'It is time for another name, my rider,' said the dragon as they gained altitude.

Maddie gazed down as the little valley grew smaller below them. 'A third name?'

'Yes.'

'Why now?'

'With your sister having departed, it's just you and me again, and I feel the time is right. 'Before that however, tell me my first two names, and who gave them to me.'

'Oh, a test to make sure I've been paying attention? Captain Hilde used to spring them on me, but gave up when she realised I *always* pay attention.'

'You're doing a lot of talking without giving me any answers.'

'Alright, your first name is Mela, and your mother called you that just after you were born, or a day or so later. Then your father named you Kaula when you were two years old. I have a theory about what this says about the kind of society the dragons live in if you want to hear it?'

'No, thank you.'

'Well, was I right? I mean, I know I was, but I'd like to hear you confirm it, please?'

'You were correct.'

'What do the names mean?'

'Mela is a word used to describe the dark beauty of a moonless, night sky; and Kaula means a lone warrior, a fighter who charges into battle without heeding the danger.'

'Reckless?'

'I prefer courageous.'

'Why did your father call you that when you were only two?'

'I had not long learned how to fly, when I saw a large flock of gulls over the coast near my home. I decided to attack, even though I was the same size as each one of them, and my father had to rescue me from being pecked to death.'

'Could you not have burned them?'

'Our fire powers do not reveal themselves until the onset of adulthood, which was wise of nature, considering the behaviour of young dragons.'

'So you were nearly killed by seagulls?'

'They were herring gulls with a wing span of a yard and a half, but yes, they almost killed me.' She quietened for a moment as they banked towards the east, the mountain peaks below them. 'And now for my third name, given to me when I was sixteen by my hunting mentor, who also happened to be my mother's older brother. He was the most magnificent dragon I had ever known; he was grey, and his scales shone like burnished steel.'

'And what did he call you?'

'Nathara.'

'What does it mean?'

'She who cannot be taught.'

'Oh.'

'Indeed. I may have been a rather recalcitrant student.'

'I can't say I'm very surprised by this news.'

'In later years, my uncle tried to claim that he had meant it a good way, that I was unteachable because I was a natural, but believe me when I say: that was not how he intended it at the time. It shamed me, but I knew I deserved the appellation, and it was by this name that I was known by many in my youth.'

'So you're Mela Kaula Nathara?'

'Yes, and now you have my three given names.'

'I thought you said you had many names? Three isn't many.'

'The others are earned rather than given. Every dragon has three given names, but they must perform some act of bravery or leadership in order to earn more. Some go through their whole lives without ever earning another name. I however, was a mere twenty-eight when I earned my first.'

Maddie shrugged. 'I'm only nineteen.'

'You are, my rider, but that would equate to an age of roughly sixty or seventy in dragon years. Most dragons are considered juvenile until they reach one hundred.' She paused as she gazed down. 'We are reaching the end of the mountain range.'

Maddie glanced down, and saw that the peaks were lower and more rounded, and were barren. She looked ahead, and it was the same, a landscape devoid of any life excepting the one beast who dominated, the greenhides. They were swirling in a great mass, like a turning wheel, and streams were breaking off, most of which were heading into the mountain passes leading to the City. Others were heading sunward into the desert, or were circling further east. Maddie shook her head as she watched them. The swirling mass measured several miles in each direction; a single, dense concentration of flesh. The dragon soared high above them as the last of the hills flattened into a plain, and Maddie stared ahead as something came into view. She squinted. It seemed at first like a rocky outcrop standing amid the ocean of greenhides, but as they came closer it more resembled a squat tower.

'Is that a building?' she said.

'Of sorts,' said Blackrose. 'You'll see when we get closer.'

They crossed another mile of greenhides, and Maddie realised that the tower was natural, a large mound of rocks and earth that rose almost a hundred feet into the air. Its steep flanks were covered in greenhides, who were issuing from a large hole in the top of the mound. Blackrose flew over, banking a little lower as she went, and Maddie glanced directly down into the dark abyss. Greenhides were pouring out from it to join the millions wheeling on the plain.

'We are at the very centre of the mass,' said Blackrose as she hovered over the mound. 'This is the source you were looking for.'

Maddie started to feel dizzy as she gazed down. She knew she should look away, but she couldn't tear her eyes from the mound. Blackrose drifted down even lower, and the noise of the greenhides' claws clacking off the stony ground echoed up to Maddie's ears as a cacophony. For a terrifying moment, she imagined falling off the dragon's back, and hurtling down into the black pit below her, and she gagged.

'Mela,' she gasped; 'take us home.'

Despite the warmth, Maddie shivered by the fire. She picked up a long branch and poked it into the embers, and sparks lifted into the air, carried on the light breeze into the red sky of evening. Blackrose was lying on the grass close by, stretching her limbs.

Maddie glanced at her. 'You knew what we'd find, didn't you?'

The dragon continued to inspect her wings. 'As you are aware, I have previous experience of greenhides.'

'What was it?'

'A nest.'

Maddie frowned. 'You mean, like ants?'

The dragon turned to her. 'Yes, my rider; very much like certain species of ants. There are three types of greenhide, and it is the warriors that you are familiar with. They have workers too, who mostly dwell in the tunnels they burrow under the ground.'

'How big can these nests be?'

'I'm not an expert, but I would say as least as big as the swirling mass on the surface. It will run deep as well as wide.'

'And what's the third type?'

'Think of ants again; how do they reproduce?'

'They have a... queen?'

'Exactly. There will be a dominant queen at the centre of the nest, and she will have a personal bodyguard of younger queens who, if they survive, will one day go off to found their own colony.'

Maddie lowered her head. 'No.'

'Yes.'

'But that means... there could be other nests?'

'There is no "could" about it, Maddie; it's a certainty. This world is utterly infested. The Grey Isle is the safest place to be, unless there are other islands elsewhere. Each nest will send out new colonies until there is no more land available, then they will fight each other, if left to their own devices. Even if almost every greenhide in this world were killed, it would only take one queen to restart the whole process.'

'How long does it take for a queen to build up a new nest?'

'It might take her a few decades to get it to a decent size.'

'And how far away would the next nest be?'

'So many questions, Maddie; as I told you, I'm not an expert in greenhide studies.'

'Then take a guess.'

The dragon glared at her. 'Maybe two hundred miles? Any closer, and their soldiers would be continually fighting each other.'

Maddie nodded. 'We can do this.'

'Do what?'

She got to her feet. 'This might work.'

'You're rather excitable this evening, rider. I don't smell any alcohol on your breath, so I'll assume the sight of so many greenhides has left you light-headed.'

'I have an idea.'

'I thought you might.'

'If, somehow, we could destroy that nest, then we would be able to seal up the passes in the mountains, and then, that would only leave those who have already got through; no more would be coming, ever.'

'Sit down,' said Blackrose. 'Maybe you should have a drink, then perhaps you would start speaking sense.'

Maddie scowled at her, but sat back down by the fire.

'Let's examine your plan in detail,' the dragon went on; 'how would we destroy the nest?'

'You would use fire, I guess.'

The dragon laughed. 'Thank you for thinking that I'm powerful enough to burn every greenhide round the nest. There will be many more soldiers below ground as well, and even the workers will fight if the nest is attacked. And how would we get to the queen? If I tried to enter the nest, I would barely last a minute.'

'We could still try.'

The dragon growled in anger. 'No.'

Maddie raised an eyebrow. 'Why are you losing your temper with me? It's a sensible suggestion; why don't we try? At the very least, we'll able to see just how many greenhides you can burn.'

'I know how many greenhides I can burn; I've fought them before.'

'Then show me.'

Blackrose turned her head away. 'I do not wish to discuss this any further.'

'Yeah, but I do,' said Maddie. She paused for a moment. 'Are you scared?'

'Don't be ridiculous.'

'I notice that you didn't actually answer the question.'

'Foolish questions do not deserve to be answered.'

'Come on, say, "I'm not scared".'

'You're beginning to anger me,' said the dragon; 'you would be wise not to.'

'Wow, so you are scared. I didn't think you were scared of anything except getting chained up, which is a perfectly reasonable thing to be afraid of. I'm not judging you; there so much about your life that I don't know, but I'd like to understand.'

'You understand nothing.'

'But I want to. I've been thinking all this time that you hated the City so much you'd be happy if it was destroyed, but if your reluctance is down to fear, then that changes things. You said you fought the greenhides before, when they were sent to your world; I'm guessing that it must have been terrible to see the islands of your realm devastated.'

Blackrose opened her jaws and stared at Maddie, her eyes lit with a dark red fire. Sparks flickered from her lower teeth like tiny forks of lightning.

Maddie edged back a little, her heart pounding. 'Did I go too far? Are you going to burn me?'

'If I did, it would be your fault,' growled the dragon; 'you provoke me with your continuous niggling and questioning. You are testing our bond, rider, and while you owe me loyalty, you give me nothing but trouble.'

Maddie hesitated for a second as the dragon stared at her. She knew it would be safer to close her mouth and let Blackrose win the argument, but her stubborn Jackdaw blood refused to back down.

'I am your rider,' she said; 'you owe me an explanation.'

The dragon's eyes hardened with rage, and Maddie saw flames lick the inside of her mouth, catching the sparks that were leaping across her teeth. Blackrose tilted her head at the last moment, and a stream of flames burst forth from her jaws as Maddie dived to the ground. The flames passed over her, incinerating a stand of trees twenty yards away, their branches engulfed in the thick, broiling fire. Maddie gasped as she watched the flames rise into the evening sky.

'See what you made me do?' the dragon said, her voice strained and dripping with anger.

Maddie lifted her head from the grass. 'Your own temper made you do that, not me.'

The flames from the trees started to drop as most of the wood was consumed, and the fires died away.

'I thought you were loyal to me, rider.'

'I am loyal, Mela,' Maddie said, scrambling to her feet, 'but unquestioning loyalty is not what you need.'

'What do you want from me?'

'Honesty.'

'You are wrong about many of your assumptions.'

'Then tell me the truth, or get rid of me now. I'm not going to be bullied into changing.'

The dragon broke off her stare and lowered her head down to the grass. 'You were right about one thing; the assaults upon my world were devastating. Island after island fell, with the accursed gods using Quadrants to transport the greenhides across the sea. Each place they appeared was left lifeless and desolate; like locusts, they would devour everything in their path, until all that remained was dust and dry bones. The hatred I felt for the greenhides at that time obsessed me, and I battled daily, burning the lands they had taken, over and over. In the end we had to capitulate, for the invading gods had made it clear by their actions that they would annihilate everything on my world if they could not possess it.'

'So you surrendered,' said Maddie, 'to save your people?'

'I didn't save them; I failed. The gods enslaved my people, both dragons and humans, as soon as we submitted to them. I too was enslaved, cast down from my throne and wrapped in chains. I was sent to Lostwell as a prisoner, mocked and ridiculed, but even then, my spirit remained defiant. In order to break me I was taken to a vast city that sprawls along a polluted coast; a city more populous than your own, from where the gods of Lostwell rule. There, with my wings clipped, and my jaw forced closed with chains, I was forced to fight in the slave pits for the entertainment of the crowds. Each day, I would be forced into an arena, where I would be confronted with packs of starving greenhides, with only my claws to protect me. They would crawl over me, their teeth and talons ripping through my scales, yet somehow my body survived. My spirit did not. Ten years of this torture I endured, as I regressed from a queen into a savage beast. The physical scars from that time may have faded, but the mental ones remain.'

Maddie watched as the dragon fell into silence. She remembered her last sight of Buckler, struggling beneath the weight of dozens of greenhides as they dragged him to the ground, and shuddered. To think that Blackrose had gone through that every day for a decade seemed too horrible to imagine.

'Is that when you were brought here?'

Blackrose glanced at her. 'One day, for no particular reason, I gave up. I refused to enter the arena, and when they forced me in, I refused to fight. I let the greenhides swarm over me, and resigned myself to death. Despite the agony, it was the closest I had felt to a state of peace since being captured. But the crowd didn't like it, and the fight was finished before the greenhides could complete their work. My owner then decided to sell me; I was of no further use to him. I was too wounded to understand what was happening to me, but I remember waking up in a desert, far from the city by the polluted sea. My injuries had been tended, but I remained in chains. That's when I was told by my new owner that I would be leaving Lostwell forever, to become a so-called champion for a place I'd never heard of.

'Young Buckler had been in the fighting pits too; he was born on Lostwell, and knew no other life, and for him the chance to come here represented a fresh start, a way to redeem and prove himself, whereas for me it was just another owner, another war, another world where I would have to fight greenhides, so I refused to help.' She glanced at Maddie. 'And now you, my bonded rider, are also demanding the same of me; demanding that I save those who have treated me so foully.'

'I won't do it again,' said Maddie. 'What you went through sounds like a nightmare; I understand. Buckler's death… I realise that…'

'I am not afraid to die,' said the dragon; 'I fear being trapped. The greenhides crawl and swarm; the feel of their claws and teeth on my skin; it is too much.'

'Alright.'

'You think me a coward?'

'No, of course not.'

'You do. I am a coward.'

'No, you're not. You are Kaula, a brave, impulsive warrior who takes no notice of danger.'

The dragon lowered her eyes. 'I wish I were. My father may once have been correct, but he would be ashamed if he saw me now.'

'You are a mighty queen.'

'I was.'

'And you will be again. I believe in you.'

'I have failed you, my rider; my fear has paralysed me.'

'Don't be silly.'

'If I did this, would your faith in me be restored?'

Maddie frowned. 'I haven't lost faith in you.'

'You have. There is no need to play the truth game; I can see it in your eyes, and I do not blame you for it. I have disgraced my name and my family. I should have died in the pits.'

'But you didn't, and I'm very happy about that. You have nothing to prove to me.'

'On the contrary, I have everything to prove. Very well, we shall assault the nest.'

'What? You said it couldn't be done.'

'And you said we should try.'

'There are too many of them.'

Blackrose glanced up at the sky as the stars appeared. 'There might be a way.'

'Might there?'

'Yes. It's dangerous, and if I fall, you'll fall with me, rider.'

'I understand that.'

The dragon let out a long breath. 'The salve in the cave; you said there was a lot of it?'

'Yes, tons.'

'Do you remember when I told you that it affects mortals and gods differently? In small doses it heals mortals, repairing their wounds and soothing their pains. In extremely high doses, it does something else. Normally, the substance is so rare and expensive, that this effect is hardly seen.'

'What effect?'

'It heightens the subject's strength and energy, to staggering levels, increasing their aggression, and making them almost impervious to pain. The ruling gods have elite companies of mortal soldiers, who are dosed with salve from a young age to almost mimic battle-vision. There is a cost, of course; exhaustion, injury, even madness can result; I have seen this among these soldiers, they go berserk, and lose all control. I must warn you, if we try this, the same may happen to me.'

'It sounds too dangerous.'

'It is too late, Maddie; I am decided. I shall need to hunt for a day or so, to prepare my body, to give it strength before I take the salve.'

'Are you sure?'

'Yes,' said Blackrose. 'I will prove to you that I am worthy of being a queen, of being a dragon, and to have you as my rider. Thank you.'

Maddie raised her hand to the dragon's face, feeling the scales under her fingertips. 'For what?'

Blackrose closed her eyes. 'For making me face the truth.'

CHAPTER 16

TRANSFORMATION

Icehaven, Medio, The City – 26th Amalan 3420

Aila's fingers gripped the top of the wall, her knuckles white as she stared down at the area before the Icewarder defences. For nearly two hours she had stood on the crowded battlements, her heart racing as she watched Corthie fight the greenhides. It was terrifying, but she couldn't drag her eyes away; she wanted to run into a dark room and hide, and she felt her nerves stretch to breaking point every time the claws swung at him. He was wielding the Axe of Rand with both hands, cleaving the flesh of every greenhide within reach, over and over, leaving their corpses scattered in piles across the broken, blood-stained ground.

She shouldn't have come to the walls to watch, she realised; it was too much. No matter how fast Corthie moved, one mistake would be enough to end him; even a moment's pause or hesitation would be enough. After an hour, the hordes of the enemy in the area before the walls had learned to fear him, but instead of holding the line, Corthie had gone out further to seek them, charging at them wherever they gathered, throwing himself into their midst among the teeth and claws and blood.

Belinda was out there too; and though there was no doubt that she was a formidable and mighty warrior, she had paled next to Corthie. She had recognised the truth quickly, and had ceased trying to stay close to the champion, instead consolidating the ground that he had won, allowing the teams of workers to carry out their repairs to the wall.

The voices of the crowds packing the battlements roared out with every greenhide that fell to Corthie's axe, their cheers echoing up into the sky of another perfect summer's day. Aila hated them all at that moment, wishing she could somehow pluck Corthie out of danger, and take him far away from the baying crowds and the shrieking greenhides. She realised that perhaps that was all Belinda wanted too, to save him, and for the first time, she felt a twinge of empathy towards the god.

'It's quite a sight, isn't it, ma'am?' said Major Hannia to her right.

Aila said nothing, her mouth frozen.

'Are you alright, ma'am? I can take you down from the battlements if you wish, and you can rest until Corthie returns?'

Aila shook her head, unable to tear her eyes away from the champion.

'It shan't be long now,' the major went on; 'the repairs to this part of the wall have been completed, and I'm about to recall him.'

'Then for Malik's sake stop talking to me and do it.'

The major blinked, then nodded. She raised a hand, and a soldier next to her lifted a horn and blew out a long harsh note. Some on the walls started booing as the sound of the horn rose up from the walls, and Aila felt rage rise within her for the ungrateful mortals on the battlements.

Down on the ground before the walls, Belinda raised her sword to show she had heard the recall signal, but Corthie was continuing to press on, his axe hacking through a group of fleeing greenhides.

'He hasn't heard,' said Aila.

'Oh, he's heard,' said the major, 'but it can take a few moments to sink in.'

The crane to their left swung out, and the large hook was lowered towards the blood-soaked ground. Belinda was close by, but she ignored the dangling hook, her eyes on Corthie. The champion cleaved the final greenhide in the group he had been chasing, then glanced around for more to kill. Aila groaned, then, without warning, he turned, and raced back towards Belinda. As a fresh surge of greenhides renewed their charge, Corthie and the god leapt up, each clinging onto the large hook with one hand as it raised them out of danger. The champion lifted the axe into the air as they were pulled up, and the crowds erupted. Corthie beamed at them, the green blood dripping from his face and scored armour, and Aila noticed traces of red from the countless small injuries he had picked up.

The crane swung back over the battlements, and Belinda and Corthie jumped down to the walkway. Corthie laughed, and gave Belinda a quick hug, then his eyes caught sight of Aila, and he bounded over. He flung his arms round her, covering the front of her robes in green blood and lifting her off her feet.

'What did you think?' he grinned.

She stared at him, unable to form any words. Someone passed him an opened bottle of brandy, and he glugged from it.

'Now,' he said to her, 'don't worry about this next bit; it always happens when I finish using so much battle-vision.'

She frowned. 'What do you...'

Corthie's eyes went blank, and he slumped against the battlements, then crashed to the ground, his armour scraping off the rock.

'It's fine,' said the major, seeing the expression on Aila's face. She signalled to a team of soldiers who had been standing by, and four of them lifted Corthie up, and started to carry him down the steps.

Belinda joined Aila's side as they followed.

'I am having difficulty with this,' the god said to her.

Aila turned. 'What?'

'Corthie's powers,' she said. 'I knew he was going be to be special, but I wasn't prepared for this.'

'You're a fine warrior too, Belinda,' said Aila.

'I know that.' She shook her head. 'And to think I came here today to watch his back; how ridiculous that sounds now. I did nothing out there to help him in any meaningful way.'

'Don't feel bad.'

'How can I not?' said Belinda. 'I volunteered to come here to search for him, and Karalyn agreed because I was the best fighter out of the three of us; the one most able to protect him, but he doesn't need me for that.' She lowered her eyes. 'I thought he'd be so happy to see me, but he only has eyes for you.'

Aila glanced at the god as they descended the stairs, surprised at Belinda's words. Despite her manner, she clearly had feelings.

'I've seen the way you look at each other,' the god went on, 'and now I have a problem. What if Corthie's happy here? What if he doesn't need to be rescued?'

'I guess that's his choice,' said Aila.

Belinda glared at her. 'And I suppose you're going to try to persuade him to stay?'

'I don't know. After seeing him fight, I just don't know. I want to be with him, but I don't want him out there every day, while I watch helplessly from the walls, waiting for him to make the one mistake that'll get him killed.'

They reached the bottom of the stairs, and stood by as Corthie was carried into a small chamber in the side of the walls. The soldiers unstrapped his armour, while others took custody of the Axe of Rand, then they withdrew.

'You go in,' said Belinda; 'it'll be you he'll want to see when he awakens. I'll get cleaned up and take a carriage back to the palace.'

Aila nodded as Belinda turned and strode away. Major Hannia approached her. 'Ma'am,' she said, 'usually someone cleans and dresses his wounds at this point, but as you are here, I felt it would be appropriate to ask if you wish to be alone with him?'

Aila glanced around. She had no desire to see his wounds, but dozens of faces were watching her across the packed courtyard.

'Yes, thank you.'

The major bowed, and gestured to the entrance. Aila stepped into the dark chamber, and the door was closed behind her. An oil lamp was burning from a wall sconce, and its light flickered across the bed where

Corthie lay unconscious. The clothes he had worn under his armour were stained with sweat, and with blood of two colours, red and green. Next to the bed was a table, where a bowl of steaming water sat by a large sponge and a pile of clean bandages. She leaned forward, moved some hair from his face, and kissed his cheek.

She felt weary, and collapsed into a chair, as if her love for him was physically exhausting. Her heart was still racing from having watched him from the wall, and her anxiety was increasing at the thought he would be doing it all over again the next day, and the day after; forever, if Lady Yvona had her way. Not that Aila blamed her cousin; she wanted to save her people, so it was natural that she would wish Corthie to stay, but to Aila the thought seemed revolting. Corthie wasn't a machine, he was a fragile mortal who happened to have a gift that inspired jealousy and awe in equal measure. She thought back to when she had known him before, when she had lived in the Circuit, and he was fighting before the Great Walls. She had known then what he did, but it had seemed abstract, and she hadn't worried about his safety. From the moment she had seen him from the walls that morning, she knew that was no longer the case; she would always be worrying about him.

She picked up the sponge, dipped it into the hot water, and began to wipe the blood from his face.

Aila frowned out of the carriage window as the crowds lining the street struggled to get a glimpse of the champion, their cheering and shouting almost drowning everything else out.

'Are they always like this?' she said.

'Aye,' said Corthie, 'but today was only my third time out there. I'm sure they'll get bored of it soon enough.'

Aila nodded. 'I bet there are a thousand women in Icehaven right now who hate me.'

'Don't say that. Everyone loves the image of me, but they don't know me. You know me.'

'Do I? Last night I thought I did, when we stayed up talking, and drinking wine, and... the other thing, but after seeing you today I'm not sure any more.'

Corthie smiled. 'I especially enjoyed the "other thing". We should do some more of that when we get back to the palace.'

'Something tells me you're not taking this seriously.'

'I don't think I understand what's bothering you. You say you don't really know me, and maybe you're right, but that's fine, because we're getting to know each other. I learned loads about you last night that I didn't know, and I'm looking forward to learning the rest.'

'I just... well... I find it hard to equate the Corthie I was speaking to last night with the Corthie I saw out there this morning. In fact, I don't think I can come to watch you again; it's too much for me to take.'

'Because you think I'm going to get killed?'

'Yes, there's that. Also though, you seem like a different person when you're fighting the greenhides; a scary person. You made Belinda look moderate and demure, and she's neither of those things.'

Corthie's smile faded. 'You think I'm a monster?'

'No, but there's a well of violence within you that I hadn't seen before, which runs counter to the man you seem to be when you're not fighting.'

'It's how I was trained to cope with it,' he said. 'For the four years I spent on Lostwell, I had to separate the two halves of my life, and keep them shut away from each other. There's no middle ground. This is who I am, but when I pull on battle-vision and go out to fight, I become that other person, as if I'm in a trance. No, not a trance. I'm focussed, concentrating on everything around me, and I let my body's reactions take over.'

'You enjoy it, Corthie; I saw you.'

'Aye, that part of me does enjoy it. It's intensely liberating. Some people need fear to motivate them to fight, but I'm never afraid out there.'

'That's not normal.'

He smiled. 'I know.'

Aila glanced out of the window and saw the large bulk of Alkirk Palace approach.

'I'm going to change the subject,' Corthie said, 'because we're nearly back, and there's something you should know. I wanted to tell you last night, but to be honest I was so happy to see you that it slipped my mind. I've been sworn to secrecy, so Lady Yvona might get annoyed, but I'm not going to keep anything from you.'

Aila narrowed her eyes a little as she glanced at him. 'Go on.'

'Princess Yendra is alive, and she's in Alkirk Palace.'

She stared at him, but he didn't seem to be joking. 'That's not possible, Corthie; someone's playing a trick on you.'

'I knew you wouldn't believe it,' he said, 'but I'm glad you think me gullible rather than a liar.'

'She was executed three hundred years ago; I was there.'

'You didn't see the execution though, did you?'

'Well no, but the God-King and God-Queen were taking her back to Ooste for that.'

Corthie smiled at her. 'They didn't do it. Instead, they locked her in a prison on the Grey Isle, and Yaizra found her.'

'Yaizra? But Naxor read her mind. If she'd seen Yendra, then he'd know.'

'Aye. I thought it interesting that he asked to speak to Lady Yvona alone yesterday when you arrived.'

Aila thought back, and her frown deepened. It couldn't be true. It was impossible.

'No prison would ever be able to hold her,' she said, 'she was a great warrior like you.'

'She's not the same as she was. She looks old, and frail, but Yvona has been able to slowly heal her a bit over the last few days.'

'Why would Yvona need to heal her?'

Corthie's expression turned more serious. 'Have you ever heard of a god-restrainer mask?'

Aila barged into her cousin's rooms. 'Naxor, you little weasel, are you in here?'

'Cousin Aila,' he said, from where was standing by a window with a glass in his hand; 'how was your trip to the walls?'

'Never mind that. Is there something you want to tell me?'

'There is as a matter of fact, now that you mention it. A delegation sent by Prince Marcus arrived in Alkirk while you were gone, demanding the arrest of you, me, Corthie and Belinda. Apparently the prince returned to Ooste and saw what had happened to our dear old grandmother. The God-Queen herself is believed to be in a foul mood.'

'Oh. And what did Yvona say?'

'She told them to get stuffed. She did it in that polite way that she has, of course. She's always had better manners than you. A "little weasel", indeed.'

'That's very interesting, but wasn't there something else you were supposed to tell me?'

He sipped from his glass. 'No, I don't think so.'

'Really? Corthie talks.'

'But he would never break a vow, surely?'

'Well, he did. He said he wasn't going to keep secrets from me.'

'I see. I suppose we'd better pay Lady Yvona a little visit then.'

He finished what was left in the glass and strode towards Aila.

'You lie to me effortlessly,' she said.

'Thank you.'

'It wasn't a compliment.'

'Maybe not, but I'll take it as one. You don't give out many, so I'll treasure it close to my heart.'

'Asshole.'

'Thank you. No, wait; that was an insult, wasn't it?'

He opened the door and they went out into the hallway.

'And where is the young champion?' said Naxor as they walked towards Yvona's quarters.

'Still having lunch,' she said. 'Did you know how much he can eat?'

'And yet he doesn't have an ounce of fat on him.'

'He burns it all off killing greenhides. My mind is still swirling about watching him in action.'

Naxor smiled. 'You do look a little giddy. How was your night with him?'

'None of your business.'

'Oh come on, cousin; don't make me read your mind.'

She clenched her fist and raised it to his face. 'If I even catch a hint that you've been rooting around in my brain, I will use this, repeatedly, to remodel that face you love so dearly.'

'Such aggression,' Naxor smirked, 'you and Corthie are obviously well suited for each other.'

They stopped at the door to Yvona's study, and Naxor rapped it with his knuckles.

'One moment, please,' came a voice from inside the room.

Naxor leaned against the wall by the doorway. 'It's a pity you missed Marcus's delegation.'

Aila frowned. 'Why?'

'You were referred to as "the dearest wife of our beloved prince" several times. It was most amusing.'

'Ha ha. From a legal point of view, what's the quickest way to get a divorce?'

'Oh dear,' said Naxor, 'haven't you read up on the matrimonial laws of Ooste? They use the same code as Tara: divorce is prohibited. You should have got married in Pella if you wanted a divorce. And an annulment's out of the question, as you'd have to post the papers in person in Ooste to apply. No, you'll be married until one of you is dead.' He smiled. 'Oh, and infidelity is a crime in Ooste too. Maybe I should have mentioned that to you last night.'

Aila sighed. 'So I'm stuck being married? Has the God-Queen recovered?'

'The messenger didn't mention her Majesty's injuries; I imagine they'll cover it up. She'll be fine by now, though; remember that she's literally sitting on a salve mine.' He gazed away into the distance. 'One can only imagine her fury.'

'Belinda should have killed her.'

The door opened a crack and one of Yvona's advisors peered through. 'Lord Naxor, Lady Aila, thank you for your patience. Would you please come in?'

Aila and Naxor walked through the door. Inside, Yvona was sitting behind her desk, while a small group were on chairs in front of her. Half were Icewarder advisors, while the others were dressed in uniforms Aila didn't recognise.

'My friends,' said Lady Yvona. 'This is Lady Aila and Lord Naxor. Cousins, these are representatives of the Hammers, sent by Lord and Lady Aurelian to request an alliance with Icehaven. We have just completed the first of hopefully many fruitful discussions on how best to coordinate our efforts. I will fill you in on the details later, but I thought I'd invite you in to meet them.'

Aila nodded to the small group of Hammers, biting her tongue about the Aurelians as she did so.

'Greetings,' said Naxor; 'how is life at the Eighth Gate?'

'It's going well,' said one of the Hammers. 'The refugees are starting to move into vacant housing in the Circuit, and the Aurelians have secured supplies of food and weapons.'

Aila suppressed a frown at the broad accent. She was dying to ask about the Aurelians, and what in Malik's name they were doing leading a horde of Hammer refugees, but told herself to stay focussed on her real reason for visiting Yvona.

'My advisors,' said Lady Yvona, 'are now going to take the Hammers to visit the champion. Lady Aila, would you like to accompany them?'

'I would, cousin,' she said, 'but there's something else I need to ask you about.'

Aila watched as Naxor's eyes glazed over for a second, then Lady Yvona blinked.

'Yes, certainly,' said Yvona, her eyes tightening a little before she resumed her smile. 'Guests, thank you again for coming. Now that we have established a line of communication between the Eighth Gate and Icehaven, we shall continue to cooperate. Enjoy your visit to

Corthie Holdfast, and have a safe trip home. My agents will be in touch.'

The Hammers rose and bowed, then left the room, escorted by the group of officials.

Yvona turned to Aila as soon as the door was closed. 'I was going to tell you today.'

Aila took a seat and nodded. 'I'm not angry; I'm in denial. It can't be true.'

'It is,' said Naxor; 'I saw her last night. Yvona and I both wanted to tell you yesterday, but you were with Corthie, and we didn't want to intrude. Well, I would have, but Yvona told me not to.'

'And then today,' said Yvona, 'you left in a carriage with the champion before we had a chance to show you.'

Aila shook her head. She began to feel a slow, small, well of emotion building in her that felt dangerously like hope, and she rubbed her face. 'It can't be true.'

Yvona walked from round the desk, knelt and took Aila's hand. 'Cousin, it's true. Our princess has returned. Come,' she said, standing and helping Aila to her feet.

Yvona took a key from her pocket and unlocked a side door, leading to a small bedroom. The shutters were closed, and the interior was dim. She walked in and Naxor followed while Aila hung by the doorway, her fingers grasping the frame. The room had one bed, and upon it an old woman was lying, a blanket spread out over her. Her arms lay on top of the sheets, and a thick bandage was covering the top half of her face.

Aila choked when she saw the bandage, remembering the effect on Naxor after only a few days. She walked forward a pace.

'I don't recognise her,' she said.

'Neither did I,' said Yvona, 'but I felt the power within her. She spoke to Corthie yesterday, and to me and Naxor this morning.'

'You've spoken to her?'

'Yes,' said Naxor. 'She asked after you. Typical; you were always her favourite.'

Step by step, Aila drew closer to the bed. She gazed at the woman's hands, old and worn, then her thin arms. The line of her chin seemed similar, but nothing else. She reached out with her fingers and touched her palm.

The old woman stirred. 'Aila?'

Aila fell to her knees by the bed, unable to halt the tears any longer. 'Yendra?' she sobbed, then buried her face into the blanket, weeping uncontrollably. She felt the woman's hand move to rest on her shoulder and she lost herself for a moment, drowning in a wave of sorrow and relief.

'Everything's going to be fine,' said Yendra. Her voice was weak and low, but undeniably hers.

'She's been getting a little bit better every day,' Yvona said. 'I've been devoting all of my powers to her.'

'Belinda could assist,' said Naxor in a low voice. 'Her healing powers are extensive.'

'Then perhaps we should ask her. At the rate we're going, it'll take many months for her to fully recover.'

'Months?' said Yendra, her voice a whisper

'I'm afraid so,' said Yvona, 'and, if I'm honest, I'm not sure you'll ever be able to see again.'

Something within Aila's mind registered, and she lifted her head. She rubbed her face, wiping the tears away.

'Excuse me for a moment,' she said; 'I won't be long.'

She raced from the room and through Yvona's study, then rushed into the hallway, where Corthie's friend Achan was talking to the group of Hammers.

'Sorry, excuse me,' Aila said as she dodged her way between them, heading for her rooms.

She burst through the door and ran into her bedroom, then frowned in dismay at the mess she and Corthie had left there. Clothes were scattered across the floor, along with blankets and empty bottles of wine. She crouched down, searching for her bag.

'What you looking for?' said Corthie from the doorway.

'Hi,' she said, 'a vial.'

'A vile what?'

She blinked. 'What? No, a vial, a little glass tube.' She found her bag under the bed and pulled it out as Corthie walked over. She tipped the bag upside down, and the contents rained onto the carpet.

'Are those letters?'

'Yeah,' she said; 'from Prince Michael to Marcus. You can read them if you like.'

'No, thanks. Are they old?'

'Eh, seeing as Michael's been dead for three hundred years I would say so, yes.'

She lifted up a dress and saw the small glass vial, its silvery contents reflecting the light from the shutters.

She clasped her fingers round it. 'Got you.'

'What is it?'

She glanced at him. 'One sniff of this was what made me look younger – one sniff.'

Corthie raised an eyebrow. 'I'm hope you're not going to take any more.'

She smiled. 'It's not for me; come on.'

She hurried from her rooms, Corthie keeping up with her. They went into Yvona's study and closed the door, then walked back into the little room where Yendra lay.

Aila nodded to her cousins. 'I'm back,' she said to Yendra, 'and I've brought Corthie.'

Yvona smiled. 'I'm afraid she's gone back to sleep for now, cousin. She told me how happy she was that you were here.'

'I have something,' she said, holding up the vial. 'I think it's pure, refined salve.'

Naxor frowned. 'May I see it?'

Aila handed him the vial and he held it up to the light.

'It's much thicker than the tincture I sell on Lostwell, much more gloopy.' His hand went to remove the stopper.

'No,' cried Aila, 'don't open it. I made that mistake in Ooste, and look what it did to me.'

'You drank it?'

'No, I sniffed it.'

Naxor laughed. 'What? Are you saying that your youthful looks came from breathing the vapours?'

'Give it to me, if you please, cousin,' said Yvona, her hand outstretched.

Naxor looked a little reluctant at first, then passed the vial to Yvona. She strode to the bed, and held out the vial next to Yendra's nose and open mouth.

'Wait a second,' said Aila. 'Just a tiny bit at first; it might be dangerous.'

Yvona nodded, and took a breath. Corthie, Aila and Naxor edged closer to the bed as Yvona moved her other hand round to the stopper.

'Here goes,' she said, and removed the plug.

Aila counted one, two, three seconds in her head, then Yvona resealed the vial as they stared at the bed. Nothing happened for a moment, then Yendra's body began to tremble, then shudder, her arms flailing around, and her head lolling.

No,' cried Yvona, a hand to her mouth; 'what have I done?'

Aila took one of Yendra's hands and held it to the bed, then she gasped as she saw the skin on the god's fingers start to change, the wrinkles smoothing.

Corthie's eyes widened. 'It's working.'

Aila glanced up. Yendra had ceased shaking, but her skin was transforming. The lower half of her face was changing too, looking younger as the salve worked its way through the god's body. The rate of change slowed to a halt, and the room fell into silence.

'Take off the bandage,' said Naxor.

Yvona reached forward, and lifted the white cloth that shielded the upper half of Yendra's face. Her eye sockets were pulsating with fresh blood, and Aila caught a tiny glimpse of an eyeball beneath the bubbling red liquid. Yvona lowered the bandage back into place, then fell into a chair.

'Her eyes are starting to heal,' said Corthie. 'What now?'

Naxor glanced down at Yendra. 'I'd estimate that she looks twenty years younger. Should we do it again?'

'Tomorrow,' said Yvona. 'For now, she needs rest and food.' She glanced at the vial in her hand, then passed it back to Aila. 'This belongs to you.'

'Thanks,' she said. 'Shall I bring it back in the morning?'

'Yes,' she said, 'and thank you, Aila. This could change everything. Do you realise what it could mean if Yendra regains her strength?'

Aila's memories of the last days of the Civil War came thundering back to her, and she remembered Yendra battling Michael in the Circuit, when the future of the City had hung in the balance.

She slipped the vial into her pocket. 'I don't know if I'm ready for another civil war.'

'Then you've come to the wrong place,' said Yvona, 'for it has already begun.'

CHAPTER 17
CASUS BELLI

Icehaven, Medio, The City – 28th Amalan 3420

Corthie stepped down from the carriage, raising his hand to acknowledge the crowds that formed by the palace gates every afternoon to welcome him back from the Middle Walls. Cheers rose up as they saw him, and he smiled despite the pain from the bruises covering most of his body.

Belinda climbed down next to him, her eyes narrow as she glanced at the crowd.

'Is this why you do it?' she said. 'For the applause?'

'No,' he said, 'but I don't mind it. You should have seen what they were like in the Bulwark; many of them used to pray to me.'

She rolled her eyes as they began walking towards the rear doors of the palace.

'Remember,' he said, 'best not to mention to Aila about the wall collapsing on me this morning.'

'Why not? Are you keeping secrets from her?'

'No, I'll tell her; just not right away. She'll see the bruises anyway.'

'Not if I heal you first.'

'You're working in the hospital today; keep your powers for that. Regardless, thousands of people watched it happen. Funny, how I was nearly killed, but not from any greenhide attack, but by a damn wall.'

'Yes, I'm sure Aila will find it hilarious.'

Corthie raised an eyebrow. 'Was that sarcasm, Belinda?'

She smiled and nodded. 'What did you think? I've been practising. I'm still bad at telling when other people do it to me, but I think I'm getting better at doing it myself.'

'Aye, it was pretty convincing.'

'Thanks. I do try to act normally. It's not like I go around upsetting people deliberately.'

'I know.'

'You are one of the very few people who understand me, Corthie. Everyone else here looks at me like I'm crazy. Aila, for example; I think she's scared of me.'

'She is.'

'Why? I rescued her from the Royal Palace, and helped free Naxor too. The God-Queen was going to put her into a restrainer mask; but instead of gratitude, all I get are shifty glances and suspicion.'

Corthie nodded to the guards as they entered the ground floor of the palace.

'They don't know you,' he said. 'They see violence and power that they don't understand, and it frightens them.'

Belinda frowned. 'Then why aren't they scared of you?'

Corthie said nothing as they ascended the stairs to their quarters.

'Do you know the answer, and don't want to say,' said Belinda, 'or are you still thinking?'

'I'm not sure, to be honest. Let me think about it some more.'

They stopped outside the doors to their rooms.

'I'm going to see Aila now,' he said. 'I'll tell her about the wall.'

'Good. If you love her, then you should be honest.'

He nodded.

'Corthie,' she said, 'I've been avoiding this since we arrived, but it's nearly time for a conversation about leaving.'

'I know.'

'Later today?'

He nodded. 'Alright.'

'See you soon.'

He knocked on Aila's door, then entered.

Aila glanced up from a chair, and exhaled. She stood as he closed the door behind him.

'You're alive,' she said. 'Yay.'

He laughed. 'Another shift done.' He pulled off his overcoat and slung it onto the back of a chair.

She frowned. 'Was that a grimace? Did you get hurt?'

'Aye, a little bit.'

'Where?'

'All over.'

'Let me see.'

He unbuttoned his shirt, revealing the huge bruises covering his abdomen.

Aila raised a hand to her mouth. 'Malik's ass; what happened?'

'I got viciously assaulted by a falling wall. Luckily, I'd already cleared the vicinity of greenhides, otherwise things might have got ugly.'

She reached out with a finger to trace one of the bruises down his side, then sat down and picked up a half-full glass of brandy.

'I wish I'd never gone to watch you that time,' she said. 'Before that, I allowed myself to live in blissful ignorance about what you did out there, but now I can barely think of anything else.'

He sat down next to her. 'What have you been doing today?'

'You mean, apart from getting drunk while I wait for you to get back? I visited Yendra, and watched as Yvona gave her a fourth dose of salve. It's working, but it's also utterly exhausting her at the same time, so we didn't have much of a chance to talk. I was worried that she would have forgotten much after three hundred years in the mask, but she remembers everything. I told her about the shrine in the Circuit built in memory of her three daughters.'

'Where we first kissed.'

'Yes.' She smiled. 'I told her that too. Then I tried to tell her about Khora, but she drifted back off to sleep. After that, Naxor annoyed me for a while, going on about how my vial of salve was worth more in gold than the entire City, and how we could be very rich if we sold it on Lostwell. I suggested that he use it to buy ten more mortals like you with battle-vision, so that you could retire.'

He laughed. 'There are no other mortals like me.'

'I thought that many mortals on your world had powers?'

'They do. One of the peoples on my world are called the Holdings, and many of them have battle-vision, as well as other vision powers; that's my mother's side of the family. But I got my strength and height from my father's side, and as far as I know, I'm the only person alive who has both. I think that's why I was taken in the first place.'

She glanced at him. 'Naxor was very interested in learning more about your world. I suspect he believes that there's an opportunity there, to recruit mercenaries or something.'

'That's what the god who kidnapped me was trying to do. I was her first sample. They failed though; Belinda told me that all of the gods who invaded my world were killed. Except for her, of course.'

Aila nodded. 'Do you trust her?'

'Aye.'

'Even though she attacked your world?'

'She's not the same person as back then; she had to start all over after my sister wiped her mind. We had to teach her to speak again, then read and write.'

'Hmm.'

'Give her a chance, Aila.'

'She wants to take you away from me.'

'Aye, but it'll be my decision.'

'And have you decided?'

'No. I love you, and I love my family too. If you were to come with us...?'

'I can't, Corthie. All my life I've been fighting for this damn City; I can't just abandon it.'

He nodded. 'Belinda says it's time for a "conversation" about leaving.'

Aila glanced away. 'Don't let me hold you back.'

'What?'

'I love you, Corthie, and that means I don't want to see you torn to shreds by a thousand greenhides. If your world is now at peace, then at least you'd be safe there.'

'You think I should go?'

'Yes.'

'Then look at me when you say that.'

She closed her eyes. 'I can't.'

He felt his good mood drain away as they sat in silence. He understood what Aila meant, but it still hurt to hear it. He longed for her to look him in the eye and tell him to stay; that one word would change everything, and he would do it, for her. Instead, everyone else was begging him to stay, while the woman he loved wanted him to go.

He stood, and tried to smile. 'I'd better eat something before I collapse from exhaustion. Do you want to come?'

She kept her eyes closed and shook her head.

'Alright,' he said; 'I'll see you later.'

He walked to the door and went into the empty hallway, then entered his own quarters. The servants had been round, and the table was covered in plates and bowls of food for him, along with ale and a bottle of brandy.

'Hey, Holdfast,' said Yaizra from a chair; 'what's the matter?'

'Nothing.'

'Come on, your face looks like you've been chewing a wasp. Is it Aila? What's she done to you now?'

Corthie sat at the table and picked up a fork, but his appetite had deserted him.

'Malik's ass, it must be serious,' said Yaizra as she walked over. 'Gone off your food? Right, I'm heading next door to have a little word with Lady Aila; nobody messes with my big lump and gets away with it.'

Corthie glanced at her as she strode towards the door. 'No, wait.'

She ignored him and left the room. He shook his head and stared at the piles of food in front of him, then heard the door open again a moment later.

'Don't do that to me, Yaizra,' he muttered. 'I thought you were being serious.'

'I'm sorry?'

He glanced up and saw a woman standing by the door. She was tall and powerfully built, and had a demigod sheen about her, though she looked a little older than Aila and Yvona; perhaps as if she were in her thirties. Her eyes were staring right at him, and he raised an eyebrow.

'Hello,' he said; 'can I help you?'

'Are you Corthie Holdfast? I assume you must be. I've come to say thank you in person.' She walked over to the table. 'Do you mind if I join you? I'm a little hungry myself.'

'Be my guest,' he said. 'There's plenty.'

She smiled and sat.

'I'm sorry,' he said, 'it must have slipped Major Hannia's mind to let me know I would be having a visitor, and I don't know who you are.'

'And yet you let me come in and sit down to share your food?'

'You said you were hungry.'

She gazed at him for a moment with her striking eyes, then nodded. 'I did.'

'And there's no need to thank me for whatever it is you're here to thank me for. I'm just doing my job out there beyond the walls, and I'm glad I'm able to help.'

'I'm not here to thank you for that,' she said, pulling a plate towards her, 'though from what I hear, you deserve all the thanks you've received.' Her stomach rumbled and she laughed.

He smiled, and picked up a chunk of bread.

'I was also told that you were always cheerful,' she said, 'but I can see from your eyes that it isn't true, at least not all of the time.'

'I don't really want to discuss it.'

'Love?'

'It's personal, sorry.'

'I think I understand. Love between mortals and those who live forever is fraught with pain. I wish I had some useful advice for you both that would fix everything, but nothing is ever that simple. Believe me though, when I say that my niece feels just as awful as you do.'

Corthie's eyes widened. 'Your niece?'

She nodded. 'You still haven't figured out who I am? You, who saved me from three hundred years of torture?'

'Yendra?'

'Yes.'

Corthie reeled backwards, almost falling off the chair. 'But... you...'

'I am healed,' she said. 'Not completely, but my strength is returning.'

'Your eyes; you can see again.'

She nodded. 'My vision powers are still faint, but my sight has come back. I remember your voice from the prison, when you told me that you wouldn't leave me.' She paused for a moment. 'I doubt I will ever find a way to express what those words meant to me; the first kind voice in three centuries of pain.' She reached out and took his hand. 'Thank you.'

'You're welcome.'

'So,' she said, 'you are a mortal with battle-vision? Naxor and Yvona have filled me in with the history of the champions, though I'm sure I still have much to catch up on. You are also immune to the powers of the gods, I believe, and you are in love with Aila. I loved a mortal man once, so I have a little experience of what my niece is currently going through. We had three daughters together, and then, before I had time to understand what was happening, he grew old and died. We spent forty years side by side, and even though I am now nearly thirteen centuries old, I still remember it all. I do not envy the pain that Aila is going through.'

'Then you think we should end it?'

'No. Absolutely not. I mourned, but I do not regret a single moment. I spoke to Aila about you this morning, while you were fighting the greenhides. She loves you with the same passion that I loved my husband Laven.'

Corthie frowned. 'She told me she thought it would be better if I left the City and went home.'

'Yes, because she loves you. She said the same thing to me this morning, but it would break her heart if you were separated again. She just wants you to be safe.' She paused. 'Is Belinda here?'

'Yvona has her working in the hospital today. You know about her, then?'

'Yes. From what Naxor told me, I believe she's an extremely old god, from an earlier generation. You have powerful friends.'

He smiled. 'Wait until you meet the rest of my family.'

'The famed Holdfasts? The god-killers?'

'Does that not worry you?'

'I slew my own brother, Prince Michael. I am a god-killer too.'

'And you love mortals?'

She smiled. 'Not all of them. I was condemned because I thought they should have the same rights as the gods and demigods. They are not our slaves, they are the very people we are supposed to protect, and by "we", I include you; the powerful, the strong. It is our duty to defend the weak, not oppress them.'

'Yvona was talking about a new civil war.'

'Yes, it is coming, but first, however, we must deal with the greenhides. There's no use in fighting each other if the City ends up being destroyed.'

The door to Achan's bedroom opened as Corthie was nodding.

'Hey,' Achan cried as he rushed out, a folded letter clutched in his hand, 'have you read this? The Just used to belong to the Aurelians! Michael stole it from them.'

'Did he?' said Yendra.

Achan glanced up and frowned. 'Who are you?'

'This is Princess Yendra,' said Corthie.

Achan stared at the god, then sank to his knees in front of her as tears appeared on his face.

'Please,' she said, looking a little uncomfortable; 'there's no need.'

'But,' Achan said between sobs, 'you're healed.'

'I thought you didn't like gods or demigods?' said Corthie.

'This is Yendra,' Achan cried, 'the only one who ever cared.'

'I remember you from the boat,' she said. 'It was you who removed the mask from my face.'

'It was,' he wept, 'and I will serve you in any way I can, I swear it. I love you, every Hammer loves you, and every Evader, everyone in this damn City who has nothing loves you...' He descended into tears and hid his face in his hands.

Corthie glanced at him as he sobbed, his eyes wide. Yendra put down her fork and walked over to where Achan was kneeling, then crouched beside him and gave him a hug, enfolding him in her strong arms.

'We're going to fix the City, Achan,' she said, 'be brave.'

There was a noise by the door and Corthie turned to see Yaizra and Aila standing there.

'What is going on?' said Yaizra. 'Not another one; why's *he* crying?'

Corthie glanced at her. 'He's just happy that Princess Yendra's better.'

Yaizra frowned, but said nothing. Yendra stood, lifting Achan to his feet as she did so, then she walked him to a chair and sat him down.

She turned to Yaizra. 'Now all three of my rescuers are here together, let me say thank you. You could have left me in that prison to rot, but you didn't.' She glanced at Aila. 'And you, my beloved niece, come here.'

Aila smiled and walked over to Yendra. They stared at each other for a moment, then fell into an embrace.

'So, she's recovered then,' said Yaizra to Corthie.

'Aye.'

She glared at him. 'And now I need to have a few words with you, big lump. I went into Aila's room, and found that you'd left her there in tears.'

'Everyone,' said Yendra, 'let's sit by the table. We are all friends, and whether our tears are those of joy or sadness, we can share them together.'

They all sat round the plates and bowls of food. Corthie tried to catch Aila's glance, but she was keeping her eyes lowered.

'Am I invited?' said a voice from the door.

Yendra turned her head. 'Are you Belinda?'

'Yes.'

'You are a friend of Corthie's; of course you are invited. Please sit.'

'I thought you were in the hospital today?' said Corthie.

'I was,' said Belinda; 'it doesn't take long to clear a ward.' She walked over to the table, a suspicious look on her face as she glanced at the others. 'I came in here to talk to Corthie about leaving.'

Yendra nodded. 'Then do so.'

Belinda sat and glanced at Corthie. 'We should do this alone.'

'I have nothing to hide,' he said.

She shrugged. 'Fine. Alright, I want to leave as soon as possible.'

'Why?'

'Several reasons.'

Corthie picked up the bottle of brandy and filled a glass. 'Anyone else want any?'

'Yes, please,' said Aila.

He smiled at her and poured out another measure. 'Right, Belinda; let's hear your reasons.'

'First, there's you and Aila. When we arrived I could see what you meant to each other, but if you're ever going to leave, then the longer you take to do that, the worse it will be, for you and her. If you cut it short now, it'll be painful, but you'll get over it. Next, I've been studying the strategic situation of the City over the last few days, and I've come to the conclusion that it's doomed. You could kill a thousand greenhides every day for a hundred years and it wouldn't make any difference, so whether you stay or not makes no difference either, in the short or long term. Third, even if the threat from the greenhides were extinguished, the divisions that exist in the City are insurmountable. Perhaps I should have killed the God-Queen when I had the chance, but that would have been wrong too. It's not my place to interfere in the politics of another world, and the politics of this world are corrupt and degenerate. In summary, staying here any longer than necessary is a waste of time.'

Corthie exhaled, then took a drink of brandy. 'I'm not sure how to even start trying to answer all that.' He glanced around the table, half-hoping that someone else would say something, but every face was gazing at him, waiting for his words. 'Bollocks,' he muttered, 'alright, I'll try. The greenhides. You're right, I guess, but the Great Walls held for a thousand years, so if we managed to kick them out of the Bulwark, the City could last another thousand. As for the divisions in the City, you and I could probably sort that out between us. I'll take out Marcus and Kano, and you can get the God-Queen; there, job done. Um, me and Aila? I don't really have an answer except to say that she's the woman I want to be with and I'm not leaving her.'

Belinda sat in silence for a long moment, her eyes on him. 'So you're never leaving? Is that your decision? Do you want me to go back and tell your family that you're happy where you are?'

Corthie closed his eyes as images of his family went through his mind. For years, all he had wanted was to return to them, but now that it came to it, he realised that his love for Aila was stronger.

He nodded. 'Aye.'

Aila's eyes turned to him and he met her glance.

'Well, that's ironic,' said Belinda, 'because I can't. Actually, was that ironic? I'm still having trouble with irony.'

Corthie frowned. 'What do you mean you can't? I thought you had the God-Queen's Quadrant.'

'I do,' she said, 'but I don't know how it works. I asked Naxor to explain it, but so far he has been avoiding me every time I bring it up.'

'Then why did you insist on having this conversation today?'

'Because I wanted to know where you stood, and if you'd agreed to leave, then we could have asked Naxor to take us.'

'You were bluffing?'

'Was I?'

'Aye,' he said, 'so you can add that to sarcasm as another of your new skills.'

Belinda turned to Aila and Yendra. 'Would you speak to Naxor for me? Make him show me how to use the Quadrant.'

'And then you'll leave?' said Aila.

'That's what you want isn't it? You win; he has chosen you over me, his sisters, his brother and his mother. Are you satisfied?'

'I know you are in pain,' said Yendra, 'but do not blame my niece for loving Corthie. I listened to your reasons, and I listened to his rebuttal; and a middle ground can be found if we search hard enough for it. Let it go for now, and I will talk to my nephew about the Quadrant. Much has already changed in a short time, and none of us sitting here know how the future will unfold. I know you must long to leave, Belinda, but I ask for your understanding and patience.'

'For how long must I be patient?'

'In a few more days I will have completed my recovery, and will be ready to make a move. May we postpone this discussion until then?'

Belinda nodded. 'And you will speak to Naxor in the meantime?'

'I shall, you have my word.'

Belinda nodded, then stood. She glanced over the people at the table, then walked from the room, passing Major Hannia, who was entering at the same time.

'Your Highness,' the major said, bowing as soon as she saw Yendra. 'Lady Yvona has asked me to fetch Corthie and Lady Aila. A fresh delegation has arrived from Prince Marcus with a new set of demands, and my mistress would like them to attend.'

Corthie got to his feet. 'Sure.'

Aila and Yendra also stood.

'There is something I need to do,' the princess said to her niece, 'but I shall see you soon.'

The major bowed again as Yendra strode from the room. Aila glanced at Corthie, and they followed the major out into the hallway.

'What do they want now?' said Corthie.

'Our complete surrender,' said the major. 'Marcus is threatening a full scale invasion of Icewarder territory if Lady Yvona does not capitulate.'

They went downstairs to a large hall. Yvona was sitting upon a high throne, dressed in long flowing robes of gold and yellow, and was surrounded by her guards and officials. In front of her stood a contingent of Blade officers, who turned as Aila, Corthie and the major entered.

'Please come forward,' said Yvona, 'and let the representatives of Prince Marcus see that you are here of your own free will.'

Corthie and Aila walked through the group of Blades, then turned before the throne.

One of the Blades stepped forward. 'Lady Aila, we are here to return you to your rightful husband. In his mercy, he has decided to overlook your errors if you renounce the treachery of Icehaven and come back with us today.'

Aila nodded. 'And if I refuse?'

'Then a state of war shall exist between Icehaven and the rest of the City. You are hopelessly outnumbered. All roads leading from the town are blockaded, and our ships have cut off your harbour from the outside.'

'Marcus would attempt an invasion of Icehaven, while the Bulwark lies in ruins and the City is under threat?

'His Highness wishes to have his beloved wife by his side.'

'Yeah? Well, if he wants me, tell him to come and get me.'

'Aye,' said Corthie, 'tell them all to come. We're not afraid of the clown who thinks he's a prince. You're Blades, do you remember me? I don't want to fight you; I'd rather be killing greenhides, but I will if you attack.'

The Blade officer scowled. 'You are the traitor who murdered Princess Khora.'

Corthie laughed. 'Are you still saying that, even when you know it's not true?'

'My brother Kano killed her,' said Aila. 'I saw him do it.'

'You Blades have a decision to make,' Corthie said, 'either you continue to follow the leaders who have brought this City to its knees, or you open your eyes and join the side that's actually fighting the greenhides.'

'Thank you, champion,' said Lady Yvona. She glanced at the Blades. 'There; I think you have your answer.'

'Then it's war,' said the officer. He glared at them. 'Understand this – our forces are ready to move up from the port of Fishcross, and across the slopes of the Iceward Range. Your people, Lady Yvona, will be slaughtered because of your foolish intransigence. Corthie Holdfast cannot be everywhere at once; he will not be able to defend your borders.'

The doors of the large chamber swung open, and a huge figure appeared in the entrance, clad in full battle armour, a great sword held in both hands, its tip resting on the flagstones. For a split second Corthie thought that Marcus had arrived, then he gasped as he realised who it was.

'Tell the usurping prince that Corthie Holdfast will not be fighting alone,' said Yendra, 'for I shall be at his side.'

The Blades backed away, their mouths hanging open.

The officer squinted at her. 'Who are you?'

'I am Princess Yendra, the youngest child of the God-Queen.'

'Princess Yendra? But that's impossible; she's been dead for centuries.'

She smiled, but her eyes were like iron. 'I have returned, and once again stand ready to defend the people of this City. I have message for my mother; we do not submit, and we will not be surrendering anyone into your hands. Tell the God-Queen that I look forward to finishing what we started three hundred years ago. She defeated me then, but the war goes on, and I am here to end it.'

CHAPTER 18

RUMOURS

Eighth Gate – Middle Walls, Medio, The City – 30th Amalan 3420

'I'll only be a few hours,' said Emily.

Daniel frowned. 'Do you really have to go the estate today? We're expecting word from Icehaven about the Yendra rumours.'

Emily glanced around the busy office. Hammers and Reaper clerks were working at desks, while Quill stood close by, ready to accompany Emily wherever she went.

'If it's a hoax,' she said; 'it's a cruel one.'

'It must be a hoax,' said Daniel; 'she's been dead for three hundred years.'

Emily smiled. 'Just remember what they said about us. I'm sure many thought that was a hoax too.'

'My lord,' said a clerk, bowing before Daniel, 'I was hoping you would have some time to glance over the plans for the new marketplace that I have prepared.'

'Yes,' said Daniel; 'give me ten minutes and you can show me.'

'Thank you, my lord.'

Daniel turned back to Emily. 'Why do you need to go?'

'Because one of us has to sign off on the latest purchases of grain and wine, and the only secure way to do that is to go in person.'

'But it's getting riskier every day. The gates on the Union Walls leading to Auldan are swarming with Blades and Roser militia; it's not worth the risk.'

'It has to be done, Danny. The government might decide to completely seal the gates, and we have to move as much food as possible into Medio before they do so, otherwise the Hammers will start to go hungry. It'll be fine; I can be very sneaky.'

He smiled. 'I've no doubt. Just be careful.'

Emily glanced at Quill. 'Let's go.'

Quill nodded, then staggered as if someone had pushed her. She put a hand to her head.

'What?' she said. 'Who? But... where... oh.' She glanced up at Emily and Daniel. 'Uh, I think Lord Naxor is in my head. He says he's looking out from my eyes at you now.'

Emily blinked. 'Lord Naxor the demigod?'

'He does have vision skills,' said Daniel.

'Tell him to prove it's really him,' said Emily.

Quill frowned. 'What? Did you hear that? Why am I speaking out loud? Oh.'

'Perhaps we should go somewhere more private for this,' said Emily, glancing at the clerks in the large room.

'I agree,' said Daniel.

Emily took Quill's hand, and led her to a small chamber next to the office. Daniel closed the door behind them, and they sat by a window overlooking the narrow streets of the Circuit.

Quill nodded. 'Alright. Lord Naxor says he's sitting next to Lady Aila, and apparently she once threatened Daniel in Pella.' Quill raised an eyebrow. 'Does that make sense?'

Daniel frowned. 'Yes. I remember that.'

'Lady Aila threatened you?' said Emily.

He nodded. 'She was Adjutant in the Circuit when I... was posted there.'

'I see,' said Emily. 'I hope she's aware of everything you've done since then.'

'Naxor says he has a message to deliver,' Quill went on, 'from Lady Yvona of Icehaven to Lord and Lady Aurelian of the Hammers. Greetings, I have chosen Lord Naxor to speak through Sergeant Quill as the news I bear is of the utmost urgency and secrecy. Princess Yendra has returned, and is alive and well in Icehaven.'

'What?' cried Daniel. 'How can that be possible?'

'Hush, Danny, let's listen,' said Emily.

'Imprisoned for over three hundred years,' Quill went on, 'Princess Yendra has now recovered from her grievous injuries, and has made common cause with Lady Yvona in her resistance to the greenhide invasion, and together they stand with you against the illegitimate regime headed by Duke Marcus. With Icehaven blockaded by land and sea, an assault will be carried out upon the Blade positions by our forces, to facilitate the entry of Princess Yendra into the Circuit, her home. While we do not ask you to carry out any military activity, any action which diverts Blade forces away from the territory of the Icewarders would be very welcome. Until then, we request that you fuel the fires of rumour, spreading the news into the Evader communities of the Circuit, that Princess Yendra is returning home.' Quill nodded. 'Uh-huh. Right, that's Lady Yvona's message, as relayed by Lord Naxor.'

'Thank you,' said Emily. She glanced at Daniel. 'I assume we accept?'

'Yes,' he said, 'though I'm still struggling to believe it.'

'Sergeant Quill,' said Emily, 'please tell them that we acknowledge their message, and will carry out their requests.'

Quill smiled. 'He can hear what you say, ma'am, and he can see you, remember?'

Emily waved. 'Hi, Naxor.'

'He has a question from Corthie; yeah... Alright, though I can answer this one myself. Where is Blackrose? Good question, Corthie. She was last seen flying iceward from the City with Maddie Jackdaw on her back. Yes. I know because I was there, and so were Emily and Daniel, I mean Lord and Lady Aurelian. Yes, we waited, all night.' She glanced up. 'Do you have any questions?'

Emily gave a wry smile. 'Any suggestions on how we deal with Lady Jade? She's occupying almost a square mile of the Circuit, and has forced every resident out, or killed them. Or worse.'

Quill went quiet for a moment, then she nodded. 'Princess Yendra says that she will deal with Lady Jade when she arrives in the Circuit.'

'Excellent,' said Emily. 'I couldn't have asked for more; thank you. Before you go, there's one more thing I want to tell you. I was in Tara a few days ago, and I heard a rumour. I don't know if it's true, but the source is someone I trust. Apparently, there is a faction within the government that wants to seal the gates in the Union Walls, and then allow the Middle Walls to be breached, so that the greenhides will destroy everyone in Medio.' She paused. 'As I said, I don't know if it's true, but I do know what the Taran aristocracy are like, and I believe they are capable of carrying this out.'

Quill nodded again. 'Naxor has passed your message on, and Lady Yvona thanks you for it, and for your alliance. She bids you well, and will be in contact soon. Farewell.' She blinked. 'He's gone; Naxor's gone.'

Emily glanced at Daniel. 'Princess Yendra's on our side?' She smiled. 'That'll put the fear up Marcus. They called him "duke", did you hear? We should do the same.'

He glanced at her, his features muted. 'Once they hear the rumours have been confirmed, the Evaders are going to erupt. The only thing that's been keeping them fairly settled are the huge numbers of Blades on the streets. Many of the Hammers will get involved too, there will be no way to stop that.'

Emily frowned. 'Then we'd better be prepared. They didn't give us any indication of when their assault was going to occur, but I assume it'll be in the next few days.' She glanced at Quill. 'This knowledge is for us three only, no one else must know. We can organise some diversions without telling anyone why.'

Quill nodded. 'Yes, ma'am.'

'How do you feel?' Emily said. 'What was it like having Lord Naxor in your head? Did he ask permission first?'

'He did, but it was still a shock. I mean, he had to come into my head to ask if it was alright to come into my head. He didn't pry, though, well, at least he said he didn't.'

Emily nodded. 'We should go.'

'Are you still going to travel to the estate after that?' said Daniel.

'I have to,' she said, 'Yendra or no Yendra, the Hammers need to eat.'

The summer sky was streaked in pinks and reds, with a band of blue overhead. Emily, Quill and two Hammer guards took a cart from the Eighth Gate, and joined the main road that led from Port Sanders to Tara. Groups of Sander militia were based on the roads that led sunward, blocking any Hammers from approaching the town walls of Port Sanders, but they were too few in number to stop the spread of refugees over the rest of their territory.

The four occupants of the cart were posing as Sander peasants, dressed in the simple, almost rustic clothes worn by that section of the tribe. Emily could do a passable Sander accent, and had instructed her three companions from the Bulwark to leave the talking to her. The two guards sat on the back of the cart, while Quill took the reins next to Emily on the driver's bench. They took an hour to make their way through the crowds of Hammers, and the lines of tents that criss-crossed the farm lands of Sander territory, and then they passed into the relative quiet of the road to the Union Walls.

Emily's nerves tightened a little as they approached the gate leading to Auldan. On previous days, they had gone straight through the Union Walls without stopping, but she could see a long queue stretching for at least half a mile up to the gates. Quill slowed the carriage down as they joined the back of the line.

'This doesn't look good,' she said.

'It might add an hour onto our journey, I guess,' said Emily, trying to sound nonchalant.

'Should we turn around?'

'We can't. If we don't get the purchase orders signed off, then tons of grain will be stuck on the other side of the walls.'

'But what if they're looking for us? Well, for you, ma'am?'

'They won't be; this is just the first stage in sealing the Union Walls completely.'

Quill frowned, looking unconvinced.

'It must have been nice,' Emily said, changing the subject, 'getting to speak to Corthie again. He was your friend, wasn't he?'

'He was.'

'What's he like?'

'Well, he's the best fighter I've ever seen; fearless in battle, though a bit reckless too.' She smiled. 'I think I spent more time trying to keep him out of trouble when he wasn't beyond the walls fighting greenhides. He was easily bored.'

'And what's he like to, you know, look at?'

Quill eyed her. 'Are you asking me if he's good-looking?'

'I'm just trying to get a complete picture of him in my head.'

'He's tall, like a warrior-god.'

'Though not as tall as Marcus, I'd imagine?'

'No, he's taller, by an inch or so; a fact which pleased him greatly.'

'So he's vain?'

'Not particularly, but he knew how much it annoyed Marcus. He drinks too much when he's bored, which could be irritating.'

'He has a temper when he's drunk?'

'No, the opposite; he thinks everything is hilarious, and he doesn't care what he says to anyone. It could be quite trying at times, when I lived with him.'

Emily frowned. 'You lived together? You didn't tell me this.'

'Not like that. I stayed in my own room, and we were just friends.'

'Do I sense a tiny edge of disappointment in your voice?'

Quill smiled. 'No. I did fancy him for a while when he first arrived, but he didn't really seem interested in being intimate with anyone. And beside, he had a crowd of devoted followers, many of whom were young women chasing him.'

'I bet he had the time of his life.'

'As far as I know,' Quill said, 'he didn't sleep with anyone, well, I never saw him bring anyone back to his quarters, and I lived next door. And then he met Aila.'

'You've met her too, haven't you? She must be pretty special, to have Marcus and Corthie pursuing her.'

'She's beautiful, but not really what you'd imagine Corthie's type to be like; he's loud and out-going, while she seems more like an introvert. She doesn't have that arrogant tone that Kano has, for example.'

'So we have to assume that she was forced into marrying Marcus, and then ran away at the first opportunity?'

'I would think so.'

Emily nodded. 'Icehaven seems to be growing stronger all the time. Corthie, Aila, Naxor, and now Yendra. Lady Yvona must be pleased.'

'Yeah. It would be handy if we had a few of them down here helping us.'

'Yes, but in a way I'm glad we don't. We're supposed to be representing the mortals of the City; if we had demigods helping us too closely, then it would hurt our cause. However we word it, one of our main aims is the restoration of mortal rule over the City and, though I'm glad they're on our side, I hope the immortals in Icehaven realise that.'

Quill glanced at her. 'I wouldn't worry that the Hammers will desert the Aurelians and follow Yendra instead; that's never going to happen, but the Evaders? They love Yendra. Daniel was right, the Circuit's going to erupt.'

Emily looked up as Quill urged the ponies onward. They were getting close to the front of the queue, and she could see soldiers stopping the wagons and carriages ahead of them.

'Remember to let me do the talking.'

'Yes, ma'am.'

The cart moved forward another place and a small group of Blades approached.

One glanced up at the driver's bench. 'Tribe and destination?'

'You're asking for people's tribes now?' Emily said.

'We are.'

Emily nodded. 'We're Sanders, heading towards the grain depot in the Sunward Range.'

The officer frowned. 'You sound a little posh for a Sander, ma'am.'

'My family moved there from Roser territory when I was young.'

He nodded, his eyes ranging over the other three on the cart. 'As of this morning,' he said, 'no Hammers, Evaders or Icewarders are being allowed access to Auldan. I'm afraid I'm going to have to ask your companions to bare their left arms for me.'

Emily raised an eyebrow as her heart started to race.

Quill leaned over. 'May I have a quiet word, Lieutenant?'

The officer frowned. 'You're a Blade; why are you not with your unit?'

Quill opened her clenched fist to reveal the sergeant pin resting in her palm. 'Because I'm part of a team infiltrating the Hammer rebels, sir.'

The lieutenant gazed at the badge. 'And who is your commanding officer?'

'Captain Hilde, of the Fourteenth Support Battalion, Auxiliary Detachment Number Three.'

'That's not a unit I'm aware of.'

Quill shrugged. 'That's the idea, sir. Captain Hilde reports directly to Commander Kano.'

'And your name?'

'Sergeant Jackdaw, sir.'

The officer quietened for a moment as he wrote in a small notepad. He glanced up. 'Alright, on your way.'

'Thank you, sir. You'll forgive me for not saluting; I'm supposed to be a Sander.'

The officer frowned, then waved them on. Quill gripped the reins, and the ponies started trotting forwards, pulling them under the arched entrance to the gate. They went through, and emerged back into the sunshine on the other side, where large groups of soldiers were stationed by the road. Workers were also there in numbers, swarming over the battlements and stretches of the Union Walls, carrying out repairs.

'Quick thinking, Sergeant Jackdaw,' said Emily, as they pulled away along the road, leaving the wall behind them.

'Thanks, but it's the kind of trick that'll only work once. Everything I told them will slowly make its way up the chain of command until it reaches Kano, who is one of the only Blades who knew what Captain Hilde was really doing. We're lucky they're not checking anyone trying to leave Auldan.'

They came to a junction, and Quill urged the ponies onto a track to the left that led into the Sunward Range. The vineyards and farms of Roser territory stretched across the terraced flanks of the hills, and they started to climb.

'I've been thinking about the plan that your mother-in-law told us about,' Quill said as the cart bumped along the dusty track. 'What about the Sanders? I can see the logic for the government wanting rid of the Icewarders, Evaders and Hammers, but the Sanders have always been loyal.'

'Maybe Lady Lydia has been tipped off,' said Emily; 'maybe she's repairing the walls of Port Sanders? We wouldn't know, because the Sander militia are not letting anyone get close to the town.'

'But only a quarter of them actually live within the walls of Port Sanders. Are the rest just being abandoned?'

'I don't know. If Lord Naxor enters your head again, we should ask him to make contact with his sister Lydia. If she knew the truth, she might be willing to be a little more helpful.'

'Or it could alert our enemies to the fact that we're aware of what they're planning to do.'

'I think it's worth the risk.'

Quill nodded. 'You're the boss.'

The cart pulled them down a long, winding road through a valley, and Emily could make out the start of the Aurelian estate. The large villa sat proud on the top of a low ridge, over-looking the acres of vineyards surrounding it, while Reaper peasants were out working in the sunshine. A few hundred yards down the slope from the villa was a cluster of large barns, packed full of grain and other supplies ordered by the Aurelians. The expense of feeding the Hammers was enormous, but so far Lady Aurelian's promise had held, and huge amounts had been purchased in her name, ready to be transported to Medio.

Emily glanced up at the sprawling villa where she had first met Daniel the previous summer. So much had happened to her since then that she felt like a different person.

She smiled at Quill as the sergeant steered the cart up the driveway towards the villa. 'Let's get to work.'

After three hours of checking inventory and signing purchase documents, Emily and Quill re-boarded the cart for the journey back to Medio. With the hard work done, Emily rested in the back of the cart, watching as the afternoon sky changed from pink to red. The gate on the Union Walls was as busy as ever, but with the soldiers only stopping vehicles trying to enter Auldan, they were allowed back into Medio without any trouble. They were a mile into Sander territory when the sun began to lower in the sky, casting thick shadows across the road and fields that lay to either side.

'I'm looking forward to a bath,' said Quill. 'All this dust gets everywhere.'

Emily nodded. 'I wonder how Daniel's been getting on with spreading the rumour.'

'It's not exactly a rumour though, is it? It's true.'

'Many won't believe it until they see her.'

'I don't know about that; the Evaders are pretty gullible.'

'Hey, I'm an Evader, remember?'

'Oh yeah,' Quill laughed. 'Whoops.'

The road curved to the right round the base of a spur of the Sunward Range, and entered the thick shadows by a stand of trees.

Quill squinted into the gloom. 'Something's wrong.'

Emily frowned. 'What?'

A dozen armoured soldiers sprang out from the shade of the trees in front of them, crossbows pointed up at the driver's bench. Emily turned, and saw a similar number appear behind them.

'Stop the cart!' cried a Blade officer on the road, his hand raised. 'Stop or we'll loose upon you.'

Quill glanced at Emily, then pulled on the reins, and the ponies slowed to a halt as the soldiers surrounded them.

The officer strode forward. 'Emily Aurelian, you are under arrest.'

The two Hammers in the back of the cart reached for their swords, but Emily raised her hand to stop them.

'Get off the cart,' said the officer, 'all of you.'

Emily kept her hands raised, and stepped down onto the dusty ground.

The officer nodded. 'Line up.'

Quill joined Emily by the side of the cart, and their two guards climbed down and did the same.

The officer walked up to Emily, two Blades at his back. 'Turn around and lower your hands.'

She did so, and her wrists were gripped and brought together behind her back, then a cord was tied to bind them.

'The rest of you,' said the officer, 'bare your left arms.'

Quill and the two guards complied, and the officer inspected them.

'A Blade?' he said to Quill, shaking his head. 'Treacherous bitch.' He glanced at the two Hammers, then turned to the soldiers. 'Tie the wrists of the Blade, then take these two into the woods and execute them.'

'Yes, sir,' said one of the soldiers.

The two Hammers tried to run, breaking away across the road as the Blades levelled their crossbows. The first fell almost immediately, a bolt striking him in the centre of his back, while the other made it as far as the edge of the trees before tumbling to the ground as two bolts drove into him.

'Murderers,' said Emily, her eyes glowing with rage; 'you killed them because they were Hammers and for no other reason.'

'They were traitors,' the officer said, 'as are you.'

'You are the ones betraying the people of the City,' Emily said. 'Do you think Duke Marcus gives a damn about your lives?'

The officer raised his hand and struck Emily across the mouth. She tried to suppress the pain, but could feel her eyes welling.

She spat out blood from her mouth. 'You're just a bully, like your master.'

He raised his hand again, forming it into a fist as he glared at her, then he lowered it.

'I was ordered to bring you back in one piece, but you're trying my patience.' He turned to his soldiers. 'Gag her, so I don't have to listen to any more of her childish nonsense; then get her and the Blade into the wagon.'

A small group of Sander peasants approached, walking home from work. They paused as they saw the soldiers blocking the road, watching as a Blade tied a thick cloth gag over Emily's face.

Quill turned to them. 'Lady Aurelian is being arrested. Emily Aurelian; tell everyone!'

The officer shook his head. 'Gag her too.'

The peasants' eyes widened, but they remained where they were, staring in silence at Emily, and at the bodies of the two slain Hammers.

Emily and Quill were pushed out onto the road, and led along it for two hundred yards as the sky darkened. At the far end of the bend, a large wagon was parked by the verge, and the Blades pushed the two prisoners up into the back. Soldiers piled in with them, and their ankles were bound to iron rings embedded in the thick floor planks. The officer peered into the covered rear of the wagon, nodded, then walked round to the front, and within a few seconds, the wagon got underway. It took a left and turned towards the dense outer suburbs of the Circuit.

The journey across the Circuit took hours as the wagon inched its way through the narrow streets. Due to the proximity of Lady Jade's residence, they had to skirt round several areas before turning towards the Middle Walls. All along the way, Evaders were coming out onto the streets, or taking to the flat roofs of the cramped, concrete housing blocks. They paid no attention to the wagon, apart from flinging a few insults at the Blades on the driver's bench, but their numbers were growing as the evening gave way to night.

Running battles between the Evaders and Blade soldiers started to break out around them, and civilians were hurling slabs of concrete from the roofs down onto the soldiers in the alleys below. Children and old folk were among them, as if the entire population had left their homes to take to the streets. The noise they made was deafening; drumbeats, whistles, and from thousands of iron pots and pans being banged off walls. Emily hoped the rioters would attack the wagon, but it pushed onwards, the armed Blades at the rear keeping the Evaders from getting too close.

Emily guessed that it was close to midnight by the time they reached the Sixth Gate on the Middle Walls, and she could see more than a dozen pillars of flame rising above the Circuit from the back of the wagon. Her wrists were aching, and she could taste blood in her mouth from being struck by the officer.

She kept her head raised as she was led down from the wagon into the walled forecourt of the Sixth Gate. It was packed with Blades, most of whom were staring at her and Quill. They were escorted into the ground floor of the gatehouse, and then taken down a level to a row of dank, stone chambers, their floors covered in filth and old straw. Blades lined the wall opposite the cells, each with a crossbow ready in their hands.

Emily was turned around, then the gag was removed, and she felt the cords at her wrist fall away as a knife slashed through them. She was shoved forward into a dark cell, and the barred gate was swung shut behind her. She turned, and watched as Quill was pushed into the next cell along. Many of the soldiers filed out of the passageway, leaving a squad to guard the cells, and Emily sat down on the low stone bench that ran down the side of the wall. There were no windows in the chamber, and the only light was coming from a solitary lamp in the passageway.

She prepared herself for a long wait, but barely ten minutes had passed before the door to the passageway opened, and an enormous figure strode in, wearing armour. He walked until he was standing in front of her cell, stared at her for a moment, then laughed. Emily frowned at him. He was massively-built, but his face looked fresh and young.

'Emily Aurelian,' he said, 'do you know who I am?'

She remained sitting on the bench, her back leaning against the wall. 'I'm guessing you're Kano.'

'Correct. I am Commander of the Blades,' he said, 'and you are now in my custody. Betrayed, arrested and brought to me, all in one evening. Do you want to know who betrayed you?'

'Not really.'

'It was one of your Reaper clerks,' he went on. 'He sent me a message as soon as you arrived at the Aurelian villa.' He shook his head. 'Reapers, eh? You just can't trust them.'

'Are you going to put me on trial?'

'I don't need to; I'm the sole government authority in Medio, and my word here is law. I can judge you myself. It's quite simple; if you cooperate, then I shall be merciful, but if you decide to resist, then I will torture you to death.'

'You coward. You have battle-vision, yes? How many greenhides have you killed today? While you were running away to catch a boat from Salt Quay, we were fighting in the Bulwark, trying to protect the people, in others words, doing your job for you. You're a disgrace to the City. You think you rule Medio, but you don't. The Icewarders and Hammers have slipped out of your grasp, and the Evaders will soon follow them.'

He laughed again. 'That was quite a rant. I can see I'm going to have fun breaking you.'

Emily kept her face calm, despite the burning anger she felt. 'I feel sorry for you. The only reason that Duke Marcus put you in charge of

Medio is because he plans to abandon it to the greenhides. He thinks you're expendable; either that, or he wants you to get killed.'

'Is that the best you can do?' he said. 'Make up some garbage about Medio? The Middle Walls are strong, and they'll hold; the only danger to Medio are the Aurelians and the traitors in Icehaven. Talking of which, the first thing I want you to do for me is publicly deny the absurd stories saying that Princess Yendra has returned from the grave. Consider it a little test. If you refuse, then I will hurt you.'

Emily smiled. 'You really don't know about Marcus's plan, do you? The work on repairing the Union Walls is nearly finished, and the Blades have almost sealed the gates already. Think about it, Kano, who would die if the Middle Walls are breached? The Evaders?' She snorted. 'As if anyone in Auldan cares about them. The Icewarders? The Hammers? Damn rebels, the lot of them. Do you see what I mean? Now ask yourself, knowing what you know about Marcus, would you say that he was capable of this? And if he was, would he tell you?'

The tiniest flicker of doubt crossed Kano's face. 'You're lying.'

'Has Marcus requested any units of the Blades to pull back into Auldan yet?'

Kano said nothing, his frown deepening.

'Oh, so he has? It's started, then. Ponder that, Commander of Medio.'

'You have until dawn,' he said. 'When I return, I will give you one final chance to cooperate. To be honest with you, I hope you decide to keep refusing, for I am already dreaming up ways to cause you pain.'

He turned, and strode from the passageway, leaving the squad of soldiers by the far wall. Emily closed her eyes as soon as the door swung shut, her nerves twisted into a knot of fear. She had brazened it out, but her courage had limits.

'You did well, Emily,' whispered Quill from the neighbouring cell.

'Well? Quill, I'm terrified.'

'I watched you lead the attack on the Eighth Gate; you're the bravest person I know. And listen; word will be spreading that you've been arrested. Right now, a hundred thousand Hammers will be starting to look for you; Daniel will be looking for you. Stay strong.'

Emily slowed her breathing. She feared the coming dawn, but she also knew that whatever happened, she had won. If Kano killed her, then she would become a martyr to the Hammers, if he didn't, then she would still be alive, and capable of resisting. What she would never do, she knew, was betray Daniel or the Hammers. She was an Aurelian.

CHAPTER 19

FALL OF A QUEEN

The Eastern Mountains – 30th Amalan 3420

Maddie aimed the crossbow at the tree, one eye closed as she squinted down the shaft, then loosed. The bolt flew through the air, missing the trunk by a foot as it whistled past.

'Damn it,' she muttered. She reached out with her right hand, took another bolt from the bag, then began to reload the bow.

'For five days,' Blackrose said, 'you have lain upon the grass and loosed bolt after bolt at the nearby trees. Tell me, how many times has your aim been true?'

Maddie frowned at her as she pulled the drawstring back. 'Today or altogether?'

'Let's start with today, shall we?'

'Four times,' Maddie said.

'And altogether?'

'Eh, six times.'

'Well, at least you're improving. Still, with those odds, I think I'd prefer it if you were to leave the bow here.'

'No chance,' she said. 'I'm taking the bow with us; you'll need some protection if a greenhide tries to jump on your back.'

'Yes, however it seems at present more likely that I shall be hit, rather than any greenhide.'

'Yeah, but one of these bolts would be like a pinprick to you.'

'Really? Shall I stick some pins into you so that you can feel what it's like?'

'I'm not going to sit up there on the harness without a weapon; you've got fire and claws, and I need something too, otherwise, well, I'm just a passenger.'

'Fine, you can bring it, but please, do not use it unless your own life is threatened. And you're not a passenger, you're my rider, and there is a world of difference.'

'Yeah?' She frowned. 'I don't see it. Why did the dragons on your world bother with having riders anyway? It's not like I do much up there that's of any use.'

'The roots of the bond between dragon and rider go back many centuries. Remember that, long ago, the humans were our slaves, and generations passed when their purpose was purely to serve us. To that end, dragons started carrying slaves around with them, chattel who could take care of the mundane tasks that the dragons felt themselves above doing; like gathering food, and building shelters and so on.

'The long unwinding of time transformed this into a tradition, which spawned its own rituals, and when the humans were emancipated, the tradition continued, only by that time it had already changed out of all recognition. The bond was sacred, and each dragon had one bonded rider and no other. Freedom meant that the riders could choose to refuse a bond, so the dragons had to adapt, and the master-slave relationship evolved into a true partnership. The riders of the aristocratic dragons in the court of my Realm formed a parallel court of humans, who looked after the needs of their kinfolk.'

'Hang on,' said Maddie, 'so if you... I mean, *when* you become queen again, I'll be like the queen of the humans?'

'Not exactly, but you would wield great influence.'

Maddie grinned. 'I'm liking the sound of this, though I have to warn you, nobody paid any attention to what I said as a sergeant, so I'm not sure the people on your world would.'

'You say that, Maddie, but I doubt it. I see the strength in you, even if you are blind to it.' She glanced up at the pink sky. 'It is nearly time. The attack will take place at dusk, when the greenhides will be starting to rest for the night.'

Maddie nodded, and put the crossbow down onto the grass. 'I'll get the fire built up.'

She stood, and walked up the little slope to the cave entrance, where a heap of firewood had been gathered. She reached out and lifted a bundle, then took it down to the scorched circle of burnt grass and ash by the side of the pool.

Blackrose watched as she dropped the bundle into the middle of the circle. 'Bring it all. We shall need the fire to rage.'

Maddie worked for ten minutes, until the entire heap had been moved close to the banks of the pool.

'Do you need to eat again?' she asked the dragon.

'No.'

'The goats of these mountains will be glad to hear that; that is, if there are any left; you may have driven them to extinction in the last few days with the amount that you've chomped your way through.'

'I certainly hope not, because I shall require a great deal of sustenance upon our return. And sleep; you must promise not to bother me in the slightest for a few days.'

'Goats, sleep and sunshine, sounds like a dragon's dream life.'

'I shall have earned it, if we succeed. The odds are still against that, however.'

'Stop going on about the odds. Life is a gamble.'

'Life is random, the risk lies in the choices we make.'

Maddie raised an eyebrow. 'Right. Shall I bring the salve down?'

'Yes.'

Maddie walked back up the little slope, and entered the cave. Near the back was a large crate that she had emptied, then filled with chunks of raw salve. She had spent an hour that morning, hewing out fragments from the thick seams that riddled the walls of the inner caves. She crouched down, braced her back, then lifted the crate with a grunt. She carried it out of the cave and down to the grass by the pool. Blackrose swung her head closer as she placed the crate a few yards from the heap of firewood.

'This looks like enough.'

Maddie nodded. 'So, do I just chuck it on, yeah?'

'Deposit the contents of the crate into the centre of the fire when it is blazing at its fiercest. Then, and listen carefully, you must run. Do not linger by the fire, and do not inhale the vapours. There is so much salve here that I fear you would be irreparably damaged.'

'Chuck it on then run; got it. I'll get the fire started.'

She ran over to the heap of wood, and crouched down next to the bag where she kept the matches. She put her knee down onto the grass, and lit a long wax taper, shielding it from the wind with her hand. The flame shone in the diminishing light, and she placed it next to the heap, moving it every few seconds as the dry wood took up the fire, crackling and igniting. She touched more than a dozen places, then blew on the fire, watching as it spread and grew.

Standing up, she noticed the crossbow lying on the grass, and picked it up. She grabbed the bag of bolts and slung the bow over her shoulder. It gave her a little comfort, but she had no experience of using a bow in a fight, and if she accidently hit Blackrose, she would never hear the end of it. The bow she had carried while posted in Auldan had been loosed only in training, but if Rosie could shoot greenhides from a roof, how hard could it be?

The fire grew, spreading upwards from the broad base of wood, the orange and yellow flames flickering against the reds of the late afternoon sky. Maddie stood back a pace as the heat built, but the dragon kept close to the flames, her jet black scales reflecting them with a satin glow.

Blackrose closed her eyes. 'Now.'

Maddie walked over to the crate, and heaved it up from the grass. She staggered over to the fire, the salve sparkling in the light, then she raised it as high as she could and tipped it over. The chunks of salve dropped into the flames, hissing and breaking apart as they disappeared into the heart of the fire. A waft of fumes arose, and Maddie backed away, then ran as the flames took on a silvery-blue tinge. She sprinted by the side of the pool to where the waterfall crashed down from the stream above, then turned. Blackrose had her head as close to the flames as was possible without being burned, her nostrils wide as she inhaled the cloud of fumes and vapours coming from the blazing fire.

For a moment, the dragon's head seemed to disappear amid the smoke and fumes, and her body merged with the shadows of the valley. A low groaning growl reverberated through the ground, and Maddie felt an urge to run back, to see if Blackrose was alright, but her feet remained frozen to the grass. The cloud of vapours started to lower and fall as the fire crackled and spat, its fuel almost extinguished. Red hot embers filled the air, floating up on the breeze and swirling with the plumes of smoke rising into the sky.

'Are you alright?' Maddie cried.

There was no response, so Maddie started to edge back across the grass, her eyes wary as she approached the dragon.

'Do you feel any different?' she said.

The dragon's face reared up before her, and Maddie stumbled back, falling onto the grass. Blackrose's jaws were open, and a shimmer of red flames were licking her teeth, but it was her eyes that Maddie was staring at. They seemed larger than normal, and were bulging from the dragon's head, their pupils dilated and glowing red like hot coals.

'Climb on,' the dragon said, her voice low and distorted. 'Let us kill.'

Maddie scrambled to her feet, her hands trembling as the dragon stared at her. She ran past the dwindling fire, holding her breath in case any fumes were still being emitted, and reached the side of the harness. The dragon's scales were as sleek and hard as she had ever seen them, as if they were from a model of what a perfect dragon should be like. She pulled on the ropes and climbed up to the saddle, strapping herself in and grabbing hold of the crossbar.

Blackrose extended her wings, stretching them across the narrow valley, and Maddie could see the muscles rippling like thick knots of iron under the scales.

'Can you hear me?' she cried.

'I can,' the dragon growled, 'but say nothing. Death needs no words.'

The dragon beat her wings and they ascended. The sky was lighter above the shadow-draped valley, and Maddie gazed around at the mountains as the sun lingered on the horizon. Below them, the greenhides were continuing their never-ending surge through the winding passes in the mountain range, but the dragon ignored them, and aimed directly for the nest. She powered her wings, and the burst of speed sent Maddie's hair flying, the wind biting into her face. She squinted as her eyes watered, then she gave up and closed them, and concentrated on holding on.

Maddie opened her eyes again as the dragon's speed slowed slightly, and she saw that they were already passing the edges of the mountains. She gazed down, looking for the enormous wheel of greenhides, and saw it on the plains below, whirling in a spiral of countless bodies that spread for miles. In the distance ahead of them, she could see the tall mound marking the entrance to the nest, silhouetted against the reds of the evening sky.

Blackrose started to bank, her right wing lowering as she turned from the mound. They tilted to face the sun then, without warning, Blackrose soared down, and opened her jaws. A torrent of flames burst out from her, wide and powerful, consuming hundreds of greenhides below them. Blackrose flew on, curving to the left as the flames destroyed a corridor in the huge mass of the beasts, leaving a trail fifty yards wide behind them of smoking, smouldering corpses, like blackened insects on the ground. On Blackrose flew, inscribing a circle on the plain; a dark halo of death. The roar of shrieks and screams from the greenhides rose up into the sky, pounding Maddie's eardrums. The first circle complete, Blackrose banked again, edging closer to the mound, the flames unbroken. She began to create another circle, smaller than the one before, consuming everything in her path. The greenhides were in a state of panic, trying to flee the flames by running towards the mound, where more of the beasts were still emerging. The bodies were piling up by the tall structure as the two masses of greenhides collided and merged, and Blackrose circled again, the flames ripping through the screaming wall of flesh. Round and round, with every revolution tightening the circle in a spiral that led to the mound.

Maddie choked from the stench of burning flesh as the countless bodies smouldered on the plain below them. At the farthest edge of the devastation, greenhides were trying to scramble over the heaps of blackened bodies, as if they had been called to protect the nest, but they were still far from the mound. Blackrose banked again, and inscribed the tightest circle yet, incinerating the area directly around the mound. The bodies of the screaming greenhides writhed as they fell, the flames withering their limbs and reducing them to smoking husks.

Blackrose closed her jaws, and the flames ceased as she gazed down on her handiwork. An area three hundred yards wide had been transformed into a single blackened circle of ash and corpses, the ground glowing red-hot beneath.

The dragon turned her attention to the mound. Greenhides were emerging at a quicker rate than ever, pouring up and out of the funnel that led to the caverns and tunnels below. Blackrose hovered overhead, and aimed her jaws down, unleashing a blast of fire that enveloped the whole mound, killing everything upon it, then she tightened the flames, concentrating them into a narrow stream that drove down into the mouth of the pit. The land around the mound started to smoke as the jet of fire penetrated the nest. For minutes the dragon hovered there, the flames unceasing as Maddie started to sweat from the wave of heat rising from the ground. The rocks on the mound were beginning to melt, and with a crack that rang like thunder, the entire mound disintegrated into earth and ash, its sides blowing outwards, and the mass of rock burying the entrance hole.

Blackrose closed her mouth again, and panted, her breath ragged as she gazed down.

'Did we do it?' yelled Maddie.

'All we have done, rider, is anger the queen of the nest. Now we shall await her response.'

The ground started to move beneath them, as sinkholes opened up, the corpses of the charred greenhides falling in as the earth collapsed. Creatures began rising from the holes, their short limbs scrabbling at the dirt, and within seconds, hundreds were crawling their way up to the surface.

'What are they?' gasped Maddie.

'The workers of the nest,' said the dragon, 'forced out by the heat and flames.'

'How are you? Are you alright?'

Blackrose didn't answer. Instead, she rose up above the collapsed mound, then soared down, sending a torrent of fire across the ruined plain, aiming at the sinkholes, and devouring the pale workers as they emerged from the earth. More holes opened up, faster than Blackrose could burn them, and the ground filled with a thick carpet of the workers, crawling over the blackened bodies of the soldiers. Their cries filled the air as the dragon swooped down again, incinerating hundreds in a wide swathe of destruction. The piles of dead by the sinkholes mounted and Maddie gagged from the smell and pulled her tunic up to cover her mouth and nose.

A ragged rip opened in the earth, and the largest greenhide Maddie had even seen began to emerge. It had six limbs instead of four, and the claws at the end of the forelimbs were as long as a full sized greenhide. It raised its head clear of the earth and shrieked in rage as it saw the dragon burn the plain.

'Malik's ass! The queen!'

Blackrose laughed. 'No, rider, that is merely one of her guard; a young queen.'

She circled in the air, then hovered above the juvenile queen as it hauled its bulk from the earth. Its claws reached upwards, and Blackrose opened her jaws, engulfing the beast in flames. It screamed, its voice ripping through the darkening sky as it writhed in torment. Maddie held on to the harness, her hands gripping as tightly as she could as the heat rushed upwards. Around them the ground was falling away, revealing more burnt corpses from the collapsing tunnels. Another juvenile queen emerged, then another, their claws gouging through the bodies and earth beneath them as they struggled to the surface. Blackrose sent a stream of fire towards one, as more appeared. One of the queens leaped into the air, its immense rear limbs powering it upwards, and Blackrose swung her claws, ripping through its face and neck. Another jumped, trying to reach the dragon with its own claws, but Blackrose banked and rose, and it crashed back to the ground.

Maddie stared down. Five of the juvenile queens were on the pock-marked and blackened surface, their monstrous faces tilted up at the dragon, and their talons extended. The ground rumbled by the destroyed mound, and cracks opened, sending smoke and vapours upwards, then the entire area collapsed, sending tons of earth and greenhides tumbling into the abyss. A vast figure slowly started to emerge from the pit, its head bigger than the body of any soldier green-hide, its limbs powerful and long. Its eyes flashed hatred and rage as they opened, and its mouth let out a cry that nearly split Maddie's head open. Blackrose circled upwards and the enormous beast crawled from the ground, its bulk easily five times the mass of the dragon. Blackrose soared down, sending a thick blast of flame at the queen, then diving and banking to avoid a swing from its massive claws.

Maddie stifled a scream as she clung on, her eyes glued to the gargantuan beast. Blackrose unleashed another torrent of fire, aimed at the base of the queen, and the juveniles who were flanking her, sending two of them to their deaths in the inferno. Maddie glanced around as the dragon levelled off. On the outskirts of the burnt circle of land, the soldier greenhides were rallying, and thousands were rushing towards the centre to protect their monarch.

Blackrose swooped again, aiming for the queen, but at the last second she turned, and blasted fire at the three remaining juvenile guards, and their death screams rang out amid the leaping flames. The queen lunged at the dragon, a talon just missing the inside of Black-rose's left wing, and Maddie shrieked. The dragon rose higher, then twisted her neck down, and opened her jaws, covering the queen in a flood of fire. The beast screamed in agony, and lunged upwards, its talons scraping the underside of Blackrose's body. The dragon grunted, and pulled away even higher, the unbroken torrent of flames enveloping the queen. The heat intensified, and washed upwards. Maddie buried her face in her tunic as she felt her hair start to frazzle. The leather on the harness was too hot to touch, and started to smoke, while the metal buckles burned against her skin, yet Blackrose persisted, the flames covering the centre of the plain in a conflagration that turned the dark sky into day.

Maddie felt the heat start to overcome her. She closed her eyes and retreated within her mind, her hands burnt from clinging on to the crossbar, when, without warning, it ceased, and the dragon closed her jaws. Shaking, Maddie opened her eyes, and gazed down at the ground. The rocks were glowing red, and smoke was billowing up from a thousand charred corpses. In the centre lay the body of the queen. Its limbs were blackened, and its body smouldered, and a pale green liquid was seeping from a dozen places over its scored and scorched torso. Its head was burnt beyond recognition, its features a twisted mass of scorched and loose flesh, the bones beneath cracked and split. Around it, nothing moved. The soldier greenhides from outside the circle were still rushing towards the centre, but the broken ground was hindering their approach.

Maddie took a breath, then nearly choked as she saw the bulk of the queen start to move. One of its broken and charred claws scratched over the earth, and its head began to lift from the earth.

'Fire is not enough,' said Blackrose. 'Hold on tight, rider.'

The dragon pointed its neck down, then hurtled towards the earth at lightning speed, her wings folded back. She landed on the vast body of the queen, the claws on her rear limbs gouging bloody trails as she ground to a halt. A talon swung out from the queen, and Blackrose lifted her left forelimb to block it. The two sets of claws collided, and Blackrose dug her heels into the belly of the beast as she was pushed back. The dragon unleashed another withering barrage of flame, scorching the queen's head and limbs, then her neck darted forward into the inferno, her jaws open. Her teeth ripped through the neck of the queen, severing its head as green blood flooded the ground.

Blackrose tipped her head back and roared in triumph. Around her, the surviving soldiers were rushing headlong towards the body of their queen, screaming out their cries of rage and grief.

'Mela!' Maddie cried from her shoulders. 'Look out!'

Dozens of greenhides scrambled up onto the vast, smouldering body of the queen. Blackrose seemed oblivious to the danger, her neck arcing upwards as she revelled in her victory, then the greenhides struck. The dragon cried out in pain as claws and teeth slashed into her, and she extended her wings, rising a yard above the queen. Greenhides leapt up, trying to pull her back down as hundreds more ran over the broken ground towards them.

Blackrose swayed in the air, greenhides clinging to her limbs, then with a roar that ripped through the evening sky, she beat her wings and rose, higher and higher. She raced upwards, shaking off the greenhides as she went, then twisted her neck and drove her teeth into the few that remained, ripping them from her forelimbs and spitting them out to hurtle to the ground below.

Blood was streaming from the wounds on her flank and limbs as Blackrose ascended. Maddie gazed down at the carnage and devastation scoring the ground beneath them. Thousands of greenhides were running in confusion, scattering in every direction. The circle of scorched and broken earth grew smaller, but in the centre the vast corpse of the queen remained visible, stretched out across the pits and smoking ruins of the nest.

Blackrose banked, and flew back towards the mountains.

'You did it,' Maddie said; 'you killed the queen.'

The dragon said nothing. They passed the edge of the hills as the sun disappeared below the horizon, a pall of smoke filling the sky behind them. Blackrose's altitude and speed began to falter, and she dropped fifty feet, then recovered, grunting, but Maddie knew her strength was fading, They followed a ravine, then turned into their little valley, Blackrose's belly grazing the tops of the trees as she sank. Blackrose extended her wounded and bloody limbs, but they gave way as she landed, and the dragon skidded across the grass, gouging a furrow behind her. She came to a halt, and lowered her head, her eyes closed.

Maddie unbuckled the singed straps holding her to the saddle and clambered down, falling the last few feet as her exhausted hands slipped on the ropes. She staggered up and stared at the wounds left by the greenhides, then she ran up to where the dragon's head was resting on the grass.

'Are you alright?' she cried.

Blackrose opened an eye a sliver, the red glow faded. 'I'll live.'

'Do you need more salve for your wounds?'

'No. If I took any more just now, my heart would stop.'

'Then how can I help?'

'Be my rider; care for me this night and tomorrow; I need water and food; and sleep, many hours of sleep.'

Maddie crouched down, and placed her hand onto the dragon's head. 'You faced your fears; you beat them; they tried to drag you down, but you didn't let them. In your world, they would have given you a new name for what you did.'

'You were there too, Maddie.'

'But I didn't do anything; I didn't even shoot my crossbow.'

The dragon smiled. 'Probably for the best.'

CHAPTER 20

ON THE BRIDGE

Icehaven, Medio, The City – 30th Amalan 3420

Yendra filled two glasses with a deep red wine, and slid one across the table to Aila.

She smiled. 'Thanks.'

'So Khora made you Adjutant of the Circuit?'

'Yes, well, after I'd finished my two hundred years of house arrest in Cuidrach Palace.'

Yendra shook her head. 'Two hundred years. How did you occupy your time?'

'I learned how to fight, and I smoked a lot of opium.'

'Opium? That disappoints me a little, but it must have been hard for you.'

Aila nodded. 'For a long time I felt oblivion was preferable to reality, but I've not had any for months. Since I met Corthie in fact.'

'He has become your new opium?'

'He has removed the need for it. Why would I want to waste my time in a daze when his life span is so short? There will be plenty of time for shutting off my feelings when he's gone.'

'Or if he leaves.'

'Do you think he will?'

Yendra sipped from her glass. 'No; at least, not without you.' She put the wine down. 'Back to the Circuit; I'd like to know how some of my other nephews and nieces have been doing. You worked for Ikara; can she be trusted? How was her governance of my old town?'

'She was corrupt and useless. She got rich taking bribes from the gangs, and let them run the place. And as soon as it got too tough, she fled.'

'She is in Pella, I believe?'

'She's hiding there with Collo and Salvor, and hoping everything will just blow over. They're cowards; well, maybe not Salvor – he helped Corthie escape the day Khora was murdered. He won't stick his neck out for us though, there are too many Blades in Pella. Doria and Mona are on our side, but they're stuck in Ooste.'

'I shall appeal to my brother Montieth in Dalrig, though I doubt he or his daughter Amber will help.'

'That's it for Auldan. We could try talking to Lydia in Port Sanders, but I think she would be too frightened to go against the God-Queen. Then there's Jade and Kano in the Circuit, both dangerous.'

'Don't forget the mortals.'

'Yeah, the Aurelians. I don't know what to think of them.'

'They saved the lives of a hundred thousand Hammers. Even if the rest of their lives are riddled with mistakes, then this one act alone has earned them respect. We should treat them as our equals.'

'Achan has been corresponding with the Hammer leadership. Did you know that they want to abolish rule by the gods and demigods?'

'Not quite, they want rule with the consent of the ruled; no slavery, no serfdom, and an end to automatic positions of authority for the Royal Family. I find it hard to disagree with any of that. Why should Kano or Ikara hold power when there are many more suitably experienced mortals who could do a better job? On the other hand, look at Lady Yvona; she would likely win any election held in Icehaven, and deservedly so.'

'It's more radical than what we dreamed of three hundred years ago.'

'Yes, but it's also fairer. More importantly, the movement is being led by mortals, whereas in the Civil War we spoke and acted on their behalf. It is better this way. They are fighting for their own freedom, rather than having it imposed upon them.'

Aila nodded.

'Can I ask something that might be a little painful?'

'Yes,' said Aila.

'Were you and Khora reconciled before she died?'

'Yes, though barely. That's why I was in the palace that night, to make my peace with her. I wish I could change things, but the fact is that I spent hundreds of years hating her. I'm still angry that she didn't tell me she had been tricked by Michael, instead of letting me believe that she'd betrayed you.'

'And who told you that she had been tricked, if not Khora?'

'Mona. She and Khora were close friends.'

'She was the only one of Michael's children that I could abide, although I wish she were a little more decisive.'

Sounds filtered through from the bedroom door, and a moment later Corthie appeared, dressed in a pair of shorts and scratching his head.

'Morning,' he said.

'It's nearly evening,' said Aila from the couch. 'You've been sleeping all afternoon.'

He raised an eyebrow and walked into the sitting room, pulling a shirt over his broad shoulders.

'Hi, Yendra,' he said, sitting heavily into an armchair. 'You look even stronger than yesterday, and a bit taller too.'

'Yes,' she said. 'I have ceased the daily doses of salve, but its effects are still working their way through my body.'

'Have you tried battle-vision yet?'

The god smiled. 'I have.'

'Feel good?'

'It did indeed, Corthie.' She exhaled. 'I have also successfully attempted line and range-vision, and have seen as far as the edge of the hills over-looking the Circuit. By tomorrow, I hope to be able to reach Ooste and Tara.'

Corthie smiled, then picked up an apple from a bowl on the table. 'That's good news.' He took a bite then turned to Aila. 'Do you fancy leaving the palace and getting dinner in a tavern tonight? Somewhere in town; we could eat fresh fish by the harbour. You could use your powers to disguise what you look like.'

'And what about you?' she said. 'Malik's ass, imagine if the locals saw you out in a tavern.'

'Aye, it could be a laugh. Remember when I used to visit you in the Circuit? It'd be like that.'

'I'd rather stay in,' she said, 'though we can visit the Blind Poet next time we're in the Circuit. I'll be Elsie, of course.'

Yendra rose from her chair. 'I think I'll leave you both to it. Aila, it was lovely talking to you.'

There was a knock at the door before Aila could respond.

'Sorry for the interruption, your Highness,' said Major Hannia, 'but Lady Yvona is requesting everyone's presence in her study to discuss an urgent matter.'

'Us too?' said Corthie.

'Yes, champion, you and Lady Aila also.'

They got to their feet, Corthie swiping another apple as he passed the bowl. They followed the major through the hallway to Yvona's quarters and entered. Naxor was already sitting there, along with Belinda, while Yvona was in her usual chair behind the desk.

'Thank you for coming so swiftly,' said Yvona; 'Naxor has some news.'

Yendra, Aila and Corthie sat, and Naxor turned to face them.

'The Blades are starting to pull out of Medio,' he said. 'Company by company, they're withdrawing through the Union Walls into Auldan. It seems that Lady Emily might have been correct.'

'What is the status of Kano?' said Yendra. 'Has he also withdrawn?'

'No. This is the strange part; Kano has a division of around ten thousand Blades under his personal command, and he's based them at the

Fourth, Fifth and Sixth Gates along the Middle Walls. None of them have budged an inch; it's the rest of them who are leaving, all the squads that patrol the Circuit, and most of the battalions that have been blockading Icehaven; gone.'

Yendra nodded. 'So what do we surmise from this?'

'That my brother doesn't know about Marcus's plan, yet,' said Aila. 'If it's true.'

'Or,' said Belinda, 'he might be remaining in position so he can breach the walls. I won't pretend to know how he thinks, but if he's loyal to Marcus, and if these are Marcus's orders, then he might be the one appointed to carry them out.'

Aila sagged in her seat. She wanted to argue with Belinda, but she half-believed the words the god was saying.

'Has Kano so truly lost his way?' said Yendra. 'He was beloved to me, loyal, kind, and brave. I know Marcus has twisted him, but would he really be capable of opening the walls to the greenhides?'

No one in the room spoke.

Aila glanced up. 'I don't believe he would do it.'

'I'm afraid I disagree,' said Yvona.

'I also,' said Naxor. 'I have listened to rumours and tales about his cruel behaviour; he is not the same man as he was before. He's done things that, well, I don't think you can come back from.'

'It disheartens me to hear this,' said Yendra. She glanced round the room. 'A decision needs to be taken. I am of the mind that speed will help us greatly here. Our assault was planned for the day after tomorrow, but there is good reason not to wait. If the Blades are withdrawing from the streets of the Circuit, then we should act, now. I propose that we go directly to Redmarket Palace and take possession of it, tonight.'

'Tonight?' said Yvona 'But the troops aren't in position.'

'I was thinking of a much smaller force. Myself, Aila, Naxor and a squad of your best soldiers.'

'Me?' said Aila.

'I need you; your powers will be invaluable in getting us through the Blade lines, while Naxor can keep our communications open.'

'This sounds like a fun trip,' said Corthie. 'Am I not invited?'

'I'd rather you remained close to the walls for now, champion,' said Yendra; 'to protect Icehaven, and so you can move down quickly if a breach does occur. Belinda, if you're happy to help, I would ask you to assist Corthie.'

Belinda nodded. 'Alright, but that's what I was going to do anyway.'

'Thank you,' Yendra said. 'Are we agreed, or would anyone else like to make a proposal?'

'So I'm losing you, Aila and Naxor tonight?' said Yvona.

Yendra smiled. 'It's a little earlier than planned, I know.'

Yvona glanced at her. 'I'm going to miss you, my princess.'

'Our friendship shall last the ages,' said Yendra, 'and I will never forget the kindness you showed me when I arrived. My vision powers are nearing their full restoration, and it is my fervent hope that I will be able speak to you from Redmarket.'

Naxor leaned forward. 'Should I try to talk to Sergeant Quill again? Do we let the Aurelians know what we're up to?'

'Yes,' said Yendra. 'I would be grateful if you could do that while we're preparing to leave. I think two hours should be sufficient, then we shall depart.'

Naxor got to his feet, while Yendra leaned over to talk to Yvona.

Corthie nudged Aila. 'I'm not altogether happy about you and me being separated.'

She took his hand. 'Come on; we still have two hours.'

It was close to midnight by the time Aila and Naxor were dropped off in the woods of the Iceward Range. Naxor was dressed as a soldier in a stolen Blade uniform, while Aila's appearance matched his. The covered carriage turned and sped back towards Icehaven, leaving the two demigods alone on the forest track.

'Did you try to contact the Aurelians again?' said Aila as they walked along the dark path.

'Yes, but no luck; I couldn't find Emily, Daniel or Quill at the Eighth Gate. A lot of Hammers are out on the streets, rioting with the Evaders.'

'A good old riot in the Circuit; I can't say I've missed that much.'

'Still bitter about being hounded out by the rebels?'

'A bit. I helped them for decades, but all they saw was another entitled demigod.'

They reached the top of the ridge, and looked down upon Medio. Below them stretched the long fields of the Icewarders and then, in the distance beyond, sprawled the Circuit. It was illuminated by a dozen fires burning across the Evader territory, their flames rising into the night sky.

'It'll be nice to feel the sun again,' Aila said as they gazed down the steep slope.

Naxor nodded. 'Corthie didn't look too pleased about you being sent on this little errand.'

'He's worried. I told him that I worry about him too, but that doesn't stop him from going beyond the walls every day. He didn't like it much, but it made Belinda laugh.'

'I'm not sure if that's a good thing.'

'Have you shown her how to use the Quadrant yet?'

'Nope, and I don't intend to.'

'But I thought Yendra had asked you?'

'She asked, she didn't order. If it comes to it, I can take Belinda back to Lostwell.'

Aila frowned. 'You should be careful. Belinda doesn't strike me as the kind of person who would enjoy being deceived.'

'It'll be fine. Besides, if I showed her now, then who's to say that she wouldn't just grab Corthie and go? She doesn't give a damn about the City, or us.'

'It sounds like you're trying to keep her here.'

'Of course I'm not.'

'What's your ulterior motive? You always have one.' She frowned. 'Do you like her?'

'No.'

'Come on. She's beautiful, powerful, and unlike every other god in the City, she's not related to us. You fancy her, don't you?'

Naxor frowned, and they started to descend the narrow path. 'Alright, I do like her,' he said in a low voice. 'She's all of those things you mention, but you forgot to include that she terrifies me.'

'I thought you liked a bit of danger?'

'What we're about to do is dangerous,' he muttered, 'going with Belinda could be fatal.'

They quietened as they approached the picket line marking the edge of the Blade camp. They crouched in some thick undergrowth, and Naxor's eyes hazed over. Aila peered through the branches while she waited. A wooden tower had been built over-looking the track down from the hills, and stretches of palisade wall had been erected. A few soldiers were up on the tower, but she could see no one else.

Naxor coughed. 'Yesterday, there were two hundred Blades here; a full company. Tonight, there are fewer than forty. A captain is in charge.'

Aila nodded. *You see me as a Blade major.* 'How's that?'

He smiled. 'Now we just need to deal with the guards up on the tower. Give me a moment.'

His eyes hazed over again, and a few seconds later the figures standing on the tower slumped over. Naxor and Aila got to their feet, and hurried down the track. They passed the base of the tower, and entered the camp.

Two Blades by the gate jumped to attention and saluted as Aila strode in.

'I'm here to inspect the garrison,' she announced. 'Where is the captain?'

An officer ran out from a door in the corner of the camp, and saluted.

'Good evening, Captain,' Aila said. 'Line up every soldier based at this camp; I wish to examine your state of preparedness.'

The captain suppressed a frown, and Aila could see the irritation in his eyes. 'Yes, sir.' He turned to a sergeant. 'You heard the major, get everyone out here.'

'What about the three up on the tower, sir?'

Aila sighed. 'They can remain where they are.'

'Very good, ma'am.'

There was a flurry of activity as the soldiers in the camp were roused and lined up by the palisade wall. Aila walked down the line, nodding.

'Excellent,' she said; 'clearly, you're all fine, strapping young soldiers.' She gestured to Naxor. 'My colleague would now like to say something.'

Naxor raised his hand. 'Sleep.'

The soldiers collapsed to the ground, their crossbows spilling over the trampled grass.

Aila nodded. 'I wasn't sure you'd manage forty in one go.'

'They won't be sleeping for long. Right, I'd better let Yendra know.'

His eyes glazed over again as Aila peered down at the unconscious soldiers. Yendra had asked them to kill only if absolutely necessary, not wanting to throw away the lives of any while the greenhides were at the gates. She crouched down and began to gather their crossbows.

'She's on her way,' said Naxor. 'Next stop, the Circuit.'

Yendra had chosen to make her entrance to the Circuit as a warrior. Freshly wrought plates of burnished steel had been strapped to her torso and limbs, and a long sword was slung over her back. The salve had done its work, and her stature almost matched that of Corthie. In her battle armour, she looked just as Aila remembered her from the last days of the Civil War; a goddess of war.

They had walked the two miles from the Blade camp at the foot of the Iceward Range to the border of Evader territory, a squad of veteran soldiers flanking them as they strode towards the Circuit. Naxor had shed his uniform, and Aila her disguise, and they walked by Yendra's side, keeping pace with her stride. The streets of the Icewarder suburbs were deserted and quiet, but the noise from the Circuit grew as they approached, and the glow in the sky from the fires began to light their way.

A canal marked the border, and a large group of Blades were posted by the blockaded bridge. Most of them were lined up by the side of the canal, their eyes on the Evader territory beyond, but a cry went up as Yendra was seen approaching, and they turned.

An officer stared at them, and the soldiers began forming up, loading their crossbows as they got into position by the roadblock.

'Stay back!' cried the officer.

Yendra signalled to the squad of Icewarders to remain where they were, and strode forwards, alone.

'Blades,' she called out, 'do you fight for the City, or do you fight for Marcus?'

'If you come any closer, we will shoot.'

'I do not wish to kill you,' she said, 'but I shall if you block my path.'

A crowd was starting to gather on the far side of the canal. A few excited cries rang out, and more Evaders emerged, until the edge of the canal was lined with people.

'Put down your weapon,' cried the officer. 'You are a rebel, and are under arrest.'

Yendra smiled. 'Then come and take me.'

The thrum of noise from the other side of the canal rose a notch as the lines of Blades aimed their bows at the princess.

'Behind you,' she said, 'a thousand faces are watching; the faces of my people. They have suffered under your rule, but for no longer, for that rule is coming to an end, tonight. You can either get out of my way and run to Auldan, or stand here and be killed. You have a minute to decide.'

The Blades glanced at each other as the officer swallowed. Without warning, a crossbow loosed, and a bolt ripped through the air towards Yendra. Her right hand moved faster than the bolt and she caught it mid-flight, an inch from her face. She dropped it onto the cobbles and unsheathed her longsword, pulling it from over her shoulder.

'Hold,' the officer shouted to the Blades. He glanced from them to Yendra. 'Let her pass; we can't fight a god.'

The Evader crowd on the other side of the canal let out a great roar at the Blade's words. The soldiers raised their bows and cleared the road, then a surge of Evaders rushed over the bridge, and began pulling down the barricade. Aila, Naxor and the Icewarder squad walked forwards to join Yendra as she gazed at the far side of the canal.

'There's your beloved Circuit,' said Aila. 'It hasn't changed all that much since you were last here.'

'I assume the Great Racecourse still stands?'

'It's been half-burnt and repaired many times, but it's still there, right next to a colossal statue of Michael.'

'They put a statue of Michael in the Circuit?'

'Yeah. You were made out to be the villain, and Michael was glorified like a martyr. The Evaders never believed it though; they always kept their faith in you.'

The last of the barricade was tipped over into the canal, and Yendra strode forward. She glanced at the Blade officer.

'You chose well,' she said. 'If you wish to serve the City, then disobey any orders you receive to withdraw behind the Union Walls. We have the same enemy: the greenhides, do not allow yourselves to be used as the tools of those who would destroy everything we love.'

The officer said nothing, but many of the Blades next to him had doubt flickering in their eyes. Yendra turned, and set foot onto the bridge. As she did so, another roar rose up from the crowd awaiting her on the other side. The entire bank of the canal was packed with people. Many looked in shock, while others had tears streaming down their faces. Yendra halted on the apex of the bridge and raised her sword into the air.

'I, Princess Yendra, have returned.'

The crowd erupted, the din rising into a crescendo of noise. Several in the crowd had lit torches, and the flames flickered off Yendra's shining armour as she held the sword aloft.

'I will fight for you,' she cried; 'I shall defend the Evaders of the

Circuit from all who wish to harm them, but I am not here to rule.' She paused as the crowd quietened, listening to her words. She said nothing for a moment, standing still, her armour and face reflecting the flames of the torches.

She sheathed her sword. 'The reign of the gods is over.'

It took another two hours to traverse the mile and a half to Redmarket Palace, the route lined with heaving crowds desperate to catch a glimpse of their returning warrior-princess. Not a single Blade had been seen on the way, and when they arrived at the palace, the entrance gates were in the hands of Evader rebels, who bowed before Yendra, and let her enter. The squad of Icewarder soldiers flanked her as she processed through the cheering crowds packing the large palace forecourt, while Aila and Naxor followed a few paces behind. Yendra ascended the wide steps, then crouched and knelt by the top, placing her hand onto the paving stones where her daughter Yearna had been cut down by Prince Michael. She lowered her head for a moment, her eyes closed, then she rose and turned to face the vast crowds that had gathered. She raised her hand, her face serene as she gazed out over the thousands of Evaders, then she turned and entered the palace.

Inside, several Evader rebels were waiting, along with a few squads of their militia. Signs of the destruction carried out during the uprising were still evident, with statues toppled, and tapestries ripped from the walls.

'Your Highness,' said one of the rebel leaders, bowing low, 'the Blades have withdrawn. Our forces have secured the palace for you.'

'Thank you,' she said. 'I have read the rebel constitution that you promulgated during the uprising last year. You stated that you intended to execute any member of the Royal Family that fell into your hands.'

The rebels glanced at each other. 'That was before we knew you were alive, your Highness,' said one, 'you and your daughters were the only ones who ever cared about us.'

'That is not true,' said Yendra. 'Lady Aila worked on your behalf for a hundred years, and suffered two centuries of imprisonment because she cared. There will be no more talk of summary executions, not if your administration wishes to have my support.'

The rebel blinked. 'Our administration? I thought that you... your Highness, would rule.'

'I shall lead the fight against the greenhides and anyone else who threatens us, but the Circuit shall be ruled by mortals. That means your administration for now, but once the crisis is over, we shall ask the people how they wish to be ruled.'

The rebels bowed.

'Your Highness,' said one, 'Daniel Aurelian is waiting to speak to you. He travelled up from the Hammer-held Eighth Gate when he heard you were coming.'

Aila frowned. 'Daniel Aurelian has entered the Circuit?'

Yendra glanced at the rebels. 'How is your relationship with the Hammers?'

'It's good, your Highness. They share many of the same aims as we do, and we've been cooperating closely.'

'That pleases me. Where is Lord Aurelian?'

'This way, your Highness,' he said, gesturing.

They went to a large meeting room, where a group of Hammers were standing by a grand, ornate fireplace. A man turned, and Aila recognised him immediately.

'Princess Yendra,' he said, advancing, 'thank you for seeing me.'

'I have heard much about you, Lord Aurelian,' she said; 'the good, and the bad.'

Daniel's eyes flickered over to Aila. 'What I did in the Circuit was unforgivable. I have tried to be a better man since that day, but I know that nothing will ever bring those people back. If you wish to take me into custody I will not resist.'

'Then why have you come to the Circuit,' said Yendra, 'knowing that many here wish to see you brought to justice?'

'To ask for your help. My wife has been arrested by Kano.'

'Lord Kano has Emily Aurelian?'

'Yes. She was on her way back yesterday evening from securing food for the Hammers, when Blades stopped them on the road near Port Sanders. They killed their guards, and took Emily and Sergeant Quill away.'

'Do you know where they are being held?'

'Our contacts suggest they were taken to one of the gates on the Middle Walls, probably the Sixth. There are thousands of Blades garrisoned along that section of the wall, all the way up to the Fourth Gate.'

Princess Yendra nodded. 'And what assistance do you require?'

'I need permission to bring my forces through the Circuit to attack Kano's position.'

'No,' said Yendra, 'that would cause a bloodbath, and we would lose soldiers that we will soon need to fight the greenhides.'

Daniel's eyes narrowed. 'I'm not leaving Emily there.'

'I agree, but our approach requires tact and precision, rather than blunt force.' She glanced at Aila. 'I'm leaving you here in the palace as my Adjutant. Naxor, you will assist. Work with the rebel government to ensure the Circuit is ready to defend itself as soon as the Blades have completed their withdrawal. Once the gates in the Union Walls have been sealed, then we won't have long to wait.'

Aila nodded. 'And you?'

Yendra smiled. 'I think it's time to meet Emily.'

CHAPTER 21

THE GOAT HUNTERS

Icehaven, Medio, The City – 1st Mikalis 3420

Corthie and Belinda jumped down from the crane, their boots landing on the parapet at the top of the stretch of walls.

'Well done,' said Major Hannia.

'For what?' said Corthie, as he handed the Axe of Rand to a pair of waiting soldiers. 'Seven greenhides in five hours? I barely broke sweat.'

'Another section of the walls has been successfully repaired, champion,' said the major. 'Moving your shifts to take place at night has allowed us to carry out more work.'

'And the greenhides know you're up here at this end of the Middle Walls,' said Belinda, wiping the edge of her sword with a cloth. 'They've moved sunward to avoid you.'

'That is also true,' said the major. 'After a few more shifts, all of our scheduled repairs will have been done, and perhaps Lady Yvona will decide to relocate you to a busier stretch.'

They strode past the lanterns hanging from the walls as the crane was stowed away. A crowd had gathered to watch Corthie, but it was much smaller than the ones that had assembled during the hours of daylight. They waved and cheered, but a few of them looked a little disappointed.

Belinda glanced at him. 'Do you miss having an audience?'

'No,' he said. 'Well, maybe a little. Having folk watch helps me focus, and to be honest, I was a bit bored out there tonight.'

'I noticed,' she said. 'Maybe you shouldn't taunt the greenhides so much; they recognise your voice now, and run away as soon as they hear it. Do you need to sleep?'

'No, I dropped my battle-vision an hour ago. My head's buzzing. I might get a few ales in when we get back. Want to join me?'

Belinda frowned. 'Why, because Aila isn't here? Am I her replacement?'

'You can say "no" if you don't want to.'

'I don't like alcohol.'

'Fine.'

'She's only been gone one night, Corthie. How are you going to cope if she's away for a while?'

He shrugged. 'Ale and greenhides.'

'So, your favourite things are: fighting, eating, sleeping with Aila, and getting drunk?'

'Not necessarily in that order, but aye. I'm a simple guy, I guess.'

'You mother would be so proud.'

Corthie laughed. 'You're getting good at this sarcasm business.'

'You're giving me plenty of practice.'

They reached a set of steps going down the inside of the curtain wall, and began to descend.

'I don't know why Yendra was so determined to separate us,' said Corthie. 'I'm starting to wonder if she wants to keep me and Aila apart.'

'You're being paranoid. My first reaction to Yendra's plan was that she wanted to keep me away from Naxor, so he wouldn't be able to show me how the Quadrant worked, but now I've had a chance to think about it, I believe she was just being efficient, assigning people to their most suitable positions.'

'Maybe I've been over-thinking it. That's why I wanted tonight to be busy, so that I wouldn't do that. Instead, I had nothing to do but think.'

They reached the bottom of the stairs, and Corthie smiled and waved at the crowd gathered outside the fortress gates. About eighty or so Icewarders were there, cheering and calling out to him, a number far lower than he had been getting in daylight. He strode up to the gates so they could get a good look at him.

'What are you doing?' muttered Belinda.

'It's the middle of the night,' he said, 'and they've come all this way to see us.'

A small group of young women screamed as he approached. One of them, a teenager, was waving her arms, trying to attract his attention.

'Corthie!' she yelled.

He smiled and waved at her.

'I'm Maddie Jackdaw's sister!'

He paused, his eyes widening, and turned back to her.

'Over here!' she yelled. 'I'm Rosie Jackdaw. I have a message from her big, scaly friend.'

'Rosie Jackdaw?' he said.

'Do you know her?' said Belinda.

'I know her sister.'

Belinda frowned. 'Half of these people look a little unhinged; get her to prove it.'

'How?' cried the girl from through the bars of the gate. 'I can't tell you with all these people here.'

Corthie turned to the major, who was waiting a few yards away. 'We need to let this one in.'

Hannia crinkled her brows. 'Who? This girl? She's barely sixteen, at a push.'

'Aye.'

The crowd on the other side of the gates started to jostle, and the cries and shouts intensified.

Hannia gave Corthie a cold glance. 'Very well. You are the champion.'

'Don't look at me like that,' he said. 'It's not for anything weird. I need to speak to her in private. You can be there, if you want.'

Hannia signalled to a squad of soldiers, and they moved forwards.

The gate was unbarred, and the crowd tried to surge through. The soldiers blocked them with their shields, until Rosie was pulled through the gap. The gates were pushed close as the screams and cries intensified.

'Malik's ass,' cried Rosie. 'Some of those girls were pulling my hair.'

'Aye, sorry about that,' said Corthie.

The major led the way to the row of stone arches by the curtain wall, and they entered a dark, stone chamber. Hannia lit a few oil lamps and closed the door.

'I've been trying to speak to you for days,' Rosie said. 'You're easy to find, but hard to get to.'

Belinda eyed her. 'Give us some proof that you are who you say you are.'

'Alright. Blackrose and Maddie saved my life when the greenhides breached the Great Walls. Then we went up to Tarstation, to look for you.'

'Tarstation?' he said. 'I haven't been there in months.'

'So we discovered, but it was the only information we had on your possible location. When we couldn't find you, we flew to a place about two hundred miles east of here.'

'You flew?' said Belinda. 'How does one fly in this world?'

'We went on Blackrose's back.'

Belinda raised an eyebrow. 'And who is Blackrose?'

'She's a big, black dragon,' said Corthie.

'A what?'

'A dragon?' said the major. 'I was under the impression that the only dragon in the City was killed when the greenhides broke through the walls.'

'There was another,' said Corthie.

'Right,' said Belinda, 'but what's a dragon?'

'Imagine a winged gaien back home,' he said, 'only bigger, and they can talk, and they have mage powers.'

'A talking gaien? Seems a little unlikely.'

Corthie laughed. 'That's what I thought too, until I met one.'

Rosie squinted at Belinda. 'So you're not from this world, either? Wow. Are you a champion too?'

'Let's say she is, for the moment,' said Corthie; 'keep on with the story. You flew east?'

'Yes, and we found a nice little valley in some mountains, where it's safe from the greenhides.'

'But you came back to the City, alone?'

'Blackrose dropped me off not far from here, in the Iceward Range. I wanted to look for Tom, my brother. I found him; he's serving with the Blades at the Fourth Gate. My next job was to find you. Blackrose says that you promised to help her get back to her own world.'

Corthie nodded.

'You did what?' said Belinda. 'How did you intend to do that?'

'I was going to steal a Quadrant,' he said. 'It didn't work out. The dragon had been imprisoned under a fortress for ten years; it wasn't right what the City was doing to her, so I wanted to help.' He took a breath. 'We still can use your Quadrant to help her.'

Rosie's eyes lit up. 'You have a Quadrant?'

'Yes,' said Belinda.

'Can it take us straight to the little valley?'

Belinda frowned. 'In theory.'

'What do you mean?'

'I don't know how to use it yet.'

'Blackrose does,' said Rosie, 'but I can see that's not going to help us. She'll be coming back to the City though, in another four days. I've arranged to meet her in the same place that she dropped me off.'

The major's eyes flickered. 'Four days might be too late for Medio,' she said, 'if the warning from the Aurelians is true. And, if I understand this correctly, we should be asking the dragon to help us, not assisting her to flee this world.'

'She doesn't want to help,' said Rosie.

'Then why should we help her?'

'I have an idea,' said Corthie, 'but we'll need to clear it with Lady

Yvona first. If it works, then we might have Blackrose on our side, and if it doesn't, then we'll be no worse off than we are now.'

'Does it involve you leaving the walls?' said the major.

'Aye, but only for a few hours. Just long enough to visit Blackrose.'

'But how?' said Belinda. 'I can't operate the Quadrant.'

'No, but Naxor can.'

'Are you sure this isn't just an excuse to see Aila?' said Belinda as the carriage was pulled down the dark road.

Corthie glanced out of the window. Ahead of them, the sky was brightening with the approaching dawn, and he was looking forward to seeing the sun again, after nearly ten days of living in the shadows of the Iceward Range.

'Are you listening to me?' said Belinda.

'Aye, I was just trying to think of an answer that would sound convincing.'

Rosie leaned forward on the carriage bench. 'Are you in a relationship with a demigod?'

'I am,' he said.

'Sounds romantic, but is it wise?' she said. 'Gods and demigods think differently from the rest of us. Be careful that she's not just using you.'

He smiled. 'Thanks for the advice, but I'm fine. Oh, and before you say anything else about gods, you should know that Belinda's one.'

'Why did you tell her that?' said Belinda. 'I was hoping she would say some more unguarded truths about us. The whole immortality thing still confuses me. Amalia said that she thought I was thirty thousand years old, and I don't know how I feel about that.'

Rosie's eyes widened. 'Can you not remember it?'

'I can only remember the last few years,' she said. 'I still feel young.'

'Wow. And you spoke to the God-Queen?'

'Apparently I'm an old friend of hers, though we didn't leave on friendly terms when I saw her in Ooste.'

'That's an understatement,' said Corthie. 'Aila told me you nearly sliced her in half.'

Belinda shrugged. 'Only to slow her down; it wasn't personal.'

Rosie edged back a little on the bench.

'Don't be frightened of me,' said Belinda. 'Just treat me normally.'

'You nearly killed the God-Queen,' Rosie said; 'the most powerful being in the world.'

'In this world, maybe.'

'You know,' said Rosie, 'I think you and Blackrose will get along quite well. Either that or you'll kill each other.'

Belinda smiled. 'I doubt she'd be able to kill me.'

'Wait until you see her before saying that,' said Corthie. 'She has fire powers.'

'Alright, though now I'm getting curious.'

The carriage sped up as they left the hills behind them and raced towards the Circuit. The Blade checkpoints were lying abandoned and half-dismantled, and the carriage passed through them and into the iceward districts of the sprawling suburbs. Corthie leaned back on the bench and closed his eyes, a smile on his lips as he thought about seeing Aila again.

'Corthie,' said Aila as they strode into the large, high-ceilinged office; 'what are you doing here?'

'He couldn't get enough of you,' muttered Belinda.

'We're here to see Naxor,' he said to Aila; 'seeing you was just a bonus. What's happened to the palace? It look like a rowdy crowd of rioters have passed through, which is what I'm guessing actually did happen.'

Aila nodded as she got up from her desk. 'Yes, pretty much.' She leaned in and kissed him. 'Were you out last night?'

'Aye, a five hour stretch. I had a nap on the way, though.'

'What's the situation here?' said Belinda.

'The Blades have all left,' said Aila, 'except for the division based along the Middle Walls by the Fourth, Fifth and Sixth Gates, and Redmarket fell without a fight. The rebels are back in charge; I'm just helping out.'

'Where's Naxor?'

'Sleeping,' she said. 'He's supposed to be helping me, but he went off to bed hours ago.'

'And Yendra?'

Aila's eyes tightened a little at Belinda's questions. 'She's gone to see the Middle Walls for herself. Why do you need Naxor?'

'We need his skills with the Quadrant,' said Corthie. He gestured to the girl by his side. 'This is Rosie Jackdaw.'

'Jackdaw?' said Aila. 'One of Maddie's relatives?'

'I'm her sister,' the girl said. She bowed her head a little. 'Hello, Lady Aila.'

Corthie smiled. 'She knows where Blackrose is.'

'Oh.' She beckoned one of the courtiers over. 'Could please awaken my cousin Lord Naxor and ask him to come here?'

The courtier bowed, then left the chamber.

'Take a seat,' Aila said to the others, 'and tell me what you're planning.'

'It's simple,' said Corthie; 'we use the Quadrant, and persuade Blackrose to come back and help us.'

Aila nodded. 'Is she likely to agree?'

'No,' said Rosie.

'Should I come along? I met Maddie once.'

Rosie shook her head. 'I don't think that's a good idea. She doesn't like you.'

'Who, Maddie? Why not?'

'No, Blackrose doesn't like you. She told me that you'd promised to help her, but didn't.'

Aila frowned. 'That's a little unfair. I found Naxor, like Maddie had asked me to, but he refused to help.'

'He refused?' said Rosie.

'And for a perfectly sound reason,' said Naxor, striding into the room. 'Now, don't get me wrong, I do enjoy being spoken about while I'm not around, but I take exception to being portrayed unjustly.' He stood by a table and poured himself a large glass of wine. 'What a ridiculous hour to be up. I was getting used to sleeping until midday each morning.'

Corthie glanced at him. 'So you know why we're here?'

'The courtier overheard everything, and I read it from his mind.'

'Good. Will you do it?'

'It depends.'

'On what?'

'Belinda's willingness to loan me the Quadrant.'

'Or,' she said, 'you could just show me how to use it.'

'Unfortunately, that would take too long; several days in fact. If you want to travel to see Blackrose today, the only way is to let me use it.'

'But I don't trust you.'

Naxor shrugged, sat, and sipped his wine.

Corthie and Aila shared a glance as Belinda glared at Naxor.

'Maybe Belinda could hold it,' said Aila, 'while Naxor operates it?'

'Nope,' said Naxor. 'It needs to be in my hands.'

'Alright, cousin, then swear an oath to Belinda that you'll return it to her.'

Naxor frowned at her. 'Whose side are you on?'

'I'm on the side of getting an enormous dragon to help us.'

'She won't,' said Rosie. 'Maddie and I have already tried to change her mind, but she hates the City.'

Corthie turned to Belinda. 'Let him win this one. If he betrays us, we'll never trust him again.'

'I'd go a little further than that,' she said; 'if he betrays us, I will hunt him down and kill him.'

'Let me make something clear,' Naxor said. 'I will happily ferry you to the dragon and back, but under no circumstances will I be involved in the transportation of that beast back to Lostwell, ever. Is that understood?'

Rosie narrowed her eyes at him. 'Why?'

'Because I like my life there, well, I did before the Holdfasts showed up. A dragon of Blackrose's power would smash the delicate balance that exists on Lostwell, and bring down the attention of the ruling gods.' He shook his head. 'We don't want that. Already these gods are searching for the location of the world that supplies them with salve, and the last thing we need is more attention.'

'On the subject of salve,' said Rosie, 'we found a huge source of it.'

Naxor's eyes bulged. 'Yes? Where? No need to speak, I can see it in your mind.' He beamed. 'Oh my, that is a lot. That changes things, considerably. Shall we leave now?'

Aila rolled her eyes.

'Alright,' said Belinda. She reached behind her leather cuirass and withdrew the copper-coloured device. She glared at Naxor. 'Swear that you'll return this to me when we get back to the City.'

He grinned. 'I swear.'

Belinda handed it to him.

Naxor leapt to his feet. 'Right, I'm going back to Lostwell. Goodbye.' He started to laugh. 'You should see your faces.'

'You're a bit of an asshole,' said Rosie.

'Only a bit?' he said. 'I shall need to try harder.' He bowed to Belinda. 'My thanks for your trust. Despite what you may think of me, I always keep my word.'

'You'd better,' she muttered.

He glanced at the Quadrant in his hands, his fingers tracing some of the etchings. 'It's not been used in a very long time.'

'You can tell that?' said Aila.

He nodded. 'It leaves a signature of the last place it was before here. I don't think the God-Queen's used this since she arrived in the City.' He glanced at Rosie. 'I'm going back into your mind for a moment, so I can work out from your memories where exactly Blackrose and your little valley are located.'

Aila glanced at Corthie while her cousin's eyes glazed over. 'We should probably let Yendra know what's happening; actually, does Yvona know you're here?'

'Aye, I spoke to her before we left Icehaven.'

'And she's happy with you leaving for a while?'

'It'll only be for a few hours, but no, not really. She said yes, but her eyes were saying no, if you get what I mean.'

Aila nodded.

'Is there any sign,' he said, 'that what Emily Aurelian was worried about might be coming true?'

'None apart from the Blades withdrawing, but that would be the main sign. The First, Second and Third Gates are all controlled by Icewarders, the Evaders are in the Seventh, the Hammers are in the Eighth, and the Sanders have the Ninth Gate. That leaves the middle three under Kano's command. If a breach is going to happen, it'll be there.'

Naxor blinked. 'I have the location.' His fingers glided over the surface of the Quadrant. 'I'm ready when you are.'

'It's as easy as that?' said Belinda. 'That didn't look hard.'

He winked at her. 'I'm so good I make it seem easy.'

The god gave him a look of such withering contempt that he backed away a step.

Rosie laughed. 'You should see *your* face.'

'Naxor,' said Aila, 'tell Yendra before you all go.'

He sighed. 'Fine.'

Corthie stood. 'Should I have brought a weapon? Will there be greenhides?'

'No,' said Rosie; 'the little valley is enclosed on all sides by steep cliffs. It's safe.'

Aila got to her feet and took his hand. 'Try not to look so disappointed.'

He smiled at her. 'It's good to see you again. It was only one night, but I missed you.'

'Maybe you could stay over in Redmarket when you get back; I could show you my old rooms.'

'That sounds good, though we might have a dragon with us.'

'We won't,' said Rosie. 'Sorry to always be pointing it out, but I don't want you all to get your hopes up.'

'I've told Yendra,' said Naxor. 'She approves, and wishes us well, but she doesn't want us to make any rash promises to the dragon in return for her aid.'

Belinda frowned. 'Did she specify what she meant by "rash"?'

'No, she didn't. I guess we'll have to use our own judgement.' He glanced around. 'Are we ready to go?'

Corthie nodded and reached out to grab Naxor's arm.

The demigod frowned at him. 'Why are you touching me?'

'I thought I was supposed to? That's what we used to do on my world whenever we used the Quadrant.'

'How quaint,' he said. He glanced at Aila. 'See you soon, cousin.'

'Give my best to Maddie and Blackrose.'

Corthie leaned over and kissed her, then the room dissolved into haze. It was replaced by the summer sky, then he felt himself hurtle down through the air. Mountains rushed upwards, then he hit the branch of a tree and fell onto a grassy bank. He groaned, then saw Rosie land next to him, while Belinda and Naxor crashed into a large pool of water, sending a loud splash up, and spraying Corthie as he lay on the bank.

'Malik's sweaty crotch,' he heard a voice say.

Rosie got to her feet. 'Maddie!'

'Quiet!' Maddie hissed. 'Nobody shout. Listen to me, this is very important; be quiet.'

Corthie pushed himself to his feet and glanced around. Ahead of him was a waterfall and the entrance to some caves. Maddie was standing by the side of the pool, watching as Belinda and Naxor lifted themselves out of the water.

Corthie laughed. 'What happened, Naxor? Were we supposed to plummet through the sky?'

'I might have made a small error in the calculations,' Naxor said, sitting on the bank, his hair and clothes dripping onto the grass. 'Still, better to be too high than too low.'

Maddie stormed over, waving a large stick. 'If I have to tell you one more time to shut up, I'll brain the lot of you.'

Corthie turned, then his mouth opened. In the shadows under the side of the cliff stretched the huge body of the dragon, its black scales almost swallowed up in the dim light.

Maddie eyed him. 'She's sleeping. By the way, nice to see you again, Corthie. How you getting on with Aila?'

'Good. And I met your sister, obviously. This is Naxor, and that's Belinda, a friend.'

Rosie walked over to her sister. 'I found Tom,' she said in a low voice. 'He's living in a garrison in the Middle Walls; he's fine.'

Maddie smiled. 'Thanks.'

Naxor stood and gazed at Blackrose. 'Are we going to wake her?'

'No,' said Maddie. 'She nearly died last night; she has to rest.'

Rosie's eyes widened. 'What happened?'

'Come over the to caves and I'll tell you.'

She strode away, and the others followed her along the side of the pool, then up a little slope to the entrance to a wide cave.

'This is my home,' she said as they went in and sat down. 'It's where me and Blackrose have been hiding; only we've not just been hiding. Anyway, before I get onto that, I'm guessing that you found the Quadrant, right? Is that how you got here?'

Rosie nodded. 'Naxor has it.'

'But it's mine,' said Belinda.

'Actually,' said Naxor, 'it belongs to the God-Queen, but yes, it is in our possession.'

'Blackrose is going to be ecstatic when she finds out. I can't believe it; you're going to take her home? She's been dreaming about this day for years.'

'Not exactly,' said Naxor.

Maddie's smile faded. 'What? Then why in Malik's name have you come here? And choose your words carefully, because I still have a big stick in my hand.'

Naxor glanced at Corthie. 'Maybe you should tell her.'

'We're here,' he said, 'to try to persuade Blackrose to come to the City's aid. Things are getting desperate; the Middle Walls are holding, but they could breach any day. Worse, Marcus looks like he's planning to seal off Auldan, and allow the greenhides into Medio. Having Blackrose on our side would change everything.'

Maddie shook her head. 'Do you not think I've already tried to persuade her? Every day I've been on at her about it, but she refuses. And after what she did yesterday, I'm not going to try to talk her round any more.' She sighed. 'You should leave. If Blackrose awakens to discover that you're here, with the Quadrant, but you're not going to take her home, she might kill all of you. Well, not Rosie, but the rest of you.'

'We could come to a deal,' said Corthie. 'Let me talk to her and see if anything can be worked out.'

Maddie glanced at him. 'I thought you wanted to go home too? Wasn't that the deal, you know, the one you already made with Blackrose? You promised to get the Quadrant and take her home. Have you forgotten?'

'No, but I can't abandon the City when it could fall any day. And I'm not going to leave Aila. She's the real reason, I guess, but I remember my promise. Once the City is safe, then we will get her home.' He glanced at Naxor. 'One way or another.'

'It's madness,' said the demigod, 'you can't seriously expect to drop a dragon of her might and history into the middle of Lostwell and not expect some major repercussions. The gods will find her; she'll be unable to hide.'

'She wants to go home,' said Maddie, 'not to Lostwell.'

'That's even worse,' said Naxor, 'she will reignite a war that has only recently ebbed away.'

'She's going to reclaim her throne,' said Maddie, a defiant light in her eyes, 'and you can't stop her.'

'As the only person here who knows how to use a Quadrant, unfortunately, I can.'

Maddie opened her mouth, then frowned and shook her head.

'You've been deceiving me, haven't you?' said Belinda. 'You keep making excuses not to show me how the Quadrant works, but you've absolutely no intention of teaching me. You want to keep the power all to yourself.'

Naxor shrugged. 'I am often unfairly judged.' He glanced at the dragon. 'When should she awaken?'

'Tomorrow morning,' said Maddie, 'when she'll expect a great pile of food to be waiting for her.'

Naxor took the Quadrant from his tunic. 'Then I shall return tomorrow at dawn. Goodbye.'

He vanished.

Maddie threw the stick at where he had been sitting. 'Asshole.'

'My thoughts entirely,' said Belinda.

Rosie nodded. 'Me too.'

'At least we can talk without him reading Rosie or Maddie's minds,' said Corthie. 'Did you hear what he told us? He doesn't know that Blackrose can use the Quadrant.'

'Why not?' said Maddie.

'He can't read everything from your mind at once,' said Belinda. 'He must have missed it.'

Corthie nodded. 'Then we steal the Quadrant from him when he returns.'

'If he returns,' said Belinda. 'How do we know that he hasn't just abandoned us here?'

'He'll be back,' said Corthie; 'I saw his eyes light up when Rosie mentioned the salve in the caves.'

'Alright, so we work out a plan to separate Naxor from the Quadrant, and give it to Blackrose?'

'If she agrees to help,' said Corthie. 'One or two days of her time, that's all I ask; we could seal the breaches in the Great Walls, and lock in the greenhides that are packing the Bulwark. If she agrees, we give her the Quadrant.'

'You're taking an awful risk, Corthie,' said Maddie. 'She likes you, but this might tip her into a rage.'

'I'll take my chances.'

Belinda nodded. 'Alright, I agree with this plan. If it succeeds, than I shall return with the dragon as far as Lostwell.'

Corthie gasped. 'What?'

She shrugged. 'You want to be with Aila. I'll tell your sister that you don't need to be rescued.'

He nodded, his mind swirling.

'So you're going to stay?' said Maddie. 'You must really love her.'

'I do.'

Rosie glanced out at the sunlight. 'So what will we do for the rest of the day?'

Maddie smiled. 'Do any of you know how to hunt goats?'

CHAPTER 22
PATHS OF REDEMPTION

Sixth Gate – Middle Walls, Medio, The City – 1st Mikalis 3420

Emily lay huddled in the cramped basement cell, shivering and bruised. Blades had entered the stone chambers in the middle of the night to deliver what Sergeant Quill had called a professional beating. None of their bones had been broken, and no permanent scars had been left; the Blades efficiently dispensing pain with wooden bats. It had been over in minutes, and Emily had crawled onto the filthy straw mattress while the soldiers had moved into Quill's cell to administer the same to her.

It had been standard procedure, Quill had whispered to her afterwards, a practice carried out by the Blades for countless generations to keep the servile populations of Hammers and Scythes under control. Emily had remembered when the Blades had beaten Daniel in Pella for resisting arrest, and sensed the truth in the sergeant's words. The fear she had felt when the four men had entered her cell had been worse than the actual pain they had inflicted, and she guessed that had been part of its purpose; to terrify and subdue them.

'It must be dawn by now,' said Quill, her low voice drifting through the bars of the cell.

Emily felt her fears rise. 'Don't say that.'

'No, what I mean is, it's past dawn, and Kano's not here.'

'Don't make me hope,' Emily said, her left eye opening. The passageway outside the cells was quiet. The guards were standing at their posts, as they had been for hours, while the heavy wooden door that led to the stairs was closed. 'I doubt he's forgotten about us.'

'No, but there's a chance that he has too many other things going on that need his attention; he has three gates and ten thousand Blades to look after.'

'Stop it, Quill. I know you're trying to help, but we need to steel ourselves, not get carried away by wishful thinking. We're probably going to die in these cells.'

'I thought you believed in your legend?'

'What if part of it is being martyred? Martyrs make excellent legends.'

'You're only saying that because they beat us. That's why they do it; to break your spirit. They make you feel helpless and they make you feel pain, and then you're grateful to them when they make it stop. I know all this, because I was trained to do it. I ended up in the Wolfpack, but I could just as easily have been assigned to a police battalion, patrolling the Scythes and Hammers. No wonder they hated us so much. We were taught not to see them as real people; that's the key. Good men and women can be persuaded to inflict cruelty upon others if they don't have any empathy with their victims. Kano and Marcus drilled that into the Blades for centuries; it was the only way they could keep power.'

'None of that changes the fact that we're probably going to die.'

'That "probably" means that there's still hope.'

Emily pushed herself up into a sitting position, grimacing from the bruises on her abdomen. Dried blood from her nose was streaked down her chin, and her right eye was swollen shut. She pulled her knees up to her chest, and hugged her legs. Her throat was dry, and she longed for a sip of water, but nothing had been brought for them since they had arrived.

She glanced at the thick door at the end of the passageway, through which Kano had entered the previous night. The large gatehouse stood directly overhead, and she wondered how many yards separated her cell from the greenhides. An occasional noise could sometimes be heard through the thick stone walls and ceiling, but nothing that gave any indication about what was happening.

The handle on the door turned, and Emily's terror rose as it was pushed open. A Blade officer walked in, armoured, and with a crossbow in his hands. He glanced at Emily, his features expressionless, then gestured for the four guards to leave. They saluted and trooped out of the passageway, leaving the officer alone.

He approached the bars. 'Commander Kano has given the order for your immediate execution.'

'What?' said Quill. 'He said he wanted us to cooperate.'

'The situation has… changed somewhat since he was last here.'

'So that's it?' cried Quill. 'Do you realise what murdering Emily Aurelian will do? A hundred thousand Hammers will kill every last Blade in the City. Kano's made a mistake, he…'

'Silence,' said the officer. He stared at Emily for a moment, the crossbow resting in his hands.

'Go on, then,' she said. 'Do it.'

'What I'm about to do,' he said, 'I do for the City.'

He placed the crossbow on the stone flagstones, and pulled a set of keys from his belt. He unlocked Emily's cell, followed by Quill's, then knelt on the ground with his hands behind his head. Quill rushed from the cell and grabbed the crossbow.

She pointed it at the officer. 'You're letting us escape?'

'I strongly recommend you stay where you are for the next few minutes.'

'Why?'

'You'll soon see.' He glanced at Emily, who was still sitting on the mattress. 'I'd be obliged, ma'am, if you would tell your husband that my soldiers were only obeying the direct orders of Commander Kano. I would be grateful if he spared their lives.'

Emily pulled herself to her feet, and limped over to the bars. 'Is he close?'

The door burst open, and armed Hammers rushed into the passageway, brandishing stolen crossbows.

'I surrender,' said the officer. 'I have freed the prisoners.'

The Hammers flooded the passageway, surrounding the kneeling officer.

'Don't kill him,' said Emily from the entrance of her cell, as the Hammers stared wide-eyed at the blood on her face.

Daniel appeared at the bottom of the stairs, and the Hammers parted to allow him through. He ran to Emily, his eyes anguished as he gazed at her, then he enveloped her in his arms without a word, pulling her close.

'Not too tight, Danny; I'm a little fragile.'

He glanced at her eye, and the blood on her chin. 'What have they done to you?'

'She was given a beating,' said the kneeling officer, 'on the orders of Commander Kano.'

Daniel turned to him, his eyes lit with fury. 'And you carried it out?'

'Not personally, but I passed on the order, yes.'

Daniel's hand went to the hilt of his sheathed sword.

'No, Danny,' said Emily. 'He unlocked the cell doors, when he'd been ordered to execute us.'

'Only because he knew we were coming. He was saving his own skin.'

One of the Hammers glanced up. 'Should I kill him, my lord?'

Daniel's eyes burned with hatred and anger, but he took his hand off the sword hilt. 'No, my wife is correct. We will execute no Blade who surrenders to us. Take him away and place him with the other captives.'

Quill slung her new crossbow over her shoulder. 'Thanks for the rescue, sir.'

Daniel nodded. 'I had some assistance.'

He put his arm round Emily's shoulder and helped her walk to the bottom of the stairs.

'Are there many Hammers upstairs?' she said.

'Just enough to hold the lower floors,' Daniel said. 'Kano has blockaded himself into a chamber on the top storey.'

'I don't understand. There are ten thousands Blades along this stretch of the wall; how did you break through?'

He smiled. 'You'll see.'

They went up the steps, Emily's left shin aching from the bruise that covered it. Armed Hammers were awaiting them at the top of the stairs. They began to cheer, but quietened when they caught sight of her injuries.

'Let's go,' said Daniel; 'we're pulling out of the gatehouse. Leave all captives here, unharmed.'

The Hammers began to move, leaving through the doors that led to the forecourt in front of the towering block. A huge figure in full armour was standing there, gripping a bloody sword in both hands. Hundreds of Blades were watching from each side, but none were moving, each staring at the tall warrior in silence. A dozen bodies lay littering the cobbles of the courtyard, all Blades, the blood pooling beneath them.

Emily gazed at the warrior. She was as tall as Kano, and looked just as strong, and her long dark hair was tumbling over the steel plates buckled to her shoulders.

'All those dead soldiers,' Daniel whispered; 'she killed them.'

'Who is she?'

The warrior turned. 'I am Princess Yendra.' She frowned at the sight of Quill and Emily, then turned back to the Blades. 'Do you see what the cruelty of your masters has done? Question everything Commander Kano has told you. If you receive orders to do something that you know in your hearts is wrong, then disobey. Fight for the City, not for tyrants that would treat all mortals as their slaves.'

The Blades cramming the courtyard said nothing.

Yendra gazed up at a window on the upper storey of the gatehouse. 'I know you can hear me, Kano, and I know you can see me. Do you now believe that I have returned? You were like a son to me, a beloved boy, brave and honourable. That is how I remember you. You have fallen far, and today you hide yourself; are you too ashamed to confront me? Your sister Aila still loves you, as do I, despite all of the evil that you have done. Your crimes are too many to be forgiven, but you can still change; there is still time for you to repent and fight for the people of this City. It won't bring redemption, but it may give you peace of mind. However, if you ever again lift a hand against the Hammers or Evaders, or any of the people that live here, I shall return and kill you, and you know that I always keep my word.'

She glanced at Emily and Daniel. 'Let us depart.'

The princess began striding across the courtyard, the Blades backing away from her, and clearing a path to the gates. The Hammers followed, with Quill and the Aurelians in their midst. Emily glanced around as she limped along, supported by Daniel.

'Where are the rest of the Hammers? I only see about forty.'

'That's all we brought,' said Daniel. 'Princess Yendra marched up to the gates and demanded that they be opened, and when the Blades refused, she broke the gates down and killed a dozen in a few seconds. A hail of crossbow bolts hit her, and she shrugged them off as if they were nothing.'

They passed the entrance, and Emily saw the iron gates lying on the cobbles, their hinges twisted and broken. Beyond the gates, there was a cleared area running the length of the Middle Walls, with the grey concrete mass of the Circuit on the other side. A huge crowd was waiting there, out of reach of the bows of the Blades, and thousands of faces stared at the sight of Yendra striding towards them. The moment they reached the safety of the streets, the crowd erupted in a roar of cheers, while the humiliated Blades looked on from the gatehouse.

Yendra raised her hand for quiet, and the crowd calmed. 'Behold Lady Aurelian,' she said, 'safely returned to the arms of her husband. From this moment forwards, I pledge my friendship and alliance with the Aurelians, and I ask all Evaders to treat the Hammers as their brothers and sisters.' The crowd cheered again. 'Do not hate the Blades,' Yendra went on; 'they are badly led, but they are the sons and daughters of the City, just like you. When our victory comes, it would be wise to be merciful.'

Again, the crowd cheered, though Emily noticed it wasn't as loud as before, and a few of the Evaders looked as though they disagreed with the words of the princess. She and Daniel were escorted through the streets, with Yendra leading the way as the sun rose above the roofs of the concrete houses, sending a deep red light across the Circuit. They reached a fortified compound, and left the crowds behind them as Evader militia opened the gates.

Yendra turned to Emily. 'This may seem like much to ask, but I would like you to come with me to visit someone.'

'Sorry, your Highness,' said Daniel, 'but she needs rest and a doctor.'

Emily leaned against him, taking the weight off her bruised shin. 'Visit who?'

Yendra gazed at her. 'Lady Jade.'

'What?' said Daniel, his eyes widening. 'But she could kill Emily in a second.'

'She won't,' said Yendra; 'trust me.'

'Alright,' said Emily.

'Thank you.'

'How will we get there?' said Emily. 'She lives about three miles from here, and I don't think I can walk that far.'

'There is a canal at the rear of this compound,' she said, 'and I have a barge waiting for us.' She turned to Daniel. 'I would like you to return to the Eighth Gate, with the Hammer soldiers you brought. I will drop Emily off there later.'

'I'm not happy about this,' he said. 'We only just saved her from Kano, and now you're taking her to see the Circuit's other resident mad demigod.'

'She will be safe with me, Lord Aurelian, of that you can be assured.'

Daniel shook his head. 'Fine. I want a minute alone with my wife before you leave.'

Yendra inclined her head, and walked away to speak to a group of Evader officers.

'Don't worry,' said Emily.

'How can I not? I've just spent the whole night looking for you, and I feel sick thinking about what you went through in there.' He gently traced the cut on her nose with a finger. 'I want to kill the people who did this to you.'

'I'll recover,' she said. 'It's just like when the Blades beat you up in Pella; we've both been hurt for trying to do the right thing.'

'I was beaten up because I resisted arrest.'

She smiled. 'Whoever tells our story can miss that part out. How did you get Yendra to help?'

'I went to Redmarket Palace and begged her.'

'You went to Redmarket, even though many rebel Evaders want to hang you?'

'I would do anything for you.'

She kissed him, and he wrapped his arms around her.

'Take care,' he said.

She glanced over, and saw Yendra waiting for her. She kissed Daniel again. 'I'll see you soon.'

She hobbled over to Yendra, who took her arm, supporting her as she walked. They went past lines of militia and came to the back of the compound's main building, where a dark canal sat. Yendra helped Emily down onto a long barge, and they sat by the stern as a squad of Evaders boarded.

'This will take us most of the way,' said Yendra as the squad pushed the barge out from the quayside.

'May I ask why you want me to visit Lady Jade with you?'

'She needs to see the future.'

'Am I the future?'

Yendra smiled. 'I think you already know the answer to that, Emily. An Evader, brought up as a Roser, and married to the heir to the oldest house in the City?'

'You know I'm an Evader? One of your people?'

'One day you shall rule, if you wish it, and I will support you.'

'You don't know me.'

'I know enough.'

'What about Daniel?'

'He is tainted by his past, though I have seen how hard he has striven to redeem himself. To rule, he will need to earn the forgiveness of the Evaders, and that is out of my hands.'

'If that's what it takes, then he'll earn it. I applauded his actions at the time, you should know that. I'm ashamed of how I reacted, just as he is ashamed of what he did.'

'Shame is an appropriate response, but it is not sufficient.'

'Only by his actions will he be redeemed.'

Yendra nodded. 'At least for Daniel redemption remains possible; for Kano, there is no such path available. It tears my heart to see what he has become, but if it falls to me to strike him down, then I will not hesitate.'

Emily glanced at the princess. 'I studied the history of Prince Michael when I was younger; it was my favourite subject, and I read countless books about his life and works.'

'I hear I am portrayed rather unfavourably in these books.'

'You are the villain; the destroyer of the peace and prosperity of the City, and the one responsible for its decline. Worst of all, of course, you killed him. Seeing as how you've seemingly returned from beyond the grave, can I ask, you really did kill him, didn't you?'

'Yes. There will be no return for Michael.'

Emily puffed her cheeks. 'Thank Malik for that. Or, thank you, I should say. So, the whole execution in Ooste was faked?'

'How do the books say I was killed?'

'The God-King beheaded you, in view of the God-Queen, then they burned your body.'

Yendra nodded. 'My father took me to the Grey Isle, and attached a god-restrainer to my face. I don't recall anything after that.'

'The God-Queen left the Royal Palace soon afterwards. Do you think she knew he hadn't executed you?'

'If I had to guess, I would say that my father told my mother that he had killed me, but she didn't believe him.'

'Well, the God-Queen will know you're alive by now. It scares me to think that she might get involved.'

'Aside from the greenhides, my mother is the greatest danger we face.' She glanced up at the passing housing blocks and canal-side warehouses. 'Next to her power, Jade should be easy to deal with.'

The barge entered an area that was deserted, and the bustle and noise of the Circuit dwindled away. Abandoned houses and workshops lined the canal and an eerie silence descended.

'It's like this for miles,' said Emily. 'Jade's frightened everyone away.'

'That ends today.'

Emily grimaced as she straightened her leg. She put a hand to her face, feeling the swelling around her right eye. She wished she could lie down for a while on the bottom of the barge; her head was throbbing, and her shin ached.

'Are you in pain?' said Yendra.

'A little. That was the worst beating I've had in years.'

'You've had others?'

'A few. I just need a day or two to rest.'

'Yes. Again, you have my thanks for agreeing to accompany me today. It shouldn't take too long.'

The barge continued on, passing alongside a massive cement works, then drew to a slow halt by a quayside. Emily glanced up, and saw a row of large concrete tenement blocks. In front of one, a group of soldiers was standing, holding swords and maces.

'The residence of Lady Jade,' said Yendra, rising and extending her hand for Emily.

She took it and got to her feet.

'Stay here,' said Yendra to the militia on the barge. 'Do not endanger yourselves.' She leaped up onto the quayside, then turned and lifted Emily up from the deck.

They walked towards the high tenements, Yendra's arm supporting Emily. The group of soldiers turned as they approached, and began raising their weapons.

Yendra guided Emily to a low wall and sat her down. 'Give me a moment to put these poor creatures out of their misery.'

Emily watched as Yendra drew her sword. She had heard about the soldiers working for Jade, and had spoken to eye-witnesses who had described them to her, but she still felt sick looking at them. Their skin was peeling from their grey faces, their eyes vacant and seeping, while flies buzzed around them in the summer sun.

Yendra approached them, her long sword held in both hands. Then she moved. As fast as a blur to Emily's eyes, the princess swept through the lines of soldiers, her blade cleaving everything it touched. Limbs fell, torsos were sliced clean through, and within seconds, the group of undead were lying scattered across the flagstones. Yendra sheathed her sword, then faced the tenement.

'Jade,' she cried, 'it's Auntie Yendra. I'm coming inside, and I'm bringing a mortal with me. I'm sure you remember my old rules; don't make me repeat them. I'm just here for a chat, so let's be civil.'

She walked back to Emily and helped her up.

'What are the rules?'

'She's not to kill anyone unless it's self defence.'

'Or?'

'I take her head.'

'I see.'

They entered the tenement, and climbed the stairs to the top floor, where a door lay open. They went inside, squeezing between the crates and boxes piled up by the doorway, and walked into a large room, heaped with clothes, furniture, and boxes full of jewellery and gold. Carpets lay rolled and stacked up, alongside paintings and silver candlesticks.

Jade was reclining on a long couch, draped in bright satin robes, a tiara balanced on her brow. At each shoulder stood a grey-skinned soldier, while other undead servants were by the wide windows.

'Niece,' said Yendra, 'I see you've been busy looting the neighbourhood.'

Jade stared at her aunt, her eyes wide.

Yendra sat on a chair opposite her. 'Come now, did you think your lifestyle would go unnoticed? You've been terrorising the Evaders for months.' She gestured to Emily, who sat down beside her. 'This is Lady Aurelian.'

'She's not a lady,' said Jade; 'she's only mortal.'

'Things have changed, Jade. I will not allow you to kill anyone else for your own selfish needs; that ends today. How it ends is up to you.'

'I've not seen you in five hundred years,' said Jade, 'and you've come to bully me?

'We're handing the City over to the mortals.'

Jade laughed until tears were streaming down her face, as Yendra waited.

'Our family have governed badly, Jade,' she said when her niece had quietened. 'At first, we justified our rule because we were needed to protect the mortals from the eternal enemy, but now the God-Queen sits in Ooste while the greenhides destroy the Bulwark, and threaten Medio.'

'So?' said Jade. 'Let the greenhides eat them all. I'll be safe here. If any of those beasts come close, I'll turn them into my own soldiers.'

'No, they will kill you. You might be able to destroy the first few hundred, but their numbers will swamp you, and they will rip you to pieces. This tenement has no balcony or parapet; they will simply come up the stairs and devour you.'

'Rubbish, I could kill thousands of them.'

'And what would you eat? Face the truth, if the greenhides break through the Middle Walls, then one way or another, you will die if you stay here. Fortunately, staying here is not an option; you are moving out.'

'I am?'

'Yes. Here is your choice; consider it well, because it's the only one I'm going to offer you – either you swear allegiance to Lady Aurelian, or I kill you. But first, I want you to heal her wounds.'

Jade started laughing again, then stopped when she caught the look on Yendra's face. 'Are you joking with me? You're asking a god to kneel before an insect?'

'You're not a god, Jade, and Emily isn't an insect. You have two minutes; make your choice. If you haven't healed her within that time, I will assume your answer is no and act accordingly.'

Jade shrieked. 'What? No, I refuse. You can't kill me; I would kill you if you tried. I'd melt the skin from your face before you could come anywhere near me.'

'Do you remember what happened to Prince Michael's daughter, Lady Yordi? She tried to use her death powers on me; I ripped her heart out through her ribcage. Time is passing, Jade, and Emily Aurelian is not yet healed.'

'But this isn't fair!'

'It's perfectly fair.'

'No, it isn't.'

'Ten seconds, Jade.'

Emily glanced from aunt to niece, the pain in her body difficult to ignore. The demigod leapt to her feet, as if she was going to run for the door, and Yendra drew her sword. Jade whimpered, then raised a hand at Emily. The force of the demigod's powers blew her off the chair, sending her flying across the floor and crashing into a wall. At first the pain increased to unbearable levels, and then it stopped.

Waves of healing washed over her, and she convulsed for a moment, then lay still, her breath calming. She blinked. She felt amazing. Every part of her body was tingling with life and energy. She sat up, and laughed. Her right eye had healed, and her sight seemed to have improved. She gazed at her hands; the skin was almost glowing, and her nails were strong and blemish free.

Yendra nodded, then turned back to Jade. 'Good.' She sheathed the sword. 'Well done, Jade. Now, get on your knees.'

Jade started to cry. 'Please, not that. I'll swear loyalty to you, my princess, but to a mortal? I can't. The shame of it.'

'It's the future, and it's that or die. If we want the City to survive, we must adjust. This is your only way out, the only path you can take that might result in you keeping your life.'

Jade slumped to her knees on the floor as tears fell down her cheeks. Emily got up from the corner of the room and walked over to stand in front of the demigod.

'Do you swear allegiance to me,' she said, 'and pledge your loyalty until death? Do you swear to obey my commands, and those of my husband, Daniel Aurelian; and do you swear to protect the people of this City; honour my friends as your friends, and treat my enemies as your enemies?'

Jade bowed her head but said nothing.

Emily kept her gaze on the demigod. 'Swear it.'

'I swear.'

Emily extended her hand. Jade looked at it with contempt for a moment, then her eyes drooped, and she took it.

'Thank you for healing me,' said Emily, 'and thank you for your oath. Stand.'

Jade got to her feet, and Yendra joined them.

'This pleases me,' said the princess, 'because I did not wish to kill you, Jade. Now, Lady Aurelian, do you know what orders you will give to my niece?'

Emily nodded. 'Jade, I'm assigning you to the Seventh Gate on the Middle Walls. That stretch of the defences is under constant pressure, and the Evader garrison has been hard pressed. Your duties will be to kill as many greenhides as you can. You boasted earlier that you could slaughter thousands, and I would like to see you prove that. I will give you the entire upper floor of the gatehouse to use as your personal quarters, with food and everything you else you might require, as befits a demigod in service of the City. No one will bother you there, and you can live as you please; only, no more killing mortals, and no more turning them into your creatures. This is what I command; tell me now if you accept.'

Jade glanced at Emily. 'Of all the mortals, why you?'

'Love and fate have thrown me into this position,' she said. 'I did not ask for it, but nor do I shirk it.'

'I accept,' said Jade, 'but I have one condition.'

'Yes?'

'Will you get me a cat?'

Emily smiled. 'I'll see to it personally.'

CHAPTER 23

THE WEED-EATER

The Eastern Mountains – 2nd Mikalis 3420

Maddie's eyes flicked open. The cave was in darkness, with a dark purple patch of night sky marking the entrance. Around her lay the bodies of Corthie, Rosie and Belinda, all sleeping, the sound of their low breathing rising to her ears. She pulled the blanket over her, freeing her feet from the tangles, and closed her eyes again.

She had been dreaming about hunting goats on a wild mountain pass, or maybe they had been hunting her, she couldn't remember. She opened her eyes again, to check that Blackrose hadn't shifted position, and she peered through the darkness until her eyes caught sight of the form of the sleeping dragon. A large pile of goat carcasses lay next to her, covered by a sheet to keep the flies off, and the sound of the waterfall was the only noise coming from outside.

She turned onto her back, her mind awake as images of the previous day's hunt flashed before her eyes. Corthie, Belinda and Rosie had been ruthlessly efficient, with the champion and the god chasing and herding the wild goats down the narrow valleys so that Rosie could shoot them with the small ballista she had assembled from the components they had stored in the cave. Maddie had sat and watched from the side of a ridge, refusing to take part in the slaughter, her heart breaking from the cries of the goats. She had gone seven full days without meat, and though her sister had started referring to her as a 'weed-eater', she felt sure that no animal's flesh would ever pass her lips again.

Her eyes closed and she started to drift off to sleep, the soft sound of a goat scraping its hoofs off the ground close to her.

She sat up, her ears straining, and heard it again. Was there a goat in the cave? Maybe one of the dead goats had risen, and was coming to get them, seeking bloody vengeance for its fallen comrades. She rubbed her eyes, trying to wake herself. The sound of the waterfall was playing tricks on her, but no, she heard it again, a soft scraping noise coming from somewhere deeper in the caves. Maybe a creature was trapped inside, unable to escape due to the four bodies blocking the entrance.

It needed help, she decided, hoping it wasn't a bear. A baby bear would be alright, just not a big one. If it was a mummy or daddy bear, then she would have to wake Corthie up, as he looked as though he could wrestle one. She pushed herself up, and took a small lantern from the top of a crate. She lit it with a match, and narrowed the shutter to a small slit, just enough to light the way. She stepped over the sleeping form of Corthie, and stole to the end of the cave, where it led off deeper into the side of the mountain. She followed the winding tunnel, and the sound grew louder. A dim light appeared ahead of her, coming from the threads of salve that traced their way across the walls of the caverns. She wondered if bears liked salve.

There was a turn at the end of the tunnel, and Maddie prepared herself to meet the bear. The source of the scraping noise was close, and she placed the oil lamp down on the ground, then peered round the corner.

'You're not a bear,' she said.

Naxor turned from where he was crouching by the wall. A sack was lying open by his feet, and he was holding a knife in his gloved right hand, while score marks along the wall showed where he had been gouging out chunks of salve.

He smiled. 'No, I'm not.'

She swooped down with an arm before he could say anything else, and pulled the sack out of his reach.

'Wow,' she said, glancing inside; 'this is a lot of salve.'

His eyes narrowed. 'You're going to give me that back.'

'Eh, no; I don't think so. You could have had some if you'd asked nicely, but sneaks get nothing.'

'Be careful, Maddie; only one of us is holding a knife.'

'You're going to stab me over some stupid salve?'

'Wars have been started over salve; the death of one girl will make no difference.'

'Were you just going to abandon us?'

'No,' he said, turning towards her, the knife raised. 'This was supposed to be a quick visit to fill the sack and get out again. I was fully intending to return at dawn, only now you've ruined my plans. If you force me to kill you, then I don't think it would be wise to return. Now, put the sack down, go back to sleep, and you and I can pretend that none of this took place. I'll return at dawn, and everything will be fine. Bearing in mind that if you refuse I will slit your throat, how does that sound?'

'I used to think you were alright,' she said, 'but now I see you're just as bad as the others.'

'My dear, I'm far worse than some; give me a little credit.'

Maddie started to back away, her arms clutching the sack.

He lunged out at her with the knife, then halted as the edge of a sword appeared against his neck, its blade making a thin line of red on his skin.

'Drop the knife,' said Belinda, 'or you lose your head.'

'Come on, Belinda,' he said, 'you and me could be in Lostwell in a few minutes with enough salve to live like the gods of old. You could have your own castle; your own realm. You're a clever woman, and I know you care nothing for the people of this world.'

'You don't know anything about me,' she said. 'This is your last chance, Naxor. Drop the knife, or I'll prove how little I care about you.'

'You're hurting my feelings,' he said.

The knife clattered to the floor of the cavern, and Belinda swung her free hand, punching Naxor in the face. The demigod flew back through the cave, his head cracking off the cavern wall. He slid to the ground, unconscious.

Belinda turned to Maddie. 'Are you alright?'

'Yeah. Thanks.'

'No problem, though I'd be lying if I said I didn't enjoy that.' She glanced at the body of Naxor. 'I hate him, I think.'

'You think?'

'My feelings about this man are confused. Part of me hates him, the other part finds him... intriguing. Don't tell anyone.'

'Don't tell anyone what?' said Corthie from behind them. 'What's going on?' He saw the figure of Naxor slumped against the cavern wall. 'Oh.'

He stepped forwards and pulled Naxor's robes open, then picked up a copper-coloured object. He gazed at it for a moment, then slipped it into his clothes.

'I should have done that,' said Maddie.

He shrugged.

'If I had,' she said, 'what would you have done?'

'Tried to persuade you to go with my plan, I suppose.'

'And if I'd refused, and given it to Blackrose?'

'Then nothing. You're my friend, Maddie; I wouldn't threaten or hurt you over a stupid Quadrant.'

She nodded. 'You might wish I'd taken it when Blackrose finds out.'

Belinda crouched down by Naxor, rolled him onto his front, and started binding his wrists. Once they were secure, she ripped a long piece of fabric from his robes, and blindfolded him.

Corthie shook his head. 'I'm not surprised that he betrayed us, but I'm still disappointed.'

'I'm not sure he actually betrayed us,' said Maddie. 'His plan was to grab as much salve as he could, then come back at dawn as if it'd never happened. I guess then he would get to appear magnanimous, while knowing he already had a sack of salve waiting for him.'

'Don't try to excuse him,' said Belinda; 'he came at you with a knife.'

Corthie frowned. 'Did he? That treacherous little rat.' He leaned over and picked the demigod up, slinging him over his shoulder. 'Let's get him out of the cave.'

Maddie watched as Corthie strode from the cavern with Naxor on his shoulder, then she picked up the heavy bag of salve, and followed, Belinda walking alongside her. The patch of sky at the entrance to the cave had brightened a little, and Rosie was awake and sitting up as the others returned. Corthie carried Naxor out onto the grass, and lowered him to the ground by the cave's entrance.

'Was he trying to steal salve?' said Rosie.

Maddie dumped the sack by her side. 'Take a look.'

'And where is the... uh...?'

'Corthie nabbed it.'

'It's nearly dawn,' said Belinda; 'should we wake the dragon?'

'Let me do it,' said Maddie. 'Everyone else should wait in the cave.'

'Alright,' said Corthie.

'I'll wave when I want you to approach,' she said, 'but if I jump up and down screaming, then it means that she's decided to kill you and you should try to run away.'

She walked down the little slope without waiting for a response, then went round the side of the large pool to where Blackrose was sleeping. The injuries across her limbs and underside were starting to heal, but still looked raw and sore. She crept up by the dragon's flank, and put a hand on her head.

'Mela,' she whispered; 'it's goat-time.'

The great eyes flickered open. 'Maddie.'

'You've been sleeping for a whole day, and almost a whole night. It's nearly dawn, and I thought you might need to eat.'

'I'm too tired to hunt.'

Maddie smiled, then walked up to the mound of goat carcasses. She took a corner of the sheet covering it, then glanced to the side so she wouldn't have to look at the mangled and bloody bodies. She whipped the sheet away.

The dragon raised her head a foot. 'You did this for me? You killed all these goats for me?'

'I had a little help.'

The dragon seemed oblivious to her words as she opened her jaws and launched herself at the mound of food. Maddie took a few paces back to get out of the way as the dragon entered a feeding frenzy, her teeth ripping through the carcasses, cracking the bones like twigs, and swallowing some goats down whole. Her claws dug into the soft ground as she ate, scoring deep marks through the soil.

'Bye, bye, poor little goats,' muttered Maddie as the mound disappeared down Blackrose's throat.

In a few minutes, it was over, the dragon leaving nothing but a few scraps of fur upon the stained grass. She extended her neck, and lowered her mouth to the pool, where she drank deep.

'That feel better?' said Maddie.

The dragon turned to her. 'Maddie, that was a feast for which I will always be grateful; but tell me, when did you learn how to use the machine that killed all of those goats?'

'The ballista? Well, as I was saying before, I had a little help.'

The dragon's eyes scanned the little valley. 'From whom?'

Maddie sat on a clean stretch of grass. 'Right. Listen to me, please, and don't say anything until I have finished.'

The dragon tilted her head. 'I sense bad news.'

'Well, there's good news and bad news; a bit of both. Remember, and this is important; I am only the messenger. I'm not in favour of the "plan" that certain other people have thought up, alright?'

'Am I going to get angry?'

'Eh, I think that might be likely, yes. Maybe not, I don't know.'

'Maddie, please get on with it.'

'The good news first,' she said. 'Yesterday, quite unexpectedly, four people arrived here in our little valley. You were sleeping at the time, and I insisted that they let you rest.'

'Who?'

'My sister.'

'Yes.'

'Corthie, a demigod called Naxor, and a god that I've never heard of before; her name's Belinda.'

'Lord Naxor? Didn't he have a Quadrant?'

'That's how they got here.'

The dragon's eyes gleamed red. 'Corthie is here with a Quadrant? Where is he? Please tell me that the bad news isn't that he's fallen off a cliff.'

'No, he's alive.'

'Then where is he?'

'I told them to hide, because I've still got to tell you the bad news.'

'Which is?'

'They will take you home, but they have conditions.'

Rage flared across the dragon's face, and she bared her teeth, still red from the goats.

'These conditions,' Maddie went on, 'well, you can probably guess. Corthie wants you to fight for the City first.'

The dragon reared her head high, her eyes burning. 'Holdfast! Show yourself, or I'll burn everything in this valley.'

Corthie appeared at the entrance to the cave, his empty hands raised. He walked down the little slope.

The dragon stared at him. 'You foul betrayer. I trusted you, I loved you; you made me a promise.'

'I know,' he said, striding forwards across the grass, 'and I'm here to fulfil it.'

'Then what is this talk of conditions?'

'A couple of days, that's all I ask. Fly to the City, and burn as many greenhides as you can, and then, I will give you the Quadrant.'

'No. Nothing I do will ever be enough for you humans. "Just one more thing", I've heard these promises before. Two days ago, I killed more greenhides that every human in the City combined; you should be on your knees in front of me telling me how grateful you are, but no, you want more.'

'Maddie told me what you did,' he said. 'Destroying that nest was amazing, and it will help every person in the City, but only if the City survives. Please, after ten years of imprisonment, two days is not much to ask.'

'You have lost my trust, Corthie. You told me you would never ask me to help the City. You lied. I thought you were different, but you're not.'

'I didn't lie; things have changed. What once made sense is no longer the case. I have decided to remain in the City, and yet I still came here, so that you can find the path home.'

Blackrose laughed, a brutal, guttural sound that evoked no joy. 'You have decided to stay here? Pathetic. To think that I once thought of you as worthy of my trust and friendship.'

'It's not pathetic,' said Maddie; 'he's in love.'

The dragon turned to her. 'Stay out of this, rider.'

'It's a fair deal,' said Corthie. 'We have struggled against the greenhides, and against the rule of Marcus and the God-Queen. I should be on the walls right now, but instead I'm here, trying to help you. If you do this for me, the Quadrant will be yours, and you can leave this world.'

Blackrose lowered her head to face the champion, her jaws open. 'And what's to stop me killing you and taking it now?'

Corthie shrugged. 'Nothing.'

'Not nothing,' said Belinda as she walked down the slope and joined them by the pool.

The dragon stared at her. 'Who are you?'

'I'm Belinda.'

'I sense your self-healing powers; you are a god from an older generation.'

'So I heard. More relevantly, I came to this world to find Corthie, and I would take exception to you killing him.'

'You came here to find him, but he doesn't want to leave. Surely your duty of care has ended?'

'Don't get me wrong; I'm a little annoyed by his actions, but his sister would be upset if he died, and I owe her a considerable debt. Personally,

I think he should just give you the Quadrant, and then you can take me back to Lostwell.'

Blackrose nodded. 'A god with some sense at last.'

'So, you're a dragon?' Belinda said, gazing up at Blackrose. 'I'm impressed.'

'You should be.'

'You could probably save the City if you wished.'

'There is no "probably" about it, god.'

'Having never seen you fight, it remains a probability to my mind. Why do you refuse?'

'Because the City tortured me for years; they treated me as a slave, and now they want my help? I think not.'

'Seems reasonable to me. I'd do the same if I were you.'

Corthie frowned at her. 'Is this supposed to be helping?'

'No. The dragon has a good point; why should I keep looking out for you if you've decided to stay?'

'Um, because we're friends?'

'But, Corthie, helping the dragon is the right thing to do.'

'That's why I'm here! I'm trying to help Blackrose get home.'

'Yes, but the imposition of conditions tarnishes your motives.'

'I'm trying to save the City and the dragon. Blackrose, swallow your pride for a moment; two days, that's it. Swoop, burn, swoop, burn, and you're done. It's a good deal, where we can all help each other.'

The dragon gave him a cold stare. 'You lied to me.'

'I didn't lie! The Great Walls were breached, and thousands have already died. The entire tribe of the Scythes has been annihilated; tens of thousands of men, women and children. The Middle Walls won't hold for much longer, and then we've got Marcus at our backs, who'd be happy to let the greenhides into Medio, where they could slaughter even more people. Do you want that on your conscience?'

'The fate of the City's inhabitants leaves me unmoved.'

Corthie shook his head. 'I don't believe you. You chose your rider from among the folk who live in the City, so you know they can't all be bad.'

'Maddie is the exception that proves the rule.'

'Marcus and Kano are responsible for your imprisonment, not the ordinary folk of the City. Why should they be punished too? What about Rosie? Does she deserve to die, when she didn't even know you existed a few days ago? Sure, we humans are weak, and many of us are cruel, selfish liars, but the greenhides will slaughter good people too; they don't discriminate.'

'Your love for a demigod has twisted your thinking,' the dragon said. 'Lady Aila has poisoned your mind, casting a spell upon you to make you want to stay. You are not the same man you once were.'

Belinda nodded. 'I can agree with that.'

He turned to her. 'What? You think Aila's poisoned my mind?'

'I don't know. If it weren't for her, you wouldn't be acting this way. If you didn't love her, we'd already be back in Lostwell.'

'Maybe there's a compromise we can reach,' said Maddie.

Corthie frowned. 'Such as?'

She shrugged. 'One day?'

'No,' said Blackrose; 'I'll not compromise. I want the Quadrant, or blood will flow.'

Maddie nodded. 'Alright. Corthie, you should do as she says.'

'I agree,' said Belinda.

Corthie folded his arms across his broad chest. 'No.'

The dragon's eyes glowed with anger. 'You are leaving me little choice, Holdfast. Give me the Quadrant, or I will take it from you.'

'You'll have to go through me first,' said Belinda.

'I thought you agreed with us?' said Maddie.

'I do, but I promised his sister I would do anything to protect him.' She glanced at Corthie. 'And I keep my promises.'

'Your loyalty does you credit, Belinda-god,' said the dragon, 'but if you get in my way, I will be forced to hurt you.'

Belinda nodded. 'Do as you must.'

A dragon forelimb swept out with no warning, and it struck Belinda, batting her away. The god's body sped through the air and collided with the side of the cliff fifty yards away, where it sank into the undergrowth.

Maddie's eyes widened. 'You just killed Belinda.'

'Nonsense,' said Blackrose. 'Her self-healing powers will preserve her; I merely slowed her down for a while. Now,' she said, lowering her head to Corthie, 'if I were to do that to you, you would die. Do you want to die?'

'Not really.'

'Then give me the Quadrant.'

'I will, after you help the City.'

She opened her jaws, and Maddie saw little forks of lightning spark across her teeth. Corthie stood his ground, watching.

'You have courage,' the dragon said, 'such a pity that you have wasted it upon those who do not deserve it.'

'I promised myself that I would always fight to defend the weak, and that's what I'm doing. I don't want to fight you, Blackrose, I want you to help me. I'm begging you, please; help me. Save the City.'

The dragon glanced away, then struck. She swung out a forelimb, but Corthie was ready. He dived back out of reach as the claws missed him by inches, then sprang back to his feet. The dragon let out a low growl.

'Blackrose,' cried Rosie from the cave entrance, her eyes wide, 'don't hurt him.'

The dragon took a step forwards, her eyes on Corthie. 'If you don't wish to see him being hurt, Little Rose, then look away.'

Corthie backed off, edging along the side of the pool as the dragon stalked him. Maddie kept pace with her as her mind raced. If the dragon killed him, then Blackrose would finally be free, but what would happen to the City without the champion? Did she care?

'Stop, Blackrose,' she cried. She turned to Corthie, her hand outstretched. 'Give me the Quadrant; don't die for it.'

He caught her glance, and shook his head. 'Sorry, Maddie. It's not just Aila, though she's the main reason. I love the City, and its people. Yaizra, Achan, Quill; they're my friends. Yendra and Yvona too. They'll all die without Blackrose's help. If I give her the Quadrant now, then you'll both be gone, and Belinda too, if you take her; and the City will be destroyed.'

He edged up the little slope towards the cave entrance, the dragon shadowing him, and getting closer with every step.

'This is your final chance, Corthie,' said Blackrose. 'Give me the Quadrant or die.'

He shook his head.

The dragon's right forelimb shot out, the claws extended. Corthie sprang backwards, but tripped over the body of Naxor lying by the entrance. He fell as the claws sliced through the air above his head, landing onto the demigod. Blackrose raised her claws again, and Naxor's hand slipped up, and reached inside Corthie's leather breastplate.

They both vanished.

Blackrose arced her neck and let out a roar of rage. The trees shook, the ground vibrated, and a rock fall cascaded down a slope as Maddie and Rosie held their hands to their ears.

The dragon beat her wings and rose into the air. 'I need to kill something,' she cried, then soared away.

Maddie and Rosie glanced at each other.

'What happened?' said a voice from the cliffs.

They turned, and saw Belinda walking towards them through the undergrowth.

'Blackrose hit you,' said Rosie.

'I'm aware of that. I meant afterwards.'

'Naxor activated the Quadrant,' said Rosie, 'and took Corthie away with him.'

The god frowned. 'You mean they've abandoned me? Corthie left me here?'

'It wasn't Corthie's fault,' said Maddie; 'he had no say in it. Naxor grabbed that Quadrant, and woof, they were gone.'

Belinda lowered her eyes. 'And now we're two hundred miles from the City?'

'Yes, but we have a dragon.'

'Where is she?'

'I'm here,' cried a voice behind them.

They turned. Blackrose was descending to the bottom of the valley, her claws stained green with blood. She landed on the grass, and stared at Belinda.

The god stared back. 'You have a strong forelimb, dragon; you broke nearly every bone in my body.'

'Do you seek revenge?'

'Why would I? I'd have done the same as you. I don't take these things personally, and I think it would be advisable if we work together, given the situation we find ourselves in.'

The dragon nodded. 'I like you. For a god, you seem remarkably honest and without pretence.'

'She's lost her memory,' said Rosie. 'She's thirty thousand years old, but only remembers the last few years.'

'That is true,' Belinda said, 'and I don't particularly like the other gods I've met so far.'

The dragon wiped her claws on the grass.

'What now?' said Maddie.

'I will take Belinda back to the City, if she wishes,' said Blackrose.

'I don't want to go back to the City,' the god said; 'I want to go to Lostwell.'

'Yes, but we appear to be without a Quadrant.'

Belinda smiled. 'There's another one.'

Blackrose's eyes glowed bright. 'There is? Where?'

'Ooste, if I had to guess.'

'Explain,' said Blackrose.

The god sat on the grass in the sunshine, her features relaxed. 'I travelled to this world without a Quadrant, as Karalyn Holdfast does not require one. She needs power, but not a physical device. We were tracking Corthie on Lostwell, and found Naxor and two of his cousins in a place called the Falls of Iron. Naxor had a Quadrant with him, and he used it to flee from us before we could catch him. I followed a day later, and found him imprisoned in a tower in the Royal Palace in Ooste. I assumed that the Quadrant I stole from Queen Amalia was the same device that he had used to travel here, but do you remember what he said? He told us that the Queen's Quadrant hadn't been used in a very long time.'

'That's right,' said Rosie; 'that's what he told us. So there must be another device, the one Naxor has been using to bring back the champions.'

Belinda nodded. 'Exactly. I propose we go and get it.'

Blackrose stared at her. 'You mean fly to the City?'

'Yes. Once there, we'll do whatever it takes to find the other Quadrant. I can handle the Queen, and anyone else on the ground.'

'And what shall I be doing?'

Belinda locked eyes with the dragon. 'What would you like to do to the rulers of the City; the gods and mortals who locked you up for ten years?'

'I think you know the answer to that.'

Maddie glanced from the god to the dragon. 'No, you can't. If you're not going to save the City, then at least don't destroy it. As your rider, I say no.'

'Perhaps you should leave Belinda and myself alone for the rest of the day, rider,' the dragon said, 'so that we can discuss our plans to locate the missing Quadrant.'

The dragon turned from Maddie, and began striding towards the shadows by the far bank of the pool, Belinda by her side.

Rosie frowned. 'They could tear the City to pieces looking for the Quadrant, and they look like they'd enjoy it.'

'I won't let it happen,' said Maddie. 'Blackrose will have to take me too; I'm her rider.'

'And how in Malik's name will you stop her?'

'I don't know yet,' she said, glancing at her sister. 'If you have any suggestions, let me know.'

CHAPTER 24

LAST ACT OF DEFIANCE

The Circuit, Medio, The City – 2nd Mikalis 3420

'Please,' said Aila as she pushed the door shut; 'I just need five minutes to eat my breakfast in peace.'

One of the Evader petitioners tried to put his foot in the gap, and Aila shoved the door against his toes until he cried out and pulled away. She closed the door and locked it, then went over to the desk by the window and sat down. She was exhausted. For thirty-six hours she had been working without a break, the list of jobs endless and growing. Food, housing, water, armaments, defence works; all of it had passed under her eye since she had arrived, and she had long lost count of the number of decisions she had made.

Worse than the work, she had waited up all night for Corthie and the others to return from their meeting with the dragon, but so far there had been no sign of them. A messenger had arrived from Lady Yvona at dawn requesting information as to the whereabouts of her champion, and Aila had sent them back empty-handed. The waiting had darkened her mood as she imagined the dragon answering Corthie's pleas with a fiery inferno.

Of Yendra, there had been no sign, though the god had checked in periodically with her vision powers. Her last communication had been during the night, when she had informed Aila that Jade's move to the Seventh Gate had been successfully carried out; and that Yendra would be spending the night as a guest of the Aurelians at the next gate along. She had told Aila to remain calm about the fate of Corthie and the dragon, which had only increased the demigod's sense of frustration.

She had cursed Naxor a hundred times, for not telling her what was happening with Corthie, for leaving her alone to carry out a mountain of work, but most of all because she knew he was plotting something; she had seen it in his eyes the moment Rosie Jackdaw had mentioned that she had discovered a seam of salve. She gazed out of the window while she ate her breakfast and pondered what her cousin might be up to. The streets of the Circuit were coming to life with the dawn, and teams of cleaners were out, removing the debris from the rioting that had come to a stop as soon as Yendra had arrived. Her presence had changed the atmosphere among the Evaders in a second; from defiant to hopeful, and Aila could feel the spirit of the place lift, in a way that had never happened under Lady Ikara's rule.

The end of civil disobedience had led to a flood of new work being carried out, and Redmarket Palace was packed with people looking for money, guidance, or for a decision to be taken, and, judging from the noise outside the door, half of them were waiting to speak to Aila. She had a hundred years of experience working as the Adjutant of the Circuit, and her knowledge was so deep that the Evader rebels deferred to her with annoying consistency.

And in the background, rarely mentioned but always there, was the proximity of the greenhides. Redmarket Palace was less than two miles from the Middle Walls; thirty minutes from any greenhide breach. If it happened, the onslaught would come so fast there would be no time to evacuate with any order; and nowhere to evacuate to.

She finished her breakfast and prepared to meet the hordes of petitioners beyond the door. She picked up her bowl, and was about to stand when she noticed a group of militia running across the palace forecourt. They were heading in the direction of the main gates as someone was approaching from the other side, alone. Aila squinted through the window pane. The solitary figure was striding toward the gates, and something about her walk seemed familiar.

The militia reached the gates, their crossbows levelled, then every one of them slumped to the ground. Aila dropped the bowl and it smashed into a hundred jagged fragments upon the stone floor.

The God-Queen.

She ran to the door, and opened it wide. Dozens of Evaders were packing the corridor outside the room, and all of them started to talk.

'Evacuate the building,' Aila said, trying to keep her voice calm.

Most of them ignored her, some thrusting documents into her face, others shouting for attention. Aila took a step back.

You see me as the God-Queen, enraged and ready for battle.

The Evaders cried out in fright, their faces stricken with terror.

Aila dropped her powers. 'The God-Queen is here. Evacuate the damn building!'

The crowd in the corridor surged, as screams echoed through from the front of the palace.

'Out the back,' cried Aila. 'Head towards the canal.'

The petitioners fled, shoving their way along the wide passageway. Militia followed them, some bursting into the room where Aila stood.

'Ma'am, come with us,' one shouted from the door. 'The palace is under attack.'

Aila hurried out of the room, and the militia moved into position to flank her as they ran. The palace was emptying quickly, with militia ushering civilians and staff out through side doors.

A scream rang out behind them.

'Lady Aila,' came the voice of the God-Queen, 'stop or I will kill everyone.'

Aila skidded to a halt as the crowds surged around her, panic infecting them as the God-Queen strode down the central hallway of the palace towards them.

The militia surrounded Aila in a tight cluster, but she pushed them away.

'No,' she cried, 'it's me she's after; run.'

'No, ma'am,' the sergeant replied; 'we stick with you.'

The God-Queen approached, a serene smile on her lips. The rest of the hallway was almost deserted, as the last of the civilians fled down every available passageway, except for the small cluster of militia, with Aila in the centre.

'I surrender,' Aila said, 'spare these soldiers.'

The God-Queen laughed and raised her hand. The militia cried out as their skin fell away from their faces, rotting and peeling, their flesh withering as they collapsed to the floor.

'I hate you,' said Aila.

'I'd already gathered that, thank you,' she said. 'Now, please take me to your study on the second floor.'

'Why?'

'Do I need to inflict pain upon you first? I'd enjoy that. You've been a very naughty daughter-in-law, and your husband means to punish you, but I can get started early if you like.'

Aila said nothing, her choices racing around her head. Resist, and she would be incapacitated in a second, along with the pain that would bring. Play along, and hope for what; that Yendra might return unexpectedly? If she was at the Eighth Gate, it might take an hour for the news of the God-Queen's arrival to reach her.

She started walking, and the God-Queen fell in alongside her.

'My study, you said?'

'Yes, dear Aila.'

They walked along the deserted passageway, the only sound coming from the clack of their heels on the marble floor. They reached the grand staircase and ascended, then followed a carpeted hallway to Aila's private study. Aila opened the door and they went in.

'Get me a brandy,' said the God-Queen as she sat in an armchair, 'and close the door.'

Aila walked to her cabinet and took out a half-full bottle of brandy.

'This is my first time in the Circuit in over one and a half thousand years,' the God-Queen said, 'and I must say it's a frightful slum. You've done a terrible job of looking after it.'

Aila poured brandy into two glasses. 'Is that supposed to be funny?'

'Am I laughing? Never mind, Medio is doomed, so the aesthetics of the Circuit are somewhat moot.'

'Here,' said Aila, handing her a glass. 'Have the gates in the Union Walls been sealed yet?'

The God-Queen nodded, then took a sip of brandy.

Aila sat opposite her. 'Presumably they'll let you back in?'

'We won't be returning on foot.'

'Oh.' Aila frowned. 'You've chosen this room for a purpose, but you're not looking for anything; you seem to be waiting for something. Or someone?'

'You were always one of my brighter grandchildren; utterly useless, but bright. Yes, we are waiting for someone.'

Aila's thoughts darkened. 'Who told you they would be coming here?'

The God-Queen glanced at her. 'It took three hours in a restrainer mask before Mona would talk; I always knew she had been conspiring against me, and she told me everything. The dragon, the mountain of salve, and, of course, that Naxor is currently in possession of my Quadrant.'

'How did Mona know that?'

'Because your cousin Naxor foolishly chose to sleep in Mona's academy last night after he had fled from the dragon's mountain. Corthie Holdfast and Lady Belinda are there.'

'Wait, Naxor fled from them? Why?'

'Apparently the mood turned against him. He is a coward at heart, and his greed for salve and gold will be his undoing.'

Aila rubbed her face. 'When will they be here?'

'That is unknown. My Quadrant will be set to return to this room, since Mona told me that he left from here. We may be waiting some time, but he will come.'

The minutes dragged by. Aila's eyes shuttled between the space in the room where Naxor had triggered the Quadrant, and the window clock, which marked the time that had elapsed since sunrise. The God-Queen remained in the armchair, drinking brandy and smiling to herself.

After an hour, Aila felt a familiar sensation inside her head.

Aila, said a voice.

Yendra.

You don't need to say anything. Through your eyes, I can see what you see. I am on my way; do not endanger yourself.

But...

The voice disappeared.

The God-Queen raised an eyebrow. 'There was a subtle change in your life force, young Aila, one that I recognise well, so don't even think about lying to me. Who was it? Naxor? It won't have been Mona, as she is temporarily unable to use her vision powers at present.'

'Is she still in the mask?'

'"Back in the mask", would be more accurate. I put it back on her after she had told me what I needed to know, to prevent her from telling anyone else.'

'You're a beast; Mona's never hurt anyone.'

'On the contrary, she has hurt me grievously with her conspiring and disloyalty. I am aware of the little plan cooked up between you and her as regards your wedding to Marcus. Rest assured that Mona will be unable to assist you in any way when your marriage is finally consummated. Unlike others in this miserable family, you will be alive for a very long time to come, bearing the next generation of demigods. Eventually, after a few millennia, you may very well be elevated to the position of queen, but for that to happen, a quite severe personality adjustment will be necessary, one along the lines of what Marcus did to your brother Kano.'

'If I'm queen, where will you be?'

'This world was always temporary for me, my dear,' the God-Queen said. 'The God-King and I decided to shelter here from the unending wars, and one day, when the worlds are at peace and it is safe to do so, then I shall return. Fear not, for that day remains at some distance in the future, and I shall be here to guide you for a long while yet.'

Aila nodded. 'It was Yendra in my head, just so you know. She's coming.'

The God-Queen's face rippled with rage.

'How did it happen?' Aila went on. 'Did you know she was still alive?'

'I always suspected, but could never prove it. I would have killed her in the Circuit, right in front of all those baying Evaders; I would have made sure they all witnessed her destruction. But the God-King was weak, and Yendra could do no wrong in his eyes, even after she murdered Michael. He swore to me that he had executed her, but when I demanded proof, he was unable to provide it. When I threatened to leave him, he chose to continue with his lies, and our marriage came to an end. For a hundred years I awaited her return, but when it didn't happen, I slowly began to believe that I may have been wrong, and I let down my guard. Men lie, Aila, even those who claim to love you.

'Once the current situation has been resolved,' she went on, 'I will announce the death of the God-King to the City. I shall make it seem as though he died in service of the citizens, and encourage his worship among the mortals; a cult to rival that of Prince Michael.'

'None of that will happen,' Aila said, 'because Yendra will kill you.'

The God-Queen laughed. 'If my daughter was no match for me three hundred years ago, what makes you think she stands a chance against me today? She is strong, yes, but not as strong as I. I do not fear her.'

'And what about Belinda? I saw what she did you in Ooste.'

'Her betrayal took me by surprise; I won't make that mistake again. It breaks my heart to see what has become of my old friend. She was truly one of the most powerful gods to ever rule the worlds, and now she is a mere tool in the hands of mortal god-killers, her mind and motivations twisted by them. I have not given up on her, though; I will win her over in time, you will see.'

Aila glanced at the window-clock, then stood and gazed out at the area next to the palace. Militia forces had set up a cordon around the gates, and were keeping anyone from entering.

'Yendra will be a while yet,' said the God-Queen. 'Fetch me another bottle of brandy and sit down.'

Aila turned back to the cabinet, then jumped in fright as two figures appeared in the middle of the room. They were lying horizontally a few feet above the carpet, then they crashed to the floor.

The God-Queen moved. With her left hand she sent a surge of death powers at Aila, knocking her off her feet as her heart faltered, then she strode to the figures on the carpet, a heavy candlestick in her hand.

Corthie glanced up from where he was lying across Naxor on the floor. The God-Queen swung the candlestick, striking the side of his face, sending a spray of blood from his mouth. Naxor tried to get up, and the God-Queen quietened him with a blast of death powers that shrivelled his skin. Corthie rolled away, his face covered in blood, and the God-Queen plucked the Quadrant from Naxor's fingers, and backed off, her eyes on the champion.

'Just the two of you?' the God-Queen laughed. 'I had been expecting stronger opposition.'

Corthie spat blood onto the carpet as he pulled himself to his feet.

The God-Queen raised a finger, and pointed it at Aila. 'Do not move. If you do, Aila dies.'

Aila groaned from the floor as her self-healing battled the God-Queen's powers. She could feel her heart slowly start to recover, but her strength had gone, and she could barely keep her eyes open. Corthie glanced from her to the God-Queen. He had no weapon, but his fists were clenched.

'The dragon will be here any minute,' he said.

'You're lying,' said the God-Queen. 'Blackrose will never help the City. She hates it almost as much as I do. Where is Belinda?'

'She's coming for you, Amalia,' Corthie said. 'Take the Quadrant and go.'

'I most certainly shall,' she said, 'but I'll be taking my granddaughter back with me to Tara. Marcus has some unfinished business with her.'

Corthie's eyes darkened and he sprang at her, his arms outstretched. The God-Queen's fingers traced a line on the surface of the Quadrant, and everything around Aila went hazy and vanished, replaced by the cold, stone floor of a dark chamber.

The God-Queen laughed. 'That was the most fun I've had in centuries.'

Aila struggled into a sitting position, leaning against a damp stone wall as her heart continued to heal. 'Are we in Tara?'

'Of course not,' said the God-Queen; 'we have something important to do first.' She gazed down at Aila. 'Now, what's the best way to keep you subdued? I neglected to bring a restrainer mask with me.' She knelt down next to her and placed a hand over Aila's mouth. 'Try not to scream too much.'

Aila convulsed as pain tore through her, and she cried out. Her insides felt like they were being ripped to pieces within her, and her skin took on a greenish tinge. The God-Queen removed her hand, but the agony remained, and Aila vomited up a thin trail of bile onto the cold ground.

The God-Queen stood, and helped Aila to her feet. 'There. That should last an hour or two. However, if you interfere in any way with what I am about to do, then the mask will be getting strapped to your face the moment we arrive in Tara. Nod if you understand.'

Aila gripped her stomach and nodded, swaying on her feet. The pain had dulled enough for her to walk, but she felt a fragility that she had never experienced before, as if her self-healing powers had been damaged. Her eyes were watering, and her teeth felt loose in her mouth. She started to shiver.

The God-Queen frowned. 'Hmm. Green really isn't your colour.' She walked to a door and hauled it open. 'Follow me.'

Aila stumbled after her. They came to a deserted passageway, and climbed a set of stairs. They emerged into a large stone chamber, with windows facing a courtyard, and a dozen Blades jumped to their feet.

'Remain calm,' said the God-Queen as they stared at her. 'Where is Commander Kano?'

The Blades bowed low, some prostrating themselves on the floor.

'Commander Kano is upstairs, your divine Majesty,' said an officer, his eyes lowered.

'Show me.'

The officer nodded, and led the way through the fort. As Aila staggered behind the God-Queen, she glanced out of a window, and saw the streets of the Circuit begin fifty yards away.

'Where are we?' she gasped.

The officer turned to her, his eyes wide. 'The Sixth Gate, ma'am. Are you well?'

'Ignore her,' said the God-Queen; 'she's fine.'

They ascended another two flights of stairs, and the officer gestured to a door. The God-Queen strode forward and swung it open. Inside, Kano was sitting with his head in his hands, an empty bottle next to him as he gazed out through a narrow slit at the greenhides swarming through the Bulwark.

He turned, and nearly fell off the chair in surprise.

'Grandson,' said the God-Queen.

'Your Majesty,' he said, falling to his knees. His eyes flicked over to Aila for a second, and his mouth opened.

'Well, this is nice,' said the God-Queen; 'a brother and sister reunited. I don't believe the two of you have been in the same room since the last days of the Civil War. Is that correct?'

Kano nodded. 'It is, your Majesty.'

'It's such a shame when politics divides families.' She glanced at Aila. 'Sit down and stop trembling, girl; and if you need to vomit again, do it into your hands.'

Aila slumped into a chair, her eyes watering so much she could barely see.

'What have you done to my sister?' Kano said.

'I'm merely keeping her under control for now, in order to deliver her to her husband in one piece. He has missed her. Do you object?'

Kano bowed his head. 'No, your Majesty.'

'Do you feel sorry for her?'

Kano hesitated for a moment. 'No, your Majesty.'

'Good. For a moment there I thought your loyalty was flickering. Your sister is a traitor and, frankly, I think she think she deserves to die a painful death, but due to Marcus's misguided feelings I am obliged to keep her alive. It will be satisfying to watch her being broken, don't you agree?'

Kano said nothing.

The God-Queen laughed. 'I remember when you were one of the most notorious rebels in the City, Kano. You followed Princess Yendra around like an obedient puppy, always eager to do her bidding. Now, you are the very model of loyalty. I look forward to seeing Aila's similar transformation, and I know that Marcus is too.'

'Do you have orders for me, your Majesty?'

'You never did like small talk, did you? Straight to business, then. I have one order for you today, Kano. Open the Sixth Gate.'

His eyes narrowed.

'The time has come, Kano, for you to prove how much you love the City; for only by the annihilation of our enemies will we ever be able to rest secure. For centuries, the Evaders have rebelled, and now the faithless Icewarders and the illiterate, savage Hammers have joined them. You are surrounded by enemies, Kano, and there is only one solution. Smash down the walls that block the gates, and let the greenhides clear away all of our mistakes in a single day. Your own life will be safe, for once you have done as I command, then I shall take you and your sister back with me to Tara, where we shall plan the reconstruction of the City anew.'

Kano nodded. 'And I shall be duke, as you promised?'

'Indeed.'

'And my harem?'

'It is being assembled, and you can take your pick from the surviving female demigods. So far, Doria and Mona have been brought to Maeladh Palace, and Ikara will be there shortly. Yvona I fear will be lost to us forever, but there is still hope that Lydia will change her mind and sail to Tara before Port Sanders is overwhelmed.'

'Don't do it, brother,' Aila gasped.

He glanced at her. 'I have no choice, sister, as you will soon learn.' He stood. 'It shall be so, your Majesty.'

'Excellent. Return here once the gates are open, and we shall depart.'

Kano strode to the door without another word, and left the room.

Aila started to cry, the sight of her brother filling her with despair. She remembered what he had once been like, and mourned him as if he were already dead.

The God-Queen walked to the narrow window and gazed down at the Bulwark. 'So many greenhides, all hungry and keen to taste the flesh of mortals. I'd quite like to stay and watch what happens, but we'll have to settle for imagining the carnage. There are half a million mortals in Medio; how long do you think it will take for them all to die?'

'You are a monster.'

'No, I'm just practical. The City needed a good clear out, and the greenhides are the ones to do it. Once Medio has been destroyed, I shall remove the greenhides, and we can retake it and the Bulwark. There will be far fewer people living there of course, but at least they will all be loyal. Enslaved, but loyal.' She frowned as she glanced out of the window. 'What is taking him so long?'

She turned, and strode to the windows on the side of the room that overlooked the Circuit. Aila pulled herself up and staggered the few paces to her side. Down in the courtyard of the gatehouse, Kano was out, giving orders to lines of Blades. Some were running out through the gates into the Circuit, while others were strapping on their armour.

The God-Queen's face darkened. 'That lying rat; he has deceived me.' She glared at Aila. 'Come, we shall do this the hard way.'

She strode from the room, and Aila stumbled after her. The God-Queen raced down the stairs, and Aila followed, clutching onto the wooden banister, her legs sore and weak. She reached the bottom of the steps as the screams began. She hurried forwards a few paces, then leant against a doorway. Outside, the courtyard was filled with the bodies of fallen Blades. The God-Queen was standing in their midst, while Kano stood with a drawn sword facing her, his back to the walled-off gate.

'You think you can disobey me and live?' the God-Queen cried.

'I can't do this any more,' Kano said. 'I have killed for you, tortured innocents, and betrayed everything I once loved; but I will not open the gates.'

'It is too late for redemption, grandson,' she said, 'your soul has long since rotted away to nothing.'

'I know that.' He turned to Aila. 'I'm sorry, sister. I don't ask for forgiveness, for I know I don't deserve any; all I ask is that you remember how I died.'

He raised his sword and charged at the God-Queen.

She lifted her hand, and Kano's body exploded, disintegrating into a cloud of blood and pieces of flesh that spattered over the ground and walls in a wide circle of red. Aila sank to her knees, weeping, her heart broken for her brother.

The God-Queen turned to the bodies of the Blades lying across the courtyard. She raised both hands, and the corpses jerked, then slowly began to get to their feet.

She pointed at the walled-up gate. 'Destroy this wall, and the one beyond.'

The risen soldiers swarmed up to the wall, their boots bloodied by the remains of Commander Kano. They gripped axes, hammers and swords, and began tearing at the stone blocks in a frenzy, hacking at the mortar, and ripping chunks out to spill onto the red flagstones.

The God-Queen took hold of Aila's shoulder and hauled her to her feet as they watched. Blocks tumbled down from the wall, crushing some of the risen soldiers, but the others pressed on into the dark, arched tunnel leading to the last wall, and the greenhides. Aila was dragged back into the gatehouse, and the God-Queen pulled her up the stairs to the battlements.

'Let's watch from here,' the God-Queen said, pushing Aila against the parapet.

Aila glanced down. Below, the greenhides were in a frenzy as they gathered by the walled-up gate, the sounds from inside reaching them. A single stone block fell outwards, then others, and the greenhides clambered up the debris, their claws widening the gap, and then, like a dam bursting, they were through; a torrent of flesh, surging through the breached gate. The God-Queen pulled Aila to the other side of the battlements in time for them to see the greenhides reach the opposite end of the tunnel gate. They swept through, shrieking in triumph as dozens, then hundreds, then thousands, charged into the Circuit.

The God-Queen smiled, and gripped the Quadrant in her left hand, while propping Aila up with the other.

'It is done,' she said. 'Gaze upon the end of the Evaders, my dear Aila; the end of Medio, and prepare for your new life in Tara.'

Aila stared out at the greenhides, then the God-Queen touched the Quadrant, and everything dissolved.

CHAPTER 25

FEELING ALIVE

The Circuit, Medio, The City – 2nd Mikalis 3420

Corthie crashed into the wall of the study, landing where the God-Queen had been standing a moment before. He jumped to his feet, then cursed, swinging his fist into a cabinet and battering the door from its hinges. He turned. Naxor was lying on the carpet, convulsing in agony.

'You stupid asshole,' he muttered down at the demigod.

He grabbed a bottle of brandy from the shattered cabinet, then fell into an armchair. He pulled the stopper off and took a long swig, then touched his face. The candlestick had struck him squarely on the jaw, and he could feel the blood on his skin. He felt for his teeth to make sure they were all still there as Naxor slowly recovered on the floor in front of him, his flesh starting to re-form.

The demigod groaned in agony.

'You suffering down there?' said Corthie. 'Good.'

'I saved you from the dragon,' Naxor gasped, as blood bubbled from his lips.

'I was in the middle of negotiating with Blackrose, and now the God-Queen has Aila, and the Quadrant.'

The sound of raised voices came in through the window and

Corthie stood, keeping the bottle in his hand. He gazed out at the palace courtyard and saw a tall woman in battle armour striding towards the main entrance.

'Yendra's here,' he said. 'Don't move, Naxor; I'll be right back.'

Corthie left the study, and hurried down the flights of stairs to the ground floor. At the end of the long, wide hallway, the double doors opened and Yendra walked in.

'Corthie?' she said as she approached. 'Where is the God-Queen?'

'Gone. She was waiting for me and Naxor to get back. She's got Aila.'

Yendra's eyes smouldered. 'Where did they go?'

'Amalia used the Quadrant. She said she was taking Aila to Tara.'

The princess turned her head as a few members of the Evader militia peered through the double doors.

'The palace is clear,' she said; 'the God-Queen has gone.' She turned her glance to a heap of soldiers lying further down the hallway, their flesh stripped from their bodies. 'Take me to Naxor, Corthie.'

He led her up the stairs towards the study. Naxor was creeping out as they arrived, his hand clinging to the wall for support, his face ragged and bloody.

'I told you to stay put,' said Corthie, grabbing his shoulders and steering him back into the study.

Yendra followed them in and closed the door. 'Sit down.'

Corthie pushed Naxor into a chair, then sat back in the armchair. 'Blackrose isn't coming.'

'I feared that would be the case,' said Yendra, 'but where is Belinda?'

'This idiot,' Corthie said, gesturing with the bottle towards Naxor, 'triggered the Quadrant, leaving her behind with the dragon and the Jackdaw sisters. We arrived back here, and the God-Queen clubbed me with a candlestick, then grabbed Aila and vanished.' He took a swig of brandy. 'I have to go to Tara.'

Yendra extended her hand. 'The brandy, please.'

'Sure, here you go.'

She took it from his hand and placed it onto a table out of his reach.

He frowned. 'I thought you wanted a drink?'

'Now is not the time for drunkenness, Corthie; we need clear heads for what is coming next.'

Naxor snorted. 'You never were any fun.'

'Shut up,' said Corthie, 'none of this would have happened if you hadn't been sneaking around at night. You could have just asked for some salve, instead of trying to steal it.'

'The champion is getting confused,' Naxor said to the princess; 'he's forgetting the fact that the dragon would have killed him if I hadn't brought him here.'

'Blackrose was just playing with me; if she'd wanted to kill me I'd be dead.'

Yendra gazed at the two men. 'I shall bend my vision towards Tara, to see if I can locate Aila. Give me a moment.'

Corthie glanced at Naxor as the princess's eyes glazed over. 'I should kick your teeth in, you treacherous little runt; and if anything happens to Aila I'm going to rip your head off.'

'Why am I getting the blame? How was I supposed to know that the damned God-Queen would be sitting here waiting for us?'

'Aye, how did she know? She can't read minds, so who told her?'

Naxor frowned as his face continued to slowly rebuild itself. 'Well, I know it wasn't me.'

'Where did you stay last night?'

Yendra blinked before Naxor could respond. 'Aila does not appear to be in Maeladh Palace in Tara,' she said, 'nor the God-Queen. I did locate Lady Doria, however, imprisoned in a cell, alongside Lady Mona.' She lowered her eyes as a darkness shot across them.

'What?' said Naxor. 'Mona's in Tara? And Doria?'

'Yes, and Mona is wearing a god-restrainer.'

Naxor cried out, his eyes wide. 'I was at Mona's place yesterday evening; she knew everything.'

'That solves the mystery of how the God-Queen knew you'd be here,' said Yendra, 'but it tells us nothing about where she is right now, nor what she is doing.' She stood, and gazed out of the window. 'If not Tara, then where?'

Her eyes glazed over again and she fell into silence.

'Poor Mona,' said Naxor; 'she was only trying to help.'

Corthie stared at the floor, trying to piece together his morning. He had been so focussed on trying to persuade Blackrose to accept his deal, that everything since seemed unreal, with only the pain in his jaw a reminder that it had really happened. He had assumed that he was the one in danger, and that Aila had been safe, but she had been torn away from him. He drew on some battle-vision, just enough to dull the pain and focus his anger. Naxor was a fool, but he wasn't the enemy.

Yendra turned, and Naxor and Corthie stared up at her.

Her eyes were lit with fury. 'The greenhides have breached the Middle Walls. They are coming.'

Corthie and Yendra strode back down the deserted stairs, the princess's face ashen. They had left Naxor behind to recover, and though Yendra hadn't said where they were going, Corthie knew he would soon be fighting.

'There you are, champion,' said a voice as they reached the ground floor.

He turned, and saw Major Hannia at the bottom of the steps.

'Lady Yvona has sent me in person,' she went on. 'She requires you back at your post on the Middle Walls, and has instructed me to lead you directly there.'

He came to a halt. 'Hannia, listen to me; the greenhides have breached the Sixth Gate. Get back to Icehaven while you can and warn everyone.'

The major's face sagged. 'What? The greenhides are in Medio?'

'Aye. I'd better go.'

'Where are you going? Icehaven is the only place that will be safe.'

Yendra turned as she waited for him. 'Corthie, we have to leave.'

He glanced back at the major. 'We're going to fight the greenhides, Hannia. Wait, did you say you were going to take me to the walls?'

'Yes, but I meant the walls up by Icehaven.'

'Did you bring my armour?'

She nodded. 'And the Axe of Rand.'

He turned to Yendra. 'I'll be as quick as I can, and I'll follow you.'

The princess nodded, then turned back towards the entrance.

'Take me to your carriage,' Corthie said to Hannia, 'we haven't got much time.'

They hurried away, and the major led Corthie out of the palace via a side door and into a courtyard. Dozens of Evaders were working in the yard, oblivious to the approaching danger.

'Everyone out!' cried Corthie, his voice echoing off the side of the palace. 'Make for the Union Walls or Icehaven; the Middle Walls are breached.'

The Evaders glanced over at him.

'Out; go!' he yelled, and they started to run, spilling out of the yard, leaving it deserted in seconds.

Hannia hurried over to her carriage, where two Icewarder soldiers were sitting, staring wide-eyed at Corthie.

'Get down here and help the champion,' she cried, and the soldiers jumped from the carriage.

They unpacked the crates of armour as Corthie stood with his arms out, then the soldiers began strapping the heavy plates of steel to his body.

'Quickly,' said Hannia, keeping her eyes on the nearby streets.

A few faint cries became audible, floating over the grey, concrete rooftops of the Circuit from the direction of the Middle Walls. Corthie lowered his arms as the last piece of armour was strapped on, and took his helmet from one of the soldiers, as the other opened a large box lined in black velvet. Corthie leaned down and grasped the Axe of Rand, lifting it clear of the box.

'Now get back to Icehaven,' he said to Hannia, 'as fast as you can. Thank Yvona for the axe, and tell her I hope to return it to her in person.'

She leaned up and kissed his cheek. 'Good luck, champion.'

Corthie turned, pulled on his battle-vision, and raced off, running down the narrow lane towards the front of the palace. He reached the corner, and faced a huge crowd of Evaders who had gathered there. Some glanced at his armoured figure in shock, as if Kano or Marcus had appeared, and he pulled his helmet off.

'Where's Princess Yendra?' he cried, his eyes scanning over the heads of the Evaders.

The people in the milling crowds all seemed to be trying to find out what was happening, but there was no urgency or panic, and many looked as if they were out for a stroll.

Corthie barged into the crowd, and people scattered to get out of his way. 'Where's the Sixth Gate?' he yelled. 'Where's the princess?'

Up ahead, a tall figure turned. She was mobbed by Evaders, all trying to get close to her. Corthie pushed on until her reached her side.

She glanced at his armour. 'Evaders!' she cried in a clear voice, raising her right arm.

The crowd stilled.

'The God-Queen has breached the Middle Walls to kill us all. Those capable of fighting, make for the Sixth Gate, those unable, flee to the Union Walls, or to Icehaven or Port Sanders. The greenhides are on their way.'

For a moment, her words seemed to have no effect, then as if a match had been struck, the road erupted with cries and shouts, and Evaders began scattering through the narrow lanes and streets. Some threw themselves to their knees in front of Yendra, pleading with her to save them.

'I will do what I can,' she said to them, 'now run.' She glanced at Corthie. 'I contacted Lady Yvona and Emily Aurelian while you were getting ready. Now we must face the eternal enemy.'

He nodded. 'I'm looking forward to it.'

They set off towards the Middle Walls, walking against the current of fleeing civilians that surged past them.

'I recognise that axe,' said Yendra.

'It's one of the best weapons I've ever handled,' he said, 'and it cuts through greenhides like butter.' He glanced over his shoulder. 'I wish I could go for Aila, though. My blood freezes thinking about what might be happening to her.'

'I love her also, but we mustn't let it distract us.'

'It's fine. Once we start fighting, it'll take my mind off Aila.'

'Let me lead.'

'No. You don't need to protect me.'

'But I can withstand far greater injuries than you.'

'Then it's lucky that I'm too quick for them to catch.'

Yendra shook her head. 'One serious blow would be all it would take to kill you, and I do not want to have to explain to Aila why I let you die.'

'I've been beyond the walls over a hundred times. My biggest problem is that once I've started, I find it hard to stop. Shout loudly if you need me, otherwise I might not hear you. Oh, and I also like to fight on the front foot, so don't worry if you see me charging into them.'

'Alright,' Yendra said, eyeing him; 'side by side it is.'

They came to a large crossroads, with a broken fountain in the middle of the junction. The line of the Middle Walls could be seen rising above the housing blocks, and a tide of people were fleeing from that direction.

'We'll hold them here,' said Yendra, planting her boots onto the cobbles and folding her arms.

Corthie glanced around. The crowds were thinning, and the familiar shrieks of the greenhides could be heard over the scream and cries.

'Did you see the God-Queen do it?' he said.

'No. I had to read the mind of a Blade who had been watching from the battlements. Lord Kano is dead.'

'Good.'

'Take care in applauding the death of others without knowing what led to it. Kano died bravely, refusing to obey the God-Queen's command to breach the walls, even though he knew she would strike him down. It does not undo his earlier evil, but it deserves to be remembered.'

'Aila was right,' he said. 'When everyone else thought he would do it, she was the only one who disagreed.'

'Indeed.' Her eyes tightened and she drew her sword from over her shoulder, its long blade gleaming in the pink light of the afternoon.

Corthie pulled his helmet on and gazed ahead. The last of the civilians were fleeing down a wide road towards the junction, the greenhides at their backs. Evaders were falling with every second that passed, the claws of the enemy ripping through them from behind as they ran. Yendra began walking towards the approaching tide, and Corthie hefted the axe and followed her. He took up position five yards to her right, and pulled on a steady stream of battle-vision. His sight sharpened, and he took in every detail of the vast swarm of greenhides rushing towards them; then he charged.

The Axe of Rand felt like it was an extension of his arms as he swung it two-handed, the blade cleaving through the tough hide of the nearest beast, then they were around him, their claws slashing out and he laughed, his speed keeping him out of their reach as he delivered death with every swing. He ploughed into them, his mind standing back and letting his battle-vision-powered body take over; energy soared through him, making him feel alive and free as the green blood flowed over the cobbles. He lost himself in the rhythm of constant movement, his arms and thighs twisting and flexing as if they had minds of their own.

All too soon, the closest greenhides tried to scramble away from him, but the press from those coming from the breach kept them from fleeing. Corthie charged at the packed mass of bodies, laying them low in a frenzy of two-handed swings. He leapt up onto a small heap of corpses so he could reach more of them, then heard his name being called.

He glanced to his left and saw Yendra slashing her way towards him through the tide of greenhides. He jumped down, his axe swinging, and fought until he was face to face with the god.

'Follow me,' she cried, and they cut their way to the side of the road. Yendra kicked down a door, and they entered, then she barred it behind them.

'That will hold for a minute or two,' she said.

'Why did you pull me out? I was having fun.'

She frowned at him, then walked up the hallway and into a large storeroom. She moved a pile of boxes to the side, and uncovered a trapdoor. She pulled it open, and gestured to Corthie to enter. He stowed the axe onto his back, and squeezed through the gap, his armour barely fitting, then dropped ten feet into a dark tunnel. Yendra followed him down, and lit a lamp before striding off.

'We were being outflanked,' she said as they walked, 'and we're moving to a new position by the Great Racecourse. I think we might have been a little too effective, and the greenhides started to divert round us. I was calling on you for several minutes before you responded.'

'Were you? I might have got carried away.'

'Corthie Holdfast, you are the greatest warrior that I have ever seen in the one thousand, two hundred and eighty-six years of my life; better than King Malik in his prime, and better than Prince Michael.' She smiled. 'Almost as good as me, in fact. You should rest soon, so that you are able to fight on.'

'Here's the thing, Yendra; I can carry on fighting, but I can't rest. If I drop my battle-vision, I'll be unconscious within a few minutes.'

'I see. And for how long do you think you can fight before you succumb to exhaustion?'

'I've managed over twelve hours in training, but I think I could do longer. I'm only burning a small thread of it at the moment, just enough to keep awake. I can increase it once we start fighting again.'

'That means you have about ten hours left.'

He glanced at her. 'You mean I was fighting for two hours?'

'Corthie, do you have any idea how many greenhides you killed?'

'No. I never try to count.'

'Are there many like you on your world?'

'No, I'm a bit of a freak.'

'You are not a freak; you are the mightiest mortal warrior that has ever lived. Tell me, if we survive this, what place do you desire for yourself in the City? I heard you pledge to Aila that you wished to remain here; what part do you see yourself playing?'

'I haven't looked beyond the greenhides and Marcus, to be honest. I want the City to be safe, but more than that, I want to live with Aila in peace.'

'After witnessing you today, I'm not sure you would be satisfied with a peaceful life.'

Corthie said nothing. Although he wanted to deny it, he knew it was true. Nothing in his life matched the feeling of being free in battle to kill. If it came to a choice between that or being with Aila, he would choose Aila, but he would always feel an absence; would he be satisfied with that? Was it fair for Aila to be tied to a man who enjoyed nothing better than being in a killing frenzy?

'You're a dangerous young man, Corthie,' she said; 'should I be concerned about my niece?'

'No, I will lay down my weapons for her. I lived a good life before I started killing, and I can do it again. Not yet, though, not while the streets above our heads are pounding to the sound of the greenhides.'

'I agree. Giving up today would not be a good idea. Forget fighting and Aila for a moment; do you want power?'

'Absolutely not. My mother was a powerful leader, maybe she still is, but I don't want that life. At the Great Walls I was happy with a little team of Wolves to watch my back; I don't desire any more power than that. What about you? You seem born to lead, and yet you're giving it up; handing power over to the mortals?'

'I'll never be able to shake the concern I feel for the people of the City, but I'll be happy to fade into the shadows and let others rule.'

Corthie smiled. 'I can't see the people letting you fade into the background, not after your rebirth. We mortals will come and go; some will love you, some will fear you, but everyone will know who you are. You'd have to live like Prince Montieth, and never come out of your palace.'

She glanced at him. 'Maybe I shall.' She stopped, and set the lamp down onto the bottom of the tunnel. 'The hatch above us leads out onto the largest open space in the Circuit: the plaza in front of the Great

Racecourse. Most roads leading iceward pass through here, and the greenhides will have reached the plaza by now. Our aim is to shield those fleeing to Icehaven by boxing as many of the enemy into this location as possible. Are you ready?'

'Aye.'

She placed a hand on his shoulder. 'We could be out there for a long time. If you feel your energy flag, then you must call for me.'

'Alright.'

'Corthie Holdfast, today you will surpass all others in the legends of the City, and I am proud to fight alongside you. We cannot win, but we can make a mountain of dead; every greenhide we kill is one fewer to chase the wretched refugees that are already pouring out of the Circuit. There is a chance that we shall both fall today, but we shall make sure the greenhides never forget us.'

'I'm proud to fight next to you too, but you're wrong about one thing; we can win.'

She smiled. 'I hope you're right.'

Yendra placed her hands on the hatch and flung it open, letting in the cacophony of shrieks and claws clattering off the cobbles. The hatch opened next to a wall, upon which shadows of the beasts flickered.

'I'll take the left,' she said, 'you go right.'

She gripped the edge of the hatch and leapt upwards, clearing the gap and disappearing. Corthie stepped forwards, and raised his hands. He braced himself, then sprang up. His head lifted clear of the hatch and he got a knee up onto the surface of the road as the first greenhide attacked. Corthie rolled left, and whipped the axe from his back, stabbing out with the sharpened butt-end and driving it through the greenhide's eye. He jumped to his feet, and caught a glimpse of Princess Yendra, swinging her long sword as she cleaved her way to the left. Ahead of him was the enormous racecourse, a vast block of concrete towering high, and spreading for a quarter of a mile along its side. People were inside, staring out of the rows of little square windows; hundreds of faces, all looking down with horror at the mass of swarming greenhides on the plaza.

'Corthie,' cried Yendra.

He dived under a slashing claw and glanced over at the princess. She had a hand raised, and was beckoning him.

'Change of plan' she called to him as he worked his way through the clusters of beasts that lay between them, the axe whistling with every swing.

'Just point me where to go,' he cried.

'There are thousands trapped inside the Great Racecourse,' she said as he got closer, 'and the greenhides know it; they're trying to get in through every entrance.'

'So we go in?'

'Yes; we turn it into our own trap. The greenhides smell blood, and will hurl themselves into the racecourse, and we shall be waiting for them.'

Corthie nodded, and they charged through the greenhides separating them from the flank of the vast structure; side by side, their blades ripping through everything in their path. One of the gates to the interior had already been breached by the enemy, and they ran for it, bursting through the split planks. The passageway led straight to the arena at the heart of the racecourse, an open-air stadium, surrounded by steep banks of tiered seating, large enough to accommodate a huge crowd. Greenhides were following them as they sprinted out onto the sand, the afternoon shadows shrouding the lower half of the arena. Other gates had been broken down, and civilians were dotted everywhere, up on the stands, and some down on the sand itself.

Yendra gestured to the nearest group. 'Open every gate that leads to the arena; funnel them here.'

The Evaders stared at her for a moment, frozen with terror, then one bowed low.

'For you, my princess,' he said.

The man turned, and began running to one of the closed gates, then others followed, spreading out to the other entrances.

Yendra strode to the centre of the sand, then gripped her sword in both hands. Corthie watched as the entrances leading into the arena were opened one by one, then readied his axe and joined her, standing a few yards to her left. The first greenhides surged out though the open gates, rippling in lines towards the two armoured figures. The civilians huddled behind them, but those who had helped open the gates were cut down as they ran.

Corthie glanced at Yendra. 'You won't be fading away any time soon; these people would die for you.'

Yendra raised her sword. 'Let's earn it.'

CHAPTER 26

PAYING OFF THE DEBT

Eighth Gate – Middle Walls, Medio, The City – 2nd Mikalis 3420

Emily could make out the advance of the greenhides from the battlements of the gatehouse. The narrow alleyways of the Circuit were impossible to see, but the enemy was also swarming over the low flat roofs of the concrete blocks, like a tide of ants. A thick line of heaped dead marked Jade's location at the next gate along; a semi-circle of greenhide corpses piled high. It acted as a deterrent and as a physical barrier, and had kept the Eighth Gate safe for the two hours following the breach.

'My lady,' said a voice behind her; 'it's time to leave.'

Emily remained where she was, her hands on the parapet.

'Ma'am,' Torphin went on, 'the last of the Hammers are underway, and your carriage is waiting. If we linger here, the greenhides might outflank Lady Jade and attack us from the east.'

'Where's Daniel?'

'Lord Aurelian is downstairs, ma'am, overseeing the loading of the gatehouse's ballistae onto the wagons.'

Emily squinted into the distance, trying to catch a glimpse of Lady Jade, but the Seventh Gate was too far away to make her out. The demigod would be cut off as soon as the Eighth Gate was evacuated.

Torphin glanced in the same direction. 'We've done all we can to contact Lady Jade, and there's nothing we can do if she refuses to leave her position.'

'Can we be sure our messages have reached her? Damn it, we should have devised a better way of communicating, with flares, or something similar. If she stays there, she'll tire eventually, and the greenhides will overwhelm her.'

'Then let's not waste her sacrifice, ma'am.'

Emily frowned, unsure if Jade was aware that she was sacrificing herself. She turned, and glanced toward Medio. To her right the Circuit spread for miles, while the countryside of Sander territory ahead of her was filled with lines of Hammers, either walking or packed onto wagons, all heading west towards the Union Walls.

She nodded to Torphin, and descended the stairs to the lower levels of the gatehouse. A guard of forty Hammers was waiting for her outside, along with her carriage and a row of wagons. Daniel greeted her as she strode back out into the sunshine.

'Sergeant Quill and the first groups of Hammers should be at the Union Walls by now,' he said.

'Has there been any word from them?'

'Not yet. She'll be sending a messenger back as soon as she's evaluated the situation.'

Emily frowned, trying to keep her rage under control. 'If the Blades have sealed the gates against us, then you know what we'll have to do.'

He nodded. 'I witnessed the defences on the walls myself yesterday. They have ballistae ranged all along the battlements; and this time, they'll be expecting us.'

She clenched her fists. 'Damn cowards. If we have to break through into Auldan, there will be a reckoning, a bloody one.'

'One step at a time,' Daniel said; 'we've still got to get there.'

Torphin gestured to the carriage, but Emily shook her head.

'I'll travel on the back of one of the ballista-wagons,' she said, 'at the rear of the convoy. I don't want to be trapped in a carriage if the greenhides attack. Fill it with civilians and let it go on ahead.'

There were six wagons, each with two ballistae secured to their chassis. They stretched across the width of the road in two rows of three, with the front row spaced so that they could aim between the wagons of the rear row. Emily climbed up onto the back of the nearest wagon, and the soldiers moved round to let her sit. Daniel raised his hand, and the convoy started off. He leaped up onto the front of Emily's wagon and stood on the driver's bench as they pulled away, his eyes scanning the edge of the Circuit a hundred yards to their right.

Piles of abandoned luggage and crates lay by the side of the road, and the sight of it broke Emily's heart. After the struggle to get the Hammers through the Middle Walls, it seemed beyond unfair that they were being forced to do it again, and if Princess Yendra was to be believed, and the breach had been opened deliberately, then her anger would know no bounds. Her rage would be useless if she died however; only by staying alive would she be able to take the vengeance she desired.

They moved away from the Eighth Gate, the road behind them empty of people. Ahead, the rear lines of the refugees were only twenty yards in front of the ballista-wagons, and thick ranks of armed Hammer militia were marching between them and the rear. The pace was slow, and the first mile seemed to take forever. The farmlands surrounding them had been trampled by thousands of boots since the arrival of the Hammers, and several tents were still pitched amid the detritus of the chaotic evacuation.

Emily glanced sunward, towards Port Sanders. Lady Lydia had refused to speak to the Aurelians, and had barred the gates of the small harbour town against all other inhabitants of Medio; another name to be added to Emily's list of those upon whom she wished to take revenge. Rumours abounded that the demigod had a ship ready to sail if the greenhides penetrated the walls of Port Sanders.

The second mile was slower than the first, as streams of Evaders began to pour out of the narrow streets of the Circuit to the right of the road to join the large groups of Hammers. Militia were shepherding the civilians away from the greenhides sweeping round Jade's position at the walls. Emily had travelled the route many times, and she noticed as they passed the halfway point between the two sets of walls. Two hundreds yards after that, the first greenhides emerged from the Circuit, bounding across the open farmland towards the road and the masses of refugees.

'Prepare the ballistae!' Emily cried.

There was only a dozen of so greenhides in the group racing across the fields, and the Hammers on the wagons moved quickly, their incessant training over the previous few days paying off as they readied the huge bolt-throwers.

'Wait until they're close,' Emily said, her hand in the air as she watched the beasts run towards them. She could hear the cries of terror coming from the refugees behind her, but ignored them, her concentration on the advancing beasts.

'Loose!'

A dozen yard-long steel bolts flew through the air as the ballistae recoiled on the wagons. Seven greenhides were hit, skewered by the bolts.

'Reload.'

The remaining five greenhides surged forward as the Hammers lifted fresh bolts up onto the frames of the ballistae. Twenty yards away; ten, five. A greenhide leapt up at the rear wagon.

'Loose!'

The dozen bolts punched out, throwing the greenhides back in a hail of steel, their bodies flung to the dusty ground. Emily stared at the corpses, her heart hammering beneath her ribcage.

'Good work,' she said. 'Reload.'

The wagons pulled off again, leaving the greenhides on the road, their blood trickling into the run-off ditch.

More Evaders appeared, running from the edge of the built-up area. A militia officer caught sight of the Aurelians and sprinted across the field towards them, waving his arms in the air.

'You're being outflanked,' he cried as he approached. He pointed ahead. 'A huge number of greenhides are circling round from the west, and they're coming this way. They'll split your convoy in two.'

Daniel stared at the grey spread of the Circuit. 'And what about the Evaders? They'll be cut off too.'

The officer nodded. 'Thousands of Evaders will also be encircled, yes.' He pulled a map from his tunic. 'Here,' he said, pointing. 'The greenhides have broken through this line of canals, and there are large groups of Evaders who will be surrounded if the enemy reach the road.'

Daniel squinted at the map. 'What about these bridges? Are they standing?'

'Yes.'

'If we strike here, we could destroy the crossings, or at least hold them until the Evaders get away.'

The officer frowned. 'Get away to where? The Union Walls are sealed against us, and so is Port Sanders. There's nowhere to run.'

'We'll batter through the Union Walls if we have to,' said Emily.

'The Blades are slaughtering anyone who gets within a hundred yards of the walls, ma'am.' The officer shook his head. 'It's over.'

'It's not over,' said Daniel. He glanced at Torphin, 'I want a full company of Hammer soldiers; two hundred. I'm going into the Circuit.'

'But, my lord, the greenhides are overwhelming that entire district.'

'Yes, and if they aren't stopped, the Evaders will be massacred, and the Hammers will be next. Get the company ready to move.'

Torphin frowned, then saluted. 'Yes, my lord.'

Emily turned to her husband. 'Why are you doing this?'

He took her hand. 'It's time I repaid the debt I owe the Evaders. Keep going, Emily; get the Hammers to the Union Walls, and no matter what happens, stay alive.'

He kissed her, then jumped down from the wagon as Torphin was organising the company of volunteers. Emily said nothing. If she allowed her feelings to rise to the surface, she would collapse in a heap of tears, but the sight of Daniel walking off into danger was almost too much for her to take. She sat down on the back of the wagon and tried to control her breathing. They had both taken so many reckless risks over the previous days that she knew it couldn't go on; one of those risks was bound to end badly.

Daniel glanced back at her, raised a hand, then hurried away, leading his company across the trampled fields towards the Circuit, heading in the opposite direction to the stream of refugees.

'That's the first time I've seen a Roser do anything for the Evaders,' said the militia officer as they watched the company disappear into the distance.

'He's throwing his life away,' said Torphin; 'he should be with the Hammers.'

'Screw you,' said the officer. 'The life of an Evader child is worth the same as a Hammer.'

'But the Aurelians aren't here to save the Evaders.'

Emily turned to them. 'The Aurelians will always love the Hammers, but we'll never desert those who need our help. Every mortal deserves to be saved.' She lowered her eyes. 'And I don't like to admit it, but Daniel was right; he does owe the Evaders a debt, and if this is the only way he can settle it, then I have to accept that.'

Torphin frowned. 'But, my lady...'

'Enough,' she snapped. 'This conversation is over. Let's get on with Daniel's last command, and get everyone to the walls.'

The wagons trundled on as the long lines of refugees continued trudging westwards. Screams rang out from the edges of the Circuit with increasing volume and frequency, and the tide of Evaders thronged the road, mingling with the Hammers. The line of the Union Walls appeared in the far distance over the fields, and Emily could see it stretch up the side of the Sunward Range of hills.

With a mile and a half left to travel, Sergeant Quill arrived back from her position at the head of the convoy. She looked tired, and her face was lined with worry.

'Emily,' she cried as she hurried to the rear wagons.

'Quill,' she said, helping the tall woman climb up. 'How is the situation at the wall?'

Quill hung her head. 'About as bad as you could expect. The Blades on the battlements have already killed dozens, maybe hundreds. They've learned from what happened at the Middle Walls, and are not letting anyone get close.'

Emily glanced away as a surge of despair shivered through her. 'We'll still have to break through; it's the only way.'

Quill shook her head. 'We'd need siege towers, and catapults, and proper armour to get through this time. We have none of those things, and no time to get them. If we assault the walls, it'll be a massacre.'

'We have no choice. If we don't assault, it means complete annihilation.'

Quill said nothing.

'My mother-in-law was right,' Emily said; 'they hate us so much that they deliberately opened the Middle Walls, and now they'll watch us all die. Part of me wants the greenhides to get into Auldan, just to make them see what they have done; so they could also feel the pain. The difference is, that I would never actually do it. Compared to them, I'm weak; I lack the will to be that ruthless.'

Quill smiled. 'You say that like it's a bad thing.'

'It might end up proving to be.'

'Where's Daniel?'

'He's gone off to help the Evaders.'

'Oh.'

'Yes. He felt he had to.'

Quill nodded.

'Go back to the walls,' said Emily, 'and start moving all of the children up into the hills of the Sunward Range, along with the sick and injured, and whoever is unable to fight. I want everyone else formed into an arc at the foot of the hills, to protect the others for as long as possible. Make no assault on the wall until I reach you.'

Quill nodded. 'Yes, ma'am.'

The Blade jumped down from the back of the wagon.

'Thank you, Sergeant,' Emily said.

Quill gave her a half-smile, then ran off towards the front of the convoy, disappearing into the crowds of refugees filling the road.

The convoy moved on, slowing as it neared the Union Walls. The mass of refugees was becoming too dense to move through, and with a mile to go, the wagons juddered to a halt. Emily glanced up at the flank of the Sunward Range, and could make out lines of people climbing the gentle slopes away from the main road, moving through the neat vineyards and terraced farms. It was their final refuge, beyond which lay only the Warm Sea and the high Union Walls.

Emily stepped up onto the driver's bench and gazed around. The road behind them was deserted, and the streams of Evaders were pushing down from the Circuit. Packs of greenhides were roaming across the fields between the road and the edge of the concrete suburbs, striking out at groups of Evaders as they tried to flee. The greenhides were still too few in number for them to attempt an assault on the huge mass of Hammers, but more were running from the Circuit with every minute that passed.

'Move the ballistae-wagons,' Emily said. 'Turn them to face the Circuit.'

'Yes, ma'am,' yelled one of the ballista operators, and the team of Hammers started pulling the oxen round to face sunward, so that the ballistae were pointing toward the Circuit.

'If you have a clear shot,' Emily said; 'then loose at will.' She glanced at the closest group of militia. 'I want double lines of crossbows and slings all along the iceward side of the road. As soon as the last Evaders are through, loose with everything you've got.'

The officer in charge nodded, and they got to work.

Emily jumped down, and ran to the Hammers escorting the refugees. 'Get everyone away from the road; start making your way up to the hills.'

'But, with all due respect, ma'am, we'll be trapped up there.'

'We're already trapped; the God-Queen has seen to that.'

The officer saluted. 'Yes, ma'am.'

'Torphin!' she cried.

The man ran over. 'My lady?'

'Send runners along the road; I want my orders carried out all the way to the Union Walls.'

He nodded, and gathered his captains. Emily turned back to the Circuit. The Evaders were thinning out, and the greenhides were massing in the fields, preparing to attack the road. A sergeant was handing out crossbows to a line of Hammers, and Emily took one, and positioned herself by the wheel of one of the ballistae-wagons.

'Here they come!' cried a voice, and the Hammers got ready. The ballistae were loaded, and every soldier with a crossbow got into line by the roadside. Emily went down to one knee, aiming her bow out into the field.

A deafening shriek rose up as the greenhides started their charge across the fields, forming a mass a hundred yards wide. The last of the Evaders out in the open fell, pulled down from behind, and Emily raised her hand.

'Loose!' she cried, her voice torn from her lungs, and a hail of bolts flew out from the road, and the wagons shook as the ballistae recoiled.

Emily aimed and squeezed the trigger. Her bolt sped through the air, ricocheting off the thick hide of a beast hurtling towards them. She reloaded, pulled on the reset lever, and aimed again. Her second bolt loosed, striking a greenhide in the centre of its abdomen. It cried out and stumbled, and was trampled into the ground by the mass of beasts thundering behind.

The ballistae were launching relays of the yard-long bolts from the wagons, their crews loading and loosing as quickly as they could, and the bodies of the greenhides began to pile up over the dark earth. Emily focussed on what she was doing, trying to ignore the noise, and the fear in the pit of her stomach. The tide of greenhides got closer, surging through the hail of steel filling the air then, ten yards from the road, they broke, scattering to either side and wheeling away from the carnage. A cluster of them circled back round to the Circuit as the Hammers began to cheer, but in the other direction a large group was reforming along the road from the Eighth Gate.

Emily got to her feet, her eyes drawn to the bodies carpeting the field in front of her. Then she turned back to the road. The large group of greenhides there was growing, and starting to advance towards them. She glanced at the rows of Hammers. All were in position along the road, and there was no time to move them to face the new threat. Most weren't even aware of it, as they celebrated the retreat of the first wave.

'Turn the wagons!' she cried, pointing back at the charging greenhides on the road.

The closest Hammers wheeled to their right, and started loosing at the approaching greenhides, while the ballistae crews jumped down from the wagons and began shoving them round. Emily aimed her crossbow and loosed, then two Hammers grabbed her by the arms and started to drag her away as the greenhides closed the gap between them.

The beasts reached the wagons as they were being turned, and swept over them, carving their way through the crews and the thin line of Hammers at the rear of the convoy. Emily struggled in the grip of the two soldiers as they pulled her away from the slashing claws and bloody teeth of the beasts.

The greenhides ripped through the crowds packing the road, their claws flashing in the light of the sun as it sank close to the horizon. Emily pulled herself free of the Hammers, and lifted her bow. It was finished; the greenhides were upon them in the open, but she would die fighting.

A scream tore through the air, then increased into an ear-splitting cry of agony as every greenhide attacking the rear of the convoy collapsed. They writhed in pain on the ground, their limbs flailing, then fell silent.

Emily stared at the corpses, her mouth open.

'Look!' cried a Hammer next to her, pointing along the road.

A figure was staggering towards them, alone on the road. Emily gasped, then started running, a few soldiers joining her. They raced up the road, jumping over the bodies of the dead greenhides and Hammers.

The figure fell to the ground on the road in front of them, her long robes ripped to shreds, and her skin pale.

'Jade,' cried Emily as she rushed to the demigod's side; 'you saved us.'

'Auntie Yendra's wrong,' she gasped; 'the stupid greenhides aren't going to kill me.'

'Carry her to a wagon,' Emily said, and two soldiers picked the demigod up, her arms falling limply by her sides.

They returned to the convoy, and Emily frowned at the lines of bodies that had been pulled from the road. Dozens of Hammers had been killed in the charge, including nearly every member of the ballista teams. Next to the human dead, the Hammers were piling up the bodies of the greenhides, building a wall of them to block the road. Jade was carried up onto the back of a bloodstained wagon. Her eyes had closed, but her chest was rising and falling.

Emily glanced at Torphin. 'Give Lady Jade whatever she needs and protect her if you can. I'm going to the Union Walls.'

He nodded. 'Yes, my lady.'

Emily slung her crossbow over her shoulder and started to run, following the line of the road. The Hammers called out to her as she passed; the rows of soldiers with crossbows and slings, and the dense groups of civilians still to make their way towards the slopes of the hills. The Union Walls grew larger as she ran until she could make out the individual towers and turrets. The masses of Hammers thinned as she got to a distance of a hundred yards from the walls. Sergeant Quill was standing in the middle of the road, directing refugees to her right, towards the Sunward Range, and she saluted when she caught sight of Emily.

'Ma'am,' she said; 'thousands are moving up into the hills, while the rest of the Hammers will shield them for as long as possible. It won't do much if the greenhides launch a full scale assault, but so far we've only had a few small groups attack us.'

'It's the same at the rear,' Emily said. 'I guess Medio's too big for them to be everywhere at once, but unless we can get through those walls, the end is inevitable.' She glanced up at the hills to their left, and saw where the Union Walls snaked across the slopes, all the way to the

Warm Sea. Ahead of her, the walls had been built on level ground, and the gatehouse loomed above the battlements, its thick iron-framed doors closed.

'I'm going to speak to them,' she said. 'I have to try.'

She walked out along the road, a few patches of blood on the ground showing where Hammers had been struck down by Blades from the walls. She raised her hands above her shoulders as she approached the gates.

'Halt, or we will shoot,' cried a voice from the gatehouse.

She stopped on the road. Blades were lining the battlements in large numbers, and each one was staring down at her.

'My name is Emily Aurelian,' she cried; 'open the gates.'

An officer up on the gatehouse shouted back. 'The gates are sealed on the orders of the God-Queen.'

'A ruler who kills her own people should no longer rule. Do not be their slaves; join with us, and free the mortals of the City.'

'You are a traitor, Aurelian. Turn back, and face the destruction you have brought upon yourself.'

'Will you stand there and watch while we are slaughtered? The Scythes are already gone; the Hammers and Evaders will be next, and then the Sanders and Icewarders; why do you fight for gods who care so little about us? Where is your compassion? Look out here, at the faces of the children, and the sick and wounded, and the tired and helpless. Do they all deserve to die? Will you do nothing while it happens?' She glared at the faces looking down at her. 'You shame yourselves, and you shame the City. I curse Duke Marcus, and I curse the God-King and the God-Queen. This war is not just against the greenhides, it is against the tyranny of corrupt and cruel gods; and you, Blades, you are on the wrong side.'

By way of a response, a crossbow bolt flew out from the battlements, and skittered across the cobbles by Emily's feet. She took a breath, then turned and strode back towards Quill. Crowds of Hammers mixed with Evaders were staring at her as she walked back, packing the roadside. As one, they lowered themselves down to their knees before her. They raised their arms and began chanting her name, their voices coming together and creating a swell of noise that rang through the air.

'This is too much,' said Emily, 'I have failed.'

'You haven't failed,' said Quill. 'You've given these people hope, and every single Blade up on the walls knows it. If I was up there, I know what I'd be thinking.'

'What?'

'Just as you said; that I was on the wrong side.'

'Will it make any difference?'

Quill shook her head. 'No, the Blades are loyal, but not one of them will have any love left for Marcus or the God-Queen after this.'

Emily lowered her head. 'I was hoping for something more than a noble gesture.'

Cries sprang up from the edge of the crowd, and Emily turned. A long line of greenhides were emerging from the nearby streets of the Circuit, with more coming behind them. They were gathering in the rows of fields that led to the road, and within a few moments thousands were present, their shrieks echoing up into the darkening sky.

'Crossbow lines!' cried Quill, and the Hammer militia rushed to get into position, filling the road as the rest of the civilians ran, streaming up the farm tracks towards the hills. Emily pulled her crossbow from over her shoulder. She glanced at the battlements of the Union Walls, where every Blade was watching in silence, then turned to face the eternal enemy. The mass of greenhides now extended for over a quarter of a mile, all the way along the road, the thin lines of Hammers all that stood between them and the thousands of civilians fleeing for the hills.

Emily's thoughts turned to Daniel as she aimed down the stock of her bow. She wasn't afraid to die; with any luck it would come swiftly, but her heart ached for her husband as she realised that she would probably never see him again. Had it all been for nothing? All the struggle, all the pain, only to die a wretched death by the walls of Auldan?

The greenhides charged.

Emily aimed, and loosed.

CHAPTER 27

THROWN

The Eastern Plain – 2nd Mikalis 3420

The sun was sinking towards the horizon as Blackrose flew over the plains. On her shoulders sat Maddie, Rosie and Belinda, the wide harness having been adjusted to fit three riders. Maddie sat in the middle, with her sister to her left.

'I'm envious of you,' said Belinda to her right, her eyes wide as she gazed down at the greenhide-infested lands rushing past; 'you get to do this whenever you want.'

'Not quite whenever I want,' said Maddie, 'but nearly every day since she got her freedom back. Before that, it was just once; it was probably the best night of my life.'

'Why did Blackrose choose you? What did you have to do to become her rider?'

'I think I just wore her down, to be honest; there was no examination or anything. We spent a lot of time together when she was chained up, and I used to spend hours mopping the floor or changing the straw, chatting to her. I mean, I was given the job because I'd been thrown out of every unit that I'd joined; it was either that or the Rats, which was weird if you think about it, because I ended up in the Rats anyway.'

'I think I get it.'

Maddie frowned. 'You do?'

'You got close to her; it makes sense.'

Rosie snorted. 'Maddie made sense? There's a first.'

'Be quiet or I'll push you off,' said Maddie; 'we should have left you in the valley.'

'Why, so you could conveniently forget to come back for me, and leave me there while you disappear off to another world?'

'I wish. Unfortunately, Blackrose would make us come back for you.'

Belinda leaned over. 'Do you know where we should drop you off, Rosie? Your home was in the Bulwark, wasn't it?'

'Yes,' she said. 'I guess the Iceward Range again would be fine, that way I can walk down the hill to the Middle Walls and see Tom, to let him know I'm back. I still have some gold left, and a big bag of salve, so I should be fine.' She glanced at Maddie. 'And then it'll be goodbye?'

Maddie stared at her sister, her mouth drying up.

'If we find the Quadrant,' said Belinda.

Maddie blinked. 'Where will we look first? The Royal Palace?'

Rosie narrowed her eyes and glanced away.

'Maybe you should talk to your sister,' Belinda said. 'We can discuss the Quadrant later.'

'I don't want to think about saying goodbye,' Maddie said. 'It seems so final.'

'It doesn't have to be,' said Rosie; 'you'll come back one day, won't you?'

'How can I say for certain? Look, as Belinda said, we might not even find the Quadrant, but if we do, then... then, well, actually I have no idea what'll happen next.'

'You'll disappear.'

'Yeah. I'll leave the City.'

'We're not in the City now.'

'You know what I mean. I don't have a name for this world. It's just the City, or not the City.'

'I'll miss you. It won't be like when you were working in Arrowhead. I never saw you then either, but I always knew you were there. Can you fit in five minutes to speak to Tom before you go? He'd love to see you, and I don't know how I'm going to tell him that you've left.'

Maddie frowned. 'I don't know; maybe.'

'We shall see if it's possible,' said Blackrose. 'There is somewhere I wish to stop for a few minutes.'

'I had somewhere else too that I wanted to visit quickly,' said Maddie. 'Where do you want to go?'

'You'll soon see; we are approaching the City.'

Maddie peered ahead. The sky was a vibrant purple, deepening sunwards, and the plains glimmered in the evening light. Greenhides covered the ground, stretching for miles in every direction. When they had left the valley a few hours previously, the high mountain passes had been almost empty of the creatures, the destruction of the nest having cut off the stream of young greenhides. Despite that, the plains remained packed with them, each bound towards the City. In the far distance she began to make out a low line on the horizon, and as it got bigger she realised it was the Great Walls, stretching from the Cold Sea to the Warm Sea, a structure that had sealed off the peninsula beyond for a thousand years.

'It looks incredible from here,' said Belinda; 'I have never seen a wall like it.'

'You might have,' said Rosie, 'only you've forgotten.'

'You're right; imagine all the things that I've seen and have no memory of. Thirty thousand damn years.'

'Don't dwell on the past,' said Maddie, 'think about the fact that, give or take an accident involving decapitation, you'll still be alive thirty thousand years from now.'

Belinda went quiet, and her glance fell.

Maddie turned back to gaze ahead of them. The dark line on the horizon was getting bigger, and she made out a couple of large lumps along the walls.

'Is that Arrowhead in front of us?' she said.

'It is,' said the dragon, 'and Stormshield is to the right of it.'

'Good, because it's Arrowhead where I want to stop off for a few minutes.'

'Are you going to visit my old lair?'

'No, I want to pick up a bag from my quarters. It has some letters in it; some stuff I want to keep to remind me of home. The Rats lived under the Wolfpack Tower, so anywhere in the forecourt would do. We could fly over and see if there are any greenhides first.'

'Very well.'

'I'll come with you,' said Belinda. 'I could do with a new sword; is there an armoury?'

Maddie smiled. 'There is, though I've thought of something better we could take.'

Maddie and Belinda spent a total of nine minutes inside the fortress of Arrowhead, once Blackrose had ensured that no greenhides were lurking inside the curtain wall, and then they clambered back onto the dragon in the forecourt, Maddie clutching her bag, and Belinda carrying a sack of weapons she had taken from the Wolfpack Tower.

'Thank you for being swift,' said Blackrose as she beat her wings and lifted into the air. The sun was touching the horizon to their left, and the light was starting to dim.

'What have you got there?' said Rosie, as Belinda opened the sack.

Belinda withdrew a large, vicious-looking weapon. 'Maddie called it the Clawhammer.'

Rosie glanced at her sister, her eyes wide.

'It belonged to Corthie,' she said. 'It was hanging up in the Wolfpack common room. I showed Belinda and she took a fancy to it.'

'It's too large for me to use,' the god said, 'but I'd like to practise with it.'

'Are those real greenhide claws at the end?'

'Yeah,' said Maddie. 'Corthie got them on his first day, if I remember right, and he had the armourers make them into a weapon.'

'I also picked up several decent swords,' said Belinda, 'a few throwing knives and a couple of axes.'

Blackrose banked, and turned back towards the Great Walls.

'Where are we going?' said Maddie.

'To the place I wish to stop for a moment,' said the dragon. 'It is time to do something I have been putting off.'

Maddie glanced down as the dragon turned to fly along the line of the Great Walls. There were no greenhides inside the channel between the outer and inner walls by Arrowhead, the beasts having discovered that going through Stormshield was the quickest way into the Bulwark. With a lurch, she recognised the place where they were going. A stream of greenhides were entering the channel through an open gate in the outer wall, and in the moat to the right, the body of Buckler came into view.

'Is that it?' said Belinda, pointing down. 'Is that how they're getting in?'

Maddie nodded, through her gaze remained fixed on the fallen dragon. Blackrose soared past, and Maddie felt sick at the sight of the dragon carcass. The moat had dried up, and the remains of Buckler lay slumped at the bottom. The greenhides were still using it as a bridge, but half of the body had gone, the ribs visible, and a giant skull lay detached by the moat wall.

Blackrose let out a low, mournful cry as she banked and circled over the fallen red dragon.

'Farewell, young kin brother,' she said, then she surged down, opened her jaws and let out a fierce blast of fire, incinerating the greenhides scrambling over the remnants of Buckler. She beat her great wings and hovered above the moat, flooding it with fire, then turning her neck, sending flames over a wide arc, and clearing an area fifty yards in diameter. The greenhides scattered, fleeing the inferno, then Blackrose focussed on Buckler's body, incinerating it to ash and blackening the sides and bottom of the moat until nothing remained.

As soon as the flames died down, Belinda unstrapped herself from the harness.

'I'll be five minutes,' she cried, then she leapt down from the side of the dragon, landing onto the smouldering ground between the moat and the outer wall.

The dragon glared at the god, her eyes burning with anger.

'What's she doing?' yelled Rosie.

'Malik's sweet ass,' cried Maddie; 'I think I know.'

The god raced across the ground, dodging the areas still burning and drawing one of the new swords she had picked up in Arrowhead. There were no greenhides close to her by the moat wall, but many were crowding the area beyond the open gate. Belinda raised her sword and charged into them, bursting through the opening in the outer wall, and lunging out with her blade.

'Help her!' cried Maddie. 'She's trying to close the breach.'

'No,' said Blackrose; 'I did not agree to this.'

'But you destroyed the nest; what's the difference? You've already helped the City once; just one more time, please.'

'No.'

Maddie glanced back down. Belinda was holding her own by the open gate, but a surge of greenhides was approaching from the direction of Stormshield, and debris was blocking the door, stopping her from closing it.

'You can't let her die,' Maddie said.

'She has made her choice. And I'm giving her the five minutes she requested. I believe she has one remaining.'

'But you need her, or you'll never find the other Quadrant.'

The dragon said nothing, her eyes on the figure of the god battling by the open gate. Maddie felt helplessness tear through her as she watched, her knuckles white from gripping the crossbar. Belinda was fighting well, fast and sleek, but she lacked the range of Corthie, and the greenhides were getting closer and closer to her.

'Time's up,' said Blackrose, and she soared upwards, and began turning for the Bulwark.

'No,' cried Rosie, 'we can't leave her.'

'Calm yourself, Little Rose,' the dragon said; 'I have no intention of leaving her.'

Blackrose swooped down over the channel that ran between the outer and inner walls and filled it with flames, burning through the charging mass of greenhides. The flames swept over Belinda, and she fell, her clothes on fire, then the dragon continued on, incinerating every greenhide from the open gate halfway to Stormshield. The dragon closed her jaws and circled back, flying low over the devastation along the channel, until she reached the place where Belinda was slowly getting to her feet.

Blackrose lowered herself to the scorched surface of the road that ran along the channel, and watched as Belinda's skin re-formed.

'I may have singed you a little,' she said, tilting her head at the god.

Belinda glanced at the dragon, a wry smile on her lips, then turned and started removing the stone rubble keeping the gate from closing. Maddie clambered down Blackrose's flank, landing on the hot ground.

'I need to help,' she said, running towards Belinda. 'I was here when they got through.'

Belinda threw an enormous boulder out through the gate, and Maddie hauled away the remains of a dead Blade.

'We'll both do it,' said Belinda as she gripped the side of the large, wooden gate. Maddie nodded, and reached out with her hands, and together they dragged the door free, then slammed it shut. Belinda picked up a long bar that had been left lying by the wall, and rammed it home, locking the gate.

Maddie leaned her head against the closed gate as tears fell down her cheeks. She was standing in the exact spot where the nightmare had begun, the nightmare that she still partly blamed herself for. She had failed to close the gate, and thousands were dead in the Bulwark. At least the rest of the City was safe, she thought. And at least she had helped seal the breach.

'Are you alright?' said Belinda.

'These are tears of relief.'

'Are there any other breaches?'

'No, this was the only one.' She lifted her head from the gate. 'Thank you, Belinda.'

'It was nothing.'

'You had to fight a hundred greenhides, then got half-burnt by Blackrose; it's not nothing. Can I hug you? Would that be too much? I do feel like hugging you; I think you might have just saved the City.'

Belinda looked away awkwardly for a moment, then opened her arms. Maddie reached out and embraced the god. She started to cry again, but didn't care.

She felt a nudge in her back and turned to see the dragon's giant nose poking her.

'Are you quite finished?'

Maddie stretched out her arms and hugged the dragon's nose. 'Thank you for helping Belinda.'

'It was just as you said, I need her to find the Quadrant. Now, please, get off me, and climb aboard. I do believe our next stop is to locate your brother.'

Maddie nodded, then she and Belinda walked round to the dragon's flank, and started to climb.

'Rosie knows where he's based,' Maddie said as she strapped herself into the harness.

'He's at the Fourth Gate on the Middle Walls,' Rosie said, 'but I don't think we should fly there. Maybe you could drop us both off on the Iceward Range, and we could walk.'

The dragon turned her head to look at her. 'That sounds like it would take a lot longer than the five minutes you mentioned before.'

'Maybe you and Belinda could look for the Quadrant in that time?'

'Perhaps,' the dragon said as they lifted up from the ground; 'we shall see.'

They rose above the Great Walls, and Maddie glanced at the area by the moat. Greenhides were racing along by the moat wall looking for the breach. They swept past the gate that had been re-sealed, ignoring it.

'Thank Malik they're so stupid,' said Rosie.

'Individually they are,' said the dragon, 'but the queen of the nest was aware of the City, even though she had never seen it. Without her, the survivors will become more disorientated over time, their attacks less focussed.'

'You sound like you have experience of these beasts,' said Belinda.

The dragon said nothing for a moment, then tilted her head. 'A little.'

'She means a lot,' said Maddie; 'they destroyed much of her world.'

Belinda narrowed her eyes. 'They exist on other worlds?'

'I think so. Is that weird? Don't other animals, like cat and dogs, exist in other places?'

'And humans, obviously,' said Rosie.

Belinda pursed her lips. 'I don't know; I'm not an expert on the creation of worlds. Apparently I once had a partner who was an expert, a god called Nathaniel, but he's one of the many things I can't remember.'

'I have heard of this god,' said Blackrose; 'he was a renowned creator of worlds; the last great builder, but the most famous thing about him is that he became a rebel in the wars; he and a loyal band of gods fought against the rulers of the worlds for centuries before being defeated.'

'I think I might have been one of his loyal band,' said Belinda. 'Malik and Amalia might have been with us too. Dragon, do you know what we were fighting for?'

'It's more what you were fighting against. The rulers of the worlds wanted nothing less than the total control of every known realm. They destroyed countless civilisations, justifying the slaughter by claiming that if they could not control a world, then no one else should be allowed to. Nathaniel held them back for a long age, but with his death the resistance crumbled, and the ruling gods emerged triumphant. My world was one of the last to fall, and only those hidden away out of their reach remain free from their control. This world is one such hidden realm, and I believe that Corthie's world might be the same.'

'Nathaniel made them both,' said Belinda, 'as refuges from the wars; somewhere for the rebels to hide.'

Rosie frowned. 'Is that what the God-King and God-Queen have been doing here; hiding from a war they were losing?'

'I think so,' said Belinda; 'that's what Amalia told me.'

Maddie glanced down as Blackrose headed iceward along the line of the Great Walls. 'Where are we going now? The Middle Walls are on the left.'

'I do not wish to be seen by anyone,' the dragon said. 'We shall fly iceward, then circle back over the Cold Sea to the Iceward Range. There I shall drop you and your sister off so that you can say goodbye to your brother.'

'Alright,' said Maddie.

The dragon picked up speed, and they soared over the abandoned outer defences of the City. To their left, greenhides were roaming freely within the Bulwark, and Maddie guessed that thousands were in the territory of the Blades, filling the circular plazas, and heading in a steady current towards the Middle Walls. Then the iceward wall swept under them and they passed over the dark waters of the Cold Sea. The air chilled, and Maddie shivered in the wind. Blackrose began to turn in a wide arc, banking to the west as the miles raced by.

The sun was setting as they turned back to face the City, and the dark form of the Iceward Range loomed into view. At its base twinkled a large cluster of lights.

'Icehaven,' said Belinda. 'That's where Corthie and I were staying.'

Blackrose swooped down to fly over the town, and Maddie could see a vast building by the harbour, which seemed to be shimmering with a silvery glow in the reflected light of the many streetlamps. Next to it, the roads and squares were packed with people, and as the dragon passed over the town walls, Maddie could see hundreds more trying to get in. She frowned. Every gate into Icehaven had a long line of people outside, and more were arriving, coming up the coastal road from Fishcross, or crossing the tracks over the hills of the Iceward Range.

Rosie glanced at her, an eyebrow raised. 'Something's going on.'

Maddie nodded. 'Why is half the City trying to get into Icehaven?'

The dragon climbed higher as they reached the steep slopes of the hills, passing the thick woodlands, and the crater-like quarries and mines. Men, women and children were swarming over the surface like a tide, some running, others trudging along the forest tracks; all of them heading in the same direction. Blackrose reached the top of the highest peak along the range, and the rest of Medio spread out before them.

The sun had disappeared below the horizon, and the sky was streaked with reds and purples. Ahead of them the vast sprawl of the Circuit began, then Blackrose banked and began to circle, her head lowered as she scanned the ground.

'It is far too busy to land here upon the Iceward Range,' she said.

Maddie ignored the dragon, her gaze fixed on the countryside separating the Circuit from the hills. Streams of people were surging iceward, heading away from the concrete suburbs and slums. They were too high for any sounds to reach them, but many looked as though they were running.

Belinda frowned. 'Blackrose, could you take us low over the Circuit for a moment?'

'Why?' said the dragon. 'There will be no suitable landing places there.'

'I think the situation below us may have changed since we were last here.'

The dragon wheeled round to face the Circuit, hovering over the sunward slopes of the hills. She directed her gaze down, her eyes on the City.

'What's happening?' said Rosie.

Blackrose said nothing for a moment, then started to ascend. 'I don't think landing would be advisable.'

Maddie tried to glance down as the dragon continued to climb. 'Why not?'

'The greenhides have breached the Middle Walls, and Medio is being overrun. I suggest we go to Ooste with all haste, and search for the Quadrant before Auldan also falls. The City is finished.'

'No,' Rosie cried out, her eyes wide.

'But what about all the people down there?' yelled Maddie. 'We can't abandon them.'

'I have never been part of this City, so it is impossible for me to abandon it.'

'I asked you to fly low over the Circuit,' said Belinda, 'would you do this for me?'

'There is no point; you know what you will see.'

'And yet I wish to see it.'

The dragon emitted a low growl, then stopped her climb. She angled downwards, and soared past the slopes of the Iceward Range, speeding across the countryside, her underside barely brushing the tops of the trees. Maddie clung on as Blackrose hurtled through the air towards the Circuit. Below them the masses of fleeing humans were packing the roads, and their cries and screams rose up around them. More people were emerging from the edge of the Circuit, but greenhides were bursting from the narrow lanes and streets also, chasing the humans, their claws and teeth slashing through any they caught. The dragon began to pass over the dense concrete landscape and Maddie gasped in horror. The greenhides were everywhere, tearing their way through the narrow streets, and swarming over the flat roofs. Heaps of dead Evaders were scattered down every alleyway, and lay floating in the canals. Some of the greenhides were grouped in clusters, feasting on the flesh and bones of their victims, while others were continuing the chase.

Rosie whimpered next to her and put her hands over her face, while to Maddie's right, Belinda gazed down, her eyes darkening.

They approached an enormous structure, the largest for miles around – a long, rectangular edifice that rose high above the neighbouring streets. Around it was a wide plaza, where a gigantic statue of Prince Michael stood, and the entire area was swarming with greenhides. They were concentrating by the many entrances to the building, squeezing in through each doorway.

Belinda raised an eyebrow.

'It's the Great Racecourse,' said Maddie. 'This is the first time I've ever seen it, but it must be.'

'Why are so many greenhides trying to get in?' she said. 'Blackrose, take us over the racecourse.'

'You are not my rider, god; you don't get to tell me what to do.'

'I'm asking, not ordering.'

'Please,' said Maddie.

'If you wish to see your own people being slaughtered,' said the dragon, 'then very well.'

She banked, and turned to pass directly over the top of the race-course. There were three open-air arenas within the centre of the complex; two were deserted, but the third, and largest, was filled with greenhides.

'That's where they're heading,' said Belinda. 'Lower, dragon. Please.'

Blackrose swooped down.

Maddie squinted as she realised that the majority of the greenhides inside the arena were dead. Vast heaps of them were piled up, and standing amid the carnage were two tall figures in armour. Greenhides were still pouring into the arena through the many entrances, and they were throwing themselves up the mounds of corpses to face the two armoured warriors. Both were swinging their weapons, their feet planted on the piles of the dead. One was a woman, wielding a notched and bent sword, while the other was a man with an axe.

Belinda frowned. 'Corthie.'

'Yes,' said Blackrose. 'He fights well, as does the god battling next to him.'

'They're tiring,' Belinda said, her voice low.

'I can see that,' the dragon said. 'They have slain hundreds, but their time is almost over.'

'We have to help them,' cried Maddie.

'No,' said Blackrose. 'Corthie Holdfast decided to tie his life to the City, rather than to me as he had promised. This is the fate he chose for himself.'

'No, it isn't,' said Maddie, her frustration growing; 'this is the fate you've chosen for him, because you're angry and hurt. I know that Corthie disappointed you, but if it was the other way around, do you think he would abandon you?'

Blackrose said nothing, her gaze directed downwards as she hovered over the arena. Yendra was fighting like the god she was, but her blade was almost broken, while a few yards from her, Corthie was swinging his axe in a blur of movement, but his armour was battered and scored, and blood was streaming down the side of his face.

'Mela Kaula Nathara,' Maddie said; 'I am your rider. Help them.'

'As my rider, I hear you,' the dragon said, 'but I will not comply. If today is the appointed day for the City to fall, then I shall not interfere.'

'Then take us lower,' said Belinda.

The dragon laughed. 'Do you think I am a fool? I remember well the trick you played on me at the Great Walls, when you jumped from my back. You shall not do so again.'

'I won't,' Belinda said, 'I promise. I want to drop Corthie's Clawhammer to him. Surely you wouldn't begrudge him dying with his own weapon in his hands?'

'Very well. If you jump, Belinda, I will be leaving you behind; do you understand?'

'I do.'

Blackrose tilted her head, then soared down, causing Corthie and Yendra to glance up as her shadow flickered over them. Belinda gripped the Clawhammer over her lap as they descended, her eyes on the approaching ground, and the thousands of greenhides swarming across the arena. Maddie leaned over and watched as the god got ready to throw the weapon down to Corthie, who was directly below. Belinda glanced at her, and Maddie noticed that the god also had a knife clutched in her left hand.

'Maddie,' she whispered; 'I'm truly sorry about this, but I can see no other way.'

Belinda flung the Clawhammer over the side of the dragon, then her hand flashed out, cutting through the straps holding Maddie to the harness. She gripped Maddie under the shoulders and lifted her clear of the saddle, then turned, and threw her from Blackrose's back, sending her hurtling through the air towards the waiting greenhides below.

Maddie saw the ground approach, and screamed.

CHAPTER 28
THE ETERNAL ENEMY

Tara, Auldan, The City – 2nd Mikalis 3420

Aila watched the sun set through the narrow slit window, and the chamber darkened as the last rays of daylight ebbed away. Next to her, on the hard wooden bench, Doria was weeping, while Ikara paced up and down by the barred gate at the end of the room. For a cell, the chamber was spacious and comfortable, and had its own latrine in a tiny room near the window.

'Doria,' Ikara cried, 'stop whining; that noise is going to drive me crazy.'

'Leave her alone,' said Aila. 'No wonder she's crying, the City is falling.'

'Only Medio,' her cousin said, 'we're safe here in Auldan.'

Aila frowned. 'From the greenhides maybe; I'm not so sure about the God-Queen.'

'You're right; I should have said "I'm safe", because everyone knows you're a rebel at heart; you always have been. Whereas I, on the other hand, have always been loyal. If Marcus wasn't obsessed with you, then you'd have been executed by now, or you'd be like Mona, and have a restrainer strapped to your face.' She smiled. 'I'll be getting out of here soon, once the God-Queen realises that I'm loyal.'

Doria lifted her face. 'Have you seen Mona?'

'I saw her when I was brought here,' said Aila. 'She's being kept in a cell by herself a couple of floors below us.'

'Is she... suffering?'

Ikara laughed. 'It's no wonder you were hidden away in the Royal Palace for centuries, Doria. She's wearing a god-restrainer; they're designed to cause suffering.'

'But it's not fair,' said Doria, 'she didn't do anything worse than Aila or I, and we're not wearing them.'

Ikara looked at her younger sister as if she was stupid. 'It's so she can't use her vision powers to help the rebels in Medio. Once everyone's been annihilated, I'm sure the God-Queen will take it off. Just be thankful that you don't have any vision powers.'

'I also saw Salvor and Collo on the way in,' said Aila. 'They're sharing a cell just like we are. The God-Queen has rounded up every demigod she can get her hands on, and has brought them all to Maeladh Palace.'

'She's going to form a new government once this is over; a government that I'll be part of.' Ikara smiled at Aila. 'While you'll be required for only one thing: breeding ugly little babies for Marcus. I always knew you were a degenerate, Aila, but imagine marrying your own cousin.'

Aila said nothing and glanced back out of the window. She knew the God-Queen held Ikara in contempt, but she couldn't muster the spite to tell her. It seemed trivial, pathetic even, compared to everything else that was happening. She wondered how many people had already been slaughtered in Medio in the seven or eight hours since the Middle Walls had been breached. There were only a few people in the world that Aila truly loved, and all of them were in the Circuit; Corthie, Yendra and Naxor; would any of them be alive by sunrise?

Hey, idiot sister,' Ikara said to Doria; 'what job do you think you'll get in the new government? Cleaning the toilets? Scrubbing the God-King's underwear?'

Doria burst into tears.

Ikara laughed. 'Maybe those jobs are a bit too complicated for you to handle.'

'The God-King's dead.'

Ikara blinked and frowned. 'What? Don't talk garbage.'

'It's true,' said Aila. 'Doria and I were there; Marcus chopped his head off.'

'You're lying. The Royal Palace made a statement saying that the God-King and God-Queen had reconciled.'

'Then why's she back in Tara without him?'

'I don't know; maybe they had another argument.'

Aila smiled. 'You carry on believing that.'

Ikara stopped pacing and sat down, her eyes on the stone floor of the chamber.

'The God-King was very ill,' said Doria, 'poisoned by salve. I think it was partly a mercy killing.'

'Shut up,' snapped Ikara.

The sound of footsteps in the well-lit passageway outside the chamber echoed through, and a squad of Roser militia appeared with another demigod in their midst. The heavy, barred gate was opened, and Lady Lydia entered.

She stood in silence with her chin held high as the soldiers locked the gate behind her.

'Sisters,' she said; 'cousin.'

Aila, Ikara and Doria watched as Lydia walked over to a chair and sat down without another word.

'Well?' said Ikara.

Lydia raised an eyebrow. 'Well what?'

'Are you joking? What's happening out there? You've come from Port Sanders?'

'Yes.'

Ikara stared at her. 'Is that it?'

'She's embarrassed,' said Aila; 'she's abandoned the Sanders to be ripped to pieces by the greenhides, and she's acting all proud to hide the fact that she's burning with shame on the inside.'

Lydia turned her stern gaze to Aila. 'I bowed before necessity. Medio is a charnel house, and my death would have made no difference. I filled every boat in the harbour with Sander families and children before I boarded the final one.' Her voice almost broke, and she took a breath. 'Staying would have been easier, for now I have to live with the knowledge of what has been done to my people. Believe me, I will never forget.'

Ikara snorted. 'That sounds like you're planning revenge. I'd be careful if I were you.'

'You are a fool, sister. The God-Queen and Marcus engineered the murder of our mother, and have opened the Middle Walls to the greenhides, and yet you would still bow before them?'

Aila glanced at her cousin. 'I'm sorry I said you were embarrassed, Lydia; I misjudged you.'

'No, you were right. I'm embarrassed to be part of this family. I should have opened the gates of Port Sanders to Yendra, only I was too afraid.' She glanced around the chamber. 'Now here we are, the most useless of all the demigods, slaves to the God-Queen, while the best of us are dying in Medio. Even Jade has shown more bravery than us.'

'So what do we do?' said Aila.

'There's nothing you can do,' said Ikara. 'You saw Mona on the way in. That's what you'll get if you resist.'

'Someone might break through the Union Walls,' Aila said. 'Corthie and Yendra, or maybe the Aurelians; we can't lose all hope.'

Lydia shook her head. 'Corthie and Yendra were surrounded somewhere near Redmarket the last I heard, while the Hammers and Aurelians were being overwhelmed as I left Port Sanders. Every Blade is lining the Union Walls; no one will get through.'

Doria sobbed, and the chamber fell into silence.

Footsteps sounded along the hallway again, and more soldiers from the Roser militia appeared.

'Lady Aila,' said an officer, as a guard opened the barred gate, 'come this way.'

'Where's she going?' said Ikara.

The officer glanced at the demigod. 'The God-Queen has summoned her.'

Aila got to her feet and started to walk towards the gate.

'What about the rest of us?' Ikara said. 'I want to speak to the God-Queen; I'm completely loyal. Tell her that; make sure you tell her.'

The officer said nothing as Aila left the chamber. The barred gate was closed and locked, and the squad moved off.

Ikara ran to the bars. 'When are we getting out of here? I've done nothing wrong.'

The soldiers ignored her. They followed the hallway to its end, with Aila flanked on either side, then descended a flight of stairs. They went past another barred chamber, where Salvor and Collo were sitting. They glanced up as the soldiers passed, but Aila was escorted away before she could speak to them. They went down more stairs, and Aila began to hear the tortured cries of Mona. The guards led her past the cell where the demigod was chained and masked. She was writhing on the floor in torment, blood covering the lower half of her face, and the guards seemed to linger for a second, and Aila imagined it was to ensure she knew what could lie in store for her.

They emerged from the base of the prison tower into a small, lamplit courtyard, then the guards escorted Aila into a wing of the main palace complex, and along wide, marble floors, where oil-lamps burned brightly from the walls. She was led to a long wood-lined room with a great window over-looking the bay and the coastline by Pella. The sky outside was darkening, with a purple glow sunward all that remained of the day's light. A large number of elegantly dressed Taran nobles were assembled, drinking white wine from tall glasses and chatting, while, upon a wide marble dais with three thrones, the God-Queen was sitting, in the central, largest throne.

The militia led Aila to the foot of the dais, then bowed low before the God-Queen.

'Lady Aila,' she said, as the nobles in the room quietened and turned to listen; 'I'm thrilled you could join us. How are the three lovely daughters of Khora enjoying their confinement? Let me guess – Ikara is pledging her undying loyalty to me, Lydia is simmering with rage, and Doria is weeping. Am I close?'

'And what did you imagine I was doing?'

'Oh, knowing you, my dear, I would have expected you to have been plotting my destruction. Of course, it's too late for that; right now, the greenhides will be spreading out to every corner of Medio. Expert opinion varies, but my advisors estimate that it will take between two to three days for the greenhides to hunt down and kill every last citizen in Medio, though Icehaven has a small chance of holding out for a little longer.'

Aila folded her arms. 'Why did you summon me?'

The God-Queen smiled. 'We are due to receive news from the Union Walls soon, announcing that the greenhides have reached every section of the battlements protecting Auldan. Once that occurs, then we can be assured that no rebel force will be able to attempt to break through. I thought you might like to be here for that.' She gestured to a pair of guards standing off to the left. 'Bring the prisoner forward.' She turned back to Aila. 'There's someone I'd like you to meet; a woman who, like yourself, I have summoned here to witness this historic occasion.'

The two soldiers were carrying crossbows, and they escorted a woman from the side of the room over to stand in front of the God-Queen.

'Lady Aila,' she said, 'meet Lady Aurelian. She is the real one, not the Evader imposter who tried to lead a rebellion against me.'

The woman kept her face impassive. 'Emily Aurelian speaks for me, and she is married to my son; she is not an imposter, your Majesty.'

'Maybe not, but regardless, she will soon be dead, that is, if the greenhides have not already torn her to pieces. And your rebel son, too; what a pity.'

'I am proud of my son,' said Lady Aurelian; 'unfortunately, one cannot say the same about our current government. Shame springs to mind, but not pride.'

Aila nodded. 'I was thinking much the same. Medio is surrounded by monsters, and not all of them are green.'

'Quite,' said Lady Aurelian; 'some of them sit on thrones.'

The God-Queen's face darkened as the room fell silent. 'You will die for that, Aurelian, but not yet. I want to look into your face when you realise that your line has been extinguished forever; I want to see the pain in your eyes, and then you will beg me to end it, but I will make it linger.'

Lady Aurelian kept the gaze of the God-Queen. 'With such a compassionate ruler, the City is in safe hands.'

Amalia turned to the guards. 'Take these two creatures away from me; they're souring the celebrations. Keep them in the chamber, but somewhere I can't see them.'

The soldiers nodded, and escorted Aila and Lady Aurelian over to the far left of the long room, where there was an empty space by the window.

Aila glanced out at the dark bay. 'You're probably the first mortal to have spoken to the God-Queen like that since... maybe ever.'

'I'd like to think that the last mortal prince said similar things to her.'

Aila smiled. 'He probably did.'

Lady Aurelian turned to face her. 'So you're the famous Lady Aila; the woman for whom Marcus brought the City to its knees?'

'That's me.'

'I don't envy your future.'

Aila glanced back out of the window. 'I still have hope.'

'Come now, Aila, don't fool yourself. The God-Queen and Marcus have wrought a calamity upon this City that will change everything for the worse. A mountain of dead, and for what? So the Gods and Rosers can enslave everyone else.'

'But you're a Roser.'

'I am, and I have never felt so ashamed of that in all my life. Look around this chamber; glance at the satisfied, smug faces of the Taran nobility, my peers. Don't you want to kill them all? Right now, my husband is languishing in a dungeon, and my son and daughter-in-law are... out there, beyond the walls. There is no hope to be had.'

'There is Yendra, and Corthie Holdfast.'

'A hundred Yendras wouldn't be able to kill every greenhide in Medio. I'm sure she will slaughter many, but they'll get her in the end. As for the Holdfast boy, champion or no champion, he's a mortal and, as I'm sure you've noticed over the centuries, mortals die.'

Aila closed her eyes as despair threatened to grip her. She knew she was foolish to have any hope left, but she clung to it. Corthie would break down a gate in the Union Walls, or he would flee with Yendra to Icehaven and they would take a ship to Dalrig. And Naxor too, he was so sly that surely he wouldn't allow himself to be cornered by the greenhides.

'I fear that my words have touched a nerve,' Lady Aurelian said. 'I have let my own despair infect you.' She put a hand on Aila's shoulder. 'Hold on to your hope.'

The doors to the chamber opened and a royal courtier entered with a bow towards the throne.

'I bear tidings from the front,' he exclaimed.

'Enter,' said the God-Queen, 'and tell us your news.'

The courtier bowed again, then approached the dais, as the ladies and gentlemen of the Taran aristocracy watched.

'Your divine Majesty,' he said; 'reports have arrived from the forts along the Union Walls, and the news from every fort, bar one, is the same; the greenhides are at the walls.'

The Tarans raised their glasses and cheered.

Lord Chamberlain stepped forward. 'Excellent news, but you said "bar one"? Pray tell us, which fort is the exception?'

'The Sunward Fort on the cliffs of the Warm Sea, my lord,' the courtier said; 'for there the masses of Hammer refugees are pressed tightly, hemmed between the cliffs and the walls, and the greenhides have yet to pierce their lines. However, my lord, it takes two hours for a fast carriage to travel from that particular fort to Maeladh Palace, so by now the situation may have changed.'

'We shall not wait for the news from the last fort to arrive before we begin our celebrations,' said the God-Queen, 'for the outcome is inevitable. I therefore declare Auldan to stand alone, as it once did in bygone years, before the Middle Walls were built, and before the Evaders arrived. It also falls to me to announce the sorrowful passing of my husband, God-King Malik.'

The chamber fell into a deathly silence.

'His Majesty's end was peaceful, and the people can be reassured that his divine, undying spirit shall watch over them always. Auldan shall mourn for ten days, and in that period I shall allow the greenhides to purify Medio and the Bulwark, and then I shall begin the process of removing them, so that we can reclaim the land up to the Great Walls.

'As for the government, I shall return to Tara once the greenhides have been liquidated, and shall hand over complete power to my grandson, Prince Marcus. It is he who will decide the dispositions of the surviving members of the Royal Family, and he who will appoint the mortals who shall assist in the running of the City.

'Tomorrow we shall begin the mourning period for our beloved God-King, but for now, celebrate this great triumph with us here at the palace, my home.'

Lord Chamberlain raised his glass. 'A cheer for our magnificent God-Queen, radiant in her power, saviour of the true City!'

The Tarans cheered and applauded, then turned to each other as they began to chat.

'You're right,' Aila said to Lady Aurelian; 'I do want to kill them.'

'The Sunward Fort, did you hear?' said Lady Aurelian. 'That's where Daniel and Emily will be.' Her composure cracked for a moment, and Aila could see the pain that lay behind her eyes. 'I thought all hope had gone, but this... this is agony.'

The pale blue shutters were closed along the length of the window as night fell, and more lamps were lit in the chamber, their light flickering over the gold-trimmed wooden panelling. An officer approached, and gestured to Lady Aurelian.

'We've come to escort you back to your cell, ma'am.'

She turned to Aila. 'If I die, and by some miracle Danny or Emily survive this night, tell them I was very proud of them both, and that I went to my death with nothing in my heart but love for them. Will you do that?'

'Yes.'

'Thank you.' She half-smiled. 'The Sunward Fort. Farewell, Aila.'

She turned, and was escorted through the crowd of Taran nobles. She held her head high, and looked at no one, while the nobles all turned and stared. Aila watched her leave the room, then glanced at the other doorways. Each was guarded by soldiers, and she had her own little detachment of crossbow-wielding militia standing watching her from a few yards away. She frowned. Maybe if she ran at them, they would shoot her and put her out of her misery.

The tall doors opened again, and courtiers entered. The central one raised his hand in a flourish. 'Behold, the Prince of Tara.'

The courtiers scurried to the side as Marcus strode into the chamber, wearing his pristine battle armour. The crowd of Taran nobles cheered loudly, and he smiled and nodded at each as he passed.

'Welcome, grandson,' said the God-Queen. 'We are victorious.'

He stopped in front of the throne and bowed his head. 'We are, grandmother. The greenhides are scouring Medio clean, and the Union Walls stand firm. In a short while we shall be living in a city free from rebels and traitors, and it is all thanks to your divine wisdom and foresight.'

'I simply saw what needed to be done, grandson; the execution was all yours.'

He smiled and turned to the nobles. 'Ladies and gentlemen of Tara; the cream of the Roser nobility, my thanks for coming here tonight for our celebration.'

They cheered.

'There is a banquet planned for later, but before that begins, I shall be begging your leave, for I wish to reacquaint myself with my new wife, and show her much I've missed her.'

The nobles cheered and a few gentlemen laughed into their wine glasses.

He turned to Aila and extended his arm. 'If you would, my lady?'

Aila stood frozen for a moment as every face turned to her. She wondered what Stormfire would do. She would probably smile, to pretend everything was fine, and then accompany the prince to his rooms where she would murder him... But how? She had no weapon. Maybe she could bash him over the head with a candlestick, the way the God-Queen had done to Corthie.

She smiled and started to walk towards the prince.

'There you are,' he beamed as he took her hand in his, clasping it tight. He began to lead her from the chamber, and the crowd of nobles parted, smiling as they passed. A small group of courtiers and soldiers escorted them as they strode along the ancient passageways of the palace. They stopped at large door of dark oak, and a courtier bowed and opened it.

The prince gestured, and Aila walked in. Lamps had already been lit, illuminating a luxurious suite of oak-panelled rooms, with sunward-facing windows that had been shuttered against the night air. A large fireplace stood cold, but the room was still warm from the summer sun. Through an open door, she could see the bedroom, and her blood chilled.

'Would you like a drink?' Marcus said.

She turned to him. 'Yes.'

'How's brandy?'

'Brandy will do.'

He walked to a table, where a large crystal decanter sat, and poured measures into two glasses. He passed her one, then began unstrapping his armour, laying his glass down onto a little table by the wooden armour-stand.

He glanced at her. 'How was your day, my dear?'

'Screw you, Marcus. You've murdered hundreds of thousands of people, and you ask me how my day was? Do you think we're going to have a civilised little chat after what you've done?'

He hung his breastplate on the stand, his eyes remaining fixed on her. 'Are you trying to provoke me into violence?'

'It doesn't take much; I saw that last time. You're a vile bully.'

His cheeks started to redden with anger. 'If it weren't for me, my grandmother would've had you in chains with a restrainer mask on your face by now, or worse, she would have chopped your head off. I'm the only thing keeping you alive, and you should try to remember that.'

She squinted at him. 'Am I supposed to be grateful to you? A man who celebrates when thousands of people are torn to pieces by greenhides? You disgust me.'

He ripped the armour from his arms and threw it to the floor, his eyes darkening. 'You don't understand what you're saying. What I did today was necessary. The City was ill, diseased, and I have used a knife to cut out the part that was rotten.'

She narrowed her eyes. 'So all those people mean nothing to you?'

'The mortals are tools,' he cried, taking a step towards her, his fists clenching; 'nothing but disposable tools. The greenhides are the same. I have nothing to justify; I was merely using one set of tools to solve a problem with another. The only problem I have left to solve is you.'

'The greenhides aren't tools, you smug idiot, they're demented, ravenous beasts.'

He shook his head, a cold smile descending onto his lips. 'They are both, Aila, and things become much easier when you understand that. I think it's time you learned the purpose of the greenhides, and where they came from.'

She backed away a step as he continued to edge closer to her.

'Have you never wondered about how fortunate it was for the City that the God-King and God-Queen arrived only a few years after the greenhides first invaded? I thought you were supposed to be clever, Aila.'

He took another step towards her, and her legs bumped against a table as she backed away.

'How do you keep a population of mortals docile over millennia?' he said, his eyes boring through her. 'The greenhides are the perfect solution; an external threat, an eternal enemy. Something for the mortals to fear and hate.' He smiled. 'And something we can use, if the mortals ever threaten to rebel. The God-Queen is a true visionary;

she knew how difficult it would be to rule here for such a long time, and so she and the God-King brought the greenhides here to this world.'

Aila's mouth opened as she tried to sift through Marcus's words. The notion sounded too ludicrous to be true, but the more she thought about it, the more she realised that it fitted in with everything she knew about the rule of the gods. If they could open the Middle Walls, then there were no limits to their cruelty and ruthlessness.

'They brought them here?' she repeated, her mind whirling.

'They did,' he said, taking another step forward, 'and just like you, my beautiful wife, the people of the City are trapped, with nowhere left to run.'

He lunged at her, and she ducked out of his reach, scrambling away. The table toppled over, sending the decanter and a dozen glasses falling to the floor with a crash. Aila backed away, her eyes looking for a way out, or for something she could use as a weapon.

He shook his head at her as if making light of it, but she could see the rage in his eyes. 'Let me be frank,' he said; 'I intend to sire at least a dozen children from this marriage, but your attitude will require some correction first. It took me nearly a hundred years to fully break your brother Kano, so as you can see, I'm a patient man.'

He extended his arms to either side as he took a step towards her, boxing her into the corner of the room.

'I hate you,' she said as he approached; 'I loathe you. I will never love you.'

'I have learned to live with the knowledge that you do not love me, but I do not require your love; only your submission.'

He sprang at her, and she grabbed the large decanter and swung it at his head, cracking it off the side of his face. He roared in pain, and reached out with a large hand, grasping her shoulder and throwing her across the room. She tumbled through the air, crashing into the armour stand with a clatter. She fell to the floor, wincing from pain, and feeling something jab into her side through her clothes. She rolled over as Marcus strode across the room, and tried to crawl away, but he leaned down and grabbed one of her ankles, and began dragging her towards him.

Something jabbed into her side again and, on instinct, her hand went to the pocket on her shirt, the same shirt that she had been wearing since Redmarket, and her fingers went round something small and hard.

'No one will pay any attention to your screams,' he said as he stood over her; 'you are mine.'

She pulled the vial from her pocket and yanked out the stopper. Marcus reached down for her with his hands, and she threw the contents of the vial into his face. The liquid splashed over him, burning through his skin like acid, and he screamed.

Aila wriggled backward as Marcus clawed at his face with his hands. The concentrated salve was eating through his features, dissolving his nose, and turning his eyes red with blood, while his teeth smoked as they were reduced to blackened stumps. The salve from his face was spreading to his hands as he tried to rub it off, and the skin on his fingers withered and peeled off.

Aila backed up against the wall, her eyes wide. Marcus howled in pain and fell to the carpet, leaking blood from a dozen places, his limbs flailing. Aila pulled herself to her feet. Her gaze went to the broad, steel breastplate that she had knocked over. She picked it up in both hands, feeling its weight, then staggered over to where Marcus was writhing on the floor.

She lifted it high over his head.

'Farewell, husband,' she said, then slammed the sheet of steel down with all the strength she could muster, the edge striking his throat, and cleaving halfway through his neck. The screams quietened, but he was still writhing, and his throat was starting to heal. Aila lifted the breastplate again, and brought it down, severing his spinal cord. His head rolled to the side, the eyes open and staring, the salve still burning through what remained of the flesh. Aila fell to her knees, staring at the massive body lying before her.

Stunned and exhausted, she sat on the carpet, as if waiting for

Marcus to get back up and attack her again. She rubbed her face. She had done it.

A loud knock came from the door. 'Your Highness, is everything all right?'

Aila jumped, her eyes going to the door. She sprang into life, getting to her feet. Her eyes scanned the floor, then she ran over and picked up the vial, and pushed the stopper back in. Barely a tenth of the concentrated salve remained, and she dropped it into her pocket.

You see me as Prince Marcus.

She went to the door and opened it a crack. Outside, several courtiers and guards were standing.

'You dare interrupt me?' she cried.

The courtiers bowed.

'Apologies, my lord,' said one; 'we heard screams.'

'What goes on inside my quarters is of absolutely no concern to you, do you understand?' She edged out of the room into the hallway, closing the door behind her. 'Get out of my way. After your crude interruption, I require some fresh air for a moment.'

The courtiers glanced at her, but said nothing.

She strode down the hallway, heading for one of the palace's many smaller entrances. Guards bowed and scrambled out of her way as she passed, and she had almost made it to a large outside courtyard when the shouts and cries of alarm rose up behind her. She dived into the shadows.

You see me as a guard in the Roser militia.

She increased her pace, reaching the wide door that led outside. She pushed it open, seeing the dark sky above, then stepped out onto the gravel driveway. Ahead of her were a set of gates, and then the large mansions where the nobles of Tara lived. She forced herself not to run, suppressing her instincts. She just had to keep her nerve for a few more moments.

'Trying to flee, Aila?' came a voice from behind her.

She turned as her breath caught in her throat. The God-Queen was standing a few yards away, her face raw with tears and rage.

'There will be no forgiveness for you,' the God-Queen said. 'For a thousand years I will torture you for what you have done.'

She raised her hand and Aila felt a pressure grip her heart. She fell to her knees on the gravel, the pain travelling out from her heart to reach every part of her.

'I will flay the skin from your body,' the God-Queen said as she approached, 'every day for a century. There will be no escape for you, Aila.'

Aila tried to keep her eyes open, but the agony became unbearable.

The God-Queen reached her, and gazed down with venomous hatred. 'Welcome to an eternity of pain.'

CHAPTER 29

THE CLAWHAMMER

The Circuit, Medio, The City – 2nd Mikalis 3420

Corthie swung the axe, driving the blade through the face of a greenhide lunging at him. His shoulders and arms were moving freely, but blood was getting into his eyes and he could feel his body tiring. He shifted his feet, climbing higher up the mound of dead as it continued to grow, and glanced over to where Yendra was fighting a few yards away. She looked as strong as she had been when she had started, but her sword was bent and notched, and her armour was covered in scores and dents.

A shadow flickered over his head, and he looked up, realising that the sun had set. The dark night sky hung overhead, casting most of the arena into thick shadows, and only a few scattered lamps were providing any light.

The shadow passed overhead again as Corthie's axe bit deep into the flank of a greenhide, and then a scream tore through the air. A large object landed a yard from where he was standing, crashing into the piles of dead, and then, moments later, a figure also fell.

Corthie blinked, then turned to fend off another greenhide as he heard a cry of terror and pain come from behind him. He cleaved through the greenhide's neck, then risked a glance over his shoulder.

Maddie Jackdaw was lying sprawled over the thick corpses on the slopes of the mound of dead, her eyes wide in shock. A greenhide saw her, and raced round the edge of the mound, its claws clacking. Corthie launched himself backwards, and kicked the greenhide in the face as it sprang at her, then brought the edge of the axe swinging down through its neck as Maddie screamed.

Corthie steadied his feet on the side of the mound as the swarm of greenhides jumped down at him and Maddie. He punched up with the tip of the axe, piercing the neck of a beast, then grabbed Maddie and pulled her down the slope with him. As they descended, he caught sight of a large wooden handle poking out from the heap of dead, and he smiled.

'Yendra!' he cried.

'I'm here,' she said. 'I saw the girl fall from the sky.'

He threw her the Axe of Rand. 'You look like you could do with a new weapon.'

She caught it, then swung her arms, wielding the axe two-handed, and slicing through the waists of two lunging greenhides. Corthie gripped the wooden handle he had seen, and pulled the Clawhammer from the heap of dead.

Corthie and the god stood back to back protecting Maddie as the massed ranks of greenhides encircled them.

'Now would be a good time,' said Corthie.

Yendra frowned. 'For what?'

'For a dragon,' said Maddie.

The arena lit up as a blast of flames poured down from the sky. The greenhides shrieked and screamed as fire covered them, blistering their thick skin and transforming them into smoking ruins. Another blast descended, and the greenhides surrounding the three figures in the centre of the arena were incinerated. Corthie raised a hand to shield his face from the heat of the inferno, then glanced up to see Blackrose hovering overhead.

Greenhides were still entering the arena through several gates, and the dragon circled the edge of the sand, sending fire down each entrance tunnel until nothing moved. The flames died down, leaving thick, oily tendrils of dark smoke drifting upwards from the charred corpses. Corthie helped Maddie get to her feet as the dragon began to descend.

'Are you alright?' he said.

'That might have been the most terrifying two minutes of my life.'

'How did you fall?' said Yendra.

Maddie frowned. 'I was pushed.'

They glanced up as Blackrose landed onto the heap of dead. Belinda jumped down, and the dragon bared her teeth at her.

'You tricked me, again.'

'I'm not sorry,' said Belinda.

'I should burn you to ash.'

'Do as you must.'

'Wait,' cried Yendra.

The dragon turned to her.

Yendra went down onto one knee. 'Your Majesty,' she said, 'my grateful thanks for rescuing us.'

The dragon snorted. 'I didn't do it for you; I did it to save the life of my rider.'

'Nevertheless, Corthie and I owe you our lives. I was imprisoned by the same gods that bound you with chains. For three hundred years I was their captive; they wronged me grievously, just as they wronged you.'

'Then why are you fighting for them?'

Yendra's eyes hardened. 'I am not. I'm fighting for every oppressed mortal in the City, to free them from the gods who have treated us both so shamefully. I swear to you that I shall not rest until those who made us suffer are dead. I also swear that, if we join together to do this, then I will deliver a Quadrant to you.' She lifted her hands in supplication. 'My fight is your fight, your Majesty; let us stand up for the weak, and tear down the tyrants.'

The dragon said nothing, her eyes steady as she gazed at the princess.

Corthie staggered back a step, and pulled on more of his battle-vision to keep going. In the lull from fighting, he had been relaxing, and he knew that he would fall unconscious within seconds if he dropped his powers.

Maddie touched his arm. 'Are you tired?'

He nodded. 'Aye, but I've still got a bit left in me.'

The dragon raised her head and sniffed the air.

'I have a plan,' said Belinda.

'No one asked you,' said Blackrose.

'I know.' She turned to Yendra and Corthie. 'We sealed the breach in the Great Walls on our way here; no more greenhides will be getting into the City.'

Corthie puffed out his cheeks.

'You did this, Belinda?' said Yendra, her eyes narrow.

'We all did it,' the god said. 'Here's what I propose. Corthie and Yendra will strike out on foot for the Sixth Gate, in order to close the breach there. Blackrose flies overhead, and clears the way, then burns every greenhide she can see.'

'Out of the question,' said Blackrose.

'Are you still not willing to help us?' said Corthie.

The dragon lowered her head. 'No, I am willing; Yendra's logic is undeniable. If she can fight those who imprisoned her, then so can I; and if she fights to protect all those wronged by my oppressors, then I should do the same. My problem is with Belinda; she has shown that I can no longer trust her. She must remain on the ground with you, for I shall not allow her on my back again.'

'I can live with your hate,' Belinda said. She glanced at Yendra. 'I would be happy to fight on the ground by your side.'

'I'm not,' said Corthie. 'Aila's in Tara; that's where I need to be going. With Blackrose, we can fly right over the Union Walls, and she could drop me off there.'

'You know I greatly love Lady Aila,' Yendra said, 'but the lives of the thousands in Medio outweigh her one life; I'm sorry, but if the Queen of the Dragons helps us, then she must confront the greenhides first.' She glanced at the dragon. 'Do you agree?'

'I do. Corthie, do not be downhearted. Take Belinda's space upon my back, and I will take you to Tara once I have dealt with the greenhides.'

Corthie nodded. He knew they were right, but it had been hours since the God-Queen had taken Aila. He hadn't noticed the passage of time while he had been absorbed in killing greenhides, but his nerves were jangling afresh at the thought of what could be happening to her.

'Come on,' said Maddie. 'I'll show you how to climb up.'

He turned to Belinda and Yendra. 'Good luck.'

'You too,' said Yendra, 'and when you get to Tara, be sure to give my greetings to the God-Queen.'

'We'll give you five minutes,' said Belinda, 'then we'll leave the racecourse.'

Corthie climbed the mound of dead, and Maddie led him round to where ropes and knots ran down the dragon's flank. She gripped on and leapt up, and he followed, scrambling up onto the wide shoulders of the dragon.

'Hi, Rosie,' he said. 'I hadn't noticed you from down there.'

'Are you settled?' said Blackrose.

'Just a moment,' said Maddie as she pulled the straps round Corthie's waist. 'Done.'

The dragon extended her great wings and rose into the air, and Corthie took a tight grip of the harness. He glanced down, and saw the two gods standing where he had left them. Yendra raised the Axe of Rand high into the sky as the dragon ascended above the arena.

'Which way's Tara?' he said, as Blackrose began to bank.

Maddie shrugged.

'That way,' said Rosie, pointing west.

He grasped the Clawhammer as Blackrose dropped without warning. She soared over the remainder of the Great Racecourse, then turned towards the enormous plaza that ringed it. The area was filled with greenhides. They were no longer trying to get into the massive building, and were whirling out in other directions. Blackrose swooped down and opened her jaws, sending flames blasting out over the plaza. She circled the racecourse in one long loop, raining an unbroken stream of fire down, then she turned sunward, following the line of a wide road. Jets of flame burst down at every large cluster of greenhides they passed, and within a few minutes, the Circuit was carpeted with the smouldering remains of charred bodies.

Corthie watched open-mouthed as he began to understand the true power of the dragon. The greenhides howled and shrieked, but there was nothing they could do to stem the tide of death that Blackrose delivered upon them. The dragon swept up and down the length of the Circuit from iceward to sunward, and she was completing their second run when Maddie pointed.

'Over to the right,' she cried; 'beyond the houses and streets.'

The dragon tilted her head to show that she had heard the words of her rider, and banked, increasing her speed as they rushed sunward. The edge of the Circuit passed by in a blur, and they flew over the fields of the territory of the Sanders. The ground was littered in human bodies, and the cries from a slaughter reached Corthie's ears. Masses of refugees were crammed into a small area, between the high cliffs bordering the Warm Sea and the line of the Union Walls. At their fringes, greenhides were launching incessant attacks, each one killing more civilians, and ripping through the small number of soldiers trying to protect them.

Blackrose soared down, and unleashed a torrent of flames onto the thick lines of the greenhides, from the base of the Sunward Range, all the way up the flank of the hillside, then she banked into a tight turn, and did the same thing downhill, driving the greenhides from her path in a chaotic panic of fire and death. The beasts fled back towards the streets of the Circuit, and the dragon pursued them, chasing them with flames as they ran for their lives.

'That will relieve the pressure for a while,' said the dragon. 'Now, let us go to Tara.'

She banked left, and turned towards the west. They soared over the Union Walls as Blades on the battlements stared upwards at them, then they passed over the peaceful farmlands of Roser territory. To their right, the huge suburbs of Pella lined their route, and after a moment, the cliffs of Tara could be seen in the distance. They whipped over the coast of the Warm Bay, and flew low over the water as the harbour of Tara came into view, lit by lines of streetlamps.

'Head for that palace on top of the cliffs,' yelled Maddie.

The dragon angled upwards, and they soared over the boats in the harbour, climbing until they reached the top of the cliffs that ran next to the town. Great villas and mansions were spread out among the trees, and to their left was an enormous, sprawling palace. They circled over it.

'Is this Maeladh Palace?' said the dragon.

'Yes,' said Maddie; 'I recognise it from a picture in a book.'

'And Aila will be inside somewhere?'

'I think so,' said Corthie.

'So I shouldn't burn it just yet?'

Corthie glanced over the side of the dragon. The palace was huge, with towers and domes, and long wings that stretched over the width of the ridge.

'Damn it,' he muttered; 'she could be anywhere.'

'Where are all the soldiers?' said Maddie. 'I thought this place would be crawling with them.'

'They must be on the Union Walls,' said Corthie. 'I don't think they're expecting a dragon.'

Blackrose descended a little and circled again, gliding over the palace.

'Should I set you down?' she said. 'I shall be needed over Medio again.'

'Alright,' he said, gripping the handle of the Clawhammer. 'Any roof will do.'

Blackrose descended again, wheeling over the domed roof of a wing of the palace, and Corthie unbuckled the straps holding him to the harness. Maddie flung an arm over his shoulder.

'Go get her,' she said, kissing him on the cheek.

'Blackrose,' he cried. 'I'm ready.'

The dragon soared down, then hovered over a wide, flat roof. Corthie crouched on her shoulders, then leapt, jumping free of the dragon and landing onto the roof with a thump. Above him, the dragon started to ascend, then she raced off east, back towards the Circuit. Corthie glanced around, and ran to the edge of the building. Below him was a small, square courtyard, with windows and doors on all four sides. He frowned. He had no idea of where to start looking. He was about to jump down into the courtyard when he heard a scream of agony rise up from somewhere behind him. It was a man's voice that had made the cry, but Corthie turned, and ran over the roof. He followed the length of a wing of the palace, clambering over walls and chimney stacks, then paused as he reached another yard, much larger than the first, and only bounded on two sides by the palace. Sounds of alarm echoed up from the building around him, and soldiers of the Taran militia were running across the large courtyard. He looked down to the right to see where they were going, and gasped. Fifty yards away, the God-Queen was dragging a body across the gravel by an ankle.

It was Aila. Her arms were trailing limply as Amalia hauled her towards a side entrance of the palace. The soldiers reached them, and watched in silence as Aila was pulled into the building.

Corthie leapt down from the roof, his boots landing on the gravel, then he sprinted towards the side door. The Roser militia turned, their eyes widening as they saw the huge armoured figure approaching them. Corthie's armour was scored and covered in green blood, and as he raised the Clawhammer he saw the terror in the soldiers' eyes. He charged into them, swinging the ferocious weapon, its greenhide talons ripping through the light leather hauberks of the Rosers and cutting them down. They fled, scattering in a panic as Corthie struck another, slicing him down the back.

He watched the rest of them run for a moment, four ripped bodies lying by his feet, then he turned to the entrance. He pulled his helmet off so that he could hear and see better, and flung it to the gravel. His energy was flagging, and he knew that he didn't have long left. He wiped the blood from his eyes and walked into the palace, the Clawhammer gripped in his right hand.

Servants cried out and ran at his approach, dropping trays of dishes and fleeing down the hallways. A soldier stepped out to block his way, then stared, his mouth opening. Corthie punched him in the face with his left fist, sending him flying back into the room he had emerged from. He turned a corner, and saw soldiers disappearing through a set of tall doors.

Corthie narrowed his eyes, and picked up his pace. He reached the doors and stepped through. Inside was a long hall, with a window that stretched along one side. Through it the City could be seen, illuminated by a line of glowing red flames that rippled across the horizon, covering the entire length of the Circuit. A large group of well-dressed Rosers was staring out at the flames, transfixed by the sight.

A soldier ran up to them. 'My lords and ladies, an intruder is in the palace!'

Corthie walked forwards. 'Here I am. Where's the God-Queen?'

The aristocrats turned in alarm, their eyes widening.

Corthie nodded to the window. 'Do you see what's happening?'

'The Evaders have set fire to their own town, again,' said a man, stepping forward from the crowd; 'they perhaps think it will save them from the greenhides, but they are mistaken. Now, one must assume that you are the notorious traitor who once bore the title of Champion of the Bulwark. If you mean to intimidate us, you shall not succeed. Medio has fallen; it is over. Kneel before me now, and I shall perhaps show clemency.'

Corthie burst forwards, wielding Clawhammer two-handed. He cut down the soldiers protecting the Roser nobles, hacking through them in seconds, his battle-vision thrumming. The man who had spoken backed away in fright as fear swept through the nobles. Corthie swept his arms back, and with a great swing cleaved the man's head off, the greenhide claws slicing through his neck.

The aristocrats screamed and started scattering, running for the doors.

One pushed a woman behind him and drew a sword. 'Do you know who you just killed, you filthy savage? That was Lord Chamberlain, the most powerful mortal in the City.'

Corthie smiled.

The man lunged forward with the sword. Corthie stepped to the left, and gripped the man's wrist, squeezing until he cried out and dropped the weapon. The woman he had been shielding remained where she was, her back to the window, her eyes wide.

'Where are the God-Queen's quarters?' Corthie said. 'Tell me, or I'll kill everyone in the palace until I find her.'

The man glared at him in defiance. 'Her divine Majesty will destroy you.'

Corthie shrugged. 'Then what's the harm in telling me? Those flames over the Circuit were caused by a dragon, who'll be coming here when she's finished killing the greenhides. Tell me how to find the God-Queen, then maybe you'll be spared when Princess Yendra arrives tomorrow.'

The man pulled a knife from his robes and slashed out at him. Corthie let the blade turn harmlessly against his steel armour, then gripped the man by the throat and broke his neck. He dropped the body to the floor, and turned to the woman.

'Was that your husband?'

She stared at him. 'It was.'

'Are you going to tell me where the God-Queen is?'

'Will you kill me if I don't?'

'No.'

'Is it true about the dragon? Is Princess Yendra really coming?'

'Aye.'

'Do you know if Emily Aurelian is still alive?'

'What's that to you?'

'I'm her mother.'

Corthie glanced down at the body by his feet. 'Did I just kill Emily's father?'

'You did,' the woman said.

He frowned.

'My name is Lady Omertia,' the woman said, 'and I will take you to the God-Queen's quarters, if you tell me the fate of my daughter.'

'I don't know for sure. I saw a lot of refugees by the sunward end of the Union Walls. If she's alive, then that's where she'll be.'

'Did she really do all of those things they say she did? Did she lead an entire tribe to safety?'

'Your daughter's a hero, ma'am. If she lives, she'll be queen; if she's dead, then every mortal in Medio will mourn her.'

A tear slipped down the woman's cheek. 'Follow me.'

They walked through the deserted hall and took a long passageway along a low wing. Servants and courtiers fled at the sight of Corthie as they crossed the palace. A squad of militia burst round a corner towards them, but broke and ran as soon as Corthie raised the Clawhammer and charged at them, dropping their shields and crossbows and fleeing.

'I didn't realise I was that scary,' he said.

Lady Omertia glanced at him. 'You're a giant; your armour and face are smeared with blood of both colours, and you're carrying that... thing with you. You look like a demon from their worst nightmares.'

'Then why are you not scared?'

'I'm terrified, but maybe it takes a demon to fight a demon.'

They reached a set of stairs, and the woman pointed. 'The God-Queen's quarters are down there.'

Corthie nodded. 'Go home,' he said, 'and wait for the storm that will descend upon Tara tomorrow. I'll mention your name to Princess Yendra, and... sorry about your husband.'

'You may look like a demon,' she said, 'but people like my husband were the real monsters. For years, Emily and I lived in fear of him, but no more. Now go, and do what has to be done.'

Corthie descended the stairs. The hallway at the bottom was deserted, but he could hear voices coming from a door to the left, so he approached it, making no noise. He opened it a crack. Inside, courtiers were gathered around the large body of a man lying on a bed, cleaning it. The head was detached from the rest of the corpse, but the flesh had almost completely melted away from the face, rendering it unrecognisable.

'Look what you did,' growled a voice. 'Don't turn away, Aila, look at your handiwork; look what you did to my beautiful boy. Every dream I had for the City is in ruins because of you, and I want you to suffer as you watch what I do next. I will destroy everything that you love; I shall smash the Union Walls, and let the greenhides devour every last mortal on this world, while I slowly flay the flesh from your body. And then, when you beg me for death, I will deny you, for you shall be coming with me when I depart this world; your suffering shall never end.'

Corthie pushed the door open. The God-Queen was standing a few yards from the bed, her right hand gripping Aila's throat. The courtiers turned, and froze as they saw Corthie.

'Out,' he said to them, raising the Clawhammer.

No one moved for a moment, then the courtiers ran for the door, pushing each other in their haste to flee. Corthie stepped aside to let them pass, then faced the God-Queen.

'Let her go.'

'You don't scare me, mortal,' the God-Queen said. 'If you touch me, I will kill Aila.'

'And then I will kill you.'

She pulled back her outer robes to reveal a copper-coloured metal device. 'Do you see this? You know what it does. With one touch, I will be...'

Corthie sprang forward. He swept his arm up, and brought the Clawhammer down, cleaving through the God-Queen's right arm. She screamed, and Aila collapsed to the floor, Amalia's severed hand still gripping her throat. Corthie pulled the Clawhammer back and aimed at the God-Queen's head. The talons whistled towards her neck, then swept through nothing but air as the God-Queen touched the Quadrant and vanished.

Corthie dropped the Clawhammer and fell to his knees by Aila. Her skin was sallow and green-tinged, and her eyes were closed. He lifted her head and shoulders and pulled her towards him, his palm on her cheek. He pulled the bloody hand from her throat and threw it to the floor.

'Aila,' he whispered.

The demigod didn't respond.

He buried his face into her hair, trying to keep his eyes from welling as his energy slipped away. He clung on to the last threads of battle-vision, as exhaustion and dizziness started to cloud his mind. If she died, he would swear undying vengeance and hunt the God-Queen down, but his heart gave way at the thought, and he felt tears slide down his face. If she died, he would be desolate, and alone, and no amount of vengeance would change that.

She coughed in his arms, then opened her eyes. 'Corthie?'

He gazed at her, his eyes widening as her skin started to heal. Corthie tried to speak, but the swirl of emotions within him were impossible to put into words.

'You came for me,' she whispered. 'The God-Queen?'

'Gone. Blackrose came back, Aila; she saved the City. And you killed Marcus.'

'Yes. My husband is dead.'

'Do you want a new one?'

She smiled. 'Are you proposing?'

'You are everything I want, Aila, everything I need; I love you.'

She touched his face, wiping away the tears, and they kissed.

'My heart is yours, Corthie,' she said, 'forever.'

CHAPTER 30

THE FATED BLADES

The Union Walls, Medio, The City – 2nd Mikalis 3420

'Stand fast,' cried Emily as the greenhides renewed their assault on the Hammers. 'Fight to the end!'

She lifted her crossbow and loosed, striking a beast square in the chest, but it continued charging up the hillside towards her, trampling over the mounds of dead on the slopes of the Sunward Range. Emily reloaded as the greenhide lunged at her, and loosed again, straight into its face. The beasts were swarming all over the hillside, ripping into the massed crowds of Hammers and Evaders, pulling refugees from the lines and tearing them to pieces.

Emily scrambled to her feet. 'Fight!' she screamed.

Quill jumped at her, pulling her down to the blood-soaked grass. Emily struggled, then cried out as flames burst over her head, sweeping across the slopes in a tide of fire. Greenhides shrieked as the inferno enveloped them, then more flames poured down, pushing the greenhides off the slopes, and sending them scattering in terror back towards the Circuit.

'Did you see that?' yelled Jade to her right. 'A flying snake!'

Quill got off Emily and rose to her feet, staring up into the sky. 'The dragon came back.'

Emily joined her, and glanced down the smoking hillside. The flames had burned the human dead as well as the greenhides, and the slope was covered with bodies. In the distance, flames were rising up all over the Circuit.

'Quill,' she said, 'round up forty soldiers, anyone still able to fight.'

'Yes, ma'am.'

Emily jumped up onto a grassy ridge and glanced back at the mass of refugees huddled behind her. In less than an hour, the greenhides had slaughtered their way through about thirty thousand of the civilians that had sheltered between the cliffs of the Warm Sea and the Union Walls, a mixture of Hammers and Evaders. Many of them stared at her as she gazed at them.

'Jade,' she said, 'do you have any reserves left?'

'Not really,' said the demigod; 'enough to kill a few a greenhides if they get close.'

'Thank you for everything you've done today, Jade; you've been wonderful. Now, I need to ask for your help one more time this evening.'

Jade frowned. 'What do you want?'

'I want you to come with me and the soldiers Quill is organising.'

She lowered her eyes. 'Fine.'

Quill appeared by Emily's shoulder. 'I have the force you asked for, ma'am.'

Emily glanced at them. The men and women of the Hammer and Evader militia that the sergeant had gathered looked exhausted. Their uniforms were ripped and several were bleeding from scratches and cuts. When she looked into their eyes though, she saw the fire that burned within each.

'We're going to the Sixth Gate,' she said; 'the dragon has cleared the way. We'll ignore every greenhide we see, unless they attack us, and we'll stop for nothing until the breach is sealed. Sergeant Quill, lead the way.'

The tall soldier saluted, and the force began descending the slope. Emily and Jade caught up with Quill, while the militia formed a double column behind them. They picked their way through the heaps of smouldering carcasses, and Emily noticed that the smell was no longer bothering her. She felt every ache and bruise on her body, and was so tired she knew that if she were to lie down and close her eyes, she would be asleep within seconds.

Quill glanced at her. 'When I saw the dragon burn the greenhides, I was expecting you to gather a force.'

Emily smiled. 'Am I becoming predictable?'

The sergeant shook her head. 'I thought we were going to be searching for Daniel, ma'am.'

Emily felt her shoulders sag, as if her sorrow had physical weight. 'It's my duty to put the people first. Maybe once we've sealed the gate.'

'Have you given up hope for him?'

'No. Take us by the canal bridge he was trying to defend, but if he isn't there, we'll have to press on.'

Quill nodded. She gestured to the soldiers behind them as they reached the bottom of the slope, and with the narrow, burning streets of the Circuit before them, they started to run.

The Circuit was a smoking cauldron of death. Charred greenhide corpses lay over the ripped remains of civilians, and the canals were blocked with bodies. Many houses were wreathed in flames, and the smoke stung Emily's eyes amid the oppressive stench of burning flesh. After a mile or so, the dragon reappeared, soaring overhead; a black silhouette against the flames engulfing Medio. The greenhides were in full retreat, racing towards the breach in the Middle Walls to escape the destruction, and civilians were starting to emerge from cellars and tunnels all over the Circuit. Emily and Quill directed any they met to withdraw to Sander territory, then pushed on, following the trail of devastation left by the dragon.

They reached a canal, and Quill pointed towards a bridge. A blackened pile of greenhide corpses stretched along the far bank of the waterway, and the bodies of soldiers were scattered across the cobbles.

Emily ran forward, and noticed that some of the dead were wearing the uniform of the Hammer militia. Her heart pounded as she passed among the slain, glancing at each face.

'He's not here,' she said, putting a hand to her face.

Quill, Jade and the militia stood round her in silence. She felt like giving up, then remembered the people she was responsible for. She had to see it through, no matter the pain.

She lifted her eyes. 'To the breach.'

They set off again, sprinting down alleys and scrambling over the low roofs where the streets were blocked. Groups of exhausted Evaders passed them, carrying those too wounded to walk, while on every side, blackened greenhide carcasses carpeted the ground.

As they approached the Middle Walls, the fires grew more intense, as the dragon concentrated on the area around the breach. Emily and the squad crawled along a roof to watch as Blackrose soared down by the Sixth Gate. The greenhides were streaming back into the Bulwark, and the dragon was encouraging them, by sending short bursts of flame at those lagging behind.

Quill leaned against the low wall surrounding the edge of the roof.

'The dragon,' said Emily; 'she's amazing. I wonder how Maddie persuaded her.'

'I honestly couldn't care,' said Quill, 'but I'll be buying her a drink when I see her.'

'Can you get me a dragon?' said Jade.

'I don't think they're like cats,' said Emily; 'you have to ask their permission first.'

'Get ready,' said Quill; 'the dragon's moving off, and there might be a few stragglers to take care of.'

Jade frowned. 'I can't see any gate, just a knocked down old wall in the archway. How are you going to close it?'

'No idea,' said Emily; 'come on.'

She got to her feet and climbed down from the roof. Ahead of her was the walled courtyard that backed onto the gate, and the gatehouse where she had been held captive by Kano was directly behind it. The courtyard was filled with the bodies of greenhides, stretching back through onto the road. Emily gestured to the militia, and they ran forward. A greenhide leapt out from the shadows to their right, and Jade raised an arm. The beast's eyes turned black, and it collapsed to the cobbles.

'Thank you, Jade,' said Emily.

'I like killing them.'

They moved across the road towards the courtyard, and as they did so, another group, far larger than Emily's, burst out from the streets to their left. At their head strode Princess Yendra, leading a host of Evaders. Emily raised her hand in greeting, and Yendra lifted a great axe above her head, then turned her face and said something to the people behind her. A man broke out from the crowd of Evaders, and raced over the cobbles towards Emily.

'Danny,' she cried, as he swept her up in his arms. She forgot where she was for a moment, her hands gripping his back as she cried into his chest.

'You're alive,' he said.

'I thought I'd lost you.'

'How did you survive?'

'Blackrose saved us; she saved the Hammers.'

Yendra approached. 'I think you may have had something to do with that too, Emily. Now, as happy as I am to see you here, we have a gate to close.'

They filed between the bodies filling the courtyard. Emily walked up to the broken entrance, glancing at the rough blocks that had sealed the arched tunnel. At the other end, she could make out a patch of light marking the beginning of the Bulwark, while halfway along the tunnel was a door.

She turned to Yendra. 'I think we might need to borrow your strength for the next part.'

They broke through the door, and climbed the steps to the old portcullis room. As it had been at the Eighth Gate, the massive, wrought iron structure was standing propped up by chains and pulleys, its base a few inches from the wide slot built to accommodate it.

Yendra instructed everyone to stand back, then she sliced through the chains with her axe. She gripped the portcullis with both hands and heaved it across the floor, edging it towards the slot, as Emily, Daniel, and a few others watched. The princess moved it until it was almost hovering over the edge, then she picked up one of the wooden props and drove it under the base, wedging it in place.

'What are you doing?' said Daniel. 'Don't stop.'

Yendra shook her head. 'It must be you. Remove the wedge, and the portcullis will fall.'

Emily stepped forward, and placed her hand on the prop. 'Danny?'

He nodded, and joined her. Together, they gripped the wedge and ripped it free, and the massive portcullis slammed downwards, bursting through the slot and driving down to the ground below, sending a dull clang echoing around the room.

When they emerged from the gatehouse a few minutes later, an enormous crowd of Evaders had gathered, filling every available space.

A woman was waiting for them. 'Are these the mortals you were talking about?' she said, gazing at Emily and Daniel.

'Yes, Belinda,' Yendra said; 'it is to them that the power in the City shall pass.' She noticed Jade standing close by. 'Niece, your heroism today has not gone unnoticed. You have made your auntie very proud.'

Jade smiled, and her face flushed.

Yendra led Emily and Daniel out to the front of the crowd.

'Behold,' she cried; 'Lord Daniel Aurelian, and Lady Emily Aurelian. They have sealed the breach.'

The crowd roared.

'It is time for mortals to rule the City,' Yendra went on. 'There is still much to do, but when the City is once again at peace, then it will be up to the people, all the people, to choose the government that rules them. But the City also needs a new king and a new queen, and they should be mortals.' She went down on one knee as the crowd silenced. 'Long ago, the last Prince Aurelian was a champion of the people, so I now nominate Daniel and Emily Aurelian to be our sovereign King and Queen; a Roser and an Evader, together, to heal the divisions of our City. They have proved their love for the people, and their courage. To my mind, there is no one fitter.'

She raised her arms. 'Daniel and Emily Aurelian, do you accept my nomination?'

Daniel took Emily's hand.

'We do,' she said.

The crowd erupted, as thousands of Evaders cheered. From every rooftop and balcony, and from the banks of the canals to the packed streets, their voices lifted into the night sky, where a shadow flickered, as Blackrose circled overhead.

Emily opened her eyes, the summer sun sending shafts of light across the large bedroom. She yawned and stretched her arms, then glanced down at the figure of Daniel sleeping next to her.

She nudged him and he groaned.

'Why are you awake?' he said. 'You used to be terrible in the mornings.'

'Yes, but that was before I was queen.'

He smiled up at her. 'You're not queen yet.'

'Then how come your mother calls me "your Majesty"?' She slid her legs off the bed and stood, then walked to the shutters and opened them so she could gaze at the view of the Warm Bay. Tara lay a few miles to the left, with its towering statue of Prince Michael, and Ooste lay directly ahead, the white façade of the Royal Palace shimmering in the morning light.

Four days had elapsed since they had sealed the breach in the Middle Walls, and it was Emily's third dawn waking up in Cuidrach Palace. The harbour of Pella glistened below her, and the quayside was busy with fishing crews, and Reapers going to work.

She felt Daniel by her side.

'Don't say it,' she said.

'Say what?'

'You were going to tell me that this is your favourite view in the whole City.'

He laughed. 'It is.'

'I know,' she said; 'its mine too.' She kissed him. 'It's ours.'

She dressed and left her quarters, the Hammer guards saluting as she passed. She walked to a small kitchen, where baskets were being prepared, and saw Quill standing next to her mother-in-law, who was directing the staff.

'Morning, ma'am,' said Quill.

Emily smiled. 'Good morning.'

Lady Aurelian bowed her head. 'Did you sleep well, your Majesty?'

'I did, King-Mother, thank you.'

'And when are you making me a King-Grandmother?'

'You'll be the first to hear.'

A line of six servants bowed, each with a loaded basket in their hands, and Emily picked up a seventh.

'Is delivering breakfast the role of a Queen-elect?' said Lady Aurelian.

Emily shrugged. 'I think it should be.'

She led the servants out of the kitchen, and they climbed a spiral staircase to the roof, where Blackrose was sunning herself in the morning light. Maddie and Rosie were sitting by the edge of the roof with Captain Hilde and their brother Tom, on leave from the Blades. Belinda was standing by the dragon, talking to her.

'Good morning,' said Emily, gesturing to the servants to lay the six baskets before Blackrose.

The dragon turned her head. 'Thank you, miss soon-to-be-queen.'

'You're welcome, miss soon-to-be-queen-again. How was the Bulwark last night?'

'Almost empty of greenhides. It should be safe for the Blades to re-enter in a day or so.'

'Good, thank you.'

The dragon's head turned as Yendra emerged from the stairway. 'You have returned, princess.'

'I have,' she said, 'and look who I've brought.' Yendra turned to the stairs. 'Come on, nephew; I'm sure Blackrose won't bite your head off.'

Naxor appeared at the top of the steps. He gave a nervous smile.

The dragon glared at him. 'I'm making no promises.'

'I found him,' said Yendra, 'by the Royal Academy in Ooste, attempting to dig up the Quadrant he had hidden there after he fled from Lostwell.'

'He has the Quadrant?'

Naxor showed his empty palms. 'If the Quadrant were in my hands, o Blackest of Roses, believe me, I would not be here.'

Yendra slipped her hand beneath her breastplate and took out a copper-coloured object. She held it out before the dragon. 'For you.'

Blackrose smiled. 'A god who tells the truth and keeps their promises? Yendra, you are a wonder.'

'I tell the truth,' said Belinda.

The dragon frowned at her. 'Yes; it is what you leave unsaid that troubles me.' She turned her head to Maddie. 'Rider, come and collect the Quadrant for me.'

Belinda raised an eyebrow. 'You're giving it to Maddie?'

'I know how it works,' said Blackrose, 'but it shall be my rider who uses it. I will teach her.'

Maddie got up from the low wall and walked over. She took the Quadrant from Yendra's hand and frowned at it.

'Is it complicated?' she said.

'If you know its secrets,' said the dragon, 'then it's simple. An hour's tuition should suffice; ten minutes if all you want to do is go to Lostwell.'

Belinda glared at Naxor. 'Ten minutes? You could have shown me how to get to Lostwell in ten minutes?'

He shrugged. 'I didn't want you to leave, Belinda; I still don't.'

Belinda's face went pale for a moment. 'Why not?'

'Because I was, well... I was hoping to spend more time with you.'

'Then come with us; you can show us Lostwell.'

Naxor glanced at Yendra.

'Are you seeking my permission?' she said. 'You should ask the Queen-elect.'

'You are free to leave, Lord Naxor,' said Emily, 'but does this mean you'll be going soon?'

'We'll wait for the coronation,' said Blackrose.

Emily nodded, though she felt the pain of separation ache inside her. 'Thank you.'

'Is that basket for Corthie?' said Yendra.

'Yes,' said Emily; 'that's where I'm going next.'

'I'll come with you; I wish to speak to Aila for a moment.'

Emily nodded to the dragon, then left the roof with Yendra. They descended the stairs, then entered a wing where Lady Aila's quarters were located. Rooms had been kept aside for Aila in Cuidrach Palace for centuries, though Emily felt it a little odd that she would want to return to the quarters where she had been kept under house arrest for two hundred years. She moved the basket to her left hand and knocked on the door.

There was a yell from within, and she pushed open the door. Inside was Aila's reception room, and she was sitting on a couch leaning against Corthie, who glanced up and smiled. Opposite them were Achan and Yaizra, who had arrived the previous day from Icehaven, along with Lady Yvona, who was standing by the window.

'Good morning,' said Corthie.

Lady Yvona walked over, and curtsied before Emily. 'So this our new queen?'

Emily smiled. 'I've brought breakfast.'

'Excellent,' said Corthie, 'thanks.'

She set it down, and Corthie unpacked its contents onto the table.

'Aila,' said Yendra, 'may I have a quick word?'

The demigod looked over. 'Alone?'

'I wish Emily to be present too.'

Aila got up from the couch as Corthie, Yaizra and Achan began filling their plates, and walked towards Yendra. The princess led Aila and Emily to the small study attached to the sitting room, and closed the door.

Yendra glanced at her niece. 'I'm here to talk you into doing something.'

'Should I be here for this?' said Emily. 'If this is private, family business, then I don't mind being excluded.'

'It affects you too,' said Yendra, 'for if Aila agrees, it will weaken your reign.'

Emily frowned.

'What do you want me to do?' said Aila.

Yendra placed a hand on her shoulder. 'I have handed over the God-King's Quadrant to Blackrose; she will be leaving in a few days, with Maddie, Belinda and Naxor. I want you and Corthie to go with them.'

Aila blinked.

'You must realise that Corthie wants to go home,' Yendra went on, 'yet he has chosen to stay here, for you. While the City was in peril I was in favour of this, but now that the greenhides have been defeated, and the God-Queen has fled this world, there is no reason for you to stay.'

'There are lots of reasons,' she said. 'You, for one.'

Yendra smiled, though pain shone through her eyes. 'I will still be here in a hundred years.'

Aila glanced away.

'Corthie's time is short.'

'Stop it,' said Aila.

'I don't want to cause you pain, my beloved niece, but you have to grasp this time with him. When it ends, you can return to the City, and I will be here, waiting for you, because I understand how it feels. But as for now, go, see other worlds; see Corthie's world, and his family, and you can tell me if they are as truly powerful as the rumours say.'

Aila bowed her head.

'I'll miss you if you go,' said Emily, 'but you would have my blessing. Princess Yendra is right.'

Aila nodded, then wiped a tear from her cheek. 'Alright. It would be nice to travel, though I'm a little nervous of meeting Corthie's family.' She smiled. 'Let me tell him now.'

They left the study, and Aila strode up to the couch where Corthie was sitting.

'Grab an apple and come with me,' she said. 'There's something I need to tell you.'

Corthie pulled himself from the couch, picked up two apples, and followed her into another room.

Yendra turned to Emily. 'Thank you for your support.'

She nodded. 'I have one more stop to make.'

'I shall remain here, I think,' said Yendra, bowing her head. 'I might have some breakfast before Corthie comes back and eats it all.'

The others bowed their heads as Emily left Aila's quarters. She walked back along the passageway, two courtiers following behind, then went downstairs to a small apartment. She knocked and entered.

'Mother?'

Lady Omertia turned from where was sitting by a window overlooking Tara. She looked tired, and older.

'Come in,' she said.

Emily walked over and took a seat opposite her mother. 'How are you today?'

'My whole world has been turned upside down, my dear. The Rosers have lost power, and my girl is becoming a queen.'

'I'm still the same person I was.'

'Yes, I see that; you were always strong, even when your father was trying to keep you down. It's a pity he won't be here to see you crowned; it would have destroyed him to witness an Evader on the throne.'

'An Evader and a Roser.'

Her mother smiled. 'I'm very proud of you, but it might take some time for me to adjust to all of the changes. In the last few days alone I've seen gods, demigods and a dragon; you have made yourself some very powerful friends.'

'I'm sure you'll see more if you decide to stay. There will always be rooms for you here in Cuidrach Palace.'

'But why not Maeladh?'

'Tara sits too remote from the heartland of the people; too aloof. It's the same with Ooste. And I love Pella; I have since I first stayed here with Danny. It feels right.'

'Of course,' her mother said, 'I'll stay for the coronation. After that, I'll see.'

'Stay or leave, you would still be the mother of the Queen.'

She lowered her eyes. 'Not your real mother.'

'Don't ever say that. Who was it that defended me as a child from Lord Omertia, sometimes at the cost of a beating? I'm happy to disown him, but you I will never disavow. This is a new beginning, for all of us, and I'd prefer you by my side, so I have someone to talk to who knows me in a way no one else ever will. As your sovereign, I could command it.'

'You don't need to,' she said, 'hearing that you want me to stay is enough. I'll be here for you, my daughter, my Queen.'

Six days later, a huge crowd assembled in the gardens of Cuidrach Palace. Thousands of the City's inhabitants were crammed in, and many more occupied the streets of Pella, filling the roofs of the red sandstone houses. The noon sky was blue overhead, merging with pinks and peaches to sunward, and Emily could feel the warmth on her face as she sat next to Daniel on a raised platform. Their coronation robes had been created for the occasion, as had the slender golden bands that Princess Yendra had placed upon their brows.

Every demigod in the City was present, and each one had sworn their allegiance to the new monarchs; even Lady Amber, though her father had declined the invitation to attend. Prince Montieth was a problem that Emily knew she and Daniel would have to deal with, but that was for the future. To the left of the platform was a shaded pavilion, where her mother and Daniel's parents were sitting, while high above to the right, the dragon was perched upon a palace tower, watching down over Pella.

'People of the City,' said Yendra, standing a few steps below the level of the two thrones; 'for a thousand years before the gods arrived, mortals ruled the peninsula between the Cold Sea and the Warm Sea, and now, they do so again. Behold your new monarchs, King Daniel and Queen Emily of the House of Aurelian.'

The crowds roared out a cheer.

'As a symbol of their sovereignty,' Yendra continued, 'the great sword that Prince Michael stole from the Aurelians has been retrieved from Maeladh Palace. Transformed by Michael into a weapon of oppression, the Just has been re-forged into two, new swords. From the mistakes of the past, hope has been forged anew.' She gestured to a pair of Hammer soldiers, who approached, each carrying a large velvet cushion, upon which a sword lay.

The two soldiers knelt before the thrones, their arms raised. Emily reached out and gripped the hilt of her new sword. Daniel did the same, and they both stood.

Emily and Daniel lifted their swords high, and the thousands watching responded, their cries and cheers echoing up into the blue sky.

'Behold,' said Yendra as she knelt, 'the new rulers of the City; the Fated Blades.'

'That was beautiful, my darlings,' said Lady Aurelian as the King and Queen emerged from their rooms, having changed out of their robes; 'sending Yendra to govern the Bulwark is a fine idea, though I am intrigued, your Majesty, by what you meant in your speech by "land reform"?'

Emily smiled. 'It'll be published in due course, along with all of the other new laws we're formulating; the "Aurelian Code", I'm thinking of calling it.'

'A lawyer as a queen,' her mother-in-law said; 'Malik help us all.'

Daniel laughed. 'All those radical ideas you used to poke fun at, mother, you shall have fun watching as we put them into action.'

Quill entered, wearing her uniform as Captain of the Palace Guards. 'Your Majesties,' she said, bowing, 'Blackrose is on the roof; they are ready.'

Emily nodded. 'Thank you.' She took a breath. 'This is the part of today I wasn't looking forward to.'

Daniel gestured to Quill, and she led them up the stairs and onto the wide roof that Blackrose had been using as her palace eyrie. The dragon was there, her black scales shining in the sunlight, while Maddie stood by her head, her hands clutching the Quadrant. Luggage and supplies had been strapped to the harness on the dragon's back, enough for the six who had chosen to leave. Yendra was also present, and was talking to Aila and Naxor. Corthie and Belinda stood close by, both armoured, the champion resting the Clawhammer over one shoulder.

'Friends,' said Emily.

They turned.

'Are your preparations complete?'

'They are, your Majesty,' said the dragon. 'We are ready.'

Emily nodded. 'For those of you who are not from this world; a dragon-queen, a god and a champion, please accept my thanks, and the thanks of the whole City. We shall forever be in your debt, and you will always be welcome to return. To those of you for whom this City has always been your home, I offer my best wishes. To Maddie especially, as the only mortal from this world who shall be travelling, thank you for looking after me in the Rats. When Buckler fell and the greenhides breached the wall, I thought our world was ending, and yet here we stand today. Thank you all, my friends, without you, the God-Queen's plan would have succeeded, and I shudder to imagine what the City would look like today.'

'It was an honour to help, your Majesty,' said Corthie, 'and it makes me happy to know we're leaving the City in your hands. I'll miss it; the people, the light, and even the Blind Poet. I came here with nothing, and am leaving with friends, and the woman I love. Farewell.'

Rosie and Tom walked forward, and embraced their sister Maddie.

'Take this,' said Rosie, handing Maddie a bag, 'it's salve, from our little mountain valley. Queen Emily said it was alright for you to have it.'

Maddie wiped her tears away and nodded.

'That shall be the last salve that travels from our world to others,' said Emily. 'With Princess Yendra's advice, we have decided that the best way to keep our world hidden from the greed of the gods is to cut off their supply of salve. We do not believe the God-Queen shall return, but while she possesses a Quadrant, and knows the location of this world, she is a threat. If you happen to meet this threat on your travels, I trust you shall do what needs to be done.'

'It shall be so,' said Blackrose. She glanced at the others. 'Those leaving, step forward and stand next to Maddie. Rider, are you ready?'

Maddie nodded, as Belinda, Naxor, Corthie and Aila approached. Rosie and Tom stepped back, his arm over his little sister's shoulder as they both wept.

Maddie glanced at Emily, and smiled. 'Good luck, and keep my City safe.'

Emily took Daniel's hand and nodded. 'Farewell.'

There was a shimmer, and the group of six vanished, leaving the roof almost empty. Rosie sobbed, and Emily felt her sorrow.

'We have gained much today,' said Daniel, 'and lost much.'

'Some of them may return,' said Emily; 'until then, we have a City to rule.'

'I shall be taking the Blades back into the Bulwark tomorrow, your Majesty,' said Yendra, 'and with your permission, I have decided to take Lady Jade along with me.'

'That's a good idea,' said Emily; 'it will keep her occupied and out of trouble, as long as you remember to keep her well supplied with cats.'

Yendra smiled. 'I shall indeed, your Majesty. I think that, with a little time, Jade will thrive away from the influence of her father and elder sister. Montieth and Amber may have sworn allegiance, but they retain the potential to make trouble.'

'One thing at a time,' Emily said, her eyes gazing over the red sandstone buildings of Pella. 'Let's go downstairs; we have one more thing to do today before we start work.'

Quill led the way, and they descended the steps to the royal quarters of the palace.

'I trust everything went well?' said Lady Aurelian as they entered their reception rooms. 'I have a list of the most pressing problems facing the City, as submitted by the leadership of the eight tribes. Are you ready to begin?'

'Not yet,' said Emily. She glanced at Daniel. 'Shall we?'

He nodded and took her hand, and they strode across the chamber. Quill bowed and opened the balcony doors, letting in the roar of the crowds gathered outside. Emily and Daniel walked out onto the balcony, and the people cheered. Thousands had gathered in the streets below, and the whole harbour front was lined with Hammers and Evaders, and many from the other tribes. They raised their hands into the air, acclaiming their mortal King and Queen, their voices lifting to the sky.

Emily's heart swelled, and she smiled. 'This, Danny, is my favourite view.'

The Mortal Blade - The Royal Family

The Gods	Title	Powers
Malik	God-King of the City - Ooste	Vision
Amalia	God-Queen of the City - Tara	Death
The Children of the Gods		
Michael (deceased)	ex-Prince of Tara, 1600-3096	Death, Battle
Montieth	Prince of Dalrig, b. 1932	Death
Isra (deceased)	ex-Prince of Pella, 2001-3078	Battle
Khora (deceased)	ex-Princess of Pella 2014-3419	Vision
Niomi (deceased)	ex-Princess of Icehaven, 2014-3089	Healer
Yendra (deceased)	ex-Princess of the Circuit, 2133-3096	Vision
Children of Prince Michael		
Marcus	Duke, Bulwark, b. 1944	Battle
Mona	Chancellor, Ooste, b. 2014	Vision
Dania (deceased)	Lady of Tara, 2099-3096	Battle
Yordi (deceased)	Lady of Tara, 2153-3096	Death
Children of Prince Montieth		
Amber	Lady of Dalrig, b. 2035	Death
Jade	Lady of Dalrig, b. 2511	Death
Children of Prince Isra		
Irno (deceased)	Eldest son of Isra, 2017-3078	Battle
Berno (deceased)	'The Mortal', 2018-2097	None
Garno (deceased)	Warrior, 2241-3078	Battle
Lerno (deceased)	Warrior, 2247-3078	Battle

Vana	Adjutant of Pella, b. 2319	Location
Marno (deceased)	Warrior, 2321-3063	Battle
Collo	Khora's Secretary, b. 2328	None
Bonna (deceased)	Warrior, 2598-3078	Shape-Shifter
Aila	Adjutant of the Circuit, b. 2652	Shape-Shifter
Kano	Adj. of the Bulwark, b. 2788	Battle
Teno (deceased)	Warrior, 2870-3078	Battle

Children of Princess Khora

Salvor	Governor of Pella, b. 2201	Vision
Balian (deceased)	Warrior, 2299-3096	Battle
Lydia	Gov. of Port Sanders, b. 2304	Healer
Naxor	Royal Emissary, b. 2401	Vision
Ikara	Governor of the Circuit, b. 2499	Battle
Doria	Royal Courtier, b. 2600	None

Children of Princess Niomi

Rand (deceased)	Warrior, 2123-3089	Battle
Yvona	Governor of Icehaven, b. 2175	Healer
Samara (deceased)	Lady of Icehaven, 2239-3089	Battle
Daran (deceased)	Lord of Icehaven, 2261-3063	Battle

Children of Princess Yendra

Kahlia (deceased)	Warrior, 2599-3096	Vision
Neara (deceased)	Warrior, 2601-3089	Battle
Yearna (deceased)	Lady of the Circuit, 2604-3096	Healer

THE NINE TRIBES OF THE CITY

There are nine distinct tribes inhabiting the City. Three were in the area from the beginning, and the other six were created in two waves of expansion.

The Original Three Tribes – Auldan (pop. 300 000) Auldan is the oldest part of the City. United by the Union Walls (completed in 1040), it combined the three original tribes and their towns, along with the shared town of **Ooste**, which houses the Royal Palace, where **King Malik** lives.

1. **The Rosers** – (their town is **Tara**, est. Yr. 1.) The first tribe to reach the peninsula where the City is located. Began farming there in the sunward regions, until attacks from the Reapers forced them into building the first walled town. **Prince Michael** ruled until his death in 3096. **Queen Amalia** governs the Rosers from Maeladh Palace in Tara.

2. **The Gloamers** – (their town is **Dalrig**, est. Yr. 40.) Arrived shortly after the Rosers, farming the iceward side of the peninsula. Like them, they fought with the Reapers, and built a walled town to stop their attacks. **Prince Montieth** rules from Greylin Palace in Dalrig.

3. **The Reapers** – (their town is **Pella**, est. Yr. 70.) Hunter/Gatherer tribe that arrived after the more sedentary Rosers and Gloamers. Settled in the plains between the other two tribes. More numerous than either the Rosers or the Gloamers, but are looked down on as more rustic. **Prince Isra** ruled until his death in 3078. **Princess Khora** now rules in his stead, but delegates to her son, **Lord Salvor**, who governs from Cuidrach Palace in Pella.

The Next Three Tribes – Medio (pop. 400 000) Originally called 'New Town', this part of the City was its first major expansion; and was settled from the completion of the Middle Walls (finished in 1697 and originally known as the Royal Walls). The name 'Medio' derives from the old Evader word for 'Middle'.

1. **The Icewarders** – (their town is **Icehaven**, est. 1657.) Settlers from Dalrig originally founded a new colony at Icehaven to assist in the building of the Middle Walls, as the location was too cold and dark for the greenhides. After the wall's completion, many settlers stayed, and a new tribe was founded. Separated from Icehaven by mountains, a large number of Icewarders also inhabit the central lowlands bordering the Circuit. **Princess Niomi** ruled until her death in 3089. Her daughter, **Lady Yvona**, now governs from Alkirk Palace in Icehaven.

2. **The Sanders** – (their town is **Port Sanders**, est. 1702.) When the Middle Walls were completed, a surplus population of Rosers and Reapers moved into the new area, and the tribe of the Sanders was founded, based around the port town on the Warm Sea. Related closely to the Rosers in terms of allegiance and culture. **Princess Khora** rules, but delegates to her daughter, **Lady Lydia**, who governs from the Tonetti Palace in Port Sanders.

3. **The Evaders** – (their town is the **Circuit**, est. 2133.) The only tribe ethnically unrelated to the others, the Evaders started out as refugees fleeing the greenhides, and they began arriving at the City c.1500. They were taken in, and then used to help build the Middle Walls. The largest tribe by population among the first six, though the other tribes of Auldan and Medio look down on them as illiterate savages. **Princess Yendra** ruled until her death in 3096. **Lady Ikara** rules from Redmarket Palace in the town's centre.

The Final Three Tribes – The Bulwark (pop. 600 000) The Bulwark is the defensive buffer that protects the entire City from greenhide attack.

Work commenced on the enormous Great Walls after the decisive Battle of the Children of the Gods in 2247, when the greenhides were annihilated and pushed back hundreds of miles. They were completed c.2300, and the new area of the City was settled.

1. **The Blades** – (est. 2300.) The military tribe of the City. The role of the Blades is to defend the Great Walls from the unceasing attacks by the Greenhides. Their service is hereditary, and the role of soldier passes from parent to child. Officials from the Blades also police and govern the other two tribes of the Bulwark. Their headquarters is the **Fortress of the Lifegiver**, the largest bastion on the Great Walls, where **Duke Marcus** is the commander.

2. **The Hammers** – (est. 2300.) The industrial proletariat of the Bulwark, the Hammers are effectively slaves, though that word is not used. They are forbidden to leave their tribal area, which produces much of the finished goods for the rest of the City.

3. **The Scythes** – (est. 2300.) The agricultural workers of the Bulwark, who produce all that the region requires. Slaves in all but name.

NOTE OF THE CALENDAR

In this world there are two moons, a larger and a smaller (fragments of the same moon). The larger orbits in a way similar to Earth's moon, and the year is divided into seasons and months.

Due to the tidally-locked orbit around the sun, there are no solstices or equinoxes, but summer and winter exist due to the orbit being highly elliptical. There are two summers and two winters in the course of each solar revolution, so one 'year' (365 days) equates to half the time it takes for the planet to go round the sun (730 days). No Leap Days required.

New Year starts at with the arrival of the Spring (Freshmist) storms, on Thanalion Day

New Year's Day – **Thanalion Day** (approx. 1st March)

-- **Freshmist** (snow storms, freezing fog, ice blizzards, high winds from iceward)

- Malikon (March)
- Amalan (April)

-- **Summer** (hot, dry)

- Mikalis (May)
- Montalis (June)
- Izran (July)
- Koralis (August)

-- **Sweetmist** (humid, stormy, high winds from sunward, very wet)

- Namen (September)
- Balian (October)

-- **Winter** (cold, dry)

- Marcalis (November)
- Monan (December)

- Darian (January)
- Yordian (February)

Note – the old month of Yendran was renamed in honour of Princess Khora's slain son Lord Balian, following the execution of the traitor Princess Yendra.

AUTHOR'S NOTES

NOVEMBER 2020

Thank you for reading The Prince's Blade and I hope you enjoyed it. It was a joy to write – as was the entire 'Blade' trilogy; the first third of the Eternal Siege series. All three books of the 'Blade' trilogy were written in one long continuous flurry while we were stuck indoors, and some of the claustrophobia may well have rubbed off into the tone of the story.

Next comes the 'Lostwell' trilogy, which will follow the adventures of the exiles from the City, leaving Emily, Daniel and Yendra to enjoy some peace for a while!

RECEIVE A FREE MAGELANDS ETERNAL SIEGE BOOK

Building a relationship with my readers is very important to me.

Join my newsletter for information on new books and deals and you will also receive a Magelands Eternal Siege prequel novella that is currently EXCLUSIVE to my Reader's Group for FREE.

www.ChristopherMitchellBooks.com/join

ABOUT THE AUTHOR

Christopher Mitchell is the author of the Magelands epic fantasy series.

For more information:
www.christophermitchellbooks.com
info@christophermitchellbooks.com

Printed in Great Britain
by Amazon

59089458R00274